The Annihilation Virus

By

Jim Norman

The Annihilation Virus

This book is a work of fiction. Names, characters, places, and incidents either are products of the author's imagination or are used fictitiously. Any resemblance to actual persons, living or dead, events, or locales is entirely coincidental.

Edited by: Sarajoy Bonebright

Cover by: Rafido

"The whole earth is the tomb of heroic men and their story is not given only on stone over their clay but abides everywhere without visible symbol, woven into the stuff of other men's lives."

– Pericles

TABLE OF CONTENTS

When thinking about writing this story, I wanted something that could be believable in today's world. Not something that we all know is Hollywood make believe. With today's world wide mix of culture, this story lays out what could easily be achievable by people with corrupt motives. I think millions of people would like to believe that a Star Trek type utopia is possible to build and maintain on our planet, but with all of our differences and beliefs, and man's tendencies to become corrupt when they find themselves with too much power, I don't think that concept will ever be realized. Without a firm belief that all of our actions will one day be judged by God, the creator of our existence, man's lofty ambitions of a utopia without God is doomed to fail. This story is simply a revelation of what man is capable of if he never has to answer to the consciousness of God that is inherently within him.

Jim Norman

CHAPTER ONE

Kaziim, after checking on the latest progress of his scientists, walked from the laboratory heading for Haris's office. Knocking on the door, he could hear Haris invite him in, and entering he took a seat in front of his desk.

"The virus is perfected," Kaziim stated. "We're ready to start producing the solution in the quantities that we will need to carry out the plan."

"Good. We're still a few men short, but I have all confidence that we'll find the rest of the ones we need," Haris replied.

"How many do you have lined up?"

"Fifty-seven. We need eight more to be complete."

"And do they all know that it is a suicide mission?"

"Yes, that's why we're still a few short," Haris explained. "It's one thing to have three or four who are willing to blow themselves up, but to find sixty-five is a little more difficult, although what we're asking is a little different than squeezing a trigger. But we'll get the rest."

"Have you finalized the plans, the flights, and all of the targets?"

"We're at about ninety percent. We should have the rest finalized within the week. So far, everything is looking extremely well, and all of our computer simulations are predicting a huge success. Before long, our enemies will know true fear, and we will be watching them as they struggle against our greatest weapon."

"You do know how careful we have to be? If this thing backfires on us, it will destroy us," warned Kaziim.

"I'm well aware of the danger, but we'll be extremely careful. There is no way it will come back on us. No one will infect anyone on their exit flight, and once they're out of the country, none of them are coming back," replied Haris.

"All plans sound good in theory. Let's hope that your plans work out accordingly. What kind of kill rate do your simulations come up with?"

"With a one-hundred-percent kill rate for all who become infected and the number of cities we'll be infecting, we're predicting at least one billion dead. The infidels will be totally demoralized by their inability to stop the spread of the virus, and by the time their own scientists are able to find a cure or a vaccine, it will be too late to save their economies," crowed Haris.

"And have you run any simulations with the possibility that the Americans are unable to produce any kind of a vaccine or antidote?" asked Kaziim.

"Actually, no. We assumed that with all of their scientists and resources that they won't have a problem finding one before it's too late," reassured Haris.

"Perhaps you should run a scenario where there is no vaccine or antidote ever found. Your decision to actually begin the mission needs to be made with full knowledge of what you'll be unleashing on the world. If there's no antidote discovered, will there be a point at which the virus will eventually die out, and when would that point occur? If it infects the whole world without stopping, will we then be its last victims?"

"You are worrying too much, Kaziim. The Americans always seem to find an answer somehow. They have thousands of scientists and research facilities that would put ours to shame. How could they not find a cure? Not only that, the rest of the infidel nations will also be doing their own research. Just because our twenty-five scientists can't find a cure, that doesn't mean that they won't."

"Okay, you've made your point. I still think you should run the scenario. At least then you can make a more informed decision."

"Alright, I will. Let me know as soon as you can what your estimate will be for when the solution will be ready for implementation."

"I will."

"Come on, Son! Let's go out to the barn. I've got something I want to show you."

"Did you get a new tractor?"

"Oh, no. It's nothing like that. While you've been gone, I've been adding some upgrades around here."

"Thanks for the breakfast, Mom. That was delicious!" Rising from the table, Sean wrapped his arms around his mom, Beth. "I've sure missed your cooking."

Giving him a kiss on the cheek, Beth let him go. "You better go with your father. He's excited to show you what he's been up to."

Sean, twenty-three years old, having only been out of the marines for three weeks after a four-year service, followed his dad out the back door. His six-foot, two-inch frame was slender and athletic with broad shoulders. He still had a marine haircut, but the dark brown coloring was highly pronounced. Looking things over as they walked out to the barn, he remembered seeing the solar panels on the roof of the house as he and his dad drove up earlier that morning.

He asked, "Getting tired of paying the electric bill? How long will it take to recover the cost for going solar?"

"Several years at least, but that's not why I had it installed. More for emergency reasons—for backup power if the grid fails."

Sean could see that there had been some recent dirt work out behind the back of the barn. The growth of new vegetation in the area he could see past the corner of the building was quite a bit smaller than the surrounding grass and weeds. There was also a two-foot-wide line in the grass, also with small new grass growing, extending to the right, down the slope of the hill for a couple hundred feet.

Smiling at his dad, he asked, "Did you finally build a bathroom in the barn like you always talked about?"

"Well, sort of… with a few modifications. The way things are going, I thought it would be good to be prepared for emergencies."

"How's a bathroom in the barn going to help that? Are you planning to let homeless people stay in the barn during emergencies?" Following his dad through the barn door, Sean was intent on looking for new construction, but the old barn looked just like it always had: tack room on the right, some open space, and then stalls for the horses on the right extending to the end of the barn, with hay storage on the left. "I don't see the bathroom. Did you add it onto the back of the barn? Where's the door?"

"It's just outside the tack room, next to the outside wall." Sean's dad, Mitch, led the way to the corner of the tack room and then to the wall of the barn, stopping at the back of the tack room, where it met the outside wall.

Sean couldn't see a doorknob or latch of any kind, nor even a door anywhere on the wall. Smiling, he asked, "You put a trick door on the bathroom?"

"Something like that. Don't want just anybody using it. Watch how I do this!"

There were several dowels mounted along the wall of the tack room, with a hand saw hanging from one and a couple of old pieces of harness hanging from others. The last two were empty. Sean watched as his dad pulled the right one down and then pushed the left one up. There was a slight click, and a small panel opened about an inch. Both dowels then went back to their previous position. Opening it wider, a small numerical keypad was exposed.

"Mom's birthday is the code." Entering it, Sean could hear another click, and a large door opened slightly.

"Spring loaded. When the lock is released, the spring pushes the door ajar. There's a finger slot right behind the edge here." Pulling the door open, Mitch reached inside to turn on a light switch, and then stepped back and beckoned for Sean to enter. As Sean stepped up to the door, he could see that it was a metal door with a wood veneer on the outside surface. Beyond the door, there was a stairway going down to a landing, turning to the left, and then continuing down.

"Really, Dad? You built a bunker?"

Mitch could hear the disapproval in his son's question. "And why not? The way society is falling into the toilet you never know what might happen. All it takes is one big catastrophe and a lot of people will turn mean. For instance, just look at that Ebola virus. If that ever got a good foothold in the U.S., things would get nasty in a hurry. So many people are so stubborn and selfish that they won't even self-quarantine until they're past the danger point. Most people will be in denial until they've already infected a whole mess of people. With a death rate between thirty and forty percent, how fast will it deplete the population?"

Sean could hear the excitement in his dad's voice as he was getting warmed up to the subject. In the past several years, he had been involved in many conversations with his dad about doomsday prepping, especially after the television series came out, but his dad now had even more ammunition for his argument with the recent onset of the Ebola virus. Grudgingly, Sean admitted to himself that there were some legitimate concerns with people's reactions to the virus, and the lack of government foresight on how to curb it's spread. Like the old saying goes, "If people are involved, then there will be problems."

"Okay, Dad. I know where you're coming from, and I admit that there is some justification for the way you're thinking… but is it really worth all the money you've put into this?"

"If nothing ever happens and we never actually need this, then for now it at least provides me some peace of mind. Besides, I have enough money for all of this without hurting our financial security. We have our retirement nest egg well on the way, and with your mom's salary and benefits from her county job, we don't have anything to worry about. We only used about half of your mom's inheritance to build and supply this bunker, and when the property becomes your inheritance in the future, it'll be more valuable because of this. Then you can sell it if you don't want it. Now, do you want to see it or not?"

"Sure, Dad. It's worth a look. I never said I wasn't interested. Now that it's done, I think it's kind of cool. So let's have a look!"

As Sean walked down the stairs, he noticed all the side-walls were poured concrete with a thick coat of paint. He also knew that by the time he reached the bottom of the stairs he was beyond the wall of the barn. The stairs ended in a hallway, and at about four feet from the last step, there was a solid metal door that looked like a submarine door with a large lever handle. Beside it was a numerical keypad.

"Enter your birth date."

Punching in the numbers, Sean heard a soft click and then pulled on the handle. The door was heavy and was a little slow opening. The hallway widened past the door to over five feet and continued for another ten feet with another door of the same type but without the keypad.

"These three doors are airtight to protect the bunker from airborne biological attacks or any kind of gas attacks. They're actually naval doors that are installed in their ships. The shower head on the wall in the corner is for decontamination. There's a drain in the floor that takes the waste to the septic system," explained Mitch.

Sean could see another of the same door on the left and opening it he could see a compartment about the same size as the decontamination room with a generator and other odds and ends with intake and exhaust pipes leading to the ceiling.

"The generator is only for emergency operation if all the other power operations fail and of course it's kept in its own area for obvious reasons." Continuing through the next airtight door, Sean found himself in a ten foot long hallway. The entire left side of the hallway was lined with shelves, from floor to ceiling. Immediately on the right, a door opened into a bathroom-utility room combination. Stepping into the bathroom, Sean could see a four-foot vanity straight ahead, with a stacking washer and dryer close beside it and a dresser beside that with linen storage. In the far back corner of the room was a water heater. Water pipes disappeared into the interior wall that was of wood construction, apparently feeding the toilet and shower. Immediately to the left of the water heater was a three-foot by five-foot toilet closet with a pocket door, and a tile walk-in shower, starting just to the right of the entry door, butted up against the toilet closet. With a smoked glass shower door for privacy, and the privacy closet, more than one person could use the bathroom at the same time.

"The water heater is electric, and I have a small one above the bunker in another alcove that is a fast-recovery propane heater. If the power goes out, we'll use the small one," Mitch explained.

Leaving the bathroom to walk down the hallway, Sean stepped into a common room that was about twenty-four feet by sixteen feet. The ceilings were also poured concrete with two steel I-beams spaced evenly across the ceiling of the room for support.

The common room included a kitchen, dining area, and a living area, with a couch, a love seat, and a reclining chair. It was a little bit cramped, but it would suffice for the need it served. There was a six-foot closet against the back wall to the right behind the couch. Also, there was a thirty-two inch flat-screen television in the corner of the room to the right, facing the kitchen in the opposite corner, with a DVD player and a cable control box in a small cabinet below. A bookshelf next to the TV was completely full, mostly with what looked like how-to books.

The kitchen consisted of an L-shaped lower cabinet in the corner of the room with a kitchen sink and two sections of uppers. At the left end of the cabinet, there was an electric range, sixteen inches of countertop and then a refrigerator/freezer. A wall-mounted heater was located a couple of feet away from the refrigerator. A square four-by-four-foot table with four chairs completed the furnishings.

There were a few lines of metal conduit that were surface mounted on the concrete for the ceiling lights, while the rest of the electrical was installed normally on the framed interior walls. The concrete floor was painted with a durable thick coat of non-slip paint that Sean had seen before on garage floors. Naturally, he knew his dad would want to stay away from carpeting to avoid the chance of mold developing in an enclosed underground area. There were small LED lights mounted on the walls and two on the ceiling.

Seeing his son looking over the kitchen, Mitch replied, "The appliances run off the power grid and only the fridge will run off the solar and windmill power. We'll run the generator when we want to use the range. I've got two, one thousand-gallon propane tanks in concrete vaults in the ground. They'll run the propane water heater that's up top for quite a while. I've got the solar panels and a windmill generator set up to provide the electricity when the power goes out, but the place is also hardwired to the grid. The solar and windmill power comes directly to here, with a shut-off switch to the outside line for when the grid goes down. That way I don't lose any power to the line, and the house isn't drawing anything. If scavengers were to find a house with its own power supply, they might take up residence.

"I've got multiple replacement parts for everything that might go out and a fully stocked pantry with both freeze-dried and canned foods and other non-perishables, mostly Mountain House products. I also have, in #10 cans, flour, salt, sugar, rice, and beans. We've got gallons and gallons of cooking oil and lots of yeast for baking our own bread. Until you really start thinking about what you'll actually need, you don't realize how much stuff will be necessary for survival. Now and then, there are a few things that we'll have to rotate to keep from spoiling, but we're well prepared."

"Wow, Dad. You spent a pretty penny to get this place built, but I've got to admit: This is a really nice set-up. How did you come up with all of the ideas for the bunker?"

"Doing some research I encountered Atlas Survival Shelters. They build and sell different sizes of bunkers and deliver them all over the country. They build a very nice and efficient bunker and watching their videos on YouTube, I took a lot of their ideas to incorporate into mine. I actually contacted them and bought the gas tight doors and the air filtration system from the guys."

"It looks like you've planned for more than one scenario with all of the different aspects you're telling me about," stated Sean.

"Yes I have. We aren't sure when the power grid might go down and depending on what kind of doomsday scenario happens, the power grid may not fail for many years. If it's some kind of war, military attack, or natural disaster, the power grid could be knocked offline quickly. But if it's some kind of a contagious disease epidemic, the power grid could stay up and running indefinitely. In that case, we would use the electric appliances to save the propane and gasoline for the water heater and generator when the power grid actually fails.

"I've put a lot of thought into this and it took a lot of planning. We have an air filtration and circulation system with the top of it built into the barn wall so that it's unnoticeable. The unit is Swiss made and is installed in the back bedroom with the exit air pipe in the bathroom. That way the bathroom smell and steamy air will exit the bunker without entering the rest of the rooms. If we have to come down here to live, we'll also bring all of Beth's houseplants in with us along with the lights needed for them to grow. Helps with the oxygen replacement."

Knowing that all the plumbing was eleven or twelve feet underground, Sean had to ask the question, "How do you get the fresh water in and the wastewater out?"

"I had a well driller come out and put down a new well about fifty feet. Artesian water. Bubbles up all by itself. Piped it into an underground concrete vault that holds a thousand gallons, and the bottom of it is still five feet higher than the kitchen sink. So, everything flows on a gravity feed. We had to dig a deep ditch across the flat ground for the septic line, but once it reached the sloping ground, it evened out. The septic tank is out about twenty feet and the drain field is down the slope a ways. The whole system works on gravity and wasn't even a problem."

Moving along, the first room off the common room, with its door close to the corner to the left, was a ten-by-ten-foot bedroom, with a bed and a dresser already in place. Both of the doors on the opposite side of the common room opened into bedrooms; one was larger but with one wall lined with floor to ceiling storage cabinets. Both rooms were furnished with a bed, a dresser, one nightstand with a lamp, and a small closet. The larger room was also set up with a desk and computer, a small reloading bench, and a large gun safe. A stand-up freezer was at the left end of the cabinets.

"The combination for the gun safe is my birth date. I've got the dies and all of the reloading supplies for all of my guns and even some dies for other popular calibers, just in case. There is enough gunpowder and bullets to reload ten thousand shells and I've stocked up on extra shell casings. I keep the powder in a compartment outside the concrete wall just for safety. Every time I go to the sporting goods store, I pick up a couple more boxes of shells. I've got quite a large supply of ammo—somewhere around forty boxes of .300 Weatherby mag, ten one-thousand round cartons of 5.56, thirty or so boxes each of .243, .22-250, .270, .30-06, fifty or sixty boxes of .280 Remington, thirty cartons of 12 gauge, and forty bricks of .22 long rifle. I also have quite a few boxes of pistol ammo for my .45, .357 Magnum, 9-mm.

"I picked up a couple of crossbows with scopes and about three hundred bolts. Once you run out of them, you won't get any more. I've still got my two latest hunting bows, and I've stocked up on the arrows. I picked up a recurve the other day with some cheap wood arrows. Worst case scenario, you can make your own wood arrows for the recurve. If things get really bad, you won't be able to find any guns or ammo anywhere. Better to be safe than sorry. Like I said before, once I'm gone, you can do whatever you want with all of this, because then I won't care. But then you never know if you might need it yourself."

Sean gave out a low whistle. "Wow, Dad. I knew that you've been stocking up on guns and ammo, but that's a lot of ammo you're talking about. How many guns you got to use up that ammo?"

"I've got fourteen rifles, three 22's, three shotguns, six pistols. Like I said, someday all the guns will be worth more than I paid for them. It's a good investment any way you look at it."

"Since you've gone to this much trouble and expense for a future you can't foresee, what else have you invested in that'll come in handy?"

"Well, Son, there's a lot of different aspects for a comfortable life to be thoughtful about. It's been tough to think of every contingency that we might run into, but probably the biggest thing would be how to feed ourselves if the food industry came to a screeching halt. What would we do if there wasn't any more bread, milk, salt, sugar, vegetables, soda, beer, candy, or meat sold at the store? Could the situation ever be that bad, and why? I don't know for sure what could ever happen to make things that bad, but what if something came up that totally disrupted the food distribution? To be ready for something that drastic, you have to have enough supplies to last yourself and your loved ones long enough to be able to replenish your supplies with growing, gathering, and killing animals for fresh meat. At first, the tame animals would be killed off—easy to find and easy to kill. Of course, at the beginning there would still also be lots of people."

"Does that mean you have stores of seeds to plant that'll last for several years?" asked Sean.

"Yes, we've put aside hundreds of packets of seeds for all kinds of vegetables and grains, and we always have seed potatoes to plant. I've even built a small flour mill to turn our wheat into flour. We've already stocked up on barrels of flour and sugar and salt. I grow some wheat every year just in case we need it for ourselves, and we grow all of our own potatoes. You've seen all of the fruit trees in the orchard, so that will help if things turn out for the worse.

Mitch continued, "For us the biggest problem will be protecting what we already have. There will always be people with less, and the only way for them to survive will be to take it from people like us. Most of our neighbors will be able to survive a lot of hardships, but they're country folks. The problem will be when strangers show up."

"And being friends and neighbors you're all more apt to help each other out along the way," replied Sean.

"Yes, we would, but eventually there will be an overflow of people migrating out of the metropolitan areas, since the worst places to live will be in the big cities where there's too many people, no way to grow their own food, and no animals for fresh meat, other than pets. If the apocalyptic issues are disease, biological warfare, or military bombing, the people in big cities will receive the brunt of it. They will turn to scavenging and then to raiding and eventually killing to get supplies for themselves and their loved ones," Mitch explained.

"Where will the police and military be? Won't they be able to curb the violence?" asked Sean.

"They'll be able to early in the troubles, but when people get hungry and worried for their loved ones, they'll get mean and nasty. Just the criminals alone will have more weapons than the police force, not to mention all of the legal guns owned by law-abiding citizens. Then the riots will start, and when things begin to spiral out of control, the shooting will begin. People on both sides will be killed; martial law will be established; and there won't be any trust between the two factions."

Sean was beginning to see the picture that his dad was painting. "And the survivors, when they realize they're going to starve to death in the city, that's when they'll begin a mass exodus out of the cities into the countryside to gather or grow their own food. I would imagine most of them wouldn't know how to survive without help from country folks, especially if there's not any government or military still intact. Many of them won't have weapons or enough ammo to last very long, even if they have guns. They'll all be desperate to survive, and many will stop at nothing to get what they need for their families."

Breaking in, Mitch said, "The only protection from those types of people will be your own weapons and your own survival instincts. Civilization is a good thing, but it takes cooperation and a willingness to help and to share with others for it to flourish. If humanity is faced with the possibility of extinction, I don't think it will turn out the way Hollywood wants to picture it. I think it will be everyone for themselves."

"But you're painting a worst case scenario. What if the transition is slow enough that total anarchy doesn't happen? Is it possible that people would be able to adjust to a different life gradually enough not to turn to barbarism?" asked Sean.

"That is the million dollar question. But looking at the human behavior exhibited every time that riots occur, such as Ferguson and the Los Angeles riots in the eighties, you see people not only protesting but breaking into stores and looting them and also burning cars and store buildings. A lot of society, especially the impoverished inner-city people, are right on the verge of anarchy already. How much do you think it would take to push them over the edge?"

"Very little," Sean acknowledged. "Like you said, the first thing to go would be the food distribution. Every grocery store could be servicing between three to six thousand people, and when the production and delivery of groceries to the local market is slowed down, it would create a lot of worry. Then there would be a run on the store, with people buying up everything they could and hoarding it. The shelves would start to empty, and then riots would start because of the lack of supply. The whole scenario could snowball out of control very quickly. I see your point. It's not really a very pleasant subject to think about."

"Nor were the Y2K scenarios that everyone was pushing back in '99. There were thousands of people believing that total anarchy was right around the corner. Gas stations were running out of fuel; generators were sold out everywhere; guns and ammo supplies were depleted; and any emergency gear or equipment was sold out. It wasn't until after the Y2K thing was over that the doomsday prepping really got on its feet. Everyone that bought into the craziness of Y2K were a little sheepish about their reactions to it when they woke up the next morning and everything was running just how it was supposed to be," related Mitch.

"I remember some of that. I had some friends in school that talked about their parents buying a lot of stuff for that."

"That was actually what got me started thinking about prepping. I bought a few extra supplies, just in case the power went down for a few days and some extra fuel, but afterwards I really started thinking seriously about what would happen to society if something big did come up." Pausing to look around, Mitch was trying to think if there was anything he had forgotten to show Sean.

"Oh, before I forget, there's an emergency exit in the back bedroom. It's the last cabinet through the bottom door. There is something in the cabinet in front of the exit door so that you can't see it. The door opens into a three-foot diameter plastic pipe. Crawling room only. Four sections of twenty-foot pipe takes you just down the slope enough that you won't be seen from up by the barn. Like I said, 'emergencies only'."

Walking back to the house, Sean asked, "How many people know about this? This was a pretty big project to get done without some help."

"From the very beginning, I knew I needed to keep this quiet, so I had your cousins, Tim and Josh, come down from Portland to help with everything that we could do ourselves. I rented an excavator to do the dig-out and then a backhoe for the follow-up. I hired a concrete contractor from Portland also so that there wouldn't be any local people on to what I was building. The concrete did come from a local company, but it was from across town. No permits. Didn't see any reason why I can't build what I want on my own property without their involvement. The appliances and all of the prepper stuff I bought at stores in Salem. Paid cash too. Didn't want my name on anyone's computers or invoices to leave a trail back to here."

"You almost sound paranoid, Dad. Do you really think there's a need for all the secrecy?" asked Sean.

"Since no one knows what kind of doomsday might come, I just think it's best to keep everything on the down low. If too many people know who the doomsday preppers are, including your neighbors, you might find too many unsavory characters showing up on your doorstep when you least expect it. Helping people when you can is one thing, but fighting off people who want everything you got is quite another. I was just trying to avoid as many unnecessary encounters as I could. Being wise about things doesn't make me paranoid."

"Okay, Dad, I see your point. If things go down the way you're talking, it's best to be careful," Sean said, apologetically. Walking across the gravel turn-around between the barn and house, Sean walked up the steps of the back porch and into the kitchen. "Hey, Mom, you okay with that bunker?"

"Sure, I'm okay with it. Pretty cool, huh?"

CHAPTER TWO

A meeting was called in the offices of the CIA headquarters. The director was meeting with his top analysts about some recent intel coming out of their Paris office concerning the Middle East.

"We've been hearing whispers coming from several sources about something big that's going to happen. It was only a rumor several months ago, but now it's popping up more and more. We believe it has something to do with the gathering of key scientists that we heard about over two years ago," began Richard Miller.

"This thing has been kept pretty quiet," added William Fulton. "The bits and pieces we've put together don't add up to much, but what we're guessing is a biological attack of some kind. With the kind of mentality that they operate with, there's no telling how big this might be."

"Some of the scientists that we've lost track of were involved in genetic engineering. Others held their degrees in disease control and microbiology. Putting these three together could spell a very nasty possibility, including a currently known virus that has been altered to make it more infectious and deadly. With two years or more to work on it, we should expect it to be very deadly and formidable," continued Richard.

"Get some more people on this. We need to know what they're up to. If you get somebody who might know something about this, don't hesitate on extracting information. Do whatever is necessary. Do you understand?" asked the director.

"Yes, sir. We'll do whatever it takes."

"Keep me apprised of the situation. I'll get with the secretaries of Homeland Security and Health and the FBI director and let them know what you just told me. If anything comes up on their end, I'll let you know."

"Hey, Mom, how did Dad ever talk you into that bunker? That's a huge investment."

"Well, let's see. First of all, I remember the Y2K era and all of the turmoil and fear that was stirred up, which was brought on by only the thought that computers were going to shut down because they wouldn't understand the turning of the century on their clocks. I never did understand that part. But, still, it made people think about what they would do if something big and catastrophic actually did happen. Your dad and I talked quite a bit about it, even back then, but since a computer meltdown didn't really sound that feasible, it wasn't that scary. Just restart the stupid thing. Isn't that what we do?"

"I know what you mean. It never sounded like a legitimate concern to me either. So what changed your mind so drastically?" Sean asked.

"One day, your father told me that North Korea had been making nuclear bombs and that they had successfully made one that was different, in the sense that it would create a huge electromagnetic pulse. I didn't even know what that meant, but then he told me that if they were able to detonate it one hundred miles above the ground, over the middle of the United States, that it would be possible that the shock-wave would fry every unprotected computer chip in the whole US. It would fry car batteries and a lot of other electrical components. It would effectively shut down the electrical grid across the whole nation. No electricity for water pumps, gas pumps, refineries, oil wells… What kind of havoc would that create? I asked him if they would ever be able to do that, and he replied that it wasn't likely. They would never be able to get a missile that close. But then one day he told me that the North Koreans were successful in launching a satellite with only dead weight to simulate what a bomb weighs. And they flew their satellite right over the very spot that would be optimum for knocking out our power, and then down the eastern seaboard over Washington D.C. And then he told me they were planning to launch another satellite. It seems to me that if you go out of your way to make the one bomb that would destroy the

U.S., that you would figure out a way to use it. That was the day I decided he could build a bunker and whatever else it would take to save us. Does that give you enough of an answer?"

"It sure does, Mom. I just hope we never have to use it, because things never turn out the way you plan for them. They're usually worse."

Walking out to the shop, Sean found his dad changing the oil on his truck.

"This last week has been real good for me, Dad, but I'm going to fly back to Oceanside tomorrow and pick up the rest of my things. I'll rent a U-haul trailer to tow back with my truck. I'll be gone three or four days," said Sean.

"Do you want me to come with you?" asked Mitch. "I can take off from work for a while. I've got a good foreman who could handle things while I'm gone."

"No, Dad, that's alright. I can get some friends to help load a few things, and I'll just take my time driving back up. There won't be any hurry. I talked to Lieutenant Kelsey with the Sheriff's Office and told him what I had to do, and he said it would be fine. I just need to call him a couple of days before I'm ready to start work."

"Is the job a full-time position?" asked Mitch.

"Part time, only for three months. With some training in between, he thought there wouldn't be any problem putting me on full time, barring the possibility that I screw up something…" Sean paused to flash his dad a joking smile, then added, "You sure you and Mom won't mind me hanging around for a few months?"

"Son, we wouldn't mind if you stayed here permanently. We both love you and have really missed you these last four years. We're real proud of you, Son, so don't worry about that kind of stuff."

"I love you too, Dad. I'll give you a call when I'm loaded up and ready to come back. Mom will give me a ride to the airport in the morning."

"Are you sure you want to go to Oregon?" asked Sean.

Mike Taylor, Sean's best friend while in the marines, grinned at him. "I've been listening to you brag on Oregon for four years, and now you're trying to talk me out of seeing it?"

"It's not that. I'm just making sure you want to go. I've got a job to start right after I get back, so you'll be on your own some," answered Sean.

"Are you my mom now, thinking that I need babysitting while you're off playin' around?" laughed Mike.

"I guess if you need one, I can be. But don't start thinking I'm gonna be easy on you." Turning more serious Sean asked, "How long will it take to pack up what you need to take?"

"Not long. Less than an hour. Other than a couple of suitcases of clothes, the only other thing I have of value are my guns. Anything I leave behind, my sister can box up and put in the garage. If I decide to stick around up there, I'll just have her ship it up to me. We're all done here, so let's swing by my sister's, and we'll be on our way."

"Let's do it then! Mom and Dad will be glad to put you up until you figure out what you want to do, as long as you clean up after yourself, that is. We'll have time for some fishin', and huntin' season is just around the corner. Course, I'm not gonna be baiting your hook."

"You got yourself a girl up there yet? If you do, you'll have to point her out, so I don't end up with her," joked Mike.

"No need to worry about that. You've never seen the day you could take a girl away from me."

"Ha!" Mike playfully punched Sean on the shoulder. "Well, let's get going then, and we'll find out."

Sean and Mike made better time on the trip up to Springfield than at first anticipated. Taking turns driving, they drove all night and stopped at Mt. Shasta for a nice breakfast at Black Bear Diner. Leaving the diner, they still had four and a half hours to go to get home and were driving through Springfield just before noon on the second day. They had been in contact with his dad that morning, and so they were expected for lunch.

Mitch's property was located about fourteen miles northeast of Springfield, in a region of small farms and acreages. He had one hundred sixty acres with the Mohawk River crossing his property. He had a small bridge across the river leading up to his house, barn, and other outbuildings. A wall of oak trees with a few maples sprinkled in lined both sides of the small river, helping to shield the house and barn from the view of the road. There were also a few Douglas fir trees scattered about the property with some old growth trees close to the buildings.

The house and barn were built on the top of a small bench of ground about two hundred feet long and twelve to fourteen feet above the surrounding area. With a gentle slope leading up to the house from the front, the ground to the south and somewhat to the east fell away noticeably steeper. With the tall fir trees and a few leafy oak trees around the house for summertime shade, the place had a very picturesque quality to it. The newer built home was a ranch-style house with a large downstairs but a smaller upstairs. Facing mostly west, a veranda circled the house on three sides; across the front, along the south side and then across the back. The veranda was eight feet deep, with a roof and handrails all around. The two-car garage was on the north end of the house with a twenty-four foot concrete driveway and a short sidewalk extending to the veranda stairs leading to the front entrance. There was a large, luscious, green yard extending all around the house with several leafy trees and fir trees scattered across it. The gravel filled lane leading up to the driveway forked to the left to circle around the house on the north side out to the barn and shop behind.

As they approached the house, Mike could see a handful of horses sprinkled across the green pasture to the right of the house and down closer to the river were twelve or so cows and calves.

"What a nice looking place, Sean!" exclaimed Mike, as they were approaching the driveway. "I bet you had a lot of fun growing up here. You got fish in that creek down there?"

"Of course. Some trout, small-mouth bass, a few perch… Had lots of fun catching fish as a kid. We've got salmon and steelhead rivers close by, too," answered Sean.

Sean drove his truck and trailer around the house to the barn, where a large open area was suitable for turning around. Coming back to the front, he was able to back his trailer into the driveway to unload. Both his mom and dad came down the stairs to greet them, and his mom gave him a hug.

"Dad, Mom… this is Mike Taylor. I couldn't ask for a better friend or a better soldier to watch my back out in the field."

Mitch stepped up and shook Mike's hand. "Glad to hear you're one of the good guys. Thank you for watching over our boy. I know he needed it."

Beth stepped up, gave Mike a big hug, and kissed him on the cheek. "I'm so glad to meet you, Mike. Sean's told us quite a bit about you."

"Thank you for the welcome. I really appreciate it, and thank you for letting me stay here in your home for a while."

"It's no problem, Mike. You can stay as long as you'd like," said Mitch.

"Hey, Mom, could I take a shower before lunch? I'm feeling pretty grungy right now after that long drive."

"Sure, Honey. I'll start the burgers in about fifteen. That should give you enough time. How about you, Mike? There's two showers upstairs if you want to take the other one," offered Beth.

"Sounds great. I'll get my suitcase out of the truck and follow Sean, and thanks again."

CHAPTER THREE

"Do you have all your men lined up for the mission?" asked Kaziim.

"Yes. They all know what's expected of them. We have all of them in seclusion as we speak. There will be no possibility of anyone leaking the information before we've started," replied Haris.

"Are you absolutely sure this is what you want to do? Once it's started, there's no turning back, and we don't know how far this will go."

For a moment, Haris closed his eyes. "It is as Allah wills it."

"So be it. We have the virus perfected, but there is no vaccine or antidote. Whoever is infected will eventually die," warned Kaziim.

"We already know that. Everyone is ready to lay down their lives for this. Are all the containers ready for transport?" asked Haris.

"All the containers are hidden in the luggage, and we also have the solution in small spray bottles of mouth freshener that they will carry in their pockets. Totally undetectable."

"Alright, I'll give the order for the men to meet you in the conference room for a final briefing. They've already begun to put on their disguises to match their passport photos, so give them a half-hour to finish. Immediately after the briefing, the men will be transported to the airport for departure. Their flights out will start at two o'clock. May Allah bring us victory."

Haris stood watching from the opposite side of a viewing glass as forty men filed into the conference room and began seating themselves. There were three rows of tables with five tables each, and three men sat at each table facing toward the front of the room where Kaziim stood waiting to address them. Two tables were set up toward the front on opposite sides of the room; one had forty pairs of specially made black gloves laid out and the other with forty small spray bottles. The overhead lights were bright, and their reflection off the white painted walls gave the room a cold, harsh feel to it. Considering the reason for the meeting, the setting was a perfect match.

"To your right are the gloves you will be wearing whenever you handle your bottle of spray. Be very careful when you use the bottle, or you will be infected immediately. The solution is designed to cause the virus to absorb through the skin, so without your gloves you'll be infected immediately. You would still have up to fifteen or so days to deliver as much of the virus as you can, but each extra day that you last will mean greater success. Be very discreet when you spread the virus. You do not want to draw any attention to yourself if possible. It is best to spray as many touchable surfaces as possible, such as water faucet handles, door handles, taxicab handles, handrails, stair rails... anything that other people will be touching bare handed immediately after you. The virus will remain viable for up to one hour on almost any surface. Once you are at your destination, you will attend sporting events, concerts, public gatherings, and anything else where people gather in large numbers. Remember, wear your gloves. Now, row by row, come forward and pick up a pair of gloves, put them on, and then pick up one bottle and put it in your jacket pocket. Be very careful! As you leave, pick out your luggage with your name on it. There are new make-up kits for your disguises in your luggage. All of you know your destination, so as you leave this room, the taxis outside will take you to the airport. Good luck, my brothers."

After donning a pair of gloves and slipping a bottle of the mixture into his pocket, each man stopped at the row of luggage to pick out the one with his nametag on it, and then exited out the door. Haris watched them until they were all gone.

"So be it."

On the ride to the airport, two men were in each taxi. Halfway to the airport, with his gloves on, Hashim reached into his pocket and removed his small bottle of spray, which was disguised as mouth freshener. Looking at the bottle for a moment, he considered how much death was stored in such a small container. His fellow conspirator looked at him and then looked ahead at the road. "Put it away. It makes me nervous." Reaching for his pocket, he lifted the flap and then dropped the bottle inside.

Arriving at the airport, the two men exited the taxi from each side and made their way to the check-in counter. Before the taxi pulled away, a husband and wife with a seven year-old boy climbed in. The driver had orders to return to the compound right away, but what would it hurt to make a little more money. No one would know.

As the family was being let out at an apartment building near the center of the city, the boy found a small spray bottle in the seat. Taking it with him, he showed it to his mom and asked what was in it. She looked at it and asked him where he got it. When he replied, she dropped it to the sidewalk, explaining that it could be bad for him. As they walked away, a pedestrian strolling by kicked it into the street. A couple of minutes later, nine people walked out of the building and stopped close to the curb, laughing, and talking about where to go. Four of them were teenage boys, the rest were adults.

Another cab drove up to see if they wanted a ride, and as he came to a stop, the front tire ran over the small bottle, shattering it and causing the contents to fly up into the air, spraying all nine of the people on the sidewalk.

Of the forty men, some were flying out immediately, and others were to wait at the airport for up to several hours until their flight was scheduled to leave. Almost all of the men would have to take a second or third flight to their final destination, as their airport of origin did not have direct flights to most of the countries that they were sent to target. Final destinations included almost all of the major metropolitan areas of the world, including Washington D.C., New York, San Francisco, Los Angeles, Miami, London, Paris, Zurich, Amsterdam, Berlin, Moscow, Tokyo, Jakarta, Delhi, Shanghai, Beijing, Calcutta, Rio, Sao Paulo, Sydney, Manila, Seoul, Lagos, and Johannesburg. The goal was to try and cover as many geographic areas as possible, as well as the largest population centers, hoping that the spread of the virus would be so catastrophically fast that it would overwhelm all attempts to stop it. Of course, with their hatred of the United States, it had more initial cities targeted than any other nation. If the disease infected and killed a large number of health and emergency workers in its first big epidemic sweep, then it's future growth would be even less hampered, guaranteeing a global sweep by the end of the year.

All of the men were instructed to infect as much of their initial destinations as possible in far reaching directions and then to move on to their secondary targets if time allowed. No one knew for sure how much time was going to be needed to accomplish their goals or exactly when they themselves would finally be infected and succumb to the virus. Their leaders were hoping to infect as many people as they could before the world's top scientists, doctors, and researchers could get started on a cure or a vaccine. Their own researchers had been unable to create a vaccine or even an antidote, and the chances that there would be any way to halt the spread of the disease were slim to none.

The disease would run its course and then would, at the end of the epidemic, eventually die out as the infected were left to die or were killed outright. With no living tissue to feed on, the virus would cease to exist. As the World Health officials would learn more about the disease as time progressed, they would realize that the best defense against the virus would be isolationism. If there was no contact whatsoever between an infected person and a healthy one, then the virus would die in its tracks. But it would take time before the World Health Organization came to the right conclusion, and by then, the world's population would have suffered a catastrophic loss.

Haris knew as much about the virus as anyone on his team. He fully realized what would be happening worldwide in less than six weeks: the death of millions, the desperation of seven billion people to stay alive, the collapse of governments and nations, and the ruination of families at their foundational level. He knew, and he still sent forth his men to begin the destruction.

Haris contacted his leaders and gave the go ahead to tighten security at their borders. Flights into their airports would have certain restrictions, but the roads were to remain open for two more weeks and no foot traffic across the border after that time. He didn't want to tip his hand too early and draw attention of any kind to himself or his people.

Patrols of their borders would begin immediately. They had been storing up provisions for their people for two years in anticipation of this moment, and they would be able to survive for three years without any interaction with the rest of the world. He knew that their only hope was to remain isolated from the rest of mankind, and when the dust had settled, they would control the world and its remaining population.

CHAPTER FOUR

"You ever fish for steelhead before?" asked Sean.

"Nope. Watched a couple shows on TV though. Looks like fun," answered Mike.

"You want to try it?"

"Sure. Where at?"

"We'll try the McKenzie River. The best fishing is already over but there's still some good fish in the river. The McKenzie comes out of the Cascade Mountains to the east, runs past Springfield, and then joins the Willamette River. We'll head east upriver about twenty miles to the Leaburg Dam," Sean explained. "There's a convenience store close by that we can run over to right now so we can buy our fishing licenses and pick up some bait. Dad's got a couple poles we can use, but we'll need to replace the line and buy some tackle. We'll go out first thing in the morning."

Heading up the river at dawn, Sean and Mike were drinking coffee, talking about the farm and what it was like growing up in the area as a kid. Sean shared with him a few of his fishing stories on the McKenzie River and some of the other rivers close by. Mike was just starting to be able to see into the distance, watching farmers' fields going by as the first light was starting to spread across the countryside. Things seemed to be so alive in this area of Oregon. There was so much greenery and forest that Mike was already falling in love with the area, and with all of the rivers, streams, and hills, there was a rare beauty about the place that Mike had never experienced before. He was finding out that it was just as beautiful as Sean had boasted about, and he was seriously considering making it his new home.

As they continued up the highway, Mike could see the shine of the river every now and then through the trees and blackberry bushes. A lot of thick undergrowth everywhere made him wonder how they were going to make it to the river's edge, and he asked Sean about it.

"Anywhere you park where there's a fishing hole, there'll be trails through the underbrush to the river's edge. All along the river, there'll be open area to move around on because the high water in the spring keeps it swept bare. There will still be some close trees, so you'll have to keep from hanging up your gear when you cast."

When they reached the Leaburg dam, Sean turned onto it, drove across to the other side, and then turned downstream for about a half mile. They passed a couple of parked cars of early fishermen before they came to Sean's favorite spot. Pulling into a wide spot for parking, Mike couldn't see anything but trees and brush. The sun wouldn't be up for another half-hour, but there was enough light to see what they were doing as they climbed out of Sean's truck and gathered their gear. It wasn't freezing, but it was still cold enough to see their breath in drifting white clouds as they moved about. There were fallen leaves on the ground, some new and some rotting, with the fresh fallen dew covering them. Mike could smell the forest, especially the tang of pine or fir trees, but there was also a scent of the river, which was hard to explain, other than a fresh and clean smell. Above everything was the sound of the rushing water, echoing off the trees, reverberating through the river canyon.

As Mike followed Sean toward the wall of brush, a trail opened up through the seemingly impenetrable wall, and after only a few yards, they were looking at the river. They could see a wide smoother area of flowing, crystal clear water moving from their right to their left, from one small set of whitewater rapids to another. The riverbank was covered with small, rounded river rock, an occasional larger rock, and even small boulders, with sand in between everything. Small leafy brush was the last of the vegetation separating the river from the forest of oak, maple, and fir trees. As they neared the edge of the water, Sean explained again how to cast and drift the salmon eggs down the current and what to feel for.

After baiting up, Sean stepped into the edge of the water and showed Mike how it was done. Upriver, Mike could see two people fishing, and there was one person on the other side. Mike baited up, then stood and watched Sean on a few drifts to see how it was done.

"Go ahead and give it a shot," Sean encouraged. "Cast upstream at about forty-five degrees, reel in your slack until you can feel your weight bouncing along the bottom, and then let it drift down to about the same degree and reel in… Looks good, Mike. Cast again."

Mike could feel the bumping of the rocks on the river bottom, and then he heard Sean exclaim, "Jerk on it! That's a bite!"

Jerking his pole back to set the hook, Mike could feel the movement of a heavy fish on his line. His pole was bent over in an arc, and his drag was sizzling. Sean reached over to the front of his reel and tightened the drag just a little. All of a sudden, close to the other side of the river, a large silver shape flew out of the water and then crashed back with a huge splash.

"Did you see that? He was huge. I've never felt a fish like this before."

"Keep your tip up! He'll run right back at you, and you'll have to reel fast to keep him from spitting the hook."

For several minutes, Mike had quite a fight on his hands. He walked up and down the river a few steps, and then when the fish started to give up and he reeled him closer to the shore, Mike thought it was all over. All of a sudden, the fish took off again, heading for the other side, burning the line off of the drag, and drawing exclamations of wonder from Mike.

"Did you see him make that run? Wow, what a fish!"

After a couple of more minutes, the fish was done, and Mike was able to bring him close to shore. One of the fishermen had come walking down the river with a net to watch the play and offer the net. As he moved closer, Sean realized it wasn't a him, but a woman—a good looking woman. In the river canyon, the sun wasn't up yet, and the light out wasn't good at a distance. As the woman came closer, she looked at him and held out her net.

"I see you need a net. That's a nice fish… probably about twelve pounds…?" Even her voice was pretty.

Sean, with a slight smile on his face, looked into her green eyes and replied "It's been awhile since I netted a fish. You can go ahead and do the honors."

Mike was looking at the girl now instead of his fish.

"Keep your tip up! Now just lead him a little closer to me," she told him, as she stepped out into the water a couple of feet, holding the net just under the surface. As the fish was pulled toward her, she scooped it up. "There we go. Good job!"

It was a little cool in the river canyon, being almost September, and the girl had on a beanie cap to keep her ears warm, with her hair pulled up under it. Sean could see tufts of loose hair hanging out that let him know she was a blond. Even with the jacket and fishing vest on, Sean could see that she had some nice curves. She realized both Sean and Mike were looking her over, and dropping her eyes to the fish, she tried to keep from smiling.

"Are you guys catch-and-release types, or are you going to keep that one? Because you need to decide quick before she dies."

Sean couldn't resist the opening she gave him; it was too perfect. "I don't know about my buddy Mike here, but I'm definitely the catch-and-keep type," Sean said, with a grin to add more charm.

The young woman couldn't keep from smiling in return.

"I'm more of a keeper, too." Mike added, also smiling.

"Well, do you have a pen to mark down your fish? If you're the keeper type, you should always have one."

"I knew I was forgetting something this morning. I haven't fished for four years, so I'm a little rusty."

"You haven't been locked away have you?" she asked a little skeptically.

"No, nothing like that. Mike and I just got out of the marines about five weeks ago. This is Mike's first time fishing for steelhead."

"That twelve pounder is a good way to start… especially on only his second or third cast. You must be a pretty good teacher, or he's a fast learner."

"I'm a fast learner." Mike jumped into the conversation, wanting to draw some attention to himself. "If I had a better teacher, like yourself, for instance, I could become quite the fisherman."

She chuckled softly. "Oh, I think you'll do alright with your friend here."

"Sean. My name's Sean Dixon." Sean supplied his name before Mike could answer.

"I'm Rachel. Glad to meet you." She reached into her back jeans pocket and pulled out an ink pen. "Hand me your tag, and I'll show you how to tag a fish." Mike pulled out his license folder and handed it to her. He watched as she removed his license from it, unfolded the papers, and held them up for him to watch. "So, Mike… I see you're a non-resident from California. What brings you to Oregon?"

"If you want to call Sean a 'what', he's what brought me. We were in the marines together for four years, and all he talked about was getting back to Oregon. So when he came back to Oceanside from his parents' house to get his stuff, I decided to come along and check it out." Looking her directly in the eyes, he added, "Now that I've seen how beautiful it is and what it has to offer, I think I'm going to stay."

"That sounds wonderful. Here, watch how I do this." She showed Mike how to find the river number and species and where to write it down, and then she pulled out a small tape measure from her pocket to measure the length of his fish. "Write the length here, and it's done."

Handing him his papers, Mike began folding them up to put them away. Rachel stepped up to Sean and said, "Maybe you should keep this pen in case he catches another one." Taking his left hand in hers, she opened his palm, aware that there was no ring, and wrote her phone number. She left the pen in his hand, then looked up at him with a beautiful smile.

"If you need any more help, just call me. I'll be right up there all morning… with my dad." She turned around and started walking back to her fishing partner.

"Thanks, Rachel, for your help," Mike said.

Without turning to look back, Rachel waved over her shoulder. "Anytime, Mike!" They both watched her walk away, hip boots and all.

Mike looked at Sean. "Wow… What a woman! You notice how she didn't want to seem too forward, so she gave her number to you instead of me?"

Sean laughed. "I really hate to break it to you, Mike, but that's not why I've got her number."

"That's not fair. I'm the one who caught the fish and needed the help…" Mike complained.

Sean grinned at Mike and said, "Well, you caught the fish. I'm the one who caught the girl." Sean pulled up his sleeve and wrote the number on his arm, just in case the one on his hand started to fade.

An hour later, Sean noticed Rachel was fighting a fish, while her dad was standing by, holding the net. He nudged Mike and gave him a head nod. As they watched, Rachel reeled her fish in, and her dad netted it.

"You had it right when you said, 'What a woman!' Catches her own fish, she's pretty, sexy voice, beautiful smile, and pretty intelligent too. Look how quickly she put you in your place and chose me over you. Quite a woman!"

"Go ahead," Mike replied. "Rub it in. Maybe we should go ask her if she has a sister?"

Continuing to fish, Sean hooked up one a few minutes later. Looking up the river, he could see Rachel and her dad walking toward them with the net. Trying not to get too excited, he kept his attention on his fish. He was standing in a foot of water with his dad's hip boots on. As he turned to step past a rock, his fish took off down river, and he slipped on the slick rocks that were under water, falling sideways into a foot of cold McKenzie water. Keeping his rod up, he came out of the water sputtering. He continued reeling on his fish, fighting him back up into the hole, and after a few more struggles, the fish was his. He led it back toward shore, where Rachel stepped into the water and scooped it up.

"Burr. I forgot how cold the McKenzie could be..." Sean said with a wry chuckle.

Rachel pulled a small towel out of her jacket pocket and wiped the water off of his face.

"Wow, you've thought of everything. Always prepared, huh? Thanks, Rachel!"

"You're welcome. You put on quite a show for us. This is my dad, Kevin O'Donnell. Dad, this is Sean Dixon and his friend, Mike."

"Glad to meet you, Mr. O'Donnell. I hope my performance doesn't affect your approval of your daughter going out on a date with me."

Laughing outright, Kevin reached out to shake Sean's hand. The laugh wrinkles around his eyes were pronounced, and Sean could see where Rachel got her humorous side. "No worry of that, Son. We all fall down eventually. Now Rachel, here, is a strong-willed character herself, and I imagine she'll date whomever she wants, regardless of what I think. But I trust her judgment of character." Extending his hand to Mike, he said, "So, Rachel said you guys just got out of the marines. You staying around here close?"

"Mike's staying with my parents and me out on Marcola Road. He's thinking about staying on, if things work out. He's going to work for my dad for a while until he finds out about a job with the Lane County Sheriff's Department."

"Your dad wouldn't be Mitch Dixon, would he?"

"Yes, sir, he is. So you know him?"

"I've met him. I bought a couple steers from him last year. He's got a nice looking place out there."

"I sure like it," Mike put in. "It looks absolutely beautiful to a city guy like me."

"Well, say hello to your dad for me. I really enjoyed that beef I bought from him. Maybe I'll get to see him again."

"I will."

Sean turned to look at Rachel, expecting to say goodbye.

"When is this date I just heard about supposed to take place? I'd say the sooner the better…"

"Really? Uh… well…" Sean was so surprised and caught off guard that he was a little slow in making a decision.

"How about tonight at five o'clock?" asked Rachel, deciding for him. "We live on Camp Creek Road, this end, third house on the right. Our name is on the mailbox, and you've got my number if you need to call." Rachel had a smile on her face as she finished.

"Okay, Rachel…" Sean couldn't stop smiling. "Sounds good. I'll be there."

CHAPTER FIVE

The stewardess aboard the Pan-Am flight en route to Shanghai, noticed the man seated in 23C. He had dark hair, a beard, and was wearing dark clothes with a jacket. Nothing unusual, really, except that he looked a little nervous and seemed to be perspiring more than anyone else on the plane. She thought that it was just a fear of flying that was causing his discomfiture, but she had also noticed that he had been wearing a pair of black gloves since he had come on board nine hours ago. That seemed a little odd, so she had been keeping an eye on him for several hours.

At one point during the flight, she had to ask him to leave the galley, and his English was so bad it was hard to understand what he was saying. He had used the restroom several times, but he wasn't carrying anything with him, nor had he taken anything from his carry-on from the overhead storage compartments. She was beginning to assume that the man just had some problems, either mentally or physically, that would account for his behavior. Nothing to worry about—probably just another nut case. One thing about seeing so many people every day was that she knew there were all kinds in the world, and a lot of them were borderline weird. Other than weird, he was probably harmless enough.

A flight to Tokyo, with one of the terrorists on board, was carrying two hundred thirty passengers, and being a long, non-stop flight, almost everyone was infected by the time it landed. Once in the airport, the terrorist continued to leave the virus on escalator handrails, door handles, and anything and everything that he could see people touching on a regular basis. Not being in any hurry, he spent seven or eight hours exploring the airport, infecting hundreds, if not thousands, of people. With so many things being operated with motion sensors, such as water faucets in the bathrooms, automatic doors, and the like, the terrorist constantly had to be on the watch for productive ways to spread the virus.

Tokyo had so many people always on the move, so it wasn't hard to figure out ways to infect them. All of the most heavily populated cities presented a lot of ways to infect a lot of people quickly, and the terrorists were trained in finding those ways.

Two men arrived in Washington D.C. on a flight from London, early the second day of the mission. Both of them went throughout the airport, twice, infecting and re-infecting handrails, door handles, water faucets, and even the toilet stall door handles. The restrooms looked like the best target for a continuous movement of people in and out, and if they felt some moisture on any handles, they wouldn't give it much of a second thought, especially with all the hand washing going on.

As time moved on, one of the terrorists had to catch a flight to Chicago, which was his primary target. By early afternoon of the second day, there were two hundred infected people walking off the plane into Chicago's O'Hare airport, including Lisa Adams, who lived in Washington D.C.

Although the flight only lasted an hour and a half, Lisa saw one man in particular, who was seated across from her and two rows forward, visit the restroom three times. He was dark haired, with a dark beard, wearing dark clothes and dark gloves, and he seemed a little on the nervous side. She knew that a lot of people were extremely nervous when they flew, so she just assumed that was the case with him.

Aboard American Airlines flight to New York from Paris were two men of the original forty. While one was spraying down the restroom door handles and the faucets inside, the other one slipped into the galley and sprayed down the silverware drawer and the plates and glasses in the cabinet. One of them, upon arriving at New York, was to board a connecting flight to Boston, with a two-hour layover. The second was to catch a flight to Miami, also with a two-hour layover. That left them with plenty of time to wander around in the airport, carrying out their orders.

With some of the terrorists traveling through at least three different airports, there were many more than forty airports infected on the first day.

The rest of the forty were doing the same on all of their flights. By the time they all had reached their final destination, it was safe to assume that possibly over ten thousand people had already been infected with the virus. Add to that number a potential three to five thousand people in each major airport that they walked through, the numbers infected in the first twenty-four hours would be astounding. After symptoms started, for a period of around nine days, all of those people would be infecting others, since none of them during that time would even know that they were carrying a contagious virus. Most would assume that it was a cold or flu bug that they might have picked up while traveling, so any family members or friends that would end up taking care of them would be infected if any bodily fluids were transferred.

By the time they realized that the infected people needed hospitalization, the virus would be close to the critical stage of the patient becoming aggressive and combative, striking out at everything around them. From yelling and screaming to scratching and biting, the medical profession wouldn't know what to make of it. With every transfer of saliva or blood into an open wound such as a scratch or bite or any mucous area, the virus would be transferred. It would not be beyond the realm of possibility that every infected person would infect at least another ten people. And even those infected in the second tier wouldn't realize that they were infected until they had become ill. By that time, the Center for Disease Control may have gathered enough information to begin warning the population of the outbreak and to take precautionary measures.

Add into the mix all of the people that would be infected by the continuing efforts of the original forty at many public gatherings, and the numbers would soon rise into untold millions. Even before the first symptoms were beginning to surface, nine days would have gone by with new people being infected every day to the tune of thousands. One terrorist at a professional football or soccer game could infect ten thousand or more in one day, and in America, football season was in full swing. The rate of infection would grow exponentially with every passing day.

Sean pulled to a stop in front of Rachel's house at a quarter 'til five, and as he was walking up to the front porch, the door opened and a beautiful creature in a beige print dress stepped out. She had honey blonde hair with a soft wave in it that extended about seven or eight inches below her shoulders, the beautiful face was almost completely bare of make-up, except for a small amount of eyeliner to bring out the green of her eyes, and her womanly curves were so eye-catching and appealing that he forgot his manners and was staring.

Sean dropped his eyes to look at the floor of the porch for a quick moment to recover his composure. Lifting his gaze back to her face, looking into her eyes, he apologized, "Please forgive me for staring. You caught me by surprise. This morning you had on hip boots, pants, a jacket, and a vest, and your hair was hiding under that beanie. I never realized that you were so beautiful."

Her eyes sparkled. "What's there to forgive when you explain it like that?" Rachel reached her hand up to his face and wiped the edge of his mouth.

"Something on my face? I'm sorry."

"Just a little drool..." she teased, and she gave him another one of those smiles that he saw at the river that morning.

This girl's got a real sense of humor, thought Sean. It's gonna be a lot of fun getting to know her.

He was invited in and was able to meet her mom, Joanna, who was just as adorable as Rachel. She was about five-feet, three-inches tall with similar hair coloring, and she was as nice as could be. Rachel also had a younger brother, Steve, who was a senior in high school, and a sister, Leah, who was almost seventeen. Looking at a recent family photograph, Sean could see that Leah was growing into quite a fox herself.

Mr. O'Donnell hadn't arrived home by the time Sean and Rachel were ready to leave, so Sean turned to Joanna before taking off.

"I'll try not to keep her out too late. After dinner, we're going to catch a movie, and then I wanted to take her out to my parent's house and let them meet her. After I told them about her, they're pretty excited to meet her in person."

"Okay, Sean, that sounds fine, and I appreciate your concern for us, but Kevin and I know you'll take good care of our baby. Have a good time, sweetie."

Finding out that Rachel liked Chinese food, Sean took her to Kowloon's Restaurant close to Autzen Stadium. It was a nice establishment. The food was delicious, and the service was exceptional. Outside of the window, the late afternoon sun was lighting up the pond and trees as people walked along a path, both coming and going, with an occasional jogger trotting by. Sean could hardly keep his eyes off of Rachel and had to keep averting his gaze to keep from staring. When he returned his gaze to look at her, he noticed that she would immediately avert her gaze, as if to not let him see that she was staring back at him when he wasn't looking.

As the evening progressed and their conversation became easier, their gazes lingered longer and longer with one another. They settled into a kind of comfort with each other that belied that it was their first date.

"I've never been able to talk to a woman so easily, so it's almost unbelievable to think that we only met this morning. I can tell you Mike was really disappointed when you wrote your number on my hand."

Rachel laughed outright. "I thought he might be. He was really sweet and was trying so hard to impress me, but you seemed like you weren't trying at all and that impressed me even more. There was something about you that drew me in and excited me, and I'm not easily impressed."

"I'm glad you're not. Otherwise, you would already have a boyfriend, and then where would I be?"

"I'm sure you would have survived." Rachel paused a moment in thought. "Actually, you do strike me as a survivor. I don't think there would be many things that you couldn't handle. You seem to be extremely confident, but you don't overdo it. It's a subtle, quiet confidence that's very reassuring. It's so subtle, I'm not sure if most people would pick up on it."

"Sounds like you've been studying me," replied Sean.

Rachel gave out a quiet laugh. "Of course I'm studying you. You've impressed me so much already, and I'm trying to figure out why. If there is any potential future for us, I want to know all I can about you. Uh, I didn't tip my hand too early, did I?"

Sean started laughing. This girl… who wouldn't want to hang out with her? "No, no that's alright. To be honest, I've been thinking the same thing. I can hardly wait to know more about you. So tell me, do you work, or go to school?"

"I'm attending Lane Community College. My classes don't start for two more weeks. I'm in my second year studying to be a dental hygienist. Have you decided on what you want to do, now that you're out of the marines?"

"I've got a start. I joined up with the Sheriff's Department last week; it's only a part time job for now, and there's some classes mixed in for law enforcement. Mostly I'll just be riding along to get a feel for it and see how things are done. I actually start that tomorrow morning," Sean explained.

"Does your experience in the marines help you to become a deputy?"

"It does have its advantages. I already have weapons training, hand-to-hand combat, know how to follow orders, familiar with the chain of command, and a few other things that most policemen may never attain."

"What kind of things?" asked Rachel.

Sean could see that she had a genuine concern for everything that he said and a desire to learn who he really was. He continued, "For one, live fire situations. When there are live rounds coming at you from several locations, you can't afford to lose your head or make a wrong decision. Either one of those can get you or your team members killed. You have to do what you're trained to do and take out your enemy as quickly and efficiently as you can, so as to limit your own casualties but inflict as many casualties as you can on your enemy."

Sean's speech had slowed a little as he explained about warfare, and she knew that she was hearing from the man that he really was.

"You have to learn when to fire and when not to. Sometimes there is a fine line between the two, and it sometimes comes down to an instantaneous decision, almost an automatic reflex that is honed only in warfare situations."

"Were you good at what you were trained at?" She wanted to know.

"Mike and I were two of the best. We were careful, precise, and trusting in each other's abilities to keep our men safe. And our men trusted us and the decisions that we made. Because of that, our unit was sent out on a lot of missions. Naturally, we lost a few good men, because the brass trusted us enough to send us out on the hard ones." Sean's voice now had a tone of sadness in it, and Rachel didn't want to hear anymore.

Reaching across the table, she put her hand over his and gently squeezed it.

"I'm sorry, Sean. I know it must hurt. Please forgive me for prying."

"Rachel, it's alright. I… you need to know these things about me. If there's going to be a good future between us, you need to know who I am. But for now, let's lighten it up a little and go see that movie."

After the movie, Sean drove out to his home to show Rachel off to his parents. He knew they were going to fall in love with her; she had such a beautiful character and a sweet spirit about her that she would be accepted immediately. Her physical beauty was, of course, a wonderful bonus, but the thing of it was, her beauty on the inside matched her beauty on the outside. Coming to a stop, Sean stepped from the truck, and as Rachel slid to the edge of the seat with her feet ready to step to the ground, Sean put his hands under her arms and lifted her out of the truck with ease and set her on the ground.

His parents were expecting him to stop by with her. As soon as they were out of his truck, the front door opened and his parents walked out. He knew they were excited to meet her because of the way he had carried on about how special she was. They had been hoping for quite some time that he would find a good woman and settle down to raise a family.

Walking up the steps with Rachel holding his arm, he presented her to his parents. The sun was already down, but there was still enough light for them to see her in all of her beauty. Sean, at that moment, felt like a conquering hero returning from war with the richest of spoils.

"Mom, Dad, this is Rachel O'Donnell. Rachel, this is my mom, Beth, and my dad, Mitch."

Beth stepped up and hugged her unreservedly, and then pulled back enough to look her in the eyes. "Rachel, I'm so glad to meet you. It sounds like you've made quite an impression on Sean." She kissed Rachel on the cheek before she let go. Mitch also took his turn, wrapping his arms around Rachel, a fatherly embrace, before saying,

"Now I can see why Sean's been carrying on about you. We hope to be seein' a lot of you. You certainly have our blessing."

"Thank you both so much for the warm welcome. I can see why Sean speaks so highly of both of you. You two should be proud of what you've raised Sean to be."

"Thank you, Rachel." Beth took her hand and started leading her into the house. "Let's go in the house so we can visit and get to know you."

Sean smiled, even as he found himself standing on the porch by himself.

CHAPTER SIX

Sean met up with Lieutenant Kelsey three days after he returned from California, the day after meeting Rachel. He started taking some classes on law enforcement, and Kelsey took him to the gun range to check his skill level with firearms. Sean tested with both a pistol and sniper rifle, and Kelsey was genuinely surprised at his shooting ability, even knowing that he had previously been in the marines.

"You've definitely got some skill with firearms, and being in the marines for four years, I'm sure you've developed some wisdom on when not to pull the trigger. That's a big plus in this business, and I'm sure you'll do fine in your classes. I'm going to put you on schedule to go on a ride along with one of our deputies sometime in the next couple of days, just to get your feet wet. With your continuing classes to learn the basics of law enforcement, I think you're going to do just fine."

"Thanks, Bill. I appreciate your vote of confidence. I wanted to ask, do you have any more openings for another officer? I've got a friend who served with me, and he was wondering about it," explained Sean.

"We don't have any at the moment, but if our new bond measure passes in a couple of months, we are looking to add two more positions. If he's not doing anything else, maybe it would be a good idea to take the same classes you're taking now. Then, if he wants to come in and fill out an application, we can put him up high on the list if things turn out."

"Okay. I'll let him know. Thanks again, Bill… for everything."

Two days later, Sean was off work by three, and he gave Rachel a call to see if she wanted to go out. He found himself thinking about her all the time, which made him want to see her even more. After running home to get cleaned up, he picked her up at four, and ten minutes later, they were driving west through downtown Springfield.

As they approached the Willamette River, they turned north on Mill Street to Island Park. He had been thinking about a special place to take her, and even though they had been out together a couple of times over the last three days, he felt a long walk in the park would be ideal for learning more about who she was.

He led Rachel down the path from the parking lot, strolling under the shade trees and along the river, sharing with her a lot of his past, his upbringing, and a little more about his time in the military. He felt that she was very special and wanted their relationship to start out the proper way. If things didn't progress any further, then he didn't want any more regrets than necessary. Although the way she had already affected him with her character and charm, he knew that there would definitely be regrets.

"So, tell me why you don't have a boyfriend. What I've seen about you already tells me that guys should be knocking down your door trying to win your affection."

"Well, that's a hard question to answer. I'll try to tell it as simply as possible. I was a little overweight in high school. I had braces. I wore glasses, until Mom and Dad took me in for Lasik surgery… and so there weren't that many guys chasing after me. The ones that did found out that I wasn't an easy catch. When they realized that I wasn't going to give them what they wanted, they would back off and eventually tie up with someone else. My dad realized what was happening, so he invited me along with him all the time to make me feel better. Because of that, I fell in love with the outdoors. He taught me to fish the river, to hunt and track… but he also taught me to think for myself and to figure things out. So, the more time I spent with him and doing the things I loved, I didn't spend much time letting guys chase me."

Sean took her hand and held it as they walked along the path. "So you never found anyone special?" asked Sean.

"Not really. There were several guys that I liked, but they either didn't like me or they were already taken." She shrugged, then asked,

"How about you? If you're the catch-and-keep type, why don't you have someone hanging all over you?"

Continuing to walk, he explained, "I have had a couple that hung on for a while, but when their desire for a career became more important than their feelings for me, it ended. Joining up with the marines also became a roadblock to finding or seeking a steady girlfriend. But now that I'm not in the marines anymore..." Pausing for a moment to think, he turned his head to look at her. "Rachel, I've never met anyone quite like you before. I don't know how to explain it... the way you take my breath away, the excitement I've felt every time I've looked in your eyes, or the way my heart was beating when I pulled up to your house to see you walk out the door... I know this is sudden, and you can say slow down, but I hope that you're feeling the same way." Sean had stopped and turned toward her, looking into her eyes, as he was talking.

"I am feeling the same way." Looking up into his eyes, she raised her hands to his face, and stretching up on her tiptoes, she felt his lips come down to hers in a gentle, sweet contact. She felt his arms wrap around her in a warm embrace that felt so secure. He tilted his head back to look her in the eye for a moment, and then brought his lips back to hers in a more passionate kiss. She answered his passion with a passion of her own that she had never before shared in a kiss. When next they separated and they looked at each other for a long moment, he took her hand in his and started walking down the path once again.

While looking at the river, the leaf-laden trees, the beautiful setting of the park, and listening to the rippling of the water over the rocks, he occasionally stole a glance at her beautiful profile, trying to understand his emotions. Not saying anything for quite some time, he was trying to order his thoughts. He had never felt himself so excited about any girl in his life, especially on such short notice, and he was wondering how this could be happening so quickly. He wasn't sure of what to say to her. Her kiss felt so right—so powerful. He didn't want to say something that would scare her away.

"You're so quiet. Was there something wrong with our kiss?"

Sean could tell by her question that he had remained silent for too long. He just wasn't sure how to word his answer. He didn't want to sound romantic, but he did want to seem sincere.

"That's just it. There wasn't anything at all wrong with it. It's kind of hard to put into words, but… I've never done anything in my life that's felt so… well, right. Does that sound weird?" asked Sean.

"No, it doesn't. I felt the same way." She giggled playfully, and her eyes sparkled as she teased, " You know… I think we may need to try it again… and probably again… just to be sure, though."

This time it was Rachel that stopped and pulled his face down to her upturned lips, seeking to test his words once again.

"Sir, London officials have picked up a man, looks to be of Arab descent. He was videotaped spraying surfaces with a liquid solution out of a small spray bottle. They're running tests on the solution as we speak, but no conclusions yet. Of course, he's not talking. Not one word. No I.D., no passport, nothing. They don't know where he was staying yet, but he had a room key that they're trying to track down," explained analyst William Fulton.

"Do you think this might be what we're after?" asked the director.

"I've got a strong feeling it is."

"Contact them immediately and explain to them the situation. If that solution is a biological agent, then they need to be extremely careful. Depending on future developments, of course, see if they need our help for the interrogation. Make it clear to them that if that solution is what we believe it to be, it is imperative that they retrieve everything that he knows about it, no matter what the means they have to employ to get it."

"Right away, sir."

"I'll get a meeting with the President lined up immediately. I want you there. I'll call you with the details, but bring everything you got on this."

"Yes, sir."

Haris, turned his head to see his top scientist coming through the door and then returned his gaze out the window. As the footsteps stopped beside him, he said, "Intel has been coming in. Our men have been very successful in the areas they've been able to access. There's only one that has missed a check-in, and that was only an hour ago."

"Do you have the second wave ready to go?" asked Kaziim.

"Yes. Twenty-five more. Do you have their luggage ready to go and the conference room set up?"

"Yes, it's all ready to start," answered Kaziim.

"They've already been given their destinations and their secondary targets. If you're ready, I'll give the order for them to assemble in the conference room."

"Give me thirty minutes, and I'll be there."

Haris stood thinking for a few moments after the departure of Kaziim. The second wave of men that he was sending out would infect more flights with the virus. There was no telling where all of the infected people would end up—which country, state, city… or which geographic region in the world they were going to. They could be traveling to someplace for business, vacation, visiting family, or government purposes, or they could be heading home on the same flight as one of his men. To figure out everywhere that the virus would travel, with just even one planeload of people, was practically impossible. International air flight was certainly a boon for the spreading of an epidemic disease. There would be no stopping it.

Two hours later at the White House, the CIA director and his top analyst was meeting with the President and her department heads in the Situation Room. They had read a brief on the subject of the meeting just prior to the arrival of the director. All of them were anxious to hear the full scope of the situation. There were twenty or so people lining two sides of a long table with the President at the head of it. There were monitors and computer terminals along the back wall, with several wall-mounted TV screens around the room, for all of them to watch whenever something was needed to be shown on screen.

"This is my top analyst, William Fulton," began Director Langdon. "I'm going to let him fill you in on the details."

"Um, let me begin with… um, two years ago, we picked up intel that there was a need for some scientists. We didn't know what kind or how many or who needed them. All we were able to put together was that at least ten scientists, who were on the periphery of our radar, turned up missing. Some of them were specialists in the field of genetic engineering, some were into disease control, and some had training in molecular biology. Putting these three together under the wrong leader would be very dangerous. They've had two years or more developing whatever it is that they're using and planning how best to use it. I'm talking about biological agents in the form of viruses, diseases… some type of biological warfare."

He continued, "A lot of the chatter that we've picked up lately has been talking about something big in the works. We've had no solid evidence of anything… until today. Four hours ago, the London police picked up a man of Arab descent. No papers, no clues as to his identity. He was seen on video surveillance spraying a liquid substance on the door handles of the restrooms at the Waterloo Central Station. The police were careful in their apprehension of the suspect, and a hazmat team was sent in to clean up. London officials were notified by us of the possibilities of what they have, and they have already begun testing of the substance that was found in the bottle. Initial reports show that it is a biological virus. They still have tests to run, but it doesn't look good. All of the initial officers are being quarantined for safety measures, and if they begin to show signs of anything unusual, it'll help in the research into what this thing is." Fulton finished with a look around the room. Intent faces were looking back at him, and then one by one, they began to look away or at each other. He turned to the director and nodded his head.

"This may only be the tip of the iceberg. I think we need to assume that this is not one man working alone. We've already dispatched our two leading experts in viral diseases to London to try and figure out what this thing is and just how bad it's going to be. We've already contacted our counterparts in fifteen countries to apprise them of the situation and what to look out for. They will be monitoring hospitals for anything unusual. Until we have more intel from the suspect's interrogation, we don't know what our next step is going to be."

The President, turning to the Secretary of Homeland Security, said "John, you need to get your people on this thing right away. The CDC needs to notify hospitals, emergency rooms, and any urgent care facilities to report any unusual illnesses, or even an unusual increase in illnesses… It doesn't matter what the symptoms are—anything at all out of the ordinary. We can't assume that London was the first or the only target. If this is an attack from an Arab terrorist organization, then my guess is that the United States is very high on their list of targets. We may have already been infiltrated by agents of this organization.

"Director Langdon, start cross referencing all passenger manifests that might have anyone from the Middle East and find out what their current status is. Include anyone, of any nationality, if their point of origin began anywhere in the Middle East, even our own citizens. We can't rule out the possibility of domestic terrorists involved in this. If there is someone out there that is willing to use biological weapons on civilians in a train station, then this thing can be a real menace, especially if all it takes is to spray door handles. All of you, we need to target this thing with everything we've got. This is your top priority until it is resolved."

"Yes, Madame President."

"We're on it."

"Contact me immediately when you find out anything else, and by no means give anything to the press on this. There may be, in the future, a time to use the press to possibly find and apprehend anyone involved with this, but that time is not now. The last thing we need is an epidemic scare."

CHAPTER SEVEN

"Director, we've got that report back. It's not good. The virus is real similar to rabies. There are some minor differences, but it looks like a strain that has been genetically altered. There's no telling what those differences are until they're able to study an infected patient."

"Are you kidding? The best they could come up with is rabies? So tell me, what are the symptoms of normal rabies, and what's its outcome?" asked Director Langdon.

Looking over his papers, Fulton pulled one out of the middle and put it at the front of his stack. "Let's see. Incubation period can be as short as fourteen days and up to several months. Early symptoms are a lot like the flu: high fever, headache, chills, fatigue, insomnia, lack of appetite, anxiety, and vomiting. It lasts two to ten days, followed by aggressive behavior, thrashing or striking out, biting, agitation, hallucinations, delusions, excessive saliva, high temperature, excessive sweating... eventual paralysis, partial or complete, organ failure, and death. Once it reaches the symptomatic stage, there are only ten known cases of survival. With treatment starting before the onset of symptoms, it has a high survival rate."

"How many deaths a year are reported?"

"Between thirty-five and fifty thousand a year. Ninety-five percent of them are in Africa and Asia. There is one other important aspect you need to know. Not only is it delivered by a bite from an infected animal but also with bats in a cave it can be delivered by saliva to the eyes, mouth or nose. That may be why they chose a liquid solution for the delivery."

"Are there tests to determine if you have rabies?" asked the director. "We would have to know who to treat."

"People are only treated because they know that they've been bitten by an infected animal, like a dog, a bat, a raccoon… but if there are no symptoms, the rabies won't show up on tests. If they suspect that someone might've been bit by a bat, such as a bat found in a baby's nursery, they'd start treatment also. But once the symptoms start, it's too late to stop its progression. That's why there are so many deaths."

"This attack, then, could be very lethal. We won't know who to treat, and anyone that's not treated before we know they're infected will die. We're in a catch-22 situation. Damned if we do, and damned if we don't."

"Yes, sir. It's not a very promising scenario."

"Are our two specialists on the way back from London yet? I need to have them meet with the President and her cabinet chiefs."

Looking at his watch, Fulton took a moment before he looked up at Langdon and said, "They are still in the lab as we speak. I'll have to contact them to find out when they can pull out. With a seven-hour flight… My best guess? They could be here by ten o'clock tomorrow morning. They'll bring back samples for the CDC to get started on, but that can be sent on ahead without them. I hope they get some sleep on their flight."

"Contact them as soon as you can and let them know I want one of them at the White House as soon as possible. I think it would be best to send the other one ahead with the samples and get the research rolling."

"Yes, sir. I'll let you know as soon as I can contact them. I'll also send word to the CDC to get things in order for this. There's one other thing, sir. The suspect died. They're not sure if he was infected and it had something to do with it, or he just succumbed to the interrogation tactics. About the only useful thing he said was that, 'We are all going to die.' Sounds like he was including himself and maybe everyone else that was sent out. He may have been aware of the scope of what he was doing."

"This situation is getting worse with everything you tell me. Do you have any good news to offset the bad?" asked the director.

"No, sir."

Jill Hastings arrived at school at her regular time on Tuesday morning, and as she walked to her classroom, she realized she wasn't feeling very well. She was a fourth grade teacher at Berry Creek Elementary school on the outskirts of Eugene. She and her husband had just returned from a vacation to London the previous weekend, where they had visited his family for ten days.

With it being the first day of school, she was a little disappointed that she wasn't feeling well. She wanted the first day to be a good day, but she also knew it was going to be a little hectic getting everyone situated. For the previous few days, after her arrival home, she had been getting her classroom prepped for the starting day. If she didn't feel any better by the end of the day, she might have to get a substitute, but she hated to miss school this early in the new season. Maybe it wouldn't be bad enough to have to stay home.

The following day, since she hadn't been feeling too bad, she declined to get a substitute lined up. As the morning progressed, she began to develop a fever and a tickle began in her throat, causing her to cough occasionally. Two or three times she went around to all the children's desks to hand out papers of one kind or another. She tried to keep up on cleaning her hands with antibacterial hand gel, but her coughing was becoming quite frequent before the day was half over. She was regretting her decision to come to work only a little while into the school day, and decided to call the office to line up a substitute for the following day.

Jill's husband, Greg, a lawyer, had a case to defend in court the previous day and he too was feeling a little under the weather. The second day of court, he developed a cough that gradually worsened as the day went on. Throughout both days in court, he was submitting statements and evidence to the court, leaving his germs on everything he handled. One of his associates had to take over on the third day while he stayed home to rest, taking some cold and flu medicine that Jill had picked up at the market the night before.

Ben Curry had been a trader at the New York Stock Exchange for three years and was addicted to the fast-paced action on the floor. When Tuesday morning trading finally got under way after the Labor Day hiatus, Ben wasn't feeling well. Because of his addiction for the action and competition with his peers, he just couldn't stay away. Even on Wednesday, with a fever and a cough, he just couldn't tear himself away until he felt better. The action was in his blood; it was what gave him his identity. If he could only last until Friday, he would have the weekend to rest up. But for now, all he cared about was making money for his clients, his employer, himself, and outperforming his competition. That was all.

In Sydney, Australia, newlyweds Liam and Emma Jones had returned from their honeymoon spent in Paris. They had been home for ten days, setting up their new life together in a house that they had only rented three days before their wedding. Liam worked at a local high school as a music teacher, while Emma had been working as a checkout clerk at a large supermarket. Since they had both missed a week at work to take their honeymoon, neither of them wanted to stay at home when they started feeling ill. They both started taking cold and flu medicine to keep the symptoms at bay, but eventually, after the third day of work, they were both too fatigued to not take a sick day, which turned into several sick days…

Arriving home late, Jason Adams walked quietly around the bed to see if his wife, Lisa, was still awake. When she opened her eyes, he kneeled next to the bed and wrapped his arms around her. Pulling back just enough to be able to kiss her, he gave her a passionate kiss that let her know what he'd like to do.

"I'm sorry, honey, but not tonight. I'd love to, but I have a headache," explained Lisa.

"I'm sorry. Do you want me to get you some aspirin?"

"No… I've already taken some. Maybe tomorrow night? No, that won't work either. I told Melissa I'd come down to see her tomorrow. I wanted to stay with her one night. Her classes start next week, so I wanted to see her while she had time. Is that alright with you, honey?" asked Lisa.

"Sure, sweetheart, that's fine. I'm sorry I'm late," apologized Jason. "We've been dealing with something at the White House, so it's been all hands on deck. I think we'll be putting in long days for the next several weeks. A terrorist cell may have started an epidemic in London, and we don't have any idea how big it might get before we can stop it."

"Maybe I should stay for a longer visit then. That way you won't be sidetracked by my overwhelming charm while you're trying to figure this thing out," teased Lisa, with a grin on her face.

"Since I'm the boss of this house, let me make the decisions. You'll only stay one night. And then I'll see about this charm that you claim you have. Does that work for you?"

"Yes, honey. That works for me. I love you."

"I love you, too."

CHAPTER EIGHT

Sean wasn't on the schedule to work the next day, so he called Rachel to see if she wanted to go fishing again. Mike had also been asked, so there would be the three of them. Rachel had made it a point to ask him if he was going to remember an ink pen this time, for there wouldn't be a nice pretty fisherwoman this time to bail him out. She was having a lot of fun over it.

The three of them were on the river at dawn and spent three hours casting bait, trying to entice the elusive steelhead into biting, but Rachel was the only one to catch a fish. The season was just about over, and although there weren't many fish left in the water, time spent on the river was relaxing. They had time to think of other things, but mostly it was just enjoying the moment, the raw beauty of the river, and having the feeling of anticipation that any cast could hook up a fish.

On the drive back to town, they stopped at a small restaurant to get a late breakfast and spent some time visiting.

"So, Mike, did you and Sean know each other before the marines?" asked Rachel.

"No. Actually, we met in basic training, and after I found out what he was like, I tried to stay away from him," Mike teased. "For some reason, though, the sergeant kept putting us together. It wasn't long before my first impression was confirmed, but after a while, he started to grow on me. Of course he liked me right off, because I was so popular with everybody."

“Do I need to hear Sean’s side of the story before I believe what you just told me?” Rachel asked with a smile, as she turned to look at Sean.

“You definitely need to hear my side of the story before you believe anything that he’s got to say. Everyone in the unit had special descriptions for Mike when he was telling stories. Needless to say, I can’t repeat them here,” laughed Sean.

“You’ve already got the girl. Why can’t you let me tell it the way I want to?” asked Mike, looking like the hurt little boy.

“Putting aside the joking… How’d you two become friends?” Rachel wanted to know.

“To be honest, I could see that Sean was a nice kid. He stood up to a couple of bullies when they were picking on a smaller member of our group, and I really liked that. And then, of course there was that time we got pinned down. A couple of our guys were hit, and he came running in from the rear, dodging bullets. He also brought more ammo, and we were able to hold them off until reinforcements came. I think maybe that was when he really started to grow on me.”

“If you would have been a little more careful about where you were poking your nose, I wouldn’t have had to bail you out. Luckily, he is a fast learner, so I didn’t have to bail him out too much after that. Of course, after that, he did follow me around like a puppy on a leash. I was stumbling over him every time I turned around.”

“You didn’t mind my close proximity when we got caught in that next firefight though. I didn’t hear any complaining then,” defended Mike.

“Okay, you got me. I finally was able to look past the faults and see the good guy that was hiding underneath and that he actually could be a benefit to the team, so I took a liking to him.”

“I’m glad you’ve been able to overcome your differences and that you made it back. It’s always nice to have someone you know you can count on. Makes life more enjoyable.” Rachel took a drink of her water then changed the subject. “Do you have anything else planned for the day, or do I get to go home and clean that fish?” asked Rachel.

“Well, I could help you clean that fish, and then we could go bowling or something. It’s hilarious to watch Mike bowl.”

“Sounds like fun.”

Haris, arriving home late one evening, was approached by his wife of many years.

"Abdullah's not feeling well. He asked to see you when you got home," said A'ishah.

"It's late. Do you think he's still awake?" asked Haris.

"Yes. I was just talking to him. He came home from school yesterday with a headache, but was feeling better this morning, so he went to school again. He came down with a high fever and a cough, though, so he came home a little early today. I gave him some flu medicine around five, but it hasn't taken effect yet."

"Okay, I'll check on him."

Walking to his son's bedroom, he knocked on the door softly and pushed it open.

The bedside lamp was on, and Abdullah had a book on his chest. The hair on his forehead was damp from the fever. Haris walked up to the bedside and placed his hand on his son's forehead, feeling his temperature—extremely hot.

"Not feeling well? The medicine will start helping in a little bit."

"Father, I'm sorry I missed some school today. I'll feel better tomorrow, so I won't miss any more."

"That's alright, Son. There's nothing wrong with missing school if you're sick," explained Haris. "You'll go back to school when you feel well enough."

"I don't want you to be disappointed in me. My friend Asad is sick, too, and his dad was angry with him for getting sick." Abdullah began coughing and covered his mouth with his hand.

"I'm not disappointed in you at all. I'm proud of you for doing so well in your studies. Someday you'll be an important person among your people."

"Like you, Father?" Abdullah reached for his father's hand to hold it in his sweating one.

"Yes, Son. You'll be just like me," replied Haris.

Rising from the bed, he put his hand on the top of his son's head and gave it a little shake. "You'll feel better in the morning. Good night."

Leaving his room, he washed his hands before doing anything else.

The next morning, after checking on his son, he told his wife, "If he's not feeling any better by the middle of the day, call me. He may need some antibiotics." Haris knew that antibiotics wouldn't help the flu, but he wanted to ease his wife's concern.

Later in the day, his wife called him to tell him that his son hadn't improved any. Leaving work early, he took some medical supplies with him.

Arriving home, he immediately went to his son, and telling him what he was going to do, he drew a blood sample to take back to the lab. He kept telling himself that there was no way his son had it. There was no way. All of his men were given express orders not to infect anyone on their initial flight. They didn't want the disease to be introduced back into their country by flights that were coming and going every day. All of their men were taken straight to the airport and either flew out immediately, or waited there for their scheduled flights. No exceptions. He walked into the kitchen to look at his wife.

"I've taken a blood sample that I'm going to take back to the lab and have tested. It's probably just the flu, but I want to make sure. Go ahead and take him to the doctor. Some antibiotics will probably get rid of it. Let them know who you are, and they should be able to get you right in."

On every continent and in every nation, people were staying home from work, missing school, or going to the doctor for treatment. The wealthier people, of course, going to the doctor first and the poorer people staying home to just ride out the flu on their own. They all had the same symptoms; the doctors were not worried about it enough, yet, to take blood samples. The initial cases were scattered across all walks of life and all across the globe. Everyone that had been infected on the initial air flights of the terrorists, or their subsequent wanderings in their respective airports, went in all different directions once they reached their destination. None of the people were infectious while they were traveling, because the virus would not be contagious for at least nine days. Some of them remained in the city to which they had flown, but others had a second or third flight to take them where they needed to go, whether they were going home or had business to attend to. Even from there, many of them lived many miles from their final airport destination, so the virus was being carried to all parts of the globe.

All it would take was for one infected person to land at Johannesburg, hop on a chartered flight to Kenya, Zambia, or Nigeria, and then stay for more than ten days. If they were a healthcare worker, government employee returning home, or a tourist, it wouldn't matter. Nine days and then they would start infecting almost everyone that they would come in contact with. When any one of the newly infected people would move on to a different town or city, they would take the virus with them and start passing it on to others.

All it would take was one, but the flight that landed at the Oliver Tambo International Airport in Johannesburg, South Africa, with a terrorist on board, was carrying at least two hundred twenty infected people. Each one of them went someplace to unknowingly infect others. By the time enough people were infected that the World Health Organization was made aware of a rising care, and a health warning issued on how to protect themselves from it, it would be too late to stop it's spread. It would be the fastest spreading virus the world had ever seen. No one would realize its impact, until it was too late to stop it. It would just have to run its course, do what it was going to do, and then die out.

Not even Haris and his associates could adequately foresee or foretell the outcome of what they had started. Hoping to destroy the capitalism and imperialism of western culture that they so hated, they had planned how best to spread the disease with maximum efficiency, not realizing that they maybe went too far.

With simple mathematics and logistics, they were expecting over a billion deaths from what they set loose, but they also were expecting the world's top scientists to eventually find a way to stop it before all of mankind became extinct. In all of the scenarios that they ran, there were always isolated groups of survivors that had been able to remain at arm's length from the disease, whether by accident or design, and those groups would eventually outlast the epidemic. What would become of those groups was anyone's guess.

Driving home later than she had planned, Lisa Adams wasn't making very good time on her trip back to Washington D.C. She always enjoyed visiting her daughter, and she found it hard to leave earlier in the day. But now, it was getting dark, she had a splitting headache, and she was burning up with a fever. She stopped at a convenience store to buy some cold and flu medicine and a bottle of water. Taking the medicine before she left the store, she pulled out into traffic. She didn't see the panel truck come around the corner, but she did see the face of the man driving it just as he plowed into her driver door. It was the last thing she would ever see.

CHAPTER NINE

William Fulton was called into a meeting with Director Langdon to discuss any new developments. They were both feeling anxiety over the slow progress of the investigation, spending more time on the job than off.

"It's been seven days since London arrested their suspect. Where do they stand on their end?" asked Director Langdon.

"The policemen they have under quarantine haven't shown any symptoms yet. They've been taking blood samples every day, but nothing is showing up on any tests. They have found the motel room that the suspect was staying at and found one piece of luggage, with clothes, a make-up kit with a prosthetic nose and glue, and a half-full container hidden in the side lining of the suitcase. Same solution as the small bottle, capacity was over a gallon. One hundred seventy ounces. Still no passport or identification of any kind. He must have hidden his passport in case he was ever found out and arrested. I would assume with the make-up kit and fake nose, his passport photo may not look like him. It'll be hard to match facial recognition to a passport. They've taken the room apart, but haven't found anything. It's a possibility that he may have tied up with a local cell and had them hold his passport."

"Then why wouldn't he have stayed with them instead of a motel?"

"If not that, then he must have found a safe hiding spot close by his motel. British Intelligence has been going over all available video footage from Heathrow, and any other airport that has video surveillance, trying to place his face on anything. Nothing on that yet. Reports have been trickling in from clinics about a small increase in flu cases… not just in the U.S. but several other countries also. Nothing alarming yet, but they've been notified to keep things current with us."

"Good work, Bill. If anything else comes in, contact me immediately."

In his underground compound, Haris was bent over the microscope looking at his son's blood sample. He couldn't believe what he was seeing. No matter how many times he thought about it, he could not figure out how it would have happened. Working backwards from the time he began showing symptoms, his son would have been infected the very day they sent out their men. His son would not have been anywhere near the route the taxis had taken to the airport. All of his men had checked in at their designated times, and none had mentioned anything amiss.

The plan was to keep the virus out of their nation at all costs; to isolate themselves from the rest of the world once the disease had become known. Isolation was the only chance for survival against the virus that his people had altered to wreak havoc across the infidel nations. Now it didn't matter. Nothing mattered. It was too late to stop it. Abdullah and his friend had contaminated their classroom, if not their whole school, and the apartment building where Asad lived as well. And now the doctor's clinic… His wife… Him.

What should he do now? Could he sit back and watch the disease take his son? His only son. And then his wife? His wife would never understand what he had been doing or why. And now this. He would get all of the blame, which he knew he should.

Kaziim had asked him, "Are you sure you want to do this?"

Haris had given the order to start. He had killed his own wife and son… What now?

As Jason Adams walked into the Situation Room, following the President, Director Langdon stood up. Nodding to the President, he extended his hand to Jason.

"I just heard a few hours ago about your wife. I'm so sorry, Jason."

Gripping his hand tightly, Jason responded with heartfelt gratitude, "Thank you. I appreciate it."

Taking their seats, the President turned to Mr. Langdon. "What have you got, Richard?"

"Madame President, we've got a lead on the suspect. British intelligence has placed him on a flight from Tehran seventeen days ago. Reviewing all surveillance video from that day, the suspect was observed spraying the virus at various locations throughout the airport. Most of the time, they couldn't tell what he was doing, but now that they know, they can assume that everywhere he went he was spreading the solution. He was videotaped in the airport for two days. They captured him on the seventh day. There is no telling how many people have been infected in that time period." The director stopped speaking as he looked around the room. "That same day, on different flights, there were eight other men from Tehran that changed flights there, in London, and boarded flights to the U.S., landing in New York, Atlanta, and here at Dulles. Five of those men, after a layover, went on to Denver, Chicago, L.A., Dallas, and San Francisco. They've been in the states for sixteen days. Surveillance video at all of those airports shows them moving around to all accessible areas. In some videos, they are seen to be spraying something that we should assume is the virus."

"The bastards!" The Homeland Security director couldn't stifle his anger.

"London has cancelled all flights to and from Tehran, and after their move, all of our allies have also cancelled air traffic with Iran," added Director Langdon.

"Do we have any information on the suspects? Where they might have went?" the President asked.

"No, Madame President. We have their photo from their passports. None of them ended up where they were supposed to be, according to their visa. Some were supposed to be here for schooling, some for business reasons, two were visiting family... We can't find any of them. I've got men reviewing video at train stations, bus depots, and airports to see if the suspects have moved on to other locations, but nothing to report yet."

The room was in total silence.

Director Langdon continued, as he looked around the room at the concerned faces, "The officers in quarantine have been showing signs of the flu: fever, headache, chills, fatigue, insomnia... Of course, the last two would be normal under the circumstances."

"They were administered the treatment for normal rabies?"

"Yes, but the rabies vaccine is a twenty-eight day series of shots. It's only been ten days. They're not sure if it will do any good. Only time will tell."

"Time is one thing we don't have, Mr. Langdon. If they're targeting major metropolitan areas in our country, even as we speak, we need to find them."

The Secretary of Homeland Security entered the conversation: "We have their photos. I know they may actually look a little bit different from their passports, but it might still be helpful. It may be time to use the media to help find these men. We don't have to say why we're looking for them, other than they are persons of interest in an investigation."

"I think you may be right, John. Get the public involved. Have each man's photo given to all media outlets closest to their last known locations. Television, newspapers, and internet. Plaster their faces everywhere you can think of. I don't want to wait for the news at six; get their photos on the TV immediately with a breaking news bulletin. Just don't mention the virus."

The President took one last look around the room at the faces of her cabinet leaders. "We'd better all start praying to God that those men are found, and we find a cure for this thing."

The terrorist that landed at L.A., after seven days of moving about, spreading the virus at two NFL games and two college football games, four bus stations, numerous restaurants, subways, and supermarkets, caught a bus over to Anaheim and spent two days in Disneyland infecting several thousand people per day. Taking a short ride over to Knott's Berry Farm, he spent another day before catching a ride down to San Diego to start all over again. His supply of solution was getting low, and he had developed a fever two days before. He knew he would have to fight through the first few days of sickness to continue his work; he didn't want to have any solution left by the time he was unable to continue.

Another terrorist on the West Coast, at San Francisco, had used up half of his supply of the virus before he boarded a bus to Sacramento. He used his virus at over a hundred bars in the Bay area, wanting to eradicate all of the sin that was rampant in the region. He also attended two NFL games and caught a taxi out to Stanford to attend one of their games. He thought that it was just too easy to kill all of the infidels. No one was catching on to what he was doing. No questions were being asked. Not one person knew what was coming. His only regret was that he was going to run out of solution before he was done and had no way to get any more. The fever had already started before he was finished in Sacramento, so on the bus to Redding, he decided to save what solution he had left for rest stops and restaurants on the way. All he had to do was wipe his saliva on the door handle of the lavatory on the bus and the water faucet to take care of the other passengers.

Nine or ten days in one area was the normal duration for the terrorists to stay at their primary target, and then they would move on to a secondary target. The amount of solution that they had would probably not last long enough for a third city, but if they still had control of their faculties after infecting their secondary target, they were to move on to a third city in hopes that their own bodily infection would be enough to spread the disease even further.

"Sir, forty countries have now reported in. There is definitely an increase in flu-like cases in all cities with a major airport. By best estimates, the cases started showing up seven days ago. Not enough the first two days to raise a red flag, but now that the numbers have climbed, there is definitely something going on." William Fulton paused to look at his numbers.

"What kind of numbers are we looking at, Bill?" asked Director Langdon.

Clearing his throat before he spoke, Bill began slowly, "Um, each country has documented at least ten thousand cases; some are close to thirty thousand. We have the most, at one hundred forty-five thousand. The disparity in numbers could be that our reporting is more accurate. We have more potential large targets, such as sporting events, and like the President said, they may just be targeting us more than anyone else. The majority of our cases are mostly centered around our largest cities, New York, D.C., Atlanta, Chicago, Dallas, Denver, L.A., San Francisco, Boston, Seattle, and Miami. Considering the incubation period is ten days, our cases started being reported on day twelve and extending through day sixteen. It would suggest that there are at least eleven terrorists within our borders, each of them infecting those eleven regions simultaneously. Some nations have their cases centered around their single largest metropolitan area that has an international airport."

"Have blood samples been taken in all regions to verify that it's all the rabies virus?" asked Langdon.

"I'm not sure. They've just been reporting the increase in the flu-like symptoms. I'll double check on that. The global numbers represent the ones that have gone to the doctor. There may be more in the poorer districts that haven't progressed far enough to decide on a doctor visit yet. And the numbers have been tallied for daily counts. It's not good. Forty percent of the cases came in the day before yesterday; we don't have the numbers yet for yesterday."

The two locked eyes for several seconds. "How many cases total have been reported?" asked Langdon.

"It's closing in on eight hundred thousand. With a ten-day incubation period, the second tier of infected may start showing up at the doctor on approximately day nineteen. This is day eighteen. If everyone that is symptomatic on day ten goes into the public arena for any reason, they could potentially infect five, ten, possibly twenty people, depending on what they're doing. If the symptoms up to day three weren't bad enough to keep someone home from work or school, they would be infecting people for up to three days. So on day ten, there could be five times increase. Same number for day eleven, five times increase. But also on day eleven, you have to factor in how many people were infected on day two that would start infecting people on day eleven. Same for day twelve, thirteen, fourteen and so on. On day nineteen, the first of the second tier infected begin infecting people. At the exponential growth rate it's showing, in one more week, day twenty-five, it'll be over ten million."

"My God!" exclaimed Langdon. "How do you quarantine ten million people? How would you even round them up, because they aren't all sitting in hospitals yet; they're all scattered across the cities and countryside where they live. How many more would be infected just trying to collect them all?"

"Even if you quarantine them, there isn't enough rabies vaccine to treat even ten percent of them. We don't even know yet if the vaccine will work on this virus. By the time we find out and it's a failure, it may take months or longer to develop a cure. I'd say the shit has hit the fan, and everyone is going to get some on themselves."

Director Langdon held up his hand. "Save it, Bill. Let's go see the President."

"Madame President, the numbers don't lie. This thing is already out of control. I'd recommend that the WHO put out a notice to all infected to stay in their homes. The doctors can't help them; there is no vaccine or cure. If they won't stay indoors at the first sign of infection, they will only spread the virus."

"Do we know anything yet on whether the rabies vaccine will have an effect on this?" asked the President.

"It's still too early to tell. The London officers are on day eleven of a twenty-eight day treatment; the four or five shots are finished on the fourteenth day, but it takes the full twenty-eight to develop the antibodies in the blood to fight it. They've been infected for eleven days and have been showing signs of the disease for two days. With normal rabies, once the symptoms start, there is no cure. The survival rate is infinitesimally small. We're talking ten documented cases since documenting started. That rate is so small that it isn't even worth mentioning. We've had pharmaceutical companies pumping out the vaccine since we found out what the virus was, but there is no way they will keep up with this. To date, they have vaccines enough to treat two hundred fifty thousand people. That's eleven days of production, but by tomorrow there may be as many new cases reported in one day that they have produced vaccines for in eleven days. And it's only going to get worse." By the time Director Langdon had finished, there was a tone of desperation and pleading in his voice that was conveyed to the whole group.

"Anyone else with any ideas?" asked the President, looking around the room, seeing despair on the faces of all her cabinet leaders as they all shook their heads in the negative. "What about our own scientists? Have they discovered anything yet about this virus that will help? Any way to kill or cure it?"

"Nothing. They've had people working on it around the clock since we brought back the sample. They don't have any good news for us," replied David McCale, the Secretary of Health and Human Services.

"This is a nightmare. How did we miss this? Why did we not uncover this before it was too late?" Pausing for a moment, listening to the silence, she began to lament, "I wish now that the Israelis had nuked them several years ago when they wouldn't stop their nuclear enrichment. Then none of this would have happened."

Her cabinet heads heard the words of despair, and none of them disagreed with her.

John, the Secretary of Homeland Security, was the only one willing to try to raise some hope. "We still need to give the London officers a few more days to see if the vaccine works. Let's hope and pray that, in the next few days, they will start to recover."

"Okay, John. Let's not lose all hope just yet. Get in contact with the pharmaceutical companies and see if there is any way to increase production of the vaccine. Contact our lead virologists that are working on a cure and let them know what's at stake. Give them the numbers you just gave me. They're our only hope of stopping this epidemic. The moment we have a bulletin telling people to stay home because of a virus, there'll be a panic that we won't be able to control. The whole economy will come to a halt. We'll give our guys a few more days before we take that step."

CHAPTER TEN

Sean picked up Rachel at her house at about eleven, with a picnic lunch made up to take with them up the McKenzie River to one of the many riverside parks. Sean couldn't get enough of Rachel, and she didn't want to turn away any opportunities to spend time with him either.

Driving along the river, they talked about the future hopes and desires they each had, trying to learn as much about one another as they could. Finding out that they had many similar interests and desires, their relationship continued to blossom into something deep and lasting.

Driving to Sahalie Falls on the McKenzie River, they parked and took a walk along the trail. Rachel carried her camera to take some pictures of the magnificent falls. Fir needles covered the ground with a deep, soft cushion that silenced their steps as they walked along the trail, holding hands, listening to the roar of the falls. As they walked down the steps leading toward the river, Sean noticed that everything was covered with water from the heavy mist thrown up and drifting in the air from the falls. Small birds were flitting about from branch to branch, singing their little tweets to one another. No doubt some of them were trying to win their mates with a time-honored ritual.

As they came to the viewpoint, Rachel stepped back to take a picture of Sean with the falls in the background. After taking several, Sean pulled out his iPhone and began taking pictures of Rachel, from different angles, close-ups of her face, different poses against the beauty of the falls in the background, and inevitably a few funny face poses.

Another couple came along and offered to take a picture of them together, and after setting the camera for the closeness of the shot he wanted, Sean stepped up to wrap an arm around her and hold her hand up high between them. After three different shots, they thanked the couple and then continued on their way.

Following the trail down the river to Koosah Falls, they were enjoying the closeness and solitude of the forest, with the rushing river close by and the roar of the two sets of falls. Although it was hard to talk normally with the roar of the water overriding everything, they were just as satisfied to walk along without words, enjoying the moment, with their arms around one another.

Now and then, Sean would take a long glance at her profile, wondering how he could be so lucky as to win her affection. Stopping to pull her tightly against him for a warm embrace, he lowered his lips to hers, tasting the sweetness of a new love. Looking into her eyes, he could see the shine of happiness that Rachel felt in his presence, which strengthened his own feelings toward her.

"Rachel, do you mind me kissing you all the time? I can't seem to help myself. I could slow down some if you want."

"I think it's close to about right, but maybe I need a few more to make an experienced decision on whether you need to slow down." She smiled up at him again with that "come and get me" smile. He promptly took advantage of her words to help in her decision.

"Madame President, we've been able to ascertain with all certainty that the virus came out of Iran. Tracking flight lists and cross-referencing all of their passenger manifests in reverse from all major airport destinations where the virus has the largest concentrated number of reported cases, we've come up with forty names that we've tracked back to their original flights out of the Imam Khomeini International Airport in Iran. We are assuming that the nation's government was behind it or, at the least, was aware of the impending biological attack. There is no solid evidence that they were, but considering the resources needed to plan, develop, and execute this type of attack, especially the need for a well-managed and stocked biological laboratory, the people behind this needed to be well funded. Laboratories of the type they needed don't just pop up overnight, nor are they ramshackle affairs. Strict protocols would have to be observed to ensure the safety of the population surrounding the laboratory, so the likelihood that the leaders in the government didn't know what was going on would be very slim." Director Langdon took one last look around the room at the cabinet chiefs and a few new faces that the President thought needed to be privy to what was going on.

"Thank you, Richard. It's good to know for sure where this started. We'll have to discuss what needs to be done in retaliation, and the ramifications it will entail, but the more important matter now is to find a cure or antidote that will stop this thing before people start dying. We still don't know the full scope of what we're dealing with concerning the final outcome of this disease. Is there anything new to report from our specialists in the lab?"

"No, ma'am. They haven't had any significant progress yet on a new vaccine. They're not very hopeful, considering the time frame and the urgency that we're under. If we only had more time..."

John, the Homeland Security chief, asked, "If we know it's rabies, then I think it would be a good idea to vaccinate everyone in this room with the existing vaccine. If by chance any of us gets infected, we could infect everyone else here, and we can't afford to lose any of us. And then afterwards we can start widening the list of who else to vaccinate by letting each Cabinet member submit a list of who they think our society needs to keep safe in their respective fields."

"You may be right, John. Let's get to work on it right away. Keep on top of things, gentlemen, and keep me informed. Thank you."

In North Korea, the President called a secret meeting with his councilors and military leaders to discuss the virus and the measures they needed to use to control it.

"Sir, since our borders are more restricted than any other country, we've only had a few cases of the virus. In fact, there are only fifteen so far."

"And how safe are we? Is there any chance of the virus spreading from those that are infected?"

"There's always a chance, but we've been very careful. We've checked all flight manifests. Everyone who arrived from Beijing or Shanghai on the first three days of the terrorist attack, we've taken into custody and put them in quarantine. Some of those are the cases that we now have."

"As bad as it is around the world, we can't take any chances. Our border restrictions are what saved us so far, so we need to shut down our borders completely. I know it will cause more instability and we're short on food supplies, but we can't afford to let this get a foothold in our country."

"We can continue to receive supplies, but prohibit any shore leave by ship's personnel or any contact between people. Any contact that is necessary, have protective gear involved that would solve the problem."

"Alright. That should work for now. But with the ones that are already infected, put them down immediately, and all those that were involved with them. If they were sick when they came in, find out where they lived, take into custody all those that were living in their homes and put them down. Any more infected show up, put them down immediately, and their household also. Run a bulletin commanding anyone with the flu symptoms to report to the hospital immediately, put them down also, and follow the protocol I just laid out. Take all precautionary measures when dealing with them."

"Yes, sir. We'll start immediately."

"One other topic I want to discuss. America's people are affected with this virus more than anyone else. If we want to strike against them, this might be a good time to do so. They will be losing manpower in their military, border patrol, customs agents, and their police forces. I think we would be able to penetrate their border with one or more of our nuclear warheads, park it outside their White House, and then detonate it. Do you think we could do this without revealing that we were behind it?"

One of his military leaders stood up to answer. "I think it's possible. We could wrap it in lead to hide it from scanners, put it on a jet to Beijing, have it transferred to a flight to L.A., then somewhere close to Washington D.C. From there, we could truck it the rest of the way and then detonate it. I don't think they will ever know where it came from."

"I think this will be our best opportunity to strike back at them for everything they've done to us. I'll leave the details up to you, but make sure our strike is big enough to cause the most damage possible. I want to destroy their governing ability, and that will also lessen a counterattack. Start planning it right away, and let me know if you can make it work."

"Yes, sir."

Although the U.S. believed they were incapable of making a megaton nuclear bomb because of insufficient nuclear material, they were wrong. For years, China had been supplying them with plutonium and uranium for enrichment. Their bomb-making abilities weren't as good as the U.S. or China, but they had been able to develop two nuclear warheads with a 100-kiloton yield and a lot of smaller ones. It would be sufficient to destroy Washington D.C. As the Supreme Leader of North Korea sat thinking about the possibilities, he was beginning to smile.

By day nineteen of their operation, all of the original forty terrorists had been infected and were exhibiting symptoms of the virus. Some had started showing the flu-like symptoms as early as eleven days, while none of the rest went past sixteen. Fifty-five major airports had been walked through and infected by them before they had even moved on to their secondary targets. The next largest population center closest to the primary was the usual secondary target, and it was up to their discretion as to which mode of transportation was used to travel there.

Many times they used computer terminals in public libraries to research some of the best locations for the spreading of the virus, how to get there, and where to go next. The terrorists were all carrying smartphones to help in their navigation, and they were also using them to send back coded messages to their leaders, notifying them of their progress.

The terrorist that had started in San Francisco moved on to Sacramento, and just before he was out of solution, traveled north by bus to Redding.

The Los Angeles terrorist spent eleven days in the area, due to its size, before moving to San Diego for a few days, and then lastly, took a short flight to Phoenix to use up the rest of his solution and to await the final stages of the disease.

Lastly, on the West Coast of the United States, the terrorist that began in Seattle, Washington, when he was satisfied with his accomplishments there, moved south to Portland Oregon, spent a short time in Salem, and then his final days in Eugene.

In such a manner of operation, the terrorists were able to infect the largest amount of people in the shortest time and yet effectively spread it around to many locations. Including the second twenty-five terrorists that were sent out on day seven and their efforts, they had effectively infected over seventy nations by day twenty, and infected travelers had carried the disease into almost all of the remaining countries. No nation or people were immune to their efforts. The well-thought-out and executed plan was enormously successful and easily exceeded the expectations of the conspirators who wished to control the world in their own way.

CHAPTER ELEVEN

On day twenty, gathered in the Situation Room, were the Joint Chiefs and the Cabinet heads awaiting the arrival of the President. As she came into the room, with the White House Chief of Staff following, they all stood until she seated herself.

Turning to Director Langdon, she said "Go ahead, Richard, fill us in on any developments you have."

"Our contacts in London report that the infected officers are feeling a little better today. Their fever has subsided some and are showing signs of improvement."

"Thank God."

There were many praises, cheers, and thanks spoken around the table as relief swept the room. As they were smiling and patting each other on the back, the President waited until it calmed down before continuing.

She began, "If the vaccine is going to work, but we only have a tenth of what we need, how do we decide who gets it? Do we divide it among every nation, save the wealthy first and then the poor? Any ideas?"

"We may want to consider giving it to the healthcare workers first to keep them healthy through the ordeal. After that, we could divvy it up among the nations according to percentages of reported cases."

The Secretary of Health stood up to speak. "We've already been distributing the vaccine for the past week and the healthcare workers, who normally have the closest contact with the patients, have already begun the series of four shots. Once the series starts, it takes twenty-eight days. The initial shot is the most important, and the others are booster shots. We can give the initial shot to as many infected as possible and go from there. Hopefully, with the increased production of the vaccine, we can keep up with some of the demand. It all depends on how many people are actually infected."

"And what are the most recent numbers being reported?" asked the President.

"Our early estimates of ten million by day twenty-five have been adjusted with the new numbers, and it shows double what we earlier estimated. Twenty million infected."

"My God, David!" exclaimed the President. "That's twice what we figured earlier. If we didn't have enough vaccine for ten million, how will we ever get enough for twenty?"

"We won't. If we had more time, the pharmaceutical companies could revamp other facilities to its production, which they are working on as we speak, but still we won't have enough vaccine for even one-tenth of those infected. People are going to die, and there isn't anything we can do about it. Our toughest decision will be trying to figure out which ten percent deserve to live."

It was quiet in the room, as the gravity of his words sank in. Jason, the White House Chief of Staff, sitting next to the President, started to speak and then coughed, raising his hand to his mouth late. He took a drink of water before trying to continue.

"I believe we should concentrate mostly on our own citizens first. There are several nations that have their own pharmaceutical companies to provide for their own needs. After all the needs of our own people are met, we can pool our surplus with theirs and ship out what is left over to the countries who can't provide their own vaccine."

"That means a death sentence for all of the initially infected in about one hundred fifty countries. Are we ready for that kind of responsibility?" asked the President.

"We'll be saving their healthcare workers at least. Once this thing is over and Americans find out that we failed to vaccinate ten million of our own people because we thought the lives of foreigners were more important, how many votes will we get in the next election?" There. He said it. The politics of the situation was bound to come into play eventually.

"You're right. Not about the votes, but our first obligation is to our own people. Do we even have enough to vaccinate all of our own infected?"

"No, but it's close. One thing we need to consider is do we only vaccinate the infected, or do we vaccinate government leaders to make sure that we continue to have a viable government?" asked Jason.

John, the Secretary of Homeland Security jumped in, "What about the military, police, firefighters, doctors, and infrastructure leaders and workers? If we lose too many military personnel, we could be open to attack; and if this thing continues to grow, we may need our military to help our police forces to keep order within our own borders. Our infrastructure has to keep running, or we may not be able to continue the production and distribution of the vaccine. There are a lot of angles we need to consider before we make any decisions."

"It could use up half of our vaccine to guarantee the health and safety of all the ones you just listed," summed up the President.

"I know, but we have to consider what will happen if we lose twenty percent of our military, police force, our government workers at every level, the leaders of our economy, our healthcare system…"

"Who is important enough to save with the vaccine that we have available? And who is going to make that kind of decision?" asked Jason. "Remember, for everyone that we pre-vaccinate, there will be someone else dying."

Robert had something to add: "Let's divvy up half of our vaccines between our fifty states as the percentages of infected dictate and use the rest on our military, police, and important government workers."

"Any feedback?"

Quiet. A long moment of quiet.

"Anyone?"

The Secretary of Defense was the only one willing to answer. "I think this would at least be a good starting point. As we've never been faced with anything like this before, we can start moving forward on this now and make it known that there can be modifications as we move forward."

The President stood, looking over her leaders and advisors, trying to make eye contact with each of them. "Does anyone have any other views? Suggestions? I know how hard it is for all of you to make decisions like this, so if any of you want to write down your own suggestions and give it to me later, I'm alright with that. I also know that we're all wondering about our own families, our loved ones, and our close friends. What about vaccines for them? What if they don't fit the criteria for being important enough to save? Let us start somewhere and figure out the rest as we go."

She paused to let her words sink in.

"Start delivering vaccines to our military, ground troops first, and get them vaccinated. Also our government leaders, spouses included, healthcare workers, and any newly infected, starting tomorrow. The ones that have been symptomatic for eight to ten days, I believe we will be wasting the vaccine on, so we'll have to move on to the next wave. They might have a chance for the vaccine to work."

She continued, "There is one other matter I want to discuss before we adjourn. Since we now know that Iran or associates of theirs are responsible for this crisis, I want to discuss what our options are and what would be an appropriate action to take. My thoughts are that we need to park a nuclear submarine or two off of their coast, just for precautions. If they were hoping to weaken our defenses or those of our allies with this attack, and are planning an offensive maneuver with troops, it would be wise for us to have ships and forces in the area. Any thoughts?"

General McIntyre was the first to speak. "I agree with you completely. We need to be ready for any move that they might make. If they know we know and they see our warships, it might deter further action on their part."

She heard numerous comments, but all were in agreement.

She especially took note of her Chief of Staff's comment: "We should just nuke those bastards before they can do anything else. If they could unleash this thing on the world, then they don't deserve to live."

She found it hard to disagree.

"Make it happen, gentlemen. And may God be with us."

Haris was looking down at his son, sleeping fitfully, wondering what to do. He had come to a conclusion of what he thought would be best, what he knew was best, but he was still contemplating it. He was one of the few who actually knew what was going to happen and was okay with it… at least he was until now—until it was going to happen to his own son, his own wife, and then lastly to himself. He finally realized what he had unleashed on the unsuspecting world, but now it was too late to change it. There was no cure and there was no way to even slow it down.

He had been keeping up with the reports from his men, and he knew how successful they had been in spreading the virus. Only one of them had been captured, in London, but he had not been able to gather any information on what had happened to him. His contacts had also made him aware of the passport pictures of his original forty had been sent out to the public, trying to use the general population to locate his men.

He was assuming that the London officials had found and tested the virus and were even now trying to find a cure. For his own men, the cure had eluded them, but he also knew that the western nations had more resources and people to draw on than he had, so there was still a chance of a cure. However, even if they found one, it would be too late to save his family or himself, nor would it be in time to save the millions of people that had been infected throughout the first ten days.

Even now, his wife was showing symptoms of the disease. She was still assuming that her son only had a bad strain of the flu and that she had caught it. Haris was unsure of whether or not he should tell her what was really happening. The easiest thing to do he was shying away from.

"Father, am I going to get better?" A faint voice brought his mind back from the edge.

"Yes, Son. You'll be better in no time at all."

He watched as his son got out of the bed and walked to the bathroom. Following him to make sure he didn't fall, he helped him back to his bed. Once he had fallen asleep, Haris reached into his pocket and removed a small case. After opening it and removing a hypodermic needle, syringe, and a small bottle of liquid, he slipped the needle through the lid of the bottle, pulled back the plunger, and watched the liquid slowly fill the syringe. Pulling out the needle, he held it up and squeezed the plunger until the liquid began to squirt out a bit into the air.

Satisfied with his action, he sat down on the side of the bed and took his son's arm. He found a vein and injected the solution. As much as he hated to do it, he knew his son was right on the verge of turning into the maniacs that they had witnessed in the lab. He had waited too long already.

His son stirred, opened his eyes, and looking at his father he said, "That hurt. What was it?"

"It was more medicine to make you feel better. You can go back to sleep now, my son."

"Yes, Father."

A few minutes later, with tears on his cheeks, Haris whispered, "I'm sorry."

After being so sure that what they were doing was right, he now knew how wrong it was. It had taken the death of his own son, the first casualty, to make him see it clearly.

The London area had the first outbreak of the virus, as most of the terrorists began their campaign there, and the authorities were keeping a close eye on their patients as they neared the second stage of the rabies symptoms. The virus had reached all corners of their nation, with their three largest cities bearing the brunt of the increase. Every day, there were more patients being admitted with severe flu symptoms, and it was becoming hard to keep track of so many. The rooms were already full. All they could do now was bring in more mats for them to sleep on the floor. All of their extra beds in storage had already been brought out, which weren't many, and officials had been talking about setting up care centers in local school gymnasiums.

Still not knowing how the current strain of the virus would differ from normal rabies, they were nervous about what was coming. One of their officials had watched a video of someone in the last stages of the disease and realized that the patient was secured to the bed, to keep himself and everyone caring for him safe, as he became increasingly violent. Soon thereafter, they began securing their own patients, but there were a few that had become violent before they were strapped down. For a while, there was quite a scuffle in a few hospitals with some of the healthcare workers suffering bites and bruises. In the future, they would make sure to secure all of the patients.

Haris had arranged a quick funeral for his son, not notifying any of their relatives—only wanting to get it done with the least amount of hassle. His wife didn't understand, but she was obedient to her husband and was too lost in grief to ask too many questions. He didn't want anyone to know that his wife wasn't feeling well either. He knew what he would eventually have to do, and didn't want to have to deal with people coming over and getting underfoot. He chose rather to keep everything quiet to avoid any questions or interruptions and to spend what time he could with his wife in his own way. She would still be able to take care of herself for a couple of more days, and he wanted to get back to the compound and take care of some things. Afterwards he could spend the last few days with her, letting her know how much he cared about her.

Arriving at the compound, he went straight to his office. His chief scientist heard that he had returned and came to see him as soon as he could breakaway. Kaziim entered his office, excited and a little nervous.

"Have you heard about all the flu cases that have started to pop up around the city?" Kaziim asked.

"Yes, I have. This is the start of the flu season, isn't it?" returned Haris.

"Yes, but I became a little nervous with so many at once."

"Have you gone to the hospital and taken any blood samples, since you're nervous?" inquired Haris.

"No, I haven't. Maybe I should, though, just to make sure. If it's the virus in our country already, we're doomed," worried Kaziim.

"Calm down, Kaziim. Go to the hospital right now, get several blood samples, and look them over. There's no way that it could be the virus. If it were, they would have had to be infected the very first day. All our men went straight to the airport from here, and none of them would have infected our own airport. You've had the entirety of the solution under your control from day one. Is any of it missing?"

"No. No. I already checked. Twice." Kaziim was extremely agitated over it.

"Then go get the blood samples and get back to me when you find out. Okay?"

"Alright."

CHAPTER TWELVE

"Madame President, I have bad news. London just notified us that many of their infected that are in hospitals, have developed into stage two rabies. They've become aggressive, combatant, seemingly driven by rage, and delusional." Jason, her Chief of Staff, pulled a handkerchief out of his jacket pocket, paused a moment to cover his cough, and then continued, "The symptoms are consistent with rabies, although the one symptom missing is the fear of water. With typical rabies, the muscles of the throat go into uncontrollable spasms when the infected tries to swallow any liquid. Some patients go into spasms at the mere sight of water, and so it's believed that the inability to rehydrate the patient is partially to blame for the catastrophic organ failure that results in death. If the current virus has been genetically altered to remove the hydrophobia aspect, then the patient may live longer. As painful and agonizing as the disease is normally, it would prolong that agony. Again, there is no telling what the final outcome is to this virus, without actually observing a patient to its final conclusion, because of what the terrorists have done to alter it."

"God, help us! How could those monsters have thought that what they were doing was something that God would approve of? How could they be so twisted?"

"I don't think there will ever be an answer for those questions. The doctors have put the patients in restraints so that they can continue to minister to them safely."

"Call a meeting with the Joint Chiefs and the Cabinet, ASAP. And Jason, contact our scientists and give them the news. I also want one of them at the meeting. Make it happen."

A leading North Korean scientist scheduled a meeting with his President and his leaders. Coming up with a plan to attack the U.S. was his most rewarding experience, and he was excited to lay it out for the President.

"Sir, I think I've figured out a way to get a nuclear warhead to the U.S. We line the container with lead, to shield it from scanners, fly it out to China, transfer it to a flight to Mexico City, and then load it on a chartered flight to Jamaica, where it will be loaded on a container ship bound to Miami. Two days from there to Miami, load it on a truck, and then drive it to Washington D.C. The U.S. only scans about three percent of the total incoming containers, and those are usually ones that are from high-risk locations that are on their radar for danger. Everything else gets through without scanning, and very little inspection. They can't afford to take the time to scan eleven million cargo containers a year. It would hamper their logistics of supply and delivery enough that they won't do it. It's a possibility that if we load the device today, we can have it sitting in front of the White House in seven to nine days."

"What are the chances of success?"

"Ninety-five percent."

"What do the rest of you think of it?" the President asked.

"It sounds like it might work. Sending it by air all the way won't work now that they've tightened air cargo screening. If other legal cargo that would pass a visual inspection surrounds the package, it would probably work. They won't be expecting a bomb from Jamaica, so it wouldn't raise any flags for screening. On top of that, the virus will deplete their customs agents, and they can't halt the incoming goods that might be carrying food to their people. Once it's in Jamaica, we can load the container with bananas and other fruit so that it can be passed through quickly."

"We would have to send men ahead to take care of the transfer and truck delivery. If we can detonate it from long range and it's discovered early, we can detonate it in the port city. Whether it's detonated in Washington or the port city, they will assume one of the Arab nations was smuggling it in for retaliation. I don't think it will ever come back on us. I'm agreeable to it."

"Okay, I agree. Get on it immediately."

"Ladies and gentlemen, we've got bad news. Apparently, many of the infected in London hospitals have progressed to the next stage of the rabies symptoms, becoming violent and combative, and they have had to be restrained. No one knows how long this stage will last, how much longer they will live, or how painful it will be. Answers will only come with time and observation." The President stopped and looked around at the faces of her friends and associates. Her vision dimmed, as the tears began to fall. "Please, forgive me."

Jason handed her a handkerchief to wipe her eyes.

The CIA director walked in and stopped next to the President. Looking down at her and noticing the red eyes and the handkerchief, he realized that she needed a moment. Stepping in, he spoke to the room: "I've just been collecting reports coming in from around the globe. It's not just London, and it's not good. The first tier of infected have exploded into public. In the poorer countries with fewer hospitals, many of the infected have remained in their homes to be taken care of by their family or friends. As they've progressed to the next stage of the disease, they've become delusional, paranoid, crazy even, combative, and very aggressive, attacking everyone around them, biting, and scratching. Many of them have wandered into the streets to attack people there. There are hundreds of reports of the police being attacked when they've tried to subdue the patients. In protecting themselves, there have been many fatalities as a result as well… in the thousands."

The virologist from the CDC, a few chairs down the table from the President, stood up, looked at the CIA director, and said, "Then we can assume that everyone that gets bit is now infected. As in normal rabies, it is transferred through the saliva into an open wound. The infected that are now at stage two were the very first ones to contract the disease. Considering that London's Heathrow airport was essentially ground zero as the terrorists started their campaign, working out of the airport, London had the first reports of the stage two patients. And after that, all the destinations of the secondary flights to other major airports, would report next on the stage two infections. The earliest infected, starting at London, and then continuing on to those other countries, will all develop stage two starting three days ago and continuing on until day twenty-seven. This is only the beginning. In first ten days of this situation, there were only forty people infecting other people, but starting with the tenth day, all of the people that were infected on day one will be infecting others. The eleventh day, all of the second day infectees will be infecting others. The twelfth day, the third day infectees, and so on. The key turning point in this whole debacle will be in about five days."

The Chief of Staff asked, "What's going to happen in five days?"

The room was deathly quiet, and everyone was straining to hear his next words.

"We're going to find out just how many tier-two infected there actually are... if there's not too much confusion, that is, to gather accurate reports. Right now, the existing reports suggest we have close to twenty million infected, with a possible five million more today. This is day twenty-two. By day twenty-seven, there could be one-hundred million... by day thirty-six, over one billion... by day forty-five? Well, almost everyone."

No one moved, and the room was enveloped in complete and utter silence.

The President asked the one question everyone needed to know the answer to: "How accurate are your assumptions? Can there be any leeway or miscalculations in your evaluations?"

"There is always a plus or minus in the calculations, but at best it pushes the final outcome out an extra week or two. So, every day that goes by, there will be exponentially more infected reaching stage two. When the numbers become too many to subdue, there will be only one recourse to save humanity from extinction."

The President looked at the scientist, afraid to ask the question, or hear the answer. "Tell us. How do we save ourselves?"

He blinked once... twice... then said, "Simply put, kill or be killed. The infected are going to die anyway, sooner or later, and so, the only protection from them will be to kill them before they can infect you. We can't afford to wait and see how long it takes them to die; they're already dead. As I said earlier, the numbers of stage two infected are about to explode, and killing them outright will be the best solution... before it's completely out of control. I think the sooner the public knows this, the better off we'll be. I know it sounds harsh, but it's the simple truth."

"You mean, tell the public to execute everyone that has a runny nose? Tell them if they see anyone who looks remotely sick, to put a gun to their head and pull the trigger?" John, the Homeland Security chief was flabbergasted.

"No. That's not what I'm saying. I would suggest they maintain at least twenty feet when they pull the trigger. They don't want to get blood spatter on them, or they might get infected."

Several gasps could be heard throughout the room, as the virologist continued, "Sorry to be so blunt, but facts are facts. I would consider it a humane killing—putting them out of their future misery. Once you start seeing on the TV the suffering, painful agony, and torment that these people will be going through, you'll understand the meaning of a mercy killing."

"A mercy killing is euthanasia with a death dealing drug not a bullet to the head."

"There aren't enough euthanasia drugs available in the world to put to death all of those that need it, and it would be too time consuming to round up everyone and administer the drugs if we had them. Besides, the infected would be increasing faster than our ability to put them down with your euthanasia. Mankind's only hope is to stop the spread of the infection or, at the least, to slow it down to give us time to remove those that it is already too late to save."

"Alright, listen up. I'm not going to give an order to start executing the sick. We'll try to ease the suffering of the ones we can—the ones in the hospital who are already subdued. However… the ones that are proving dangerous, we may have to take out, but that will be the military's call as they need to. What we need to do is concentrate on stopping the spread of the virus as soon as possible, as much as possible, so contact the WHO and tell them to immediately issue orders to all infected to stay indoors, no matter what. Air TV and radio announcements immediately in every country, and print newspaper announcements with directions and phone numbers. Give out phone numbers for people to call to report their sickness so they can at least have cold and flu medicine delivered to their door to ease their symptoms. Have them say that this flu is a new strain, similar to the swine flu, and highly contagious. If anyone begins to feel the slightest of symptoms to stay home and call officials of the WHO to receive further instructions. There will be panic, but if we put out directions and explanations, it might keep it under control until we can make a decision on our next step."

As the President paused, Director Langdon, being more familiar with the effects of the disease and the numbers involved, injected one statement, "…at least until the body count starts to climb."

"We'll have to have a conference call with the leaders of every nation to let them know how serious this is and see what their thoughts are. Start making calls gentlemen and get this thing going. We also need to start gathering ideas right away on how to at least save some pockets of mankind in case this is as bad as you've made out."

"In that case, I think the first thing you need to do is immediately stop all air and ship traffic to any island or island nation. In their isolation, if they aren't already infected, it is our best immediate hope."

"Alright then, I agree. Make it happen."

CHAPTER THIRTEEN

Sean and Mike were at the sporting goods store, looking over the guns they had on display. They had come in to buy extra ammo for target practice they were starting, and since they had an extreme interest in guns, their attention naturally turned to what was on the back shelf. Joe, the owner of the store, seeing their interest, had been handing them several different guns to handle and to look over.

"That .220 Swift with the bull barrel is sure a sweet gun!" Sean exclaimed.

"It sure is. Make a great varmint gun," Mike added.

"Hey, Joe, could you let me see that Springfield XD 9mm? Four-inch and five-inch barrels."

Mike handled both handguns also and really liked the feel of the full-sized, five-inch barrel. They both decided to buy one of the full-sized models, and Sean filled out the paperwork for both of them.

When Sean and Mike walked out of the store, they were each carrying a cardboard box full of ammo, along with their two handguns, two holsters for the guns, twelve boxes of 9mm, four boxes of .45 for his semi-auto, a couple boxes each of .300 Weatherby mag, .280, .223, and .243 Remington, and two cartons of twelve gauge. Sean realized his dad's philosophy was starting to rub off on him. Returning home, Sean felt a little sheepish approaching his dad, but what the heck.

"You want to store that ammo you're not planning to use right away downstairs?" Mitch asked. "You could show Mike around if you like."

"You sure? I thought you wanted to keep it on a 'need to know' basis?"

"Yes, I'm sure. I think Mike is trustworthy, don't you?"

"Do you have to put me on the spot like this? Right in front of him? Let me think about it for a moment." Sean felt a fist slam into his arm—pretty hard, too. "Hey, take it easy. You're gonna make me biased if you keep that up. I guess we could probably trust him, but remember this was your idea."

Sean led the way out to the barn with Mike beside him. He was going to enjoy seeing Mike's reaction.

Mitch walked down to the bunker fifteen minutes later. As soon as he entered the common room, he switched on the TV. Sean and Mike were in the bedroom with the storage cabinets looking through some of the stuff; both were amazed at all the things that Mitch and Beth had stored up. They heard the TV come on and then a serious voice begin talking. The two of them immediately stepped out into the living room to hear the broadcast.

"I repeat, there is a new strain of flu that has started, and it is extremely contagious. It has spread exceedingly fast, due to the fact that many people that were infected were traveling on the airlines. We don't know how many countries are infected or to what extent, but as a precaution, we are warning everybody to remain in their home if they are feeling any flu-like symptoms whatsoever. If you have a fever, cough, chills, headache, or nausea, stay indoors. You will infect others if you go out. Call this number if you are experiencing any of these symptoms, and a relief worker will call you back to give you further directions: 1-800-555-5555. It is imperative that you remain indoors if you are feeling ill. This flu may run its course the same as any other flu, but as a precaution, you must stay indoors and call this number: 1-800-555-5555. This strain of flu is very contagious. If you have symptoms, do not have physical contact with anyone and call this number for further directions. Until we find out how serious the spread of this flu actually is, we recommend that all people stay home as much as possible in the next two weeks. Again, the number to call is 1-800-555-5555."

Sean's mom had walked in and took Mitch's hand, watching the end of the broadcast. Putting his arm around her, he said, "It's okay. It's just a precaution. If it were any worse, they would have said so." Turning to his son, Mitch asked, "Sean, what do you think?"

"It sounds like they don't want to alarm anyone to how serious it really is. To broadcast on national television a warning like that…? They already know what the reaction would be, and yet they still felt the need to do it. They know there will be a potential for panic, but they've still put out the warning."

"I agree. It's one thing to work with local officials and try to keep it on the down low, but to put out a national broadcast…? It has to be very serious," explained Mike. "What they're trying to do is to nip it in the bud before it becomes a serious epidemic, which suggests to me that it already is serious."

"Maybe we should head back down to the sporting goods store and buy a little more ammo, just in case." Sean was already beginning to take seriously everything that his dad had been telling him about prepping, and he wasn't being apologetic about it.

"I'll go with you, Son. There might be a few other things to buy."

"I'm going too. I brought a few guns with me from home, but I don't have much ammo stored up. We better go right away in case there's a lot of other people with the same idea."

"If you three go there," Beth jumped in, "then I'm going to the grocery store. If we need to stay home for a couple of weeks, we'll need some things."

"Let's take both vehicles and get them fueled up, too, after we hit the sporting goods store, just in case. Sean, would you run out to the shop and grab all of the gas cans, too?"

"Sure, Dad."

"Same for you, Beth, fill up the car as soon as you're done at the store. I'm glad the fuel company just filled our tanks the other day. And remember what that bulletin said about the sick. Try to keep your distance from everyone. Alright, let's get going."

As the three of them drove into town, Sean called Rachel to see if they had heard the bulletin. They had seen it, but her dad wasn't home yet. She hadn't been able to get him on the phone yet either. Sean found out the several calibers of weapons they had and let her know he would buy them some extra ammo.

When the three of them entered the store, Joe was behind the counter doing some paperwork, and there were a few customers scattered throughout the store with a couple of store employees helping them out. They walked straight to Joe to get things rolling before a rush started.

"Hey, Joe!" greeted Mitch.

"Hi, Mitch! Good to see you. You guys see that news bulletin a little while ago?"

"We did. That's why we're here. We wanted to buy some more ammo, and Sean was thinking about another gun. I see you've got some .280 Remington there and .45 rounds. I'll take all seven boxes of the .280, all ten boxes of the .45s, and your last seven thousand-round cartons of 5.56. You got yourself all stocked up, Joe, in case this thing is bad?"

"Yeah, Mitch. I've already set back another rifle and pistol and plenty of ammo for them, plus extra ammo for my other guns."

"You can never have too much ammo."

Sean was looking the guns over and noticed a couple with interest. "Hey, Joe, I see you have the Colt AR15 LE6920. I think it's about time I bought one of those, too. Be nice to have them if this virus thing blows up before it's all over. I think I'd also like to get that Beretta in the .357 Magnum, and I'd like to look at that Remington 870 Express Tactical shotgun."

Joe let out a little whistle. "Okay! That's a nice selection of guns, Sean. I've got those same ones in my collection, but doubled. I sold your dad two of those Colt AR15s six months ago. We'll have to be quick about this before a crowd comes in. Here's that shotgun. I'll get one in the box for you to open up and look over, and we'll start this paperwork."

"That's a nice looking shotgun, Joe," Mike commented, looking it over as Sean handled it. "How about if you double Sean's order for me, too?"

"I'd like to get that four-inch compact Springfield XD I looked at earlier too, Joe, for my girlfriend."

"Sure thing, Sean."

"You got any recommendation on a scope for the Colt?" Sean asked.

"There's quite a few on the market, but the one I have in stock that I like is the Aimpoint Pro Patrol Rifle Optic. It's a 1x32 red dot system and also the Acog 4x32. Aimpoint's about four hundred bucks. Acog twice that."

"I'll go with the Aimpoint. That alright with you, Mike?" asked Sean.

"It'll work for me."

Sean filled out the paperwork for all the guns, because not being an Oregon resident, Mike couldn't purchase any yet. As soon as they had the paperwork filled out and Joe was putting it away, the front door opened and seven guys walked in, coming straight toward the gun counter.

Mitch looked at Joe, still behind the counter, "Thanks, Joe, for this. We really appreciate it."

"Don't mention it. Just glad I could help you out."

"Joe, we're set up pretty good out at my place, so if this thing actually gets out of control and you need help, call me or come on out to the house. You got my address."

"Thanks, Mitch, for the offer. I'll keep it in mind." Shaking hands all around, they started gathering up their stuff to head out.

The three of them had their boxed guns in hand, and two cardboard boxes loaded with several calibers of ammo and shotgun shells. They ended up buying all of Joe's available ammo and extra magazines for the calibers and weapons they had, plus four holsters and cartridge belts for their 45's, 9-mm, and the .357s. Mitch had two of the boxed rifles and cartridge belts, while Sean and Mike each carried a large box of ammo, which was quite a load to carry. Joe had set Sean's three handguns, with holsters, on the top of Sean's box as he picked it up, and the three knives they purchased were on the top of the other box. Sean would have to come back in for the remaining guns. As they were walking to the door, three more guys were coming in, and outside there were another twenty or so heading for the entrance with more cars arriving in the parking lot.

"Looks like we got here just in time," Mitch commented.

"Just in time," Sean echoed.

"Let's get gassed up. After that, I'm going to meet your mom at the store and help her out."

"Okay. I'll call Rachel and have them meet us at the store and stock up on some things."

"Let's get rolling."

There were only seven cars in front of them to fuel up, so it was better than they expected. When they arrived at the supermarket, it was a different story. There were crowds of people that would rival the Christmas shopping. Sean was pushing a cart as well as Mike and Mitch, and all three were loading things in bunches. Their first stop was the bread and goodies, because those were the two they would run out of first. Lunchmeat and cheese seemed to be a big one too. Soda pop, juices, frozen concentrates, pastas, bottled water, fresh meat, canned soups and vegetables, and the list went on. They eventually tied up with Beth to see a heaping cart full of a variety of items.

Rachel, her mom, and sister came in and started gathering things. Using the phone to locate each other, Sean walked with them to help in the selection of things that might help in a prolonged emergency. After forty-five minutes of filling up carts, they had to wait thirty minutes or so to get checked out. Beth's car was loaded to the roof with the lightweight stuff and Sean's truck took all of the heavier stuff that wouldn't blow out on the way home. After helping Rachel and her mom load their two carts, Sean led Rachel over to his truck and dug out the ammo he bought them and the Springfield 9mm he picked up for her.

"You know how to use a handgun?" Sean asked her.

"Yes. Dad took me target practicing a lot. Is it that bad already?"

"Not yet, but it might be pretty quickly. Better to be safe than sorry. I know this isn't a ring, but I bought this for you." Pulling the pistol from the holster, he showed her how to load the magazine, use the slide to cock it, use the safety, and how to take a round out of the chamber. Watching her do it three times in a row, he was satisfied that she would be okay. "As soon as you get home, clean the gun to remove any excess grease that might cause it to malfunction. There'll be instructions in the box to break it down for cleaning."

"Okay, I can do that."

"Did you get a hold of your dad?" Sean asked.

"Yes. He was still at work, but he'll quit early. Sean, what do you think is going on?" asked Rachel, looking at Sean with deep concern and earnestness.

"Just what they said. A disease that can easily become an epidemic and that probably already has. They didn't say go to the doctor first, so it must be contagious enough that they don't want any contact at all between a sick person and a healthy one. I would also assume that it can be lethal, or they wouldn't have warned people to just stay at home. So, the best thing to do right now would be to go home, unload your stuff, and stay indoors. Just in case, though, keep your weapon handy."

Sean's cellphone started ringing, and as he answered it, he linked hands with Rachel, who stood by quietly, listening to the conversation. While he was conversing with what sounded to Rachel to be the sheriff, he looked her in the eye several times. When it was over, Sean pocketed his phone, and then looked at Rachel. Her mom, Joanna, had walked over to stand closely, too, listening to the conversation.

"That was the Sheriff's Office. Asked if I could come in to attend a briefing on what's happening. They also warned me not to get close to anyone that seems the slightest bit sick. Said that it would be a death sentence for me." Looking at Rachel, seeing the questioning look on her face, Sean put his arms around her and whispered, "It's okay. I'll watch over you." Just holding her for a long moment, he inhaled the comforting fragrance of her hair: fir trees and lavender.

"Rachel, honey, we'll be okay."

Pulling away enough to look her in the eye, he bent his head down to lightly kiss her on the cheek, and then stepped back and looked at Joanna.

"I'll need to go home and unload this stuff first before I go down to the Sheriff's Office. Once I know more, I'll call you and let you know what I find out. This is serious stuff. You guys need to gas up first, but don't have any contact with anyone. Do you have cash to pay for your fuel?"

"Only a few dollars. I usually use a credit card."

"Here's some more cash. Just pay the attendant as close as you can get it, but don't take back any change. Keep your windows rolled up and be careful. If you think you need it, stop at the drive through to get out as much cash as you can, but try to wear gloves when you touch the buttons. Like I said, this sickness is deadly, so be careful. I'll call you as soon as I can."

With one last quick kiss and hand squeeze, Sean turned away from Rachel and walked back to where his parents and Mike were waiting for him.

"The Sheriff's Office just called me. They want me to come in for a briefing, said to bring Mike if I could find him. He said not to have any contact with anyone who looks sick and that it would be a death sentence for me. This is serious. Let's get home and unload this stuff; then Mike and I can run down to the Sheriff's Office and find out what's going on."

"Okay, Son. Let's go."

CHAPTER FOURTEEN

Arriving at the Sheriff's Office, Sean and Mike were surprised at the number of cars that were parked everywhere. They had to park a block away and walk back to the entrance, where a deputy was standing guard. Recognizing Sean and Mike, he let them pass. Inside the conference room, it was standing room only, and Sheriff Ken Briles was speaking.

"I'll explain it again for those of you who arrived late. This came down from the office of the President two hours ago. The sickness that the bulletins on the TV and radio were talking about isn't just the flu; it's something much worse. It's a virus that an Arab terrorist organization has developed and has spread throughout the whole world by utilizing the airline industry. Almost every nation is reporting the disease—some worse than others. The U.S. has apparently received special consideration from this group, since we have reported over two hundred thousand cases with symptoms so far. Thirty thousand of them are at stage two, where they are irrational, combative, and very aggressive—almost mindless. The estimated numbers for non-symptom infected is as high as five million. Twenty million or more are reported for the rest of the world. The early symptoms of this disease are very similar to the flu: headache, fever, coughing, nausea, lack of appetite, and insomnia. Those symptoms last up to ten days, and then stage two develops. At the onset of stage two, the patient becomes very aggressive, combatant, exhibits irrational behavior, is paranoid and delusional, will begin to over-salivate, and will have a high fever with excessive sweating. The increased salivation causes excessive drooling, and they tend to bite and strike out at everything around them."

Sheriff Briles paused for a moment, took a deep breath, and then raised his voice slightly, as he said, "This is the most important thing: There is no vaccine or cure. Once you've contracted the disease, you will die. The incubation period is nine or ten days once you've been infected. In other words, you will feel fine for about nine or ten days, but on day ten, you will think you've got the flu. In order to save the men next to you, or your wife and kids, your loved ones, the moment you feel sick, stay away from everybody else. Do not spread it. If everyone stays under cover, then our job will be easier. The less this thing spreads, the greater our chance of survival."

The sheriff looked around the room, locking glances with as many of his friends as he could.

"The President's orders were to help subdue the stage two infected so that they won't spread the virus to more innocent people. We are to wear protective gear while doing so, because the slightest bite or scratch can infect us. Any saliva that lands on our face and makes contact with our eyes, nose, or mouth will infect us. This is serious people."

"If the infected will die anyway, why should we attempt to subdue them? Putting our lives on the line for the sake of subduing the walking dead doesn't sound reasonable." The sentiment of the room was agreeable to what was just said by one of the deputies.

"Why not just put them down? If they're dead anyway, why take chances?" another asked.

"We can't just start executing people. That's just not an option at this moment. If you are being attacked or see someone else being attacked, my orders to you are to use deadly force if you think it is necessary. As of now, our county has only reported about three hundred cases. That might be because we're not a large enough population center to attract the notice of the terrorists, as are New York and L.A. The big cities are reporting infections into hundreds of thousands, so there might be a possibility that we won't have to go through the worst of it. For now, protect yourselves and your loved ones, not just from the infected. We will surely see an increase in looting and robbery. When supplies run low and people are desperate, people start getting killed. Those of you that are on duty, get back to work. We're going to put on more patrols right away, and the rest of you will be notified of your new schedules."

Immediately, the noise level in the room increased by seventy decibels, as everyone started to talk to those around them. The sheriff made his way to Sean and Mike, and he signaled them to follow him. Once in his office, behind closed doors, the sheriff turned to them to see calm faces looking back at him.

"This thing is pretty serious, boys. Since I need more men that I can count on, I'm going to swear in the both of you. This is a little unorthodox, but since you've both been in the marines and have a clean record, I'm foregoing the formalities for now. We've already got two officers down with this thing, and I believe we could be facing a lot of other problems because everyone will be in a panic. Do you have anyone in your household that is showing any symptoms?"

"No. I haven't even seen anyone that's sick yet. But it looks like this thing will be hard to track, especially with a ten-day incubation period," answered Sean.

"It is. The notice I received about it indicated that there have been a lot of deaths from policemen protecting themselves. The infected are attacking anyone close to them for no reason, and it appears as if they are reduced to animal-like aggression. Even worse than just being insane, there's no thinking behind it, just straight aggression."

"So, if we run into that type of person, it seems to me to be best just to put them down, rather than take any chance with contact. This thing really sounds a lot like rabies. Being overseas, we were made aware of the disease and its effects, in case we ourselves were infected. In Africa and Southeast Asia, it's pretty common," replied Sean.

"I can't tell you not to shoot them; that has to be up to your discretion in each instance. All I'm going to say is protect yourselves. Stop by the duty desk on your way out, fill out some paperwork, and pick up your schedules. Now I'm going to swear you in and give you your badges."

Haris had been in the compound for two days straight going over reports and listening to any newscasts that were coming in. His fever had started two days after he had mercifully ended his son's life. His wife had taken it hard, not understanding how a simple flu could cause his death. And now she had the same symptoms. Haris was still deliberating on what to do with her; he cared about her very much and didn't want to see her suffer any more than he did his son. Her symptoms would be getting worse, since she was two days ahead of him in the infection.

Haris had also been keeping track of the local area, checking hospital reports of the flu, but he had not released that information to his associates or peers. In their own city, over five hundred cases of the flu had been reported. Because of the symptoms' similarity to the flu, it had been misdiagnosed, and no blood tests had been done. Within twenty more days, their total infected would probably be over ten thousand, after that, two hundred thousand… The only way to stop it would be to take every one of the infected and kill them on the first day of symptoms, and they would have to be very careful doing it. With care and thoroughness, there would be a slight chance of eradicating it.

Haris had seen the worldwide news bulletin that had been started during the night. He didn't know how much good it would do; he had better information on where all his men had spread the infection. His team had run the numbers and scenarios numerous times, and their best guess was closer to forty million worldwide. They could be wrong by a few million of course, but what difference would that make? The disease was well on its way to achieving their goal and most likely would far exceed it.

Rising, Haris left his room and made the rounds in the compound, checking on his associates and compatriots. He never let on that he had a new perspective on what they had started. Instead, he kept quiet, in order to not create any doubt about him among his men. With his climbing fever, there was no doubt in his mind that he would be infecting his own men as he moved among them, but his one thought was, It is as Allah wills it.

Retrieving his case with the syringe and the bottle of paralyzing agent from his desk, he made his way out of the compound to see his wife and to let her know how much he cared about her.

Director Langdon, sitting in his office, was looking over the reports coming in hourly. The number of deaths by police or military was up to fifteen thousand and climbing. The infected were totally losing their minds and attacking everything like rabid dogs. No one was safe.

The more he thought about it, the more he agreed with the virologist. The only way out would be to put down everyone showing symptoms before they were able to infect anyone else. If there wasn't any contact for transfer, it would die out. Putting people in the hospital only increased the chances of those in the healthcare industry to catch it, not to mention the people who would have to transport them, and anyone else in the hospital for any other reason. Isolation would be the best thing, like living in the mountains or on an island. There would eventually be some survivors, but it wasn't looking too good.

Calling his brother, he explained what was going on.

"This thing has the potential to kill ninety-five percent of the world's population in the next two months. The only way to avoid it is to isolate yourselves as much as possible. I'd recommend gathering all your weapons and ammo, camping gear, and as much food and water as you can load in your vehicles and head for the mountains. The best thing to do would be to rent a little cabin that is isolated in a small community with a fresh running water supply and wait this thing out, at least two months. By then we should either have it under control, or we'll all be dead."

"What about you?" his brother, Cliff, asked. The director could hear concern and anxiety in his voice.

"I have to stay and see if there is any way I can help fight this thing. If Mary and Josh were still here, I would probably come with you, but for now… this is what I have to do. I'll call Julie and tell her the same thing, and then you two get your heads together and get out of here. No later than tomorrow. Believe me, this is the only way to be able to survive. I love you, and take care of the family."

CHAPTER FIFTEEN

Sean and Mike decided to make one last trip through the store before everything was completely picked through or was gone entirely. At that point, there was no telling how bad it was going to be, how affected the food supply would become, or how long it would last. For all they knew, it could be the last time to buy groceries. Even as early as it was, there were a lot of empty shelves as they walked through, but some of the things that people were overlooking were the salt, flour, and yeast. If they were reduced to baking their own bread, they would need those three ingredients. Without the salt, the bread might taste a little blah, and without the yeast, the dough wouldn't rise. Mitch and Beth had probably stocked up on it, but to what degree, Sean didn't know. Better to be safe than sorry, so Sean bought a whole cart of the ingredients. They loaded up another cart with all canned goods from soup to vegetables, and a lot of beans. There were still a lot of people shopping, but not nearly as many as the earlier rush.

Once they were out of the store and driving through Springfield, he and Mike talked about what was happening and what would be best to do.

"If we're both gone, then Dad will have to watch over the place by himself. I don't really like that idea, but I can't see any other way to do it."

"Do you think we'll need to move into the bunker?" asked Mike.

"No, not yet. As soon as we move out of the house, people might think it's empty and start nosing around. I think it'll be better to save the bunker for our last option. What I'm wondering about is Rachel and her family. If we're on duty, we can't watch over them or Mom and Dad. But I don't know if we need to ask them to move in with us until this thing is figured out. I'm sure they wouldn't want to leave their place unguarded."

"Maybe it won't be as bad as they think. The main thing is to stay away from other people, so maybe it'll be alright for a while. If everyone stays inside, there shouldn't be too much trouble, except for a few of the stage two people, and it shouldn't be too hard to protect yourself from them." Mike was talking sense, and it eased Sean's worries.

"You're probably right, Mike. There aren't that many cases around here, so we might be in pretty good shape."

As soon as they arrived home, Sean called Rachel and explained the situation to her, but he also decided he would drive over so that he could talk to her dad. He wanted him to have a clear understanding of what was happening and what could happen.

"You guys are eight miles out from town, so you shouldn't have any trouble for a while. I don't think people will get too crazy just yet. There aren't that many reported cases in Lane County, and people will respect others' property until things start getting desperate. Then you might get people coming through and trying to steal stuff out of your shop or barn. It would have to be really serious for you to actually be in danger."

While Sean was at Rachel's house, the news came on the TV. Everyone gathered in front of the TV to listen and to watch the carnage that was happening around the world. There were police officers being attacked, knocked down, and bitten, with other officers pulling the attacker off only to get bitten and scratched. The attackers were fighting like wild animals—no rhyme or reason, other than to attack. Many times the police ended up shooting the attackers to stop them, and although parts were edited out, they could all see what was happening.

"That looks so bad. How can they ever stop that?" Joanna asked.

"If it gets any worse, most countries will have to declare martial law, with a curfew, and anyone doing anything suspicious will be shot before they can do any damage," Sean explained. "Hopefully, it won't get that bad around here."

The news anchor went on to say that the military was being mobilized in several countries to control the turmoil, mostly in and around the largest cities. There were only a handful of cases reported in the U.S. so far, around New York, Washington D.C., and Atlanta.

"With the bulletin coming out, did your boss tell everyone to stay home?" Sean asked.

"Yes, he did. He's got a family, too, that needs watching over." Looking Sean square in the eye Kevin asked, "Tell me, Sean, just how bad is it?"

"It's bad, Kevin. Not too bad here yet, but with the worldwide spread of it? It might be hard to hide from. The more isolated the area you live in, the better your chances. The bad part is that although we only have three hundred reported cases in the county, how many unreported cases are out there, since it is so similar to the flu? It won't be until they are so sick that they realize it's not the flu, and then they'll go to the doctor. By that time, the infected person will have infected their whole family and maybe more."

"What are we supposed to do if one of us starts to come down with the flu?"

"I would have to say, first of all, it might actually be the flu. But with it being this deadly, don't take any chances. The one not feeling well needs to immediately leave the house and live in the camp trailer until you find out if it is just the flu, lasting four or five days, or this other stuff. Don't touch them in any way and keep your distance. And immediately upon the sick person leaving the house, you should use disinfectant on everything, every surface that you can wipe down. You can take food and supplies out close to the barn for them, but keep your distance. It might be a good idea, from this moment on, to keep your distance from one another. Wash your hands with antibacterial soap often. It wouldn't even hurt to wear gloves and a facemask if you had them. The incubation period is nine or ten days, so if any one of you or me were infected today in the store, the symptoms will start on the ninth or tenth day from now. If we don't have any contact with anyone else for ten days from today, and we're all still healthy in ten days, then we're safe for a while. Hopefully, by the time we know we're good, we'll know more about the rest of the world and where we stand."

"At least that's plain talk. We didn't even get that with the news bulletin."

"I know. They didn't want to cause people to panic, so they held back too many details. If this turns out for the worse and it shuts down the economy, you need to start thinking how you'll feed yourselves once your food supplies run out. You have a freezer or two?"

"Yes, we've got a stand-up one in the utility room and a chest freezer in the garage."

"Are they full?"

"I'm not sure. Joanna, how full are the two freezers?"

"The one inside is almost full and the one in the garage is only about half full. Even with the things we bought today," replied Joanna.

"Do you think it would be worth going back to the store for more things now?" asked Kevin.

"In a situation like this, the more the better. If everyone else stays home from work, including store employees, delivery truck drivers, distribution plant workers, and food processors, the stores will run out of everything quickly… and not just the grocery stores either. If you want to take quick stock of your supplies right now, we can make a decision on whether to make another trip to the store right now. I'll go with you, and we'll be extremely careful."

"Okay, let's take a look."

After looking things over, they decided to run to the store again, just Kevin and Sean. They stopped at the small local market first, put on face masks that Sean was given at the Sheriff's Office, and then went inside. As they looked around, there wasn't much left, but they did buy all the salt, flour, and sugar that was left, brown and white. The larger market in town still had enough left to help, but it was limited. Many things that would come in useful for preparing their own foods if the stores never came back online were overlooked by the crowds, so they bought up many of those supplies. After returning to Rachel's house and unloading the groceries, Sean said his good-byes to the family and then led Rachel out onto the porch to say his farewell.

"Rachel, I'm so sorry that this had to start so soon after meeting you. I was so much looking forward to sharing a lot of fun and laughter with you, under circumstances that are more normal. I hope this doesn't put a damper on our relationship too much."

"No, Sean. We'll be fine. I'm really glad that we were able to meet before this happened, because you make me feel like we'll get through this somehow, no matter how bad it gets. I can tell my dad really appreciates you, too, like the way you've handled yourself and made decisions in helping us. My mom is glad that you're here too. She told me so while you and dad went into town."

Sean put his arms around her and pulled her in close, looking into her eyes. Gently, he placed his lips over hers, and she responded with soft kisses of her own. When he lifted his head, he could see tears in her eyes. He lifted his hands and gently wiped the tears from her cheeks as they started to fall.

"Rachel, honey, it's okay. We'll figure this out." Putting his arms around her again, he pulled her in tightly, making her feel secure and safe, like nothing could ever hurt her. "Let's give this some time, and if it gets worse, you and your family can come live with us at the farm. Dad has actually been preparing for something like this to happen, so we're pretty well set up. It wouldn't take that much to move you guys over if it comes to that, and Mike and I will be good to have around. There won't be anything to worry about."

Rachel looked into Sean's eyes for a long moment. She knew that she could trust what she could see in them. "Sean, I love you. I know that this is happening so fast, but the more I find out about you, the more I see how caring, strong, and confident you are… I'm realizing you're the man I've always dreamed about. I'm so happy we've found each other and you're here with me."

Putting her hand on the back of his neck, she pulled his head down until their lips came together, and she spent her passion upon his lips. Pulling away, she stepped to the door, looked back at him, and then disappeared inside.

The next day, Sean and Mike were on the schedule together, but they were riding with different deputies. Their training hadn't been completed yet, so they were placed with senior deputies to continue learning their duties. There were quite a few calls to stores to settle disputes between customers who were fighting over supplies, but other than that, it was surprisingly calm. After watching some more of the news that morning, Sean was thinking that this was just the calm before the storm.

The previous night, he and his dad had stayed up for a while with Mike, discussing the situation, and possible strategies concerning Rachel and her family. If it actually came to the point of moving them over, they would bring all of their supplies, their freezers, refrigerator, cars, truck, camp trailer, personal effects, and any valuables, of course, whether family heirlooms, albums, or anything else they dared not lose if the house was later looted.

Once they arrived, Mitch and Beth, Kevin and Joanna, and Rachel and Leah would move into the bunker, while Mike, Sean, and Rachel's brother, Steve, would sleep in the house. They would all be armed, and if anyone came to the house in the night, they would find more trouble than they'd want to take on. It was the best plan they could come up with until they were able to receive more insight from future developments.

Sean kept in contact with his dad and Rachel on and off throughout the day, making sure they knew what was going on and to help reassure Rachel and her family that things were going to be okay. The deputy that Sean was assigned to also called his family several times throughout the day just to be reassured of their safety. Everyone was more than a little worried.

They learned that day that the military had been given orders to make sure product deliveries to markets continued to operate on schedule. Protective gear was given out to workers in packing plants and distribution centers to help against being infected while at work. They were given instruction on how to protect themselves, and it was made clear that if anyone felt the slightest bit ill, they had to remove themselves to their home immediately. Also, instructions were going out over the TV channels about how to protect themselves and their families from the virus. All in all, it made a lot of difference for those that were scared. If anything could calm the panic, it was the knowledge of how to protect themselves and that they wouldn't have to starve to death.

CHAPTER SIXTEEN

The President and her advisors were in the Situation Room on day twenty-three, listening to the current reports coming in from around the world. As near as they could tell, the current estimated number of infected was between twenty-five and thirty million. Two million had symptoms, and the rest were infected but not at the symptomatic stage yet. Still, there was plenty of guesswork going on. However, watching what was happening in the newscasts, the numbers were believable.

As other world leaders were joining the meeting on video feeds, their individual faces were taking over TV screens, one by one, until there were twenty nations represented.

"Alright, ladies and gentlemen, I'm glad you've joined us today. We've got some very hard decisions to make, and I'm sure there will be differing views on what our actions should be to stem the advance of this virus. I'm going to open the floor to Director Langdon to fill us in on our latest reports. We will have a discussion, and then those who want to add something afterwards may take turns. Go ahead, Richard."

"Madame President, London reports that the quarantined officers again have a fever and have taken a turn for the worse. They're starting their seventh day of symptoms, but they had their final shots of vaccine yesterday. Twenty-eight days is the length of time it takes for the body to fully develop the antibodies it needs to fight the virus. In three more days, we'll know for sure if they develop stage two or start recovering. If they reach stage two, there will be no recovery."

"Thank you, Richard. How do we stand on the vaccinations for the military and our government leaders?"

"Ten percent of our military has received their first shot and about thirty percent of the government leaders. Our healthcare workers are substantially higher than that, due to the fact that they started a week ago."

"And do we need to worry about any side effects of the vaccine causing a drop in the recipient's ability to show up for work or carry out their duties?" asked the President.

"Very low risk of side effects of much consequence, but there can be allergic reactions that could turn serious. However, very few of those are expected."

"Are there any accurate reports on the number of the stage two infections?"

"We're three and a half days into the start of stage two; we have a count for two days at about seventy thousand. No reports yet for yesterday or for today. Actual current number could be closer to one hundred thousand. The ones we've been seeing on the news represent mostly those that weren't in the hospital. Once those turned, there was no one to stop them. Most of the ones in the hospitals were able to be subdued before they were completely out of control, even though there were still many cases being reported of people getting bit during the subduing. Our biggest concern now is that the hospitals ran out of room to hold more patients two days ago. They've got patients on mats on the floor. Each hospital room designed for one patient has four, and double occupancy rooms have six or seven. The staff are being overworked, and when the current stage one progresses to stage two, they will in all likelihood be overrun."

"Is there any way to alleviate that scenario before it escalates?" asked the President. "Does anyone have any ideas short of immediate euthanasia?"

There was a long moment of silence in which nobody moved, other than the turning of heads to see if anyone else had an answer. David, the head of the Department of Health stood up and proceeded to give his opinion: "This is a terrible dilemma that none of us have ever dreamed was possible. I don't think there will be any easy answers from now on, and there is no one but us to solve this issue. If we continue to sit back and watch it unfold and not take serious immediate steps to slow its progress, then we're finished. Our best hope is that the vaccine will work, but our earliest test subjects are still three days out from giving us an answer. By that time, according to our estimated numbers, there will be a possible fifteen million people newly infected on that one day. Even today, there may be as many as eight to ten million new cases. We should assume that everyone that is infected before today will not be able to be saved, which our number estimates would indicate is around twenty-six to thirty million. If those people infect only five more people, the number of infected grows to one hundred fifty million. If we euthanize twenty-six million people today, it could save the lives of one hundred twenty-five million people, give or take five million or so."

"That would be like dropping a nuclear warhead on New York City. We'd be wiping out more people than make up the entire population of the world's smallest countries. How could we possibly condone that, as the world's leaders of freedom and liberty?!" exclaimed the Attorney General.

David responded, "If we don't do it, the freedom and liberty of at least one hundred twenty-five million other people will be violated. Which situation is more desirable? Sacrificing millions to save the human race as we know it, or watching almost everyone you know die a slow and agonizing death?"

"Alright. Alright. How about an interim alternative? We already know that the stage two infected are hopeless. If we euthanize those, it stops them from infecting others, and it makes more room in our hospitals for others, who can be restrained as they near their stage two conversion. Then, if the vaccine fails, we can take measures that are more drastic. Would that work for the next three days?" asked the Attorney General.

The President noticed on the monitors that several world leaders wished to respond, and standing to her feet, she quieted the room. Some of our esteemed colleagues from other nations have something to say. Prime Minister, your nation was the first to be infected. What would you like to say?"

"We also have been vaccinating as many people as we can. However, daily, our supply runs out, and we have to wait for more vaccines to arrive the following day. The growth rate in our country is a day or two ahead of yours, and we see that there is no other solution than to immediately euthanize at least the stage two infected. Each succeeding day, there will be more than the previous day advancing to stage two. If we don't at least start today with euthanasia, we won't be able to keep up with the medications to accomplish it nor the body removal and disposal."

He paused as he looked down at his papers. Raising his eyes once more to the camera, all those who could see him on the monitor could see the heartache that he was facing.

Everyone was listening as he began again, "I know how hard this situation is and the decisions we're facing. Some of you may even have loved ones right now that are infected, but there is more at stake than just those that are closest to us. We're looking at a possible near extinction event. Drastic measures are now called for to save the world for those who survive us. We will, in our nation, begin euthanasia of the stage two infected immediately."

"Is there anyone else with a differing opinion of what has been said already?" asked the President. She could see the shaking of heads in the negative all around the room and on all of the monitors. No one had anything else to say. "I'd like to see a show of hands. I know you won't want to be put on record for your decision, but we have to do this in order to move forward. All those in favor of David's proposal of total euthanasia of all those infected, please raise your hand." The President looked down the table to see David's hand rise first and then one next to him, one across the table, and then another, another, two more, but then no others.

"All those in favor of immediate euthanasia of all stage two infected, raise your hand."

Immediately all hands were raised in the room and on the monitors, including the previously dissenting seven.

"It seems that it's unanimous. One other decision then must be made. Do we keep this decision from the press, or do we tell them immediately? Is the public ready to hear this drastic decision, or will it do more harm than good?"

Director Langdon took the floor, "All it takes is one doctor to disagree with this decision, and he will leak it to the media anyways. Then we will all be roasted for not sharing the magnitude of our decision with the public. I think it would be better to make an announcement right away. Every national leader should put out his own bulletin, for his own people, explaining the magnitude and purpose of our decision. There will be panic, but it will also wake up everyone to the importance of protecting themselves from being infected. Either way, we all need to be in agreement."

He turned it over to the President and took his seat.

David McCale, head of the Health Department stood up with an idea, "If we explain to the public that the vaccine won't work on the stage two infected, but we have developed another experimental medicine that we want to try on them to see if it can cure them, they'll never know that we're actually euthanizing them. When they die, we write it off as another failure. If the public knows that we're putting their loved ones to death, there may be an outcry, and they'll stop coming to the hospital."

"That might be a good idea, but to re-label drugs so the doctors and nurses don't catch on to it, might take too long," rebutted Langdon. "And again, if the truth came out that we misled them so that we could kill several million people they might revolt."

The President raised her hand for quiet. "Alright, we've got two choices. We either tell the public the truth, or we hide it from them. All those in favor of notifying the public of our decision, raise your hand."

Director Langdon's hand went up first, and then over half the room followed simultaneously. Another, another, several more, and then the rest of them went up. "All those opposed?" No one.

"For those of you who will be involved with this, get the word out immediately to your counterparts. Drugs need to be produced and shipped ASAP. Doctors need to be notified of the urgency of using what drugs they have on hand. Logistics need to be figured out for the disposal of bodies with the least amount of infection. Time is of the essence, people. Arrange a news conference ASAP. May God help us."

As soon as the meeting was adjourned, Jason, the White House Chief of Staff slipped away. He wasn't feeling well at all. The flu medicine he had been taking just wasn't getting the job done anymore. He left the White House, thinking about staying home a few days until he felt better. He'd had the flu before, many times in his life, and since he hadn't had any contact with anyone that was sick for quite some time, he really couldn't believe that what he had was the rabies virus that was infecting the world. There could not be any way.

CHAPTER SEVENTEEN

Sean had called Rachel and arranged for her family to come to his house for dinner and a visit. No matter how things turned out, there still needed to be a coming together of the two families to get to know each other. Sean and Rachel knew in their heart that they were never going to part, but for that night, Sean wanted to discuss the future plans of joining forces if necessary.

Sean and Mike had enough time to shower before Rachel's family arrived, and they were waiting for them on the front porch. The TV in the living room had been turned on that morning, tuned to the news channel, and left running all day. Anytime Mitch or Beth walked by, they would stop and listen to see if anything new had been reported. Everyone was anxious to hear more news of the virus.

Dinner was almost ready when Rachel's family drove up in the car. After greetings, they sat down to a fine dinner of pork chops, fried potatoes, green beans, homemade rolls, and a fresh apple pie, with iced tea to wash it all down. It was a fine start to an enjoyable evening. Shortly after dinner, before the conversation actually turned to the problems at hand, a news bulletin began. Turning to gather in the living room to listen, they could hear the announcer say, "The President of the United States."

"Good evening, everyone. As you all know, there has been an outbreak of a contagious virus throughout the world. I am here now to explain to you what has happened and what we are trying to do to escape this terrible plague. First of all, I want you to know how this virus was started. We have backtracked it to its origin. It was developed by an Arab terrorist organization in the Middle East and was sent out on airline flights with at least forty different terrorists to many different countries. They infected all those on their flights and at all of the airports where they landed. They then continued to spread the disease until they could no longer do so. As of now, our best estimates are that forty million people may be infected—the majority of those don't know it, and they won't know until they start showing flu-like symptoms. The disease is divided into two stages of development. It takes ten days to become symptomatic, and then roughly ten days of the symptoms, which include fever, headache, chills, fatigue, insomnia, and lack of appetite. When it develops into stage two, the patient becomes aggressive, combative, irrational, delusional, and the saliva glands become overactive, causing excessive drooling. We're still testing a vaccine, but the results won't be in until three or four more days."

Pausing for a moment to drink some water, the President arranged her papers before continuing. "Of the total infected, there are approximately two-point-two million with the flu-like symptoms and, of those, about two hundred thousand have developed into stage two. Our vaccine has no effect on stage two of the virus. The virus is a genetically altered strain of rabies. Stage two is very painful and agonizing for the patient; they no longer even know who they are."

The President paused, took a deep breath, and continued, "I say this with deepest regret: There is no hope for stage two infected, and we don't have the medications to help all of them through the pain until they succumb to the disease. I say again, they are past the point of any medical cure. The only way to alleviate their pain and suffering and also to reduce future infections arising from their care… I, my leaders and councilors, and our allies from around the world, have decided, with deepest regret, to euthanize all of the stage two infected, beginning immediately. Our hospitals are overrun with infected, and there is an exponential increase of new cases every day. We will continue to vaccinate those we can in hopes of stopping this disease. We advise that you have no unnecessary contact with others, and if you are feeling the slightest bit ill, stay indoors and call your doctor to report it. We are asking that people in the production, delivery, and selling of food products continue to work, with acceptable protective gear, so that our people will continue to have what they need to survive. Thank you, and may God help us all."

The women were sitting down by the end of the announcement, with their men standing close by. None of them had anything to say for a moment, while they digested the bad news. Rachel was holding Sean's hand and then stood to her feet and wrapped her arms around him. The sadness of the moment was palpable in the room.

Kevin was the first to say something. "How could those people be so stupid as to start an epidemic like this? Do they not have any feelings at all?"

"When you hate everything about another race, then mix into it a religious zealotry, you can do almost anything. But this time they've gone too far. I wonder what the response of the world's leaders will be?" asked Mitch.

"If this is as bad as they say, it might end up killing them also. The most important thing right now is to hope that their vaccine works." Sean was remembering that the sheriff said that getting infected would be a death sentence. That would suggest that the President was still running a smoke screen to prevent a total panic. The vaccine probably was going to be a no show, and if everyone knew about it, things would spiral out of control quickly. Sean decided not to say anything about his worry for the moment.

Looking beyond the top of Rachel's head, Sean caught a slight head nod from his dad, indicating the direction of the barn. Understanding that he was asking should they reveal the bunker set-up, he nodded his affirmative.

Mitch took Beth's hand and helped her to her feet, hugged her, and whispering in her ear asked, "Do you think it's a good time to show them the bunker?"

She also nodded her head in the affirmative.

"Kevin, Joanna... there's something we'd like to show you. This thing going on is by far the scariest thing we've ever faced, and we feel that since our paths have crossed and become intermingled in such a beautiful way..." his gaze shifted to Rachel, standing in Sean's grasp, "...we want to share with you something that will help all of us to survive this. Follow me out to the barn."

Mitch and Beth led the way, with Kevin and Joanna following. Leah and Steve were next, with Sean and Rachel bringing up the rear. Mike elected to stay behind, to keep a lookout and to let the two families share a moment together. Going through the hidden door and down the stairs to the next one, Kevin was impressed with what he was seeing. With a coded lock entry on the remaining door, concrete walls, and ceilings, Kevin was beginning to sense a new hope beginning to emerge. A true shelter to weather the storm in its worst moments!

Walking through the second airtight door into the heart of the shelter, Kevin saw a small kitchen and living room, with three bedrooms and a bathroom, furnishings, and well-stocked shelves. He felt such a relief from a growing, gnawing fear, that he turned and hugged his wife, holding her as she also realized what a blessing these people were showing them. Joanna started crying with relief as Kevin held her.

Steve and Leah were excited about the bunker and began looking into all the rooms, asking questions about everything. Sean watched as his dad was finally able to show off his foresight and creation in a way that he never expected: as a true refuge and fortress that may very well save all of their lives.

"We've got the range, refrigerator, room heater, and water heater. I've got two underground propane tanks to feed a propane water heater that's in another compartment that should last us quite a while, if we're careful, if the main power goes out. I believe we could live comfortably here for a couple of years if need be. As long as the power remains on, we'll use electric as much as possible. We're very well stocked with things you'd expect in a place like this, and we have an inexhaustible supply of pure water. We've got both solar and wind generated power for when the grid goes down, and outside we have cattle, hogs, a fruit orchard, and good farmland to raise enough vegetables and grain to supply our future needs. I've made a small flour mill to turn our grains into flour, and with the fruit and vegetables and fresh meat, I think that we can survive here better than anyone else will out there. We will be self-sustaining, and almost no one else knows about this bunker. I think we're set up really well."

When Mitch finished explaining his creation, Sean was extremely proud of him. Before the disease hit, he honestly thought he was wasting his money, but now, listening to him expound on his survival plan, it was the sweetest thing he ever heard—except, of course, Rachel's declaration of her love.

Joanna turned to Beth and hugged her, still teary eyed, and Kevin stepped up to hug Mitch.

"Thank you, Mitch. This means so much to us, to me. I was completely lost as to how to keep my family safe. Sean already really helped me see some hope, and now this. We can't thank you enough."

"What else could we do? Leave our future in-laws outside to fend for themselves? I'm glad that we'll all be here to help and watch each other's backs. If this thing blows completely out of control, we'll need a few extra people here anyhow. Card games can get boring after a while with only four people."

Everyone laughed at his attempt at humor, fully realizing that card games were the least of it. After walking through and showing and explaining everything to them, they made their way back up to the living room, where they all sat down to discuss their plans. Kevin was agreeable with everything that Sean, Mike, and Mitch had already planned out, and the only thing up in the air was pertaining to when they should move over. Because of not wanting to lose his house and property to vandals and thieves unnecessarily, they would continue to live there until it became unsafe. The only other decision that came from their discussion was that it would be a good idea to have Steve and Leah stay in the camp trailer as much as possible for the next few days in case they might have been infected at school. Everyone knew that sicknesses were spread rampantly inside the school districts. If either one of them became symptomatic, staying in the trailer might save the rest of the family.

Mike's cellphone rang, and he made his way into the kitchen, mentioning that it was his sister's number. All of them quieted down for Mike to talk, and although he was in the kitchen, they could hear the conversation.

"Hey, Sis, how's it going? … I've been trying to call you, too. The lines have been too busy to get through … Yes, I saw the bulletin … You sure? Have you called the doctor? … Six days? Still not feeling any better? … I'm so sorry, Sis. Is Dean sick, too? … Same day? … What about the kids? Are they alright? … I'm so sorry. No. The way it was explained the vaccine might still be able to help you and Dean. But it would definitely help the kids. … They said there wasn't enough vaccine? That's not what they said in the bulletin. … Those bastards. Why can't they just tell the truth? They're probably saving the vaccine for people that they think are important. … I love you too, Sis. … I'm doing good. Sean's family is the greatest. We're actually more in the country, so the virus hasn't had much of an effect here, yet. We're set up pretty good, and I think we have a good chance of outlasting this thing. … I wish you were here, too. … I'll tell him. Don't give up yet. Take the kids to the hospital yourself if you can. If they see the kids, maybe they'll help anyway. … Call me again tomorrow and let me know. I love you, too."

Mike sat in silence for a bit, sniffled, and wiped his tears. After a moment, he came back into the living room, eyes red, still wiping his nose with the sleeve of his shirt. Mike had lost his parents when he was thirteen years old, and his sister had just finished two years of training at a junior college when it happened. She took him in, raised him, and watched over him, until he had joined the marines. There was a close bond between the two, and now he had no way to help her.

"Hey, buddy… we heard." Sean stepped up to him and hugged him. His best friend. Friendship forged in warfare. Closer than a brother. Sean cried. Rachel, overcome with grief, seeing tears on the face of one that she saw with so much strength, wrapped her arms around them both and cried along with them.

CHAPTER EIGHTEEN

Haris had spent the last two days with his wife, taking care of her during her sickness. She realized that she would also die the same way her son had, thinking that it was a new strain of flu. She didn't know what was happening around the world with the virus. She only knew what her husband had told her, because she hadn't been listening to any TV. Her husband hadn't let anyone in the house, telling her that the flu was too contagious. During her lucid moments, she could see that her husband also had contracted the disease. First her son, then her, and now him. Why was Allah punishing them? She just didn't understand. They were good and devout people.

Haris wanted to get back to the compound before he was too sick to do so, but he found it hard to face what needed to be done with his wife. If he went to the compound and then couldn't return, his wife would have no one to take care of her, and she would succumb to the second stage of the disease, all alone in her sickness. He couldn't stand that thought either. He decided to wait one more day before he said his good-bye.

"Madame President, we received word from Russia that their President and several of their top leaders have been infected. They were hoping that it wasn't the case, but they have now tested positive for rabies antibodies in their blood. The only way for those to be present is that they're infected and the body is trying to fight it. They're two days into the symptoms already. They'll be stage two in eight more days. In future contact, they will have a new President appointed with a few new Cabinet members.

"On another matter, things are progressing as well as could be expected with the euthanasia. But there were several things that came up. Before they were able to euthanize all of the stage two, more patients began to turn. Some of them were able to get out of their rooms, and more people were infected before they could restore order. Although they had tried to keep track of the ones that were on the verge of turning, there were some that they were unsure of, about the day they became symptomatic. The rest were subdued with straps before they turned.

"Second thing, the bodies are piling up more than we were expecting. We already assumed that thirty thousand stage two were in the U.S., and after this morning's fiasco, the total number that they've put down so far, with the most recent reports, are just under forty thousand."

"My God, Richard! Forty thousand Americans are dead in less than twenty-four hours? How can this be happening? And to think this is only the beginning."

"I know. I keep trying to wake myself up from this nightmare."

"What else is there?"

"Um. The normal death rates in the U.S. total about two-point-six million annually, which equates to seventy-one hundred a day, across the entire nation—seventy-one hundred funerals per day. We are still having the normal death rate, but now we have forty thousand bodies to dispose of in one day, with most of those concentrated around eleven metropolitan regions. They're already digging mass graves to dispose of them. They've run out of body bags to transport them, so some of the hospitals have turned to dump trucks to haul away the bodies, simply wrapping them in plastic. All of the hospitals are also reporting that they have patients advancing to stage two hourly. They're running out of drugs to put them down, and the doctors are having to get creative with it."

"That is horrible! Is there any way to get the drugs produced and distributed any faster?" asked the President.

"They're working on it. They've already grabbed up all the drugs from the local veterinarians. Just think, if they can't keep up with it now, can you imagine what's going to happen, when in the next seven days, they have to put down another one-point-eight million people? They may be reduced to using pillows. In eight days, there will be almost as many deaths in the U.S. as there are normally in a year."

As the death toll was climbing, the news reports kept the public informed on the numbers. It seemed impossible that they could kill so many, and many wondered what kind of person would it take to put to death so many? It wasn't like they were putting down an injured horse or two. Because of the seeming callousness of it, many people stopped going to the hospital, nor would they take their loved ones there. It was like taking them to the slaughter. When a video of bodies being dumped out of a dump truck into a big hole hit the airwaves, there was a public outcry, but who was there to listen? It was already becoming a world of survival, and it wasn't always going to be the fittest who survived, but rather the lucky ones. Many people were becoming discouraged with the continuing reports of death and disease. Thus, when their loved ones became sick, they became their family's executioner and then committed suicide rather than going to the hospital to be put down like a rabid dog.

Sean's mom and dad continued to harvest their garden and orchard, canning as much as they could. Beth had been canning for many years, so she always had a large stock of jars and canning supplies set aside for the new harvest, but this year she wanted to fill every jar she had. She had called Rachel early that morning and invited the women over to help her with the canning. It would be a good opportunity for them to get to know each other better. Mitch had already harvested his wheat and had it in storage, waiting to sell it, but now it would probably come in handy.

Sean and Mike were on duty again during the morning to afternoon shift, and they were becoming more acquainted with the rest of the Sheriff's Department employees. Most of them seemed to be pretty good guys, but there were a couple that they could do without. Again, there wasn't much trouble other than fights in the stores when someone wanted what someone else already had. To Sean, it seemed like a precursor to what the future was bringing. There were always going to be people who wanted what someone else had, and as the law enforcement dwindled, more people became infected, and things became more desperate, some people would turn to killing to get what they needed. Additionally, there would be a lot of people willing to kill to keep what they already had. Sean knew it for a certainty, and he and Mike were ready to take the brunt of the defending upon their own shoulders. Neither of them had a problem with killing in defense of their friends and loved ones, and they wouldn't hesitate to do so.

Director Langdon, after receiving new reports, immediately called the President. She was on a call with David McCale, head of the Department of Health, and rather than having to talk to each of them separately, she turned it into a conference call.

"I just received a report listing the number of healthcare workers that have been lost to the virus. These numbers are worldwide. Some nations are worse than others, but the average percentage of healthcare workers with symptoms are fifteen percent. Three percent of those were lost during the euthanasia cleansing, and there is an average now of twenty percent of the healthcare workers not even showing up for work, nor even calling in. Some of them may be home sick or just too scared to show up for work. We can probably assume that at least some of those are already infected. The healthcare industry has been hit exceptionally hard with this."

"We've all been hit hard, even if we're not sick, but thirty-five percent of healthcare is exceptionally bad. If a new wave comes into the hospitals, how will they be able to take care of them? Have you had any word on the status of the London police officers?" asked the President.

"No change."

"And the continuing efforts to vaccinate the military and government?"

It was David's turn to answer. "Almost one hundred percent on the military, eighty-five percent on the government leaders. As with healthcare, our military is reporting a loss of eighteen percent of personnel. Since so many of them spend time in close quarters, when one got sick, it spread to most of the unit. All healthcare workers have received vaccinations, and as many of the sick that we could do with the remaining vaccines. As more is made, we can continue the booster shots of all those who have already been started, but there still isn't enough to vaccinate even a tenth of the infected. Practically everyone is out of lethal doses for the continuing euthanasia, and the pharmaceutical companies are slow to produce more, because they're trying to keep up with the vaccines."

"As long as they're doing their best, that's all we can ask. Thank you, gentlemen."

As Sean and Mike drove home that afternoon, they stopped by the Super Wal-Mart to have a look-see at what they still had available. Everyone that they encountered was wearing a facemask, and as they had been given facemasks to wear anytime they were out of the car when they were on duty, they also wore theirs into the store. They still had on their uniforms and carried their side-arms as they strolled through the store. Because of that there were a few people who stopped to ask them questions, keeping their distance of course. Pushing a cart, they would throw something in whenever they found something they thought was worthwhile that other people hadn't. There had been continuing deliveries of some things, but they were still out of many others. Even with the government wishes to continue production, delivery, and sales of products, it was still hard to get people to leave the safety of their own home.

When they arrived at the grocery section, there were a lot of empty shelves, but there had been some recent deliveries. With so many people too scared to leave their homes to shop, there was still plenty for them to choose from. A new shipment of canned goods had just come in, so they loaded up a whole cartload and then continued looking for more things. With an extra family to feed whom had nothing really stored for emergencies, Sean was glad to be able to get more in reserve. As the virus would continue to spread, eventually there wouldn't be anyone willing or able to work in any stage of the food production and distribution industry, or any industry for that matter. With a second cart, they filled up on toilet paper, cleaning products, soaps, aspirin and other medicines, and several other items that would be hard to live without. They could never have too much toilet paper.

After checking out, walking back to his truck, they heard some yelling across the parking lot. They could see a woman and two men wrestling or fighting, and then the woman screamed for help. Sean and Mike took off running, and as they closed the distance, they could see that the man now on the ground was trying to get the other guy off of him. Mike got there first and knocked the guy off, while Sean pulled his weapon. The down man jumped up and ran to his wife, while the other, when he had stopped rolling, came to his feet. Seeing Sean, he came at him flailing his arms. Sean could see a glassy look in his eye and realized that he was infected. Raising his weapon quickly, he lined up his sights and put two fast ones in the chest, dropping him in his tracks.

Keeping his eyes on the assailant, he asked Mike, "You okay? I think he was infected."

"Yeah, I think so. I clobbered him on the head to knock him off is all. No blood, no bites, and no scratches. We might want to call this in."

"Yeah, okay." Giving Mike a head nod toward the couple, Sean said, "See if they're alright and then get inside and wash your hands. Don't touch your face!"

Sean pulled his cellphone out and called the department. Explaining where he was and what had happened, he asked for the morgue to send out a vehicle for the body. There were a couple of people coming over to see what had happened, and looking at Mike, Sean saw his head shake in the negative. Looking over at their two cartloads of stuff, he mentioned it to Mike. "I'll stay here Mike. As soon as you wash up can you load our stuff?"

"Sure."

Sean stepped over to the man to see how he was, and he could see that he had several bad bites on his forearms. "Take him into the bathroom and wash those bites out with soap… several times. Be quick about it, because it might keep him from getting infected."

The two immediately took off into the store to get them cleaned out. Sean could hear a police siren and an ambulance on the way as he stepped over to look at the man on the pavement. Lying on his back, his shirt front was wet with sweat, with a large stain of blood and a dark red pool spreading out around him on the pavement. His hair was all disarrayed and sweaty-looking; his pants were dirty; and he looked like he hadn't changed them in a couple of weeks. There was a little blood at the corner of his mouth, but Sean couldn't tell if it was the victim's blood or the attacker's own blood. Just in case, Sean wasn't going to get too close, knowing how contagious the virus was reported to be. Just as Mike walked out to the truck, a city police vehicle pulled in one entrance and an ambulance pulled in another.

As the officer and ambulance personnel rushed up, Sean said, "Don't get too close. He's stage two infected. I sent a man and his wife into the bathroom to wash out several bites he received on his forearms. You need to take your kit inside and do a better job on the cleaning. It might save his life."

"Alright, I'll grab my kit."

The officer was looking at the two holes in the man's shirt. Three inches apart, one dead center, might have taken out the spine and the other close to the heart.

"He attack you?"

"Yep. Mike and I came out of the store and heard yelling and then a scream. A man and woman were here and this guy, and then we saw the two guys go down just as we were running over. I pulled my weapon, and Mike sailed over him and knocked him off. As he came up, I could see his eyes glazed over, sweating profusely, and when he saw me, he ran straight at me. I double-tapped him, and he went down. After seeing him, trying to subdue an infected person is out of the question. It's doable, but you'll most likely get infected, which is a death sentence."

"Alright. I'll get a statement from Mike, and then you guys can go. Looks pretty cut and dried. I'll get the victim's statement as soon as I get Mike's."

"Remember what I said: If you get faced with one of these, you keep your distance and take them out."

"Got it."

Haris helped his wife to the bathroom, and then back to bed. He brought in a pot of hot water and gave her a sponge bath to make her feel as comfortable as possible. She gave him a smile of gratitude and could see the pain in his face as he smiled back.

"I have some more medicine for you that I brought back from the lab. It will help you sleep and feel better. I'm sorry I don't have it in pill form; I'll have to give you a shot in the arm. It'll take effect faster that way anyhow. Are you ready?"

"Yes. I love you, Haris," she whispered in weakness, and Haris leaned in close to hear her words. "I'm so sorry about Abdullah. I know how much he meant to you. When I get better, maybe we can have another son?"

"Yes, we can have another son… when you get better."

Haris lifted her arm, tied a tube around it to find a vein, and injected her with his medicine. As she drifted off to sleep, he held her close.

When she was gone, he raised himself from her side, covered her face with the blanket, and walked to the door.

Turning back to look at her, he said, "I'm so sorry. Please, forgive me." He left his house for the last time as he made his way to the compound.

CHAPTER NINETEEN

Day twenty-five in the Situation Room was tense, waiting to hear the new numbers and looking to see who might be missing and who was still healthy. Everyone was looking tired, worn out, and had bags under their eyes from a lack of sleep. People were becoming irritable, but they were still trying to find answers, showing up for the meetings, hoping to finally hear some good news of some sort. But as they were soon to find out, there still wouldn't be any good stories.

The President stood to her feet, quieting the room, and she tried to make eye contact with as many as she could as she started to speak.

"The first thing I want to tell you today is thank you for your help. The decisions that we've made thus far… I couldn't have made without your input and counsel. For that, I'm very grateful. Secondly, I need to tell you that my Chief of Staff, Jason Adams, has become ill. This morning he tested positive for the virus."

Suddenly voices were raised with questions, throwing the room into pandemonium. Holding her hands up in the air, she waited until all was quiet.

"Unfortunately, Jason began feeling ill four or five days ago. He had not been around anyone that was sick; he had not been in any of the airports that we know had the terrorists; and he doesn't get out much other than here at work. Taking those things into consideration, he thought that he only had the normal flu. Wanting to continue to help, he couldn't stay away from his duties. He has expressed deepest sorrow for not staying away from us until he was sure of the illness, one way or the other. And yes, I am probably infected, as are some of you. There are no tests that will confirm that until we begin to exhibit symptoms, but at this point, our only hope is that we started our vaccines before we were infected. Hopefully, as in standard rabies, our early start may be enough to thwart the virus. Only time will tell. David, would you like to take the floor?"

David McCale, the head of Health and Human Services, stood to his feet. "I hate to continually give you bad numbers, but that's all there's going to be until we find out if the vaccine actually works. First, in the U.S., we're estimating the total number of infected is about thirteen to sixteen million. Sixty-five thousand of those have been euthanized as of last night. By tonight, there will be another ten thousand, at least, added to that number. Actual numbers may fluctuate according to just how many people were infected by the terrorists on day five. If they had a bad day on day five, but had a good day on day six, or vice versa, then the number of stage two infected will fluctuate accordingly. Generally on the nineteenth day of infection, the patient becomes stage two, so the first stage two started showing up on the nineteenth day, which was six days ago. The second day infected develop stage two on the twentieth day, day three on the twenty-first day, and day four on the twenty-second. Since we now have better numbers coming in, we can make better estimates on the overall picture. We estimate that there are, right now, about one million with symptoms, with another two hundred thousand coming on tomorrow, and two hundred twenty thousand the following day. Again, the numbers I just gave you reflect just the U.S.

"Worldwide, we're estimating the first day that at least sixty thousand were infected. We will call the first nine days of infection tier one, the second nine days, tier two, and the third nine days, tier three. Infected on day one, their symptoms start on day ten, and they will infect others on that tenth day; infected on day ten, they're symptomatic on day nineteen; infected on day nineteen, they're symptomatic on day twenty-eight. What we're looking at is the exponential growth of each tier. Tier one infected total we estimate at less than three hundred thousand, infected by only forty people. Tier two infected we estimate at over five million, infected by three hundred thousand. Tier three infected we estimate at one hundred million, infected by five million, and tier four infected we estimate at two billion, infected by one hundred million. Tier five, everyone else. Tier three will be complete in three days. In twelve days, there may be two billion infected."

The room was completely silent… and then a few sniffles could be heard.

David continued, "We have made a small dent in the numbers with the euthanasia we performed, so we may have prolonged our existence by another week or two. If the vaccine doesn't work, we are doomed. Even if we were able to put to death everyone that is now symptomatic, the other ones that are infected would start the process all over again. But on the other hand, it is logistically impossible to euthanize more than we already have. Our healthcare workers are depleted by thirty-five percent; pharmaceutical companies are reporting a ten percent loss in their work force; our military is reporting a twenty percent loss; and the government is reporting a twenty-five percent loss, across all sectors. Not all losses are due to illness, of course, for some are just staying home with their families or are too scared to leave their home."

The President responded, "David, I don't think I can say thank you, but… people, friends, this news is very disheartening. I don't have words to express my sorrow that this has happened. One thing that I can say, though, is that I think that we should launch a nuclear strike on the country that instigated this plague on mankind. In my mind, there is no reason that they should continue to live, while the rest of us are dying. If, by chance, they've protected themselves by closing their borders early, then they are the last ones I want rebuilding mankind after the rest of us are gone. Are there any comments?"

"I agree," spoke up Langdon.

"I agree also," said her chairman of the Joint Chiefs.

The Secretary of Defense also spoke up, "I agree."

And then complete and resounding voices of agreement started in the room. There were no dissenting voices. The President looked around the room at the faces of all her leaders. None of them wanted this plague to happen. None of them would have agreed with the nuclear strike under any other scenario, but with a loss of all hope for mankind, knowing the one who was to blame, they were out for blood. They were sick of all the turmoil that had come out of the Middle East that had caused this whole fiasco.

"I'll leave the details up to my military leaders, but I would suggest targeting Tehran, from which all of the terrorists came, and to do a good job of it, nuke the whole country to make sure that wherever they're hiding, we're sure to get all of them. Let me know of your final plans and the timing so I can give you my final approval."

In Beijing, Chinese leaders were meeting to discuss the potential possibilities that were beginning to open for the world domination that they had been working toward for many years. With the onset of the virus, many avenues were being studied and searched out.

"With the widespread effect of the virus throughout the U.S., all of our simulation programs show an almost complete annihilation of its population and ability to govern or have a viable military. If we survive this outbreak, we could take over the U.S. and all of its resources without any casualties of any consequence. However, Russia may be a different matter."

Another leader took over the discussion about Russia. "Russia, on the other hand, had only one major site of infection, and that was Moscow and its surrounding region. They also will have its sights on the U.S. to acquire all of its farmland and natural resources. When that happens, we will have to fight them for possession or forfeit our plans. If Russia gains control of the U.S., then they may become more powerful than us, especially if they obtain all of the U.S.'s ground-based nuclear arsenal."

"We can't let that happen. We've known that the U.S. would never attack us unless provoked with our own attack on them, but Russia may be a different matter. With the U.S. out of the way and up for grabs, Russia may very well launch a first strike against us. We've had a lot of cooperation from Russia, because of the U.S.'s superiority over both of us, but now that the U.S. will fall, our next big worry will be Russia. They will want the U.S. and its holdings as bad as we do. We need to run some scenarios on what we can do to thwart them in whatever stand they may take, including us making the first strike."

China's President looked around the room, letting his gaze touch all of his leaders and councilors. "I agree. If America falls, I want it in our hands. Is there a chance that Russia is already thinking the same thing?"

"It would be highly likely. They have the same information as we do. With England sure to fall, and the U.S. having eleven of their largest cities initially targeted, and the quick spread of the virus because they are so lax on travel inside their borders, Russia will come up with the same conclusions as we have. The land of the U.S. would be a ripe plum for the taking."

"Let me know as soon as you come up with some scenarios, and then we will decide. The world affairs are in a very fluid situation right now, and we need some answers before it's too late to act."

"Right away, sir."

CHAPTER TWENTY

Rachel had spent the day with Sean's parents, helping with more canning, picking fruit, and becoming better acquainted with the two of them. The hard work started when Mitch took her out to the garden to start digging potatoes. Carefully digging the shovel beside the row and then prying up the dirt to expose the brown spuds. Uncovering only a short section of row, they dusted them off and began placing them in burlap sacks that Mitch had brought from the barn, and then they continued down the row. They had ten, eighty-pound sacks filled when Sean and Mike turned onto the driveway and came up to the barn.

As soon as Sean spotted Rachel's car, he became excited—anxious to see her face again. Parking behind the house, close to the barn, he could see her and his dad out in the garden working with sacks of potatoes. Climbing from the Ford F150, they both walked out to the garden to see if they needed some help.

"Look at you, the little farmer girl."

"Don't be making fun of me. The way things are going, you'll be doing this same thing pretty soon. But I'm still glad you're here… you're just in time to carry these sacks into the barn."

"Great. Giving me orders already. Better be careful about stretching our relationship too soon," teased Sean.

"Son, take the spuds into the tack room for now. We'll dig some more tomorrow. We'll work on that stretching technique some too." Winking at Rachel, he took her hand and led her back to the house.

Walking down the stairs after taking a shower, Sean made his way into the kitchen to see his mom taking a pan of chicken over to the table.

"Smells good, Mom. I just realized how hungry I am. If I'm not careful, I'm gonna start putting on weight eating your cooking." Sean could hear a news bulletin on the TV, and as he stepped into the living room, Mike was coming down the stairs. Mitch and Rachel were already sitting on the couch, watching.

"Today, at the Olympic Street Wal-Mart Store, Lane County had its first stage two victim. The man attacked a couple in the parking lot, took the man to the ground, and was biting him. Two off-duty deputy sheriffs were coming out of the store, when they heard cries for help. Running to help, they freed the man, and when he attacked the officers, he was shot and killed. We have this video from a witness's cellphone. The following scene is graphic."

Beth had come into the room to watch, and as the scene unfolded, they could all identify Sean and Mike as the two deputies. Rachel took Sean's hand in hers and was squeezing it tightly. When it was over, they all turned to look at him.

"You alright, Son?" asked Mitch.

"I'm fine, Dad. It's not as though that was the first one. After being involved in warfare, that didn't amount to much. The only way to look at it is either it's a mercy killing or that he was an enemy to our well-being. That's the way I'm handling it. It's sad that this is what it's coming down to, but this is just the beginning. I'm sorry to have to say this, but as more of these infected come out, this is what all of us will have to do to protect ourselves. There's no other way to stop these infected without getting infected yourself. From now on, everyone needs to start carrying a weapon on them. That includes you too, Mom."

"As the numbers of these stage two infected increases, you could run into one of them just about anywhere," Mike added. "If your neighbor down the street turns and gets out of his house, he could be running through your field or up your driveway even, so you have to carry a firearm everywhere you go from now on. Everyone. Everywhere."

"Mike's right. We can't take any chances. No one leaves the house without carrying a weapon—even just out to the barn. Every time the door is opened, it would be a good idea to look out the window first, and then still be careful opening the door. I don't want to lose any of you. I know, Mom, how hard this will be for you, but it's just getting too dangerous to not use caution."

"I know, honey. I don't disagree at all. It'll take some getting used to though. Maybe it would be best to get your guns out right now and give me a lesson on how they all work again."

Mitch disappeared into his bedroom to pick out some suitable weapons, and Sean went up to his room to get a pistol with a holster, an extra mag, and a box of ammo. Seeing the AR15 leaning in the corner, he decided to take that as well. Walking down the stairs, Sean could see Mike giving Rachel instructions on his pistol. It was a different make than the Springfield that Sean had given her, and there were some minor differences, like how to work the safety, working the slide to cock it, and how to remove the clip and replace it. After giving instructions to the women on Mitch's rifles, the AR15, and three different pistols, one of them a revolver, Mitch set one rifle at each of the front and back doors. That way, anyone would have one handy if needed. After dinner, they went out back to set up a target for the women to load their own weapon, fire it, reload the mag, and also how to make the gun safe, taking a live round out of the chamber, and carrying it. Satisfied with their ability, Sean followed Rachel home so that he could talk with her family about their own protection.

On day twenty-six, Director Langdon received word that the London officers had lost the battle and developed stage two. They had been subdued with straps two days earlier, and since they were the first ones to reach stage two while receiving the vaccine, their doctors and researchers decided to keep them alive and under observation to see if the vaccine had any effects on their condition that would be different from the symptoms of untreated patients. They had also kept alive four other patients with stage two for research into the longevity of the disease and its final outcome.

Immediately after notification, Richard called the President and briefed her on the details.

"Then, most likely, I am going to die along with the majority of my personal staff and Cabinet members, and probably you too, Richard," stated the President.

"Yes, you're probably right. Although, we'll have thirteen days of treatment before the first symptoms even start. The officers only had ten days. That's going to be our next best hope to hold onto. Our bodies have had the chance to develop antibodies to fight the virus longer than they had, and it might just be enough. Four more days and then if symptoms develop, we can still make decisions for several more days, although we'll have to remain isolated from the day before our symptoms might start. We don't want to push it and infect any more of us."

"Thanks for the encouragement, Richard. There's not enough of that going around these days. Do you wish that Mary and Josh were still here?"

I've wished it many times in the past several years, of course, but now this? No. Right now I'm glad they aren't here to see this unfolding and possibly being a victim to it. That would be too hard to take," replied Richard.

"How about Cliff and Julie? Have you talked to them about this thing?"

"Several days ago, I called both of them and warned them to gather up supplies and try to rent an out of the way cabin in the mountains for two months until this thing is figured out or we're all dead. They pulled out the next day, so hopefully they can stay isolated from it."

"Do you think we should have warned the public sooner? Maybe we could have helped more of them to keep away from the virus," the President asked.

"We can second guess ourselves all day long, and it won't help any. The way this has turned out, an earlier warning probably would have slowed down the transfer of the virus. But even then, without a cure, it only would've slowed it down. You know what the bad thing is…?" asked Richard.

"Don't you mean 'one of the bad things'?"

"You're right. The way this virus spreads quietly, we can't even try to round up some uninfected to help them survive and rebuild humanity, because we don't know who isn't infected to round up and won't know until they start infecting the rest of the pool. Got any ideas on how to save some pockets of humanity?"

"That's a very good question." Pausing in thought for a moment, the President started musing out loud. "What if we picked families that aren't infected yet, hopefully, and keep each family isolated for ten days to make sure they're virus free, and then move them to a secure location, with all due precaution. If a family develops symptoms, they're removed immediately, and if we could get enough of those virus free families, set them up in a secure area with plenty of supplies and weapons, of course, for survival after we're all gone."

"Yes, I see. If we could be successful getting one group together, we could put together a lot of groups, keep them safe, and keep them isolated at all costs. We need to get some people working on this. The earlier we could implement it, the greater the success we'd have."

"Good. Get some thinkers working on this right away and keep me updated. If I get this thing and get taken out, it would be nice to know we helped in keeping humanity on the planet."

Director Langdon assigned some top scientists and brainstormers to figure out a game plan to carry out the wishes of the President concerning survivors. The plan was to try and find families with doctors, scientists, engineers, teachers, administrators, and others in useful fields for the survival and rebuilding of mankind if all else failed. The President and Mr. Langdon had hit on an excellent idea as a last resort to save humanity, and the thinkers were working overtime to work it out. They immediately sent word out to small communities that were out of the way of the mainstream of the spread of the virus to find some common families that were untouched, and to also find safe locations away from the big cities where the disease was beginning to run rampant.

Coming up with names of specialists, they would contact them to find out their status with the virus and then would go from there. Single, married, or even with a family, it didn't matter. All they needed were healthy specialists to add to the mix, and the rest of the potential survivors were for the reproduction of mankind. And that thought led to another: What about gay people? If what they needed were people for reproduction, should they try to screen out all gay people? A legitimate concern. Which was more important? The fate of the human race, or the civil rights of a few gay people? The human race was more important. They also began stockpiling supplies for when they needed them, and once they finalized some acceptable refuge areas, they could disperse the supplies. It didn't take long to start formulating a plan when there was a definite goal in mind and they had their best minds figuring it out.

Also, the CDC was locked down so that the nation's top researchers would be able to continue their work, unimpeded by the disease, on finding an answer to put an end to the virus. There wasn't much hope left, but if they stopped trying, there would be no hope at all.

CHAPTER TWENTY-ONE

It was day twenty-seven, when Kaziim put his eye to the microscope one more time. He couldn't accept the fact that he was looking at the virus that he and his team had developed to destroy the rest of the world. It was now running rampant within his own country. This was not how it was supposed to happen. He made his way to the facility's storage lockers to check on the remainder of the virus. Everything was in order; nothing was missing. He had spent the last several hours trying to figure out how the virus would have been introduced back into the country, but he could not think of any scenarios to explain it. He'd heard that Haris had come into the compound, so he turned back in the direction of his office.

There was no answer to his knock, so he opened the door to see if Haris was indeed inside.

"Hello? Haris, are you here?" Walking in further, he could see the office was empty and continued over to the bedroom door. Haris was asleep on the bed, and walking over to him, Kaziim put his hand on his shoulder to wake him.

"Haris? Haris, wake up. We need to talk."

Haris was hot to the touch, and his shirt was damp. Shaking him until he started to wake, Kaziim reached to turn on the bedside lamp. When the light came on, what he saw turned him cold. Haris was sweating profusely, his face red from a fever. Before Kaziim could pull back,

Haris started coughing. Jumping back in fear, Kaziim looked closely at Haris, evaluating what he was seeing.

"Haris…? What's wrong with you?"

Groggily, Haris turned his head to look at Kaziim. His eyes were feverish; his head was splitting; and he was so tired. He needed some aspirin, but he was too tired to get up.

"Water."

Kaziim picked up the water bottle from the floor. Opening it, he put it to Haris's lips so that he could drink. After a few swallows, Kaziim pulled the water bottle back.

"Haris, you look like you're infected. Are you?" Kaziim needed to know.

"Yes, Kaziim, I'm infected with my own virus. I think this is about day seven. It's been hard to keep track."

"What happened? How did you get it?"

"I don't know for sure, Kaziim. On day ten, my son, Abdullah came home sick from school. The next day, he went back to school, but came home early, feeling worse. When I arrived home late, I checked on him, and the next day, I took a blood sample. I found out that my own son had the disease that we so painstakingly developed to kill the infidels. His friend at school was also sick, and they had spent two days in the school infecting everyone. Kaziim, my wife was also infected."

"I'm sorry, my friend. This wasn't supposed to happen."

"I know. Kaziim, my son was infected on the day we sent out our men. He wasn't even close to the compound, airport, or the route to the airport. I haven't been able to figure it out," Haris explained.

"If you knew, why did you come back here to infect all of us? Why didn't you tell us?" whined Kaziim.

"My son was dying, ready to turn. I couldn't let that happen."

Kaziim stood there listening, not hardly believing what he was about to hear.

"Kaziim, I killed my own son. And when my wife was close to turning, I… I…"

Kaziim could see the pain on the face of his friend. He also could see Haris's handgun on the nightstand. Reaching for the gun, he took it out of the holster and flipped off the safety.

"Haris, why did you come back?" Kaziim needed to understand the reasoning behind his decision.

"It is as Allah wills it."

Kaziim raised the pistol, pulled back the slide to inject a shell into the chamber, and pointed it at Haris's forehead. Seeing Haris looking back, Kaziim said, "It is as Allah wills it." He squeezed the trigger.

Looking down at Haris, seeing the bleeding hole in the middle of his forehead, the widening red stain on his pillow, Kaziim raised the gun to his own temple and pulled the trigger a second time.

In more populated areas, the chaos was only getting worse. There were constant videos being broadcast on TV of the stage two infected running rampant through the streets, until the military or police force took them out. The numbers of infected coming into the hospitals were actually decreasing, but it was assumed that most people now looked on the hospital with fear and refused to take their loved ones into the slaughterhouse.

In the worst hit areas, the military were helping with supply deliveries to the food processing plants and then delivery and distribution into the cities, where masses of people were running out of food. The logistics of producing, delivering, and distributing the amount of food needed to supply millions of people in one city was mind boggling. The current system of supply, from farmers' fields all the way into people's kitchens, had been grown slowly, one step at a time—from one new store to another, putting in new orders to the distributor, which in turn was passed on into the production stage, which had to receive more raw goods from farmers, who had to plant more, harvest more, or new fields had to be developed and put into production. And then the virus hits and people turn up missing. From calling in sick to just not coming in to work because of fear, every facet of the food industry had been affected and the government and military couldn't fix the problem.

Society's advances to take care of the needs of a steadily increasing population were quickly crumbling into nonexistence. Millions of desperate people were about to explode onto the public scene as the supplies that were able to keep them indoors, away from the advancing virus, were coming to an end. And then the virus would have many new targets to attack.

Inside the White House, the President called a meeting of her Cabinet leaders to let them all know the latest news. David McCale, the head of the Department of Health was the first to speak.

"Madam President and Gentlemen, today is the day that we reach a milestone. There is an estimated five million infected progressing to stage two today, one million of them in the U.S. There are at least one hundred million total infected as of today, twenty million of them in our nation. Tomorrow is the start of tier four with a possibility of thirty-five million people being infected in one day, seven million of them in our nation. We're beyond euthanasia, and we're almost beyond the ability to remove the bodies of the ones the military will be forced to put down. Our attempt at a vaccine is failing; our economic infrastructure is beginning to fail; and our people are beginning to fail. Without a definite vaccine, we have little hope." Taking his seat, he lowered his head dejectedly.

The President stood to her feet and looked around the room at the faces of those who had become her friends. She felt such heartache, watching them receive such bad news.

"Friends, we've started a new objective. We're gathering people that have not been infected, mostly family units, with as many specialists as we can find, isolating them in their family groups for ten days to make sure they are virus free, and then we're going to set them up in secure locations with supplies to last through this year's winter season. If we can guarantee they stay virus free before they go, and keep all outside contact at zero afterwards, there will be a good chance of having a base of people to rebuild humanity if this virus can't be stopped with a vaccine. And we won't stop at just one group. We will try to build up as many clusters of society with the necessary specialists and place them in key areas where their survival will be the most advantageous. We've shared our plans with our allies so that they can also take the necessary steps to implement their own groups for survival. These are precautionary steps only. There may still be many small groups of people that remain unscathed by the virus. Not everyone will end up infected, and we will hope that the survivors will recognize the importance of their opportunity and work together for the greater good of humanity."

Sean and Mike, again on duty, were wearing their facemasks and gloves everywhere they went, even in the Sheriff's Office. All of the deputies were. Three more deputies had come down with the virus—two of them by stage two attackers that they had missed with their first shots and were bitten before they could kill them. There were more and more occurrences across the county of the stage two infected out in public, wandering the streets, attacking anyone who stepped into their path. The police forces soon adopted the policy to shoot to kill any that were stage two. Body removal was done in full protective gear and a complete wash-down afterwards. No one was taking any chances anymore.

Now that the attacks were escalating in Lane County, Sean and Mike came to the decision that it was time for Rachel and her family to move into the bunker. Sean gave Rachel a call to let her know that it was time and to get started loading the things they wanted to keep into the camp trailer, such as clothing, bedding, and anything else that would fit. The rest of the things they could load in the trucks that evening when Sean and Mike could get over there. Letting Mitch also know of his decision, they were both looking forward to the move. There would be a lot less worry on his part to have the woman he loved safe in his own home.

After their shift, Sean and Mike headed over to Rachel's house to get things going. As Rachel walked out of the house, Sean could see that she had the 9mm and holster attached to her belt. Of course, Mike had to make a comment about a sexy woman with a gun that made Sean laugh. The camp trailer was loaded with the light stuff and keepsakes that Kevin and Joanna wanted to keep and was already hooked up to Kevin's truck. As soon as they arrived, the women started unloading the refrigerator and freezers into boxes for the trip over, and Sean and Mike loaded them into the truck and strapped them in. The cars were loaded to the hilt already, and after loading some tools and small equipment from the shop, they were ready to head out. They were planning to return after unloading at the farm, to pick up more of the shop equipment, like the welder and big air compressor and any other odds and ends that they thought might come in handy for survival.

Arriving at home, Sean drove around by the barn to unload things into the bunker. They decided to use Kevin's stand-up freezer in the bunker, putting it in the large bedroom, and set up the chest freezer in the barn. Mitch and Beth had already moved some of their personal belongings into the bunker, and Kevin and Joanna would use the second bedroom. They still had a few days to go to make sure that no one had been infected, so Rachel moved into the bunker, while Leah would stay in their camp trailer, and Steve would stay in Mitch's camp trailer until they were all declared healthy. No use putting all of their eggs in one basket.

Returning to Kevin's house while the women and Steve continued unloading their belongings, Sean, Mike, and Kevin picked through everything that was left behind, loading up anything that would be useful.

CHAPTER TWENTY-TWO

On the morning of the twenty-eighth day, David McCale, head of the Health Department, received a report from one of his leaders. As he read the report, his stomach turned. He dropped his head, and tears started to fall. He knew he was reading his death sentence—everyone's death sentence. After several moments, collecting himself, he called the President to see if she had a few moments for a meeting. She needed to hear what he had just read.

Sean and Mike were off duty for a day, and Mitch, wanting some electrical wire and motion sensor lights, sent Sean and Mike into town to see if they could find any. Home Depot was still open for business, but just barely. There wasn't really enough customers, but they were afraid that if they totally closed up, people would break in and steal what they wanted. Sean picked up triple the wire and lights that Mitch wanted, just in case they decided there should be more light around the place. Stopping in at Joe's Sporting Goods store to check up on him, they found it locked up and shut down. He had probably sold out all of his guns and ammo, along with most of his survival and camp gear, so there wasn't much reason to keep it open. Besides, he had a family to watch over and keep safe. Sean made a mental note to give him a call, if he could get a personal number.

As soon as they arrived home, Mitch had a plan for the lights, and before noon, they had them up and working. After dark, if anything came up the driveway or close to the house or barn, the lights would come on and expose whatever was moving. Along with outside preparations, they also moved some of the groceries into the bunker kitchen for impromptu preparations or snacks, although they would still be cooking their meals in the house.

Sean was walking in absolute bliss being around Rachel most of the day, especially with not having to worry about her safety. Being able to wrap his arms around her and kiss her in the morning, steal kisses throughout the day, and then to hug and kiss her goodnight was rocking his world. She was the sweetest girl he had ever met, and she was in love with him. He had never felt so lucky.

After lunch, Sean and Mike gathered everyone out back to give some lessons on handling the firearms. Leah, Steve, and Joanna needed to go over the procedures on several guns, and Beth and Rachel needed some refreshing just to make sure they had it down. The worst time to forget how to operate a gun or change out the mag would be when they needed to do so quickly in order to save themselves or a loved one. They all needed to be proficient enough to do what needed doing, even under duress. Going over it many times with all of them, they spent the better part of an hour on it. Steve and all the women each shot a few rounds through both rifles and pistols until Sean was satisfied with their performance. He wanted to make sure that if they were entering into warfare, they knew the basics of protecting themselves. He and Mike could not always be there to protect them.

Later that evening, on the East Coast, the President's Joint Chiefs met with her and the other Cabinet members in the Situation Room in the basement of the White House. Things were ready to get under way; their forces were ready to go.

"Gentlemen, I have an announcement to make before we get underway," began the President. "Today, I received a report from David about the vaccine. One of his men was thinking about the vaccine and if there was any other way to tell if it was going to work. He started checking on the rabies virus and found out that forty thousand Americans each year are treated for rabies infection. All of them treated after a bite from a possible infected animal, or a veterinarian or dog catcher who are pre-vaccinated because they may have to handle an infected animal. Contacting the CDC for the names of all the ones who received vaccinations during the past twelve months, the same vaccine that we ourselves have been administered with, he started cross-referencing with hospital reports, and he came up with some alarming numbers." Pausing for a moment to take a deep breath and to keep her voice under control, she looked around the room to steady herself before continuing. "Out of the forty thousand vaccinated, he found two hundred twenty-eight names admitted to the hospitals with the virus so far. Seventy-nine of those were euthanized with stage two."

There was an immediate eruption of questions. Worried looks and fear were on their faces.

Raising her hands in the air to quiet them she began again, "Our assumption would have to be that they still have enough antibodies in their system to fight off normal rabies, but it had no effect on this altered strain. For all intents and purposes, the vaccine that we have been counting on is a failure. I'm sorry... so very sorry."

Turning to the Secretary of Defense, standing next to a control console, she nodded her head.

"Madame President, we await your final order on the launch." The Secretary of Defense spoke with a flat, monotone voice. "Our two nuclear subs the USS Nevada and the USS West Virginia have pulled back to a safe launching position, and we have confirmation of the removal of all of our undercover agents. We have drones in the air to send back video of the outcome."

"Make it happen."

The Secretary of Defense gave the order to his man, and he passed on the order to NORAD. Everyone in the room waited anxiously, watching the TV monitors for the final outcome of the ones who murdered the planet. After several minutes of empty sea, one Trident missile broke the surface of the water with a huge uplifting splash of whitewater, engine igniting and making its way into the sky. Following it by fifteen seconds was another uplifting of water, with the second Trident missile emerging from the showering water. Fifteen seconds and a third erupted from the froth, followed by a fourth one. Each Trident missile was fitted with eight W88 thermonuclear warheads with a yield of 450 kilotons each. The four missiles were flying at eighteen thousand miles per hour into the edge of space and then releasing their multiple independently targeted re-entry vehicles, each targeting a specific site or location. Thirty-two sites had been designated by the military and entered into the navigational computers. Some were military installations, government facilities, underground compounds, nuclear research and development facilities, and cities. Depending on the site, each warhead was set to detonate in the air or on the ground for maximum effect on each location, and some sites were targeted with more than one warhead.

The drones were flying towards Iran from several directions when the nuclear blasts started erupting. With an overhead view from satellite on monitor, the whole room could watch the total annihilation of the country that unleashed hell on earth. Once the missiles erupted from the sea, it was all over in less than twenty minutes. There were no cheers, no remarks, just silence as they watched their justice being dealt. They all knew that it was not only bad people dying in the nuclear holocaust, but also innocent men, women, and children, who had nothing to do with unleashing the virus.

Not until the mushroom clouds began to dissipate, did anyone get out of their chair to leave the room. There were no greetings or congratulations when it was over—only brief eye contact and a slight nodding of the head in the camaraderie of a tough decision. Many of the faces in the room had a look of remorse or sadness for what they were compelled to unleash on humankind, but still there was a feeling of justice among them—harsh though it was.

The President was the first to leave the room, heading for the briefing room for a scheduled press conference. The nuclear strike would only take minutes to reach the airwaves, and the world needed to know her reasons why such a drastic measure was taken.

Later, right after dinner, Mitch and his group were gathered in the living room, as Sean and Mike laid down some ground rules for the protection of the party.

"No one is to go outside without a firearm of some kind, whether you're going to the barn, the trailer, or just a stroll down the lane," Mike began. "We'll never know when an infected will show up, and if you have to protect yourself in a hand-to-hand struggle, you will get yourself infected. And then you will die. Don't put the rest of us in a position to have to kick you out or to have to put you down with a bullet in the future. Life is hard enough without having to do that. So be aware of what's going on around you at all times so that if someone does come, you'll be ready for it and not be caught unawares."

Sean took over, as Mike paused: "Another thing, two of our deputies were bitten recently because they were nervous when they began shooting and missed their first two or three shots that would have stopped or at least slowed down the infected person. So when you line up those sights on someone's chest, keep your cool and squeeze the trigger, put the sights on the chest again and squeeze the trigger again. When he goes down and he's still moving, stay back and shoot him again. If it's an infected person, you're putting them out of their misery. If it's someone who shows up to steal from us, to kill us, or to kidnap or rape the girls, then treat them the same way you would a stage two infected. If you don't, they might end up killing one of us or at least hurting our group. As time goes on, our first enemy will be the infected, but as they get killed out, our next enemy will be looters and scavengers who will want to take everything we have and leave most of us dead. Everything we do from now on is extremely important. We're a team, and it's going to take teamwork to survive."

The TV was running in the background, with the sound turned down, but one of those emergency management signals came on the TV. All of them tensed up as it caught their attention. Increasing the volume, they all sat down to listen.

The President's face came on as the announcer was saying, "The President of the United States."

"My fellow Americans, a short while ago, after much thought and deliberation with my Cabinet members and Joint Chiefs, I gave the order to conduct a nuclear strike on the nation of Iran. We have positive proof that this current virus that is spreading across the world was developed and sent forth by Iran itself or they conspired and abetted with those who did. All of the terrorists who spread the virus came out of Iran, from their international airport. They were trying to protect themselves from the virus by restricting incoming flights to their nation before we were even aware of the virus. It was my opinion and that of my Cabinet and Joint Chiefs that if this virus is not contained, that the world would be a better place without those terrorists here to rebuild it in our absence. If we made the wrong decision, may God forgive us."

Pausing for a moment to gather her thoughts, she raised a glass to her lips and took a drink of water. "There is one more thing I'd like to share with you before I go. My Chief of Staff came down with the virus on day twenty, and we have to assume that I, and many of my Cabinet members, have also been infected. This is day twenty-eight, so tonight, tomorrow or the day after, we will probably begin showing symptoms. Beginning tonight, we will be in isolation until we find out if we are indeed infected. Once the symptoms start, we may be able to continue to make decisions for several more days, but toward the end of stage one, we will pass the torch of leadership to another. Thank you, America, and may God help us through this. Goodnight."

CHAPTER TWENTY-THREE

Mitch was the first to speak, "This thing is just getting worse and worse. I hope the other Arab nations don't have any nukes or they might send them back at us."

"Dad, I don't think we have to worry about the Arabs as far as nukes go," Sean explained, "because I don't think they have any. No telling about ground troops though, but who knows? They might be just as pissed at Iran for starting this as the rest of us. There's no telling how many of their own people they'll lose to the virus either before it's all over."

"I hope you're right, Son."

Steve entered the conversation with his opinion, "I think it was the right thing to do. They needed to be punished, and now, the rest of them will know what happens if you piss off the United States."

"I agree with you," Mike put in. "If things ever turn around, maybe this will make them rethink their hatred and what it has led to. But then again, it might be best to nuke all of them."

"Boys, let's not become barbaric. Let's just hope this will bring about some change," Beth said reprovingly.

"If this virus gets much worse, there won't be any reason to drop any more nukes. The thing on my mind right now is how much longer should Mike and I keep working for the sheriff? Every day we go out, we take a chance of getting infected, and that might mean a death sentence for all of you," explained Sean.

"I know what you're saying, Son, but if you're cautious, and he still needs you, I think you should keep at it. There's no tellin' how many people you guys might save by continuing to patrol. If the population is dying off as bad as the President implied, we'll need all the people we can to rebuild humanity."

"Your reasons are good, Dad, but still my first concern is for us and our own survival. We can continue, but I'm not making any promises for how long. The moment I think that it's over, I'm quitting. That sound good to you, Mike?" Sean asked.

"Sure, I think we can handle that. If it gets too bad, we can just bug out. We can put down as many as we can so that they won't continue to spread the disease, but when it comes to those that only have the flu-like symptoms, I'm not sure if we'll help much with that anyhow."

"One thing we need to figure out now is what to do if others come to us. We need to figure out a way to keep us safe until we know that they aren't infected before we can actually have them join the group. Any ideas?"

There was a moment of silent thought.

"We could set up some living accommodations in the shop. At least ten days of quarantine to make sure they're safe. If we get too many, maybe we'll have to see about rounding up camp trailers. Before long, there might be a lot of them available," Mitch explained.

"That sounds like a good idea," Kevin added. "But I'm still wondering if we're in the clear yet. All of us had a lot of interaction with other people only six days ago."

"I know," agreed Sean. "That one is still on my mind too. Steve and Leah were in the high school, and every one of the rest of us were in the store with all those crowds that we couldn't avoid touching. We've still got four days left before we can be sure we're clean, but that doesn't mean that one of us won't come down sick tomorrow from an earlier infection than six days ago. It might be best right now to try to be as separated from one another as possible. No physical touching between any of us, no hugs, handshakes… or kisses…" Sean looked directly at Rachel as he spoke the last word. "…starting later tonight, of course."

Everyone laughed at his comment; all of them had noticed how much kissing had been going on between the two.

"Mike and I could set up cots out on the porch to sleep; Mom, Joanna, and Kevin stay in all three rooms in the bunker; Dad could come back into his room; Rachel can use my room; Leah and Steve continue in the trailers. Something like that? When we wake up in the morning and we're feeling good, then that's great. Still keep our distance, and we can start wearing facemasks all day when we're close to one another. As soon as someone's done in the bathroom, take a disinfectant and wipe down all handles and surfaces for the next person. Same in the kitchen. Be extra careful around the food and refrigerator, and we should be fine. On the fourth morning from now, if everyone wakes up feeling good, we can go back to normal. Sound like a plan? Anything I miss?"

"Sounds pretty straight forward. Be a little tough, especially for you and Rachel, but it would guarantee the safety of the rest of us if someone is infected," agreed Mitch. "Anyone else have anything to add?"

"What do we do if one of us gets sick," Leah asked.

Quietly, everyone looked around at the others, waiting for an answer.

Sean felt that it was up to him to give an answer. "That, of course, would be the most horrible thing to happen, now that we're together and have worked it out this far. The best answer I could give for now is that we would separate the one that gets sick, putting them out in the shop, giving it time to determine if it's the virus or only a real cold or normal flu. Give it at least eight days to get past it. If one of us is still sick on the ninth day, that's when it's going to get real hard. If they reach stage two, they become a real danger to us all, and they will be in extreme agony of pain and torment. They will be out of their mind not knowing who they are or who we are. We can't let that happen. If that comes about, either Mike or I will take care of it. If I get sick, Mike will put me down, and if it is him, I will put him down when the time comes. Mike and I have seen things in war that we can't even begin to explain to you, and we've had to cope with things that none of you ever will. We will do whatever is necessary. This is strong talk, but these are tough times. Let's hope it doesn't come to that."

It was deathly quiet in the room for several moments, and then Mike made a comment: "And I thought we were friends. You better hope you don't get sick first, 'cause I'll probably put you down long before the ninth day."

Everyone laughed at Mike's comment, knowing exactly why he said it.

"It's about bedtime," Mitch said. "We better start getting our sleeping arrangements in order and get the last of our hugs and kisses finished. Remember, they have to last us for the next three days. Sean, I'll run out to the shop and get those cots and cushions for you and Mike."

"Alright, Dad. I'll help Rachel bring up some of her things and get my stuff out of my room. Once everyone gets their stuff settled, let's meet back here to say goodnight."

Sean led Rachel down to the bunker, where she gathered enough clothes and personal hygiene items in a suitcase to last her for the next four days. Watching her pack clothes, Sean noticed her nightgown and was thinking how nice it would look on her.

"How many kisses would it take to be able to see you in that nightie?" Sean asked with a smile.

Turning to look at him, Rachel smiled and then went back to packing.

Sean, realizing that Rachel was uncomfortable with his question, stepped over to her and wrapped his arms around her. Whispering in her ear, he said, "I'm sorry, Rachel, if what I said offended you. I saw it and said the first thing that came to mind. Will you forgive me?"

Turning in his arms to face him, she raised her hands to his face and kissed him, long and tenderly. Leaning back in his arms, she looked into his eyes. "What is there to forgive? I love you, Sean, and I would love you to see me in it. The way you make me feel when you look at me makes me realize how much you love me and makes me feel very special."

She paused for a moment to think about how to word her next statement. "When you asked me that, Sean, I didn't know how to respond right away. No man has seen me in my nightgown, and there's never been one that I wanted to see me that way… until now."

Looking into each other's eyes for a long moment, they both could see how much they were loved by the other. Bringing their lips together in a lingering, gentle kiss and then a second one with more passion and fire, they were separated at the sound of Kevin and Joanna coming down the hallway.

Finishing with her packing, Sean carried her suitcase up the stairs and into the house. His dad already had the cots set up and was heading down to the bunker to bring up his things for the next several days.

Leading Rachel up to his room, he let her get situated, while he started gathering some of his things to take downstairs. His old sleeping bag was still in the closet, and after he pulled it out, he started carrying his things downstairs. Within a few minutes, he had his bed set up, and decided to leave his suitcase in the living room, as he could pull stuff out of it as needed for each day.

Rachel came down the stairs, and as there wasn't anyone else in the room yet, Sean took Rachel's hand, led her to the front door, and walked out onto the porch. Taking a seat on the bench, he pulled Rachel onto his lap, and her arm went around his neck.

Rachel was wondering what was happening, and looking down into Sean's eyes, she lowered her head to his and kissed him. Several times, each one becoming more passionate. With his arms wrapped around her, Sean squeezed her tightly for a long moment before releasing her and leaning his head back far enough to look into her eyes.

"Rachel, I love you. I…"

"I love you too, Sean."

She kissed him again… and again.

"Rachel, this is serious. I… I know this is fast. We've only known each other for a month, but you're the sweetest, most exciting girl I've ever met. But now I'm getting worried."

"You mean about the virus or the nuclear bombing?"

"I'm already worried about that. I don't know what I'd do without you now that I've found you, and I would do anything to protect you. But what I'm worrying about now is if we want to… you know… um…"

"Are you saying if we want to make love?" asked Rachel.

"Well, yeah, sort of, of course… but, I mean, what will we do… how do we get married if we might not be able to find a preacher to perform the ceremony?" Sean was a little tongue tied and stammering like a lovesick fool. Rachel thought that it was very sweet. What excited him enough to tie his tongue was hearing Rachel use the words "if we want to make love". Now that was exciting.

"Sean, are you proposing to me?" Rachel asked with a sweet smile on her face. "This is sudden. As fast as you work, you've never been married?" teased Rachel.

“No, Rachel! Are you going to be serious? This is important to me. I was thinking about our future, and you’re making fun of me?” asked Sean with a hurt tone in his voice.

Rachel leaned forward to kiss Sean again to let him know that she was also serious. A long, loving, prolonged kiss that spoke volumes. Pulling back from him so that she could look him in the eyes, she laid his fears to rest. “I love you, Sean, in a way I had always hoped and dreamed I would find someday, and now that I’ve met you, my love has blossomed into something I’ve never known before. Although we’ve only known each other for twenty-eight days, I feel like we’ve been together for a long time, and maybe going through these things together, we’ve looked deeper into each other than most people ever do. If you are asking me to marry you, I would say, as soon as you can find a preacher, yes, I’ll marry you. Is that serious enough for you?”

Sean pulled her to him and kissed her softly, then again more passionately. The sweetness of her kisses were so satisfying to his soul. “What do we do if we can’t find a preacher? Any ideas?”

“Well, not offhand, but I could talk to Mom about it and see what she’s got to say. If it comes to it, I’d be happy with just a ceremony with a promise between us before our parents, and under the circumstances, I think they’d be agreeable with that.”

“That sounds wonderful, Rachel, but I’ll still be looking for a preacher first. If I start looking right away, I could probably round one up. My worry was that if we waited too long, there might not be any left. Do you want to tell your mom and dad now or wait a while?”

“If you found a preacher tomorrow, I don’t want them to be surprised, so maybe it would be better right now.”

Standing to her feet, she pulled Sean off the bench and hugged him. Taking his hand, she led him back into the living room to face their parents.

“Mom? Dad? Sean has something to say.”

Standing there before Rachel’s parents, he was all of a sudden nervous. His parents, Mike, Steve, and Leah all perked up, listening and watching. The TV was still on, and as he hesitated, Rachel gave his hand a reassuring squeeze.

“Kevin, Joanna, this may seem sudden, but I’ve asked Rachel to marry me, and she said yes. May I have your permission to marry your daughter?”

Kevin and Joanna both stood to their feet, and Kevin looked Sean in the eye. "This is sudden, Sean. But I've seen the way Rachel looks at you, and she's never looked at anyone that way before. To know that you're the one that's caught her eye and her heart, to see the kind of man you are, I'd be proud to have you as my son-in-law."

Holding out his hand, Sean met it in a strong grasp of mutual respect. Joanna hugged her daughter and then turned to Sean to hug and kiss him, while the rest of the family stood to give their hugs of approval.

"With the world falling apart, I was asking Rachel about finding a preacher, because if we wait too long, they might be hard to find… and one thing led to another… and here we are. So as soon as I can, I'm going to start looking for one, because Rachel told me as soon as I could round one up, she'd marry me."

They all started laughing, especially enjoying the moment after hearing the earlier bulletin.

"In that case, buddy, I'll help you look," replied Mike, laughing as he gave Rachel a big hug.

"Alright, everyone. I think that's a good note to finish the evening with. Let's finish up the hugs and hit the sack."

Rachel gave Sean a last hug and kiss and then walked up to Sean's room. Mike had taken his things to the back porch as his cot was set up on the backside of the house. Sean followed his parents to the back porch to say goodnight, and as Mike came up, he asked about a sleeping bag.

"Mom, I got my sleeping bag out of my closet, but where's another one for Mike?" asked Sean.

"There were two in your closet, but it was probably on the other side."

"Okay, I'll run up and get the other one. Be back in a minute."

"A minute doesn't leave much time for kisses," Mike joked.

"Well, maybe two or three minutes then."

Sean hurried into the house and up the stairs, so he had the time for more kisses. As he stopped at the door, he knocked softly and then slowly opened the door so Rachel would have time to cover herself if she was undressing.

"Rachel, may I come in?" Sean asked.

Rachel was walking over to turn off the overhead light before she crawled into bed, and when she heard Sean's voice, she stood still, facing the door. She realized she had on the green nightie that Sean had seen earlier, how short it was, and how much of her it revealed, and although it covered more than her bathing suit, it carried a totally different message than swimwear. In a flash, she realized she wanted Sean to see her in her nightie, and she felt an excitement that caused her face to blush and a heat to flow through her veins. The lamp on the nightstand was still on, and as the door continued to swing open, Rachel replied in a soft, barely controlled voice: "Come in."

The door opened all the way, and Sean walked in and closed the door behind him. Turning, seeing Rachel standing under the overhead light with the lamp behind her, his heart skipped a beat.

"Rachel…" Sean could barely whisper her name. "Rachel, you're so beautiful." Looking at her in the short nightgown with spaghetti straps and the low v-cut front, almost tight across her rising and falling bosom, the overhead light revealing and accentuating her womanly curves, Sean was spellbound. His eyes roamed up and down her beautiful form, his mouth became dry and tongue-tied. He licked his lips in preparation to say something, looked one last time at her curves, and then was finally able to speak. "I came up to get another sleeping bag from the closet… and to get a few more kisses. But now, I don't think it would be safe for me to get that close."

Rachel was a little nervous about letting Sean see her in her nightgown, but as he spoke from his heart, it made her feel good to know that he cherished her so much. She walked up to him, feeling his eyes on her body, and once again, she reached up to his face and wiped the edge of his mouth.

Sean was able to take his eyes off of her lower portions and look in her eyes as he asked, "More drool?"

"Lots." She smiled, put her arms around his neck, and met his lips with a stirring passion she had never known. Sean kept his arms around her the whole time, with his hands on her back, not trusting himself to move his hands anywhere else. After several moments of kissing, Sean leaned his head back to look her in the eyes.

"Rachel, I have to go. I wasn't expecting this, and the way you just kissed me… I don't want to lose control. You've saved yourself for marriage, and I won't take that from you. We'll only have to wait a few more days. I love you."

Rachel pulled his head down one more time and whispered, “But what if one of us becomes sick before then. We’ll never be able to share what we both want so badly.”

Sean met her lips one last time and pulled her arms from his shoulders as he pulled away.

“I love you, Rachel. Everything will be alright.”

Sean turned to the closet, and sliding the door over, he reached in and grabbed the sleeping bag. He walked to the bedroom door, and as he opened it, he turned back to look at Rachel, still standing in the center of the room. He didn’t know how he was able to leave; she was irresistible. He now knew how much she loved him, and he hoped she knew how much he loved her, to be able to save her first time for her wedding night.

“I love you, Sean.”

“I love you too, Rachel. Good night.”

CHAPTER TWENTY-FOUR

Rising at dawn the next morning with the briskness of fall in the air, Sean walked into the house, picked up fresh clothes for work, and made his way to the back porch to wake Mike. As he stepped out the door, he could see Mike already standing at the edge of his cot, stretching his arms over his head.

"Refreshing, isn't it?" Sean asked.

"It is. Feels good to sleep outside in this kind of air."

There was wet dew shining on the grass, and they could feel the humidity in the cool air.

"I'm gonna go upstairs and take a shower. You can take one down here if you want, no one else is up yet."

"Alright, sounds good."

Sean stopped at Rachel's door and opened it softly to look inside. Rachel lifted her head from the pillow to look at him. "Good morning."

"Good morning, Rachel. Feel good?"

"Yes, I feel wonderful. Although, I had a hard time falling asleep after you left, and then I dreamed about you, too."

"Really? I hope it was a good dream."

"Yes, yes, it was. The only way it could have been better was for it to be real."

"I'm glad. I had a hard time sleeping, too. I couldn't get your image out of my mind. That was a dangerous thing for you to do last night."

"Do you wish I hadn't done it?"

"Definitely not. No. It was special for me, and I will never forget it, but it makes me think of things that would be better if I didn't. I'm going to take a shower, grab a bite, and then Mike and I are out of here. I love you, and don't forget to carry your pistol outside, okay?"

"Yes, dear."

At work, it was busy. There were numerous calls—a lot of them calling to report a loved one that had turned to stage two overnight, attacked, and then had escaped the house. It was heartrending to the deputies to hear the reports. The last thing to happen was that the caring spouse, parent, or child was attacked by their loved one, bitten, and bruised for their care before they were able to get away. There seemed to be so many cases. It was thought that maybe Lane County would escape most of what the rest of the world was facing, but as the new day arrived with the first of the second tier infected now turning to stage two, there were reports coming in from so many locations. The sheriff broke out the AR 15's, one for each patrol car. No one traveled alone for their own protection. Sean called home to give his dad a heads up on how many people were stage two, running wild throughout the city, and to be careful. He strongly suggested that no one should be outside alone. Two or more people would be able to watch each other's backs.

Sean heard over the radio when Mike and his partner were confronted twice with stage two people, and they put them both down without incident. There were a few more throughout the day, and Sean and his new partner, Jack Leland, eventually ran into one early in the afternoon. As soon as they stepped out of the car and started to close the distance, the woman turned and ran straight at them. Sean's partner had the AR 15 raised, lined up the sights, and squeezed the trigger. Her head snapped back, and she collapsed falling forward.

"That's cool. See any more?" he asked, looking around.

"That's cool? Really? You just had to kill someone, and it was cool?"

"What's the matter? Mad cause you didn't get the shot?"

"Jack, let's get this straight. I've killed more men than you ever thought about. Take my advice and don't fall in love with the killing. Respect it as what it is. That woman was probably someone's wife or girlfriend or even a mother last week. Show some decency."

"Alright, sorry. Never thought about it that way, but I see your point."

The morgue boys were kept fairly busy throughout the day, with driving all over the county to pick up twelve or so bodies. They had to wear full protective gear when disposing of the bodies, and they were very nervous about it. Sean was glad when his shift was over and he and Mike could get back to the house.

There were still gas stations operational, and the supermarkets still had their doors open. Every day, Sean and Mike would stop at the store and buy whatever was available to add to their stockpile. Mitch hadn't planned on two families when he started storing food products, so the more they could round up the better, especially if in the near future other people started showing up looking for safety. Sean wasn't expecting that to happen soon, but once the virus shut down the supply chain completely, there would be a lot of people out scavenging for food. When that time arrived, Mitch and Sean would have to either help people out or turn them away. Only time would tell.

Sean looked up a couple of different church phone numbers, looking for a pastor who could perform the service, but there wasn't anyone to answer. The first church that they came to on their way home, Sean stopped in to see if he could find someone, but the doors were locked up tightly. Another one was the same way. The third church they found was open, and as they walked in, they were met by a man with a pistol in his hand.

"Sorry about the gun. I heard the door open and… just in case, you know?"

"We know. It's alright. I was looking for a minister who could perform a wedding ceremony. Are you him?" Sean asked.

"No. No. He's in the office. Right back here."

The two of them followed him down the hallway to step into a large, well decorated office.

"Hey, Tom, what do we have here?" The pastor stood up to meet them.

"One of these gentlemen wants to get married and needs to talk to you about it," Tom replied.

"Great. It's nice to see that love can still flourish in these troubled times. So, which one of you is the lucky man?"

"I am. I was getting a little worried we might not find someone who could do it for us. And we both feel it's still the right thing to do."

"Good. My name's Bob Lafferty. You are?"

"Sean Dixon, and this is my best man, Mike Taylor," Sean replied.

"Alright. Do you have a date and time set? And do you want it performed in the church or somewhere else?"

"Where is a question I never asked, but we wanted to get it done in three days. Now that I think about it... probably at my folks' house would be best. With the virus and all, there won't be anyone there, except for our immediate household."

"May I ask, is anyone sick in your household?"

"Not so far. We're in a ten-day holding pattern with very limited contact for three more days to make sure none of us were infected on the day the bulletin came out. As soon as that's done, we're getting married."

"That's smart. One of you gets sick and doesn't infect the rest of you. Too bad the government didn't notify us earlier so that we all could have done the same thing. Might've saved a lot more people. I have a two hundred fifty member congregation, with seven people infected, and everyone is now afraid that they might be infected by coming to church."

"Yeah, well, everyone's afraid right now. Can't blame 'em. Besides, the best thing to do right now is to stay isolated until the virus starts to fall off," Mike responded.

"I know, I know. Just talking. Let me get your names on the license, and you can call me later with your address and the time and date you want the ceremony."

"Okay, but I can say right now that the ceremony will be on the third day from now. Probably early afternoon. I need to ask, have you been around anyone that is sick?"

"No. My family is still well, and since the warning, I haven't been to see any of the seven that are sick. Why?"

"If none of us are infected," Sean explained, "we shy away from meeting others unless we're very careful. That's why we didn't shake hands."

"Oh, yes, I see. That's the only thing that is guaranteed to work. No contact."

“That’s about it. If you have a card, I’ll give you a call this evening or in the morning. Thank you for the help, pastor.”

Shortly after leaving the church, Joanna called and asked Sean if he could stop by a doctor’s clinic to pick up a package for Rachel, explaining that she had called in and arranged it so all he had to do was walk in, let them know who he was, and they would give him the package. Giving him the address, she also let him know that everything was fine at home.

“Wonder what that’s about?” Sean asked when he explained it to Mike.

“You say Rachel’s never done it?”

“That’s what it looks like.”

“Then she’s not on birth control. It may be that Joanna wants to get her started on it right away so she doesn’t get pregnant. Imagine going through this turmoil pregnant or raising a baby in it. Probably be best to wait and see how things turn out before starting a family,” Mike reasoned.

“You’re right. That’s not something that I had thought of.”

“That’s because all you can think about is that beautiful girl of yours. Don’t blame you, though. To have someone to love you is pretty special, no matter what the circumstances.”

“Do you think we should wait to marry?”

“If you don’t, do you really think you can keep from doing it anyhow?”

“Good point. No. Last night it was real hard to not go further. It was the thought of getting married in three days that helped me to walk away. So, I think it’s best to go ahead and get married and see what happens.”

In Pyongyang, North Korea, the President sat down to a meeting with his leaders to find out about the mission.

“Sir, we’ve been successful in delivering the nuclear bombs inside the borders of the U.S. Even now, they are approaching Washington. Within twelve hours, they will be ready to detonate.”

“Good work. We will finally make them pay. The only bad thing about it is that we can’t let them know that we did it. I can’t revel in it as much if they don’t know.”

"Maybe someday you'll be able to tell them. For now, we can take pleasure in sweet revenge."

"As soon as they're ready to detonate, let me know," ordered the President. "It would be good if we had someone filming it as it happens. I would love to see the explosions for myself."

"Alright, sir, I'll see what I can do."

"How do we stand on the spread of the virus?"

"Completely in check, sir. Everyone with symptoms has been neutralized and disposed of, and all those who had contact with them are under quarantine. If any more cases are reported, we'll act immediately with the same protocol."

"Well done. I'm very pleased with your performance."

CHAPTER TWENTY-FIVE

Quarantined in the Bethesda Naval Hospital, the President was notified of recent intel concerning North Korea. On a conference call with Director Langdon and his chief analyst, the President was to learn of another impending disaster.

"Tell me again. What exactly have you heard?" she asked.

"We received intel from inside North Korea that two nuclear devices were moved out of the country more than seven days ago. No word on its destination or its payload capacity. Talking it over with all of our analysts, we're in agreement that it would have been sent to the U.S. With the world in turmoil over the virus, we think they're taking advantage of the situation to get it across our border and detonate it on U.S. soil. The most likely target would be D.C. If it comes in on a plane, we would probably locate it, but by cargo ship container, there's a good chance it could get through undetected. There are over eleven million cargo containers that cross our borders every year, and it's practically impossible to inspect and screen all of them."

"How many are actually x-rayed per year?" asked the President.

"Four or five percent. Not enough equipment, too costly, and not enough personnel. Mostly, we check cargo that's coming from higher threat locations. And now considering that we've lost ten to fifteen percent of our workforce across the board, the possibility of stopping a nuclear device at our border is looking pretty slim," Langdon explained.

"Put out an alert at all of our ports to start checking more cargo, just in case. Most likely, it would come through one of our southern coast ports, California or Texas to Florida. Last thing we need is another crisis."

The President paused for a moment to order her thoughts. "I think we need to get the rest of the Cabinet, Joint Chiefs, and the Vice President out of Washington as soon as possible. If that nuclear device is headed our way, we need to keep our leadership alive. It might be best to send them to NORAD just in case. Have we had any reports of the virus at NORAD?"

"First of all, unfortunately, the Vice President is in here with us. Several of us have it, including Robert, David, and most of your personal assistants and secretaries. The CDC still hasn't made any headway on finding a cure. As to the second part of your question, no, we haven't had any infections inside NORAD. If it started in there, we would probably lose all of them."

"Then maybe it would be better to quarantine the rest of the Cabinet and Joint Chiefs for ten days before we put them in there, but we still need to get them out of D.C."

"I agree. I'll make the call right away. How have you been feeling?"

"A fever started during the night. They took a blood sample this morning, and it turned out positive."

"Same here."

"I've about given up hope for a cure. So, about North Korea, should we send a nuclear sub over their way in case this nuclear device goes off inside our borders?"

"We've already got one within range. What do you think we should do if that happens?" asked Langdon.

"The same thing we did to Iran. Their borders are so locked down that they'll probably be untouched by this plague. Any nuclear power with a standing army left after this plague is done will potentially control the rest of the world. It would be horrific to know that the few Americans left alive would eventually be killed or become prisoners of war of a nation like North Korea."

"You're right, of course. We can't let that happen. Even if they let them live, eventually the Koreans would arrest them for speaking out against their atrocities."

"Let me know as soon as the Cabinet and the others are safely away."

"I will. Madame President, if a nuclear warhead goes off anywhere close to us, it will be over in a flash. I just wanted to say, it's been a privilege to serve under you."

Moscow officials and leaders were called into a special meeting with their new President. Intel that they had been receiving was indicating that the Chinese were gearing up for something big, and they needed to make some decisions.

"Sir, our intel, ground and satellite, show that the Chinese have moved more missile defense systems to their northern border in the last couple of days."

"What reasons would they possibly have to defend against missiles coming from our direction?" asked the President.

"Our only answer would be that they expect us to attack them with nuclear missiles. Then we have to ask ourselves: Why would they expect that? The only conclusion we can make is that they expect retaliation from us for something they are planning to do to us."

"And have you come up with a reason why they might attack us first? We're all under the same threat of the virus, just like anyone else."

"This is only a theory, but the only one I have: England is going to be wiped out by this virus, and the U.S. leadership and her population will probably be wiped out as well, because they had so many cities targeted early. That leaves all of the domain of the U.S. up for grabs to the strongest contender. If China is looking at us as a contender for the U.S. and if they see that only our largest city came under the virus attack and that we may not lose enough of our population to be out of the running for being the world leader, then we are the only ones that can keep them from attaining their own goal of world domination. If they launch a first strike against us, and it is enough to weaken our ability to strike back, especially with their missile defense set up, then they will be the world leader from now on. Imagine having all of America's farmland and machinery at our disposal, all of her military weapons for the using, her factories, food production facilities, oil wells, and other natural resources. Is that worth China trying to knock us out to gain the prize?"

"You paint a good picture, Yuri. Have you shared your theory with everyone else?"

"This is the theory that we all came up with and agree is the most probable one. We have shown no aggression toward China thus far, and yet she is posturing for attack and defense."

"Then what would be your recommendation for our response?"

"The U.S. will not launch a nuclear strike on anyone unless in retaliation for a strike against them, such as with Iran, which all of us here totally agree with. They are no danger to us, even if they do survive. There is no other nation that can or will harm us, except for China. I would recommend parking at least half of our nuclear submarine fleet all along China's coast in preparation for their attack. Put our missile defense forces on high alert and have our air force ready to fly at a moment's notice. Have our stealth bombers loaded and standing by to get in the air before their missiles drop. If their missile defense takes out a lot of our missiles, our stealth bombers will make it into their country to drop more nukes. If they do launch first, we launch all of our short-range missiles first, trying to take out their defenses just before our ICBMs are launched. Same with our subs and naval armament, fire all smaller rockets and missiles first and then the nukes. If we could fly a nuke in somehow under radar and set off an EMP, it might be enough to disrupt the electronic tracking ability of their missile defense."

"Alright. Confer with the military and get it set up. Let's get all of our targets for our nukes programmed into the targeting computers right away. Gentlemen, we are on high alert as of now. Get things worked out as soon as possible. If China doesn't launch, we may have to consider our own position for a first strike. As you said, the stakes are high. Thank you."

Arriving home and telling Rachel about the minister was going to be hard for Sean, especially with all of the kisses he had shared the night before. It was going to be hard to see her, knowing he wouldn't be able to take her in his arms and hug her. Driving up behind the house, Sean and Mike climbed out and walked into the house, not knowing what to expect as far as the eating arrangements were concerned. They were both hungry, but to have a family meal might be out. Sean left the doctor's package in the truck in case Joanna wanted to keep it on the down low. Sean and Mike didn't even look to see what it was.

Beth had dinner ready anyhow. As Sean walked up, he could see she had her mask and gloves on, and she explained her reasoning, "I'm feeling really good today, Sean, so I cooked dinner for everyone. I'll dish up what you want, give it to you, and you go somewhere to eat it. No one else touched the food or the plates, except for me. Okay?"

"Sounds good, Mom. Thank you. We're starving. I'll take a whole lot of that, a little of that, and some of that, some of that, and a roll. Are you pouring drinks too?"

"Yes, I will. Tea?"

"Sure. Ready to get your order in, Mike?"

"Sure am. Sean's plate looked really good to me, so just copy that, please."

Walking into the living room, Rachel was sitting in the chair watching the news. She was also wearing a mask, as was everyone else that Sean had seen. Good, they were all being careful.

"Hi, honey. How was your day?"

"Just fine, darlin'." He winked at her playfully. Then, with a straight face, he added, "Mike and I saw some interesting people today."

As Mike walked in and sat down, he added, "Yeah, that one guy that was dressed funny? You remember him? The one with the white collar around his neck?"

Taking several seconds to sink in, Rachel asked excitedly, "Really? You found a preacher? Did you bring him with you?"

Sean laughed at her enthusiasm. "No. We've still got three more days to go before I can hold you again."

"Oh, yeah. Well, if you would have brought him anyhow, I could have been your wife tonight. Think about that for a moment."

"Rachel, if you keep talking like that, I'll go back to town and get him right now."

"Oh, no, no..." she teased. "It's too late for that now. You'll just have to wait."

Sean turned to look at Mike, "How do you deal with that kind of reasoning?"

"I don't know, buddy, but that's your problem now." Mike chuckled.

Sean gathered his plate and drink and said, "I think I'm gonna go out on the porch to eat, okay?"

A few minutes later, Rachel walked out on the porch and sat down on the top step.

"So you really talked to a preacher? Was he okay with coming out here for the ceremony?"

"Yes, he was okay with it. He's not sick; no one in his family is sick; and he hasn't been around anyone that's sick. So, it sounds pretty simple. We just need to know if you want the ceremony in the church or out here."

"Out here would be nice. It's so beautiful out here, and it would make a nice setting. Also, it would be safer than going into town."

"Yeah, that's what I thought too. Do you have something to wear for the wedding?"

"I can pick out one of my dresses that would work."

Sean smiled at her. "You'll look beautiful in whatever you wear."

After dinner, Sean followed Joanna down to the bunker to give her the package he had picked up. Rachel was still in the house talking to Beth about the wedding, so Sean utilized his time to ask some questions.

"Joanna, does Rachel have a dress for the wedding?"

"She's got some cute ones that would work, but nothing special. Why?"

"Tomorrow I could look around and see if I can find a shop that might still be open, but I would need to know what size to get if I can find anything."

"I'll write it down for you. Do you really think there would be a shop still open?"

"Probably not, but you never know. There might still be some weddings taking place that had dresses ordered or something, so there's a chance I might get lucky. Won't know, until I try. How about a ring size, just in case I get really lucky?"

"I like your attitude, Sean. I'm glad that Rachel has found a man like you that cares so much about her."

"Thank you, Joanna."

CHAPTER TWENTY-SIX

The next day, Sean made a lot of calls to shops in the yellow pages, but no one was around to answer the phone. Looking online, he found some with cellphone numbers, and he was finally able to get an answer. Talking to the owner of the shop, Hailee, Sean was able to convince her to meet him that afternoon at her store. She had a little bit of the romantic in her, so she gave in to Sean's pleas.

At the store, Sean met Hailee, who turned out to be a dark-haired beauty, about five foot six, slender with some nice curves. She looked to be about twenty-two, maybe.

Sean was able to give her Rachel's measurements and her height, and he had a couple of photos of her at the falls that showed the profile of her body's curves. It was the best they could do without Rachel actually being there.

Sean looked at the several dresses that Hailee had available in Rachel's size. The one that he liked… he was having a hard time deciding how it would look on Rachel.

"Hailee, how close are you to Rachel for size? You look pretty close?"

"She's just a little larger than me across the front. Everything else is real close. Why?"

"Could you try on this dress so I can see what it looks like? Is that weird? You don't have to, if you don't want to. It's just that I really like this one, but I'd like to see it on someone, you know?"

Hailee hesitated for a moment, but seeing Sean's sheriff uniform, she decided it would be safe to do.

"Okay, stay here, and I'll be right back."

Three or four minutes later, she came back in, and Sean found himself staring. The dress was perfect and beautiful. Hailee twirled around slowly once and waited to hear Sean's answer.

Just as she finished her spin, the door opened, and Mike walked in. He had been walking around outside, looking things over. Hailee looked at him, also in his uniform, and gave him a shy, sweet smile.

Mike let out a little whistle. "Wow, Sean, if Rachel can make that dress look as beautiful as she does, you've got it made!"

"Hailee, this is my partner, Mike Taylor. He has a habit of talking when he should just be watching."

"Oh, I am watching… and talking." Mike winked, but then, he gave her a kind smile and added cordially, "Glad to meet you, Hailee. You look lovely."

"Glad to meet you, too, Mike. Thank you. So, you're both with the Sheriff's Office. How has it been going out there?"

"It's not real good, but not real bad yet either. At least not like the big cities. But we think it's still going to get a lot worse. How are you set up for yourself? Are you doing okay?" Mike asked, deeply interested.

"I'm living with a roommate in an apartment complex about six blocks from here. This shop was my dream as I was growing up, and I only opened it about a year ago. Now all this has happened. It's been pretty scary lately with all of the newscasts showing people getting killed constantly, but we're surviving. I haven't had the shop open for a week, because I've been too scared to come down here. We were able to stock up on some food when that first bulletin came out, but there's some things that we're out of right now."

"Do you guys have any weapons to protect yourselves if you need to?" Sean asked.

"My roommate has a little .22 pistol, an automatic. I've never shot it, though."

Mike had to ask, "Is your roommate a girl?"

"Yes, of course. I could never live with a guy. I own a wedding shop for a reason."

Mike nodded in understanding. "Well, Tell you what, if you want to follow us down to one of the stores when we're done here, we'll see if we can get you some more groceries."

"That would be so nice of you. I would really appreciate that," Hailee responded sincerely. "Well, Sean, I think I'm just a little taller than Rachel. Right now, this dress is dragging on the floor, and I'm wearing flats. I could hem it up an inch for you if you like?"

"Oh, wow... thank you. That would be great, Hailee."

"I've taken my sewing machine home, so if I do it tonight, we could meet up tomorrow somewhere."

"That would work fine, Hailee. Let's finish this up, and then we'll hit that store. Afterwards, we can follow you home to make sure you make it safely."

"Sweet girl, Mike..." Sean commented on the way home. "Did she strike a chord?"

"The most beautiful chord. Sweet music ringing in my ears. Do you think she liked me?"

"She was definitely eyeing you every time you weren't looking. Not to mention, she hardly said a word to me after you walked in."

"Told you I could get the girl," Mike crowed.

"Let's not go there. It was probably because I'm already taken, so I wasn't putting out any vibes. She, being honorable, couldn't get excited over me. Let's just say, 'You lucky devil.'"

"Okay, I'll accept that. Although, it's more than just luck. If she hasn't been out of her apartment since the night of the bulletin, she's in the same shoes we're in: waiting for the ten-day results. I could ask her to the wedding, seeing how she loves those things and the dresses and all. It was the thought of romance that got her out of her apartment, and it would only be fair for her to experience a wedding after all this turmoil. Right?"

"I'm with ya, buddy. It would be good for her to experience a wedding in the midst of all this. It might also be nice to have her there in case Rachel needs a little help with the dress. Not to mention, it's not too easy for you to meet women right now. This virus has really put a stranglehold on the dating scene. If she turns out as nice and sweet as she seems so far, she would be a good addition to the group."

Sean's comments really hit home with Mike, making him feel good and extremely fortunate. "Don't mention anything about Hailee or the dress tonight. I want it to be a complete surprise for tomorrow… unless… Should we wait for the morning of the wedding to give it to her? What do you think?"

"I think that if you give that beautiful white dress to Rachel on the morning she's to be married, when she's only expecting to wear an everyday go-to-work dress, you're gonna be one lucky guy that night. As long as there aren't any problems with it fitting of course. If there is, though, she might delay the wedding. So I'll let you make the call on that."

"We'll just make sure Hailee is there with her sewing machine and anything else she needs to do some minor alterations, is all. This is going to work out perfectly. I can hardly wait to see her face when she gets that dress."

"I can imagine how you feel, buddy. Seriously, I'm real happy for you."

As Sean and Mike got out of the truck, Mitch came down the steps to yell at them to come watch a news bulletin. They hurried into the house, just in time to see on the TV screen a mushroom cloud rising into the sky. Seconds later, another explosion took place with an identical cloud rising into the air. The two mushroom clouds looked to be only a mile or two away from each other. The caption under the picture read: "Washington D.C. Twenty Minutes Ago."

"Oh… my… God…" Mike whispered as he sat down on the couch, with his eyes still glued to the screen.

Sean turned to look at his dad. "Have they said anything about who might have done it?"

"They're guessing one of two nations might've done it: either one of Iran's allies for payback or North Korea. They weren't missiles or air dropped bombs, but rather ground bombs probably trucked in from one of the ports," Kevin spoke up. "They've already commented that the size of the explosions weren't large enough to be a bomb that Russia or China would have used, but they could easily be one that North Korea was capable of making."

"Makes you wonder what's going to happen next…" Mitch stated.

"I can tell you right now what's going to happen," Mike said, matter-of-factly. "By tomorrow night, the world will never have to worry about North Korea again. Those idiots just signed their own death warrant."

"Did they say if the President and her staff was killed?" Sean asked.

"Her and all of her staff that were infected were in the hospital there, including the Vice President. They're all gone, but the rest of the Joint Chiefs and Cabinet were already out of the city along with most of the members of Congress," answered Kevin.

"So who's next in line for the Presidency?" Sean asked.

Steve jumped into the conversation with excitement, "The Speaker of the House. Didn't you watch Olympus Has Fallen?"

For the next hour, they all sat around watching the special report, listening to the different specialists talk about what was happening. Emergency crews were already at the perimeter of the blast radius, trying to help survivors, in full radiation suits, not knowing for sure what to expect. Aerial views from helicopters flying around the perimeter after most of the smoke had cleared were revealing images of total desolation from the blast. Several miles of rubble could be seen and very few buildings were left partially standing. Smoke and fires were still rising, and there were no living souls in the midst of it all. It was hard for the specialists to measure the size or strength of the blast, since there were two of them almost simultaneously detonated, but their best guess was between eighty and one hundred kilotons each.

By the end of the evening, they were all emotionally exhausted by the reports and were glad to turn off the TV and hit the sack.

The South Korean Prime Minister was notified with an encrypted message to immediately pull all of their troops away from the DMZ by at least fifteen miles. They had twenty-four hours to do so or lose all of them to nuclear radiation.

As soon as they began to move away, word was leaked to the North Korean leadership about their departure.

Six hours later, the President of North Korea and his entire Cabinet of advisors and leaders were on a jet to Beijing, including his military generals. As their jet was crossing the border into China, they were discussing how the Chinese government would give them asylum, protecting them from the U.S.'s retaliation.

Just as they were starting to feel a little more secure as they entered China's airspace, alarms started going off. As they sat in their seats, the pilot's agitated voice came to them over the speaker, "We now have a radar lock on us, and there are three missiles approaching. You have killed us all—"

Before the pilot could even finish his sentence, the three missiles successfully destroyed their target. What was left of the fiery ball of wreckage fell to the ground, scattered over several miles of hillside. There were no cameras watching, nor was there anyone to mourn the loss of the ruling body of North Korea.

CHAPTER TWENTY-SEVEN

Stopping by the store again after work on the following day, Sean and Mike loaded another two carts with groceries and dry goods. As long as they could still find stuff that they could use, they would continue to buy and stockpile it. However, much of the things they purchased that day, they were going to give to Hailee and her roommate.

Sean and Mike arrived at Hailee's apartment with their arms full of groceries. Hailee was more than appreciative for the supplies, and she let Sean know that the wedding dress was hemmed and ready to pick up.

"Actually… we wanted to talk to you about that, Hailee," Mike told her. "Sean decided it would be best to give Rachel her dress on the morning of the wedding and that the surprise would then be complete and more rewarding. The only drawback is that if the dress is a little too tight or if it might need some minor alterations, we would need someone there who could do that. I… We were hoping that you would come to the wedding so that you could do that for us if necessary… and to also join in celebrating with us. I could come into town and pick you up that morning and afterwards bring you back home."

"That sounds wonderful, Mike! I would love to go to a wedding, especially after all the things that have been happening. I could bring my sewing machine and do the alterations too. That whole thing sounds so romantic."

"Alright, it's settled then. I'll come by tomorrow morning… around eight?"

"That'll work for me!"

The wedding dress was wrapped in plastic, and as Sean picked it up and was heading for the door, another bulletin came on the TV. They stopped to listen.

"The President of the United States."

The President walked up to the podium, and gripping the sides with his hands, he began to speak, "My fellow Americans, good evening. I'm Nathan Roberts, your new acting President, since the loss of our previous leadership in the bombing attack. I stand before you to inform you that we have retaliated against North Korea almost one hour ago for the nuclear bombing of our capital city. We had received information that North Korea had shipped out two nuclear devices, but we had no idea where they were headed. We are absolutely certain that North Korea was behind the bombing. We launched four Trident missiles from the USS Nebraska, targeting almost all of North Korea. There were no strikes within twenty miles of their borders with South Korea or China, so as to reduce unintentional collateral damage. The prevailing winds will blow the nuclear fallout into the Sea of Japan, and it will pose no threat to any other nation. Both bordering nations were given time to evacuate their adjoining borders to keep their own people safe from the blast. Needless to say, North Korea is no longer an entity in world affairs.

"Other disturbing news that we've had is that the vaccine we've been counting on to stop the spread of the virus is a failure. The virus was genetically altered enough that our current vaccine has no effect on it, and although our brightest virologists are trying to produce a new vaccine, they haven't had any breakthroughs as yet. What this means is that if you get infected with the virus, you will eventually die. If someone you know comes down with the symptoms, stay away from him or her at all costs. If you come down with the symptoms, leave those you're with, or you will infect them also. Stay indoors as much as possible, wear protective masks and gloves any time you go into public, and avoid all unnecessary contact that you can.

"We continue to encourage and to help all of those that are in the production and distribution of food supplies in order that our citizens will be able to survive until this virus has run its course and we may begin to rebuild our nation. If any businesses need military help to continue their work in the food industry, please call the number at the bottom of your screen and let us know how we can help. I ask again, food industry workers, do your best to continue providing food to your fellow Americans. Good night and may God help us."

As the bulletin subsided, Mike said, "Two out of three ain't bad."

"What's that mean?" Hailee asked.

"Two out of the three nations that hated the United States are now extinct—all because they attacked us. I wonder, if they would have known what would have happened to them, would they still have attacked us? It's weird how harboring hate for so long has now caused their own destruction."

"Who's left?"

"Syria."

"Is there any danger of them attacking us?"

"I really doubt it. As long as we have nuclear submarines hiding in the ocean, and now that they've seen what happens to those who attack us, they'll probably keep their distance."

"Why do they hate us so much? That's something I never understood."

"The U.S. has been a sort of a watchdog of the world after World War II," explained Sean. "Recognizing that if some nation had been one before that war, Germany would have been shut down before they became too powerful and tried to dominate the world. Recognizing that fact, the U.S. adopted that role. The nations that don't want to adhere to basic human decency toward their own people, or people they believe to be inferior, hate the fact that the U.S. and her allies will stop them from doing what they want to do. That's it in a nutshell. They will say that the U.S. wants to take over the world, but if that is true, they would have kept control of all the countries they set free in the war, rather than letting them return to being autonomous. Seems pretty clear to me. Live and let live, as long as they will adhere to basic human decency for all,"

"That's not the way most people look at it," Hailee commented.

"I know, but people's opinion still doesn't change the facts. So, the other announcement is big, but not something I wasn't expecting," commented Sean.

"The failure of the vaccine?"

"Yeah. The way the announcements were couched in hope whenever the vaccine was mentioned and the fact that the Homeland Security memo to the Sheriff's Office was that if you contracted it, you would die. That was over a week ago, and now it's proven out."

"What happens now? If the vaccine is useless, and people continue to die, how do we survive if we can't get any more food?" asked Hailee, with genuine concern edging her voice.

"That's the most important question you could ask," began Sean. "How to survive? Live off the land is the best answer. Before everyone is gone, most of the stored food will be used up anyhow, and the only way to get food supplies after all the processed food is gone is to grow or collect your own. And even then, the ones who can grow their own will have to survive against those who want to take all of the food they've grown or collected, because taking what others have is the only thing they're good at."

"If that's the case, then how will I and others like me survive? What hope do we have?" Hailee asked with worry.

Mike took her hand, and when she looked at him, he replied, "You have to hook up with other people who know how to survive and learn from them."

"How do I find those people? You can't just look them up on the Internet, can you?" Hailee was becoming very distressed. She had put her trust in the assertions that the vaccine would halt the virus and save the rest of the population and then the world would return to normal. Now she was faced with a reality that she was unprepared for, that no one was prepared for.

Tears started to well up in her eyes, and Mike was fighting back his own emotion as he watched her struggling with what Sean had revealed to her. Reaching up a hand to her face, he wiped away her tears, and lifting her chin so that she could look at him, he began to explain the situation.

"Sean and I aren't just deputies. We were in the marines for four years, and we have some particular talents that will help us, and anyone else that wants to tag along and help, to survive. We've got a plan already, and if we weren't confident in it, then Sean wouldn't be worrying about a wedding."

"You really have a plan? Can I get in on it?" Hailee asked with rising hope.

"We have a plan. It wasn't ours to start with, but rather Sean's dad. We're living on his farm, and he's already got a lot of things figured out for survival. But, of course, the application fee has to be paid."

Here it comes, thought Sean.

"What kind of fee? I don't have a lot of money, and I don't have much of value."

"You can afford this fee. It's only one big hug and one small kiss." Mike smiled at her to ease her fear. Hailee wiped her eyes, and there started a ghost of a smile on her face, as she realized that Mike had been setting her up.

"Do I get to choose who to pay this application fee to?" Hailee was pretty and smart.

"No, that would be against the rules. I'm the one who collects all the fees, and if you don't play by the rules, you can't join our group."

"Well, in that case…" Hailee stepped up to Mike and gave him a big hug for a long moment and then tilted her head for him to kiss her.

"Wait!" Sean interrupted the kiss. "We have to wait for the ten days to be up for that. Saliva is the best way for the virus to transfer. We all want to be safe, right?"

Mike looked down into the blue eyes that were still sparkling with moisture from the earlier tears. "He's right, Hailee. I'll have to collect that second half of the fee on the day of the wedding, with interest. I wouldn't mind another big hug now though."

"What about your roommate? Will she want to come with us?" asked Sean.

"She's got some friends that she's been wanting to go stay with, but since I was staying here, she didn't want to desert me and leave me alone."

"Hailee, pack up tonight, all the stuff you want to take with you, and then tomorrow morning when I come to pick you up, you'll be moving in with us. How does that sound?"

"Wonderful. Are you sure it'll be okay with the others?"

Sean finally joined in with an answer. "Won't be any trouble at all, Hailee. Mom and Dad won't mind taking in another lost soul."

"We'll take all of your personal things tomorrow, anything else that you can't live without, and anything in your shop that you need. We can't be certain how long this will last or if we're going to be your family for the rest of your life, but once you're out there and you think you need something else from your apartment, we can come back and get it early next week."

"Thank you guys so much. This gives me something to count on and to look forward to. I'm breathing easier already."

CHAPTER TWENTY-EIGHT

The new President, Nathan Roberts, with his Cabinet and Joint Chiefs had been moved to a secure location several miles west of the Pentagon and had just convened a meeting.

"Sir, we estimate that North Korea will be uninhabitable for the next fifty years, although at the rate of growth of the virus, there won't be anybody left to worry about that. We also estimate the total death rate of yesterday's bombing at twenty-five million people. There could be a few survivors along the borders, but within the blast zone there was one hundred percent kill rate," explained William Fulton, the CIA analyst.

Richard Miller, the other CIA analyst continued, "We're starting to get better estimates on the damage done in D.C. The first detonation was a half-mile north and a little west of the White House. There was almost complete destruction within the two-mile diameter of the blast zone, including the White House, the Capitol Building, the Washington Monument, and the Lincoln Memorial. The Pentagon was at the edge of the blast radius and had all of its windows blown out with subsequent personnel injuries. Even the windows of our headquarters at Langley were blown out from the second blast.

"The second detonation was located further northwest, a half-mile from the Bethesda Naval Hospital, in the direction of the White House. Assuming that they were aware of the President's current location in the medical center, it would explain the location of the second device. And since they were less than five miles apart, the only things left standing were smaller buildings with reinforced concrete walls toward the perimeter of each blast. Everything made of wood construction was totally destroyed, if not by the initial blast, then by the ensuing firestorm. If the detonations had occurred two thousand feet above ground level, the damage would have been more widespread but with less radiation on the ground.

"All rescue efforts will be hampered by the increased ground level radiation that didn't take place during the bombings of Hiroshima or Nagasaki. Death toll estimates are one and a half million and rising. No one survived inside the immediate two-mile zone of each detonation, but there are hundreds of thousands of injured around the perimeter, and many of those are expected to die. Death toll may reach as high as three million by the end of the week."

As he finished speaking, there was dead silence in the room as all of them absorbed the catastrophic numbers. Who would have believed that their nation's capital would be the site of two nuclear detonations?

"How are we even able to treat all of those that are injured and dying? That's so many."

"We aren't, and we can't," Fulton answered. "The radiation alone prevents adequate care because we don't have enough radiation suits, then we don't have the medical personnel to handle it, and we lost four major hospitals with all of their healthcare workers. There's just too many."

"My God! I can't believe this has happened. Why wasn't the virus killing us not enough to satisfy their hatred?" asked the President

"Maybe because it wasn't their virus. They wanted to be the one responsible for our demise, and they thought they could get away with it because the blame for the attack would fall on the Arab nations for getting retribution for Iran."

"Back to the injured, if we are currently euthanizing the stage two infected, shouldn't we just euthanize the injured that are going to die anyway? Put them out of their suffering?" asked the President.

"That would probably be best. Save the ones that they can, and don't waste any unnecessary time on the others. Even at that, with the spread of the virus to worry about too, we've got a very large and unpleasant task ahead of us."

"Just do what you can. Now, what's the latest on the virus?"

"There's somewhere between two hundred fifty and three hundred million total infected worldwide. About thirty million are symptomatic; four million have been euthanized; and police forces and military around the world account for putting down a possible two million. Of course, the U.S. has a higher percentage of the euthanization numbers and lower percentage on the military. In the U.S. alone, we've had two hundred twenty thousand stage two. Tomorrow, there may be as many as one hundred thousand infected turning to stage two, and most of them aren't in the hospital. The day after that, there may be that many again, and the day after. We're going to be overrun with crazy people, and at some point in the near future, it's going to come down to killing before you're killed." As Fulton finished painting the unbelievable scenarios, there was complete silence in the room.

"With it that bad, what can we possibly do? There's going to be so many bodies rotting in the street that we'll be fighting other diseases as well," whined the President.

"Makes you want to go crawl into a hole and hide doesn't it?" asked Miller.

Fulton had one more thing to share with the group. "On another matter, our satellites have been picking up a lot of movement on both sides of the border between Russia and China. The first to start moving was China with mobile anti-missile defenses rolling toward the border. A day later, Russia started bolstering their forces in preparation of China's preparation. I think they're both posturing to take the other out."

"Why on earth, with this virus killing everyone, are they doing that?" asked the President.

"There's only one reason that makes sense," Fulton began. "Before too long, England will no longer be a superpower and neither will we. France will be out of it. India and Pakistan will be out. North Korea is out. They will be the only two superpowers left with enough people, military, and operational nuclear armament to take over the world. Neither one of them trust the other. It's apparent that China realized that first and started taking defensive measures. When Russia caught on to it, they started juggling things around. For now, it's just posturing."

"I think what we have to consider," began Miller, "is that if the U.S. population is reduced to several million people by the time this virus is done, we won't have any standing military to thwart a land invasion by either of those countries. The whole of the U.S. will be a rich and ripe plum to be captured by the strongest contender. One of them might want to attack the other, but on the other hand, they don't want to be attacked. It boils down to how badly they will want our nation—not just our nation, but our farmland, our machinery, our factories and food processing centers, our military weapons, and our natural resources. Whichever country gets the U.S. will reign supreme over the whole world. That's what's at stake."

"As much hacking as China has been doing in the past two years in the U.S., do you think they've neglected hacking Russia's businesses, government computers, and military?" asked Fulton. "China probably knows more about everyone else than anyone does. They might believe that they could take out Russia before they get blown to bits."

"Are there any ideas to what our part in this scenario should be?" asked the President.

"One question we have to ask ourselves is which country taking over the U.S. would be better for the Americans that will still be here? Who would we rather see living with our own people, who wouldn't kill off the remaining Americans or subject them to the atrocities of conquerors that are usually perpetrated on the remaining population?" asked Richard Miller. "Any ideas?"

"What you're asking is who would make friendlier conquerors for any of us who remain?" asked the President.

"Yes, that's it. Whoever we believe will be better for our people, then that is who we should help if this breaks out into a nuclear war," explained Miller.

"I think that Russia would be better for our survivors than China. They may have had the KGB, a lot of bad and corrupt politicians, and a lot of corrupt industrialists, but China's record on human rights isn't very encouraging."

"I agree. Russia seems like they would make a better conqueror and maybe not be as cruel as the Chinese leaders."

"I agree, also."

Very quickly then the rest of the room made their recommendation and it was unanimous.

"Since we agree, then what should our plan be?" The President looked around the room at all the faces, waiting to hear their ideas.

The Secretary of Defense, Glen Williams, stood to his feet. "We could send at least half of our Trident subs to sit off the coast of China, and at the first sign of a nuclear launch, we launch half of our own missiles and save the rest for clean-up if it's necessary."

"Do you think we should contact Russia to let them know that we are with them? I'd hate for them to think we would launch any missiles against them," reasoned the President.

"That might be a good idea," began Miller. "Create an alliance now with Russia, and it might help our people in the future if Russia ends up the world leader. We would need to make sure China doesn't find out, or they might launch some missiles our way if things go sour."

"As much hacking as China has done, there may not be any way to keep that secret. We don't know what kind of spyware that they may have attached to any of our computer programs," warned Fulton.

"That's true. But if they have, how do you suggest we contact Russia?" inquired the President.

"Create a hard copy of an alliance that can't be accessed by computer spyware and sent back to China and, somehow, hand deliver it to Moscow and wait for a return missive."

"Alright. All those in favor of an alliance with Russia against China?" A unanimous show of hands.

"Anyone against?" None.

"Write up the details, let me sign it, and get it done."

The Chinese President looked at his top military general, listening to his report. Some of their intel came from the Internet, through information gathering of their spyware that they had installed on the military and government computer programs of other countries. Their expert computer hackers had infiltrated almost every government agency in all of the world's top governments and had installed backdoor programs for accessing top-secret information.

"The Russians have started moving more missile defense systems closer to our border to coincide with our own preparations. We have to assume that they are aware of our movements and that now they will be ready for any aggressive move on our part. This may make things a little more difficult. If either one of us launches an attack, then we will not come out of it unscathed. Are you ready for the retaliation if we launch first and also the repercussions for our nation if our missile defense system fails to destroy most of the incoming missiles?"

"I am if I think that launching first becomes our best alternative. This virus may kill more of our people than it does Russia's population. Where will that leave us in the end? I would rather see mutual destruction for the both of us than to be subservient to Russia, after all we've had to put up with dealing with America over the last forty years. Keep working up different attack strategies and plans and running scenarios on the computer, and let me know what our best course of action might be."

"Yes, sir."

"What's the latest on the virus?" asked the President

"We've been continuing to round up the infected as fast as we can and putting them down immediately before they can infect others. We then quarantine those from their household to see if they are infected before they are allowed back into society. The process seems to be working so far on controlling the spread of the virus. Our three largest cities were infected heavily to begin with, but since our working class inside the cities don't have that much contact with the peasants in the outlying districts, the disease hasn't spread as much across our nation as it has in the U.S. By all accounts, we've lost about two million people, and we estimate that there may be another three to five million infected. We're hoping that most of them are already in quarantine so that it doesn't spread much further."

"What about the rest of the world?"

"We estimate that twenty-five percent of the UK's population of sixty-seven million is infected, with one point five million having symptoms. Their reports indicate that they've lost one hundred thousand people already, and their stage two conversions will have transitioned to thirty-two thousand today. At their current rate of growth, and because they won't deal with the virus as quickly and effectively as we are, in six more days, their infected population will be around sixty-six percent, and two days after that, their entire population. With the added warnings and the fear factor causing people to stay indoors, the increase may be somewhat lower than the numbers I just quoted, but still, once the disease reaches the exponential growth rate of the fourth tier, the numbers fly off the charts."

"And the U.S.?"

"In the progression they're at, they have thirty-eight million infected now, with another twenty-two million more today; four million with symptoms, with an additional two million more today; they've lost almost four hundred thousand to stage two, with another two hundred thousand turning to stage two today. In seven more days, their entire population may be infected. In twenty-five days, their entire population will have developed stage two, of course within the parameters that I previously mentioned. The more they lose and the more separated the survivors are, the more likely that there will be minuscule pockets of people escaping the virus. But probably not more than several hundred thousand for the entire nation."

"It looks like the U.S. will get knocked out by the virus before anyone else. The terrorists did a better job with the virus than they ever imagined."

"They did. Actually too well. We'll be lucky to stop the disease ourselves before we lose a tenth of our own population."

"That just means we'll have that many less to feed. If you need to mobilize the army to round up the infected and remove them, then do so. It is imperative that we keep it under control at all costs."

"Yes, sir."

CHAPTER TWENTY-NINE

Arising early on his wedding day, Sean made sure that Mike was awake and then took his shower. Afterwards, he had to see Rachel to make sure that she was feeling well and that everything was okay. Tapping softly on her door, he opened it to see if she was awake, and walking to her bedside, he watched her for a couple of minutes as she was sleeping. The sun was just coming up and starting to shed some light through the curtained window, and Sean, standing there spellbound, watched her face as the light continued to grow. Looking at the dress hanging from the top of the closet door that she had picked out to wear, Sean was elated and pleased with himself that he was able to find her a real wedding dress.

"Rachel," whispered Sean. He leaned over her and whispered her name again. "Rachel. It's your wedding day." Her eyes fluttered open, and when they focused on Sean's face, she gave him the most beautiful smile.

"Good morning, darling. To think from now on I get to wake up to your face every morning."

"That's not any better than me waking up to your beautiful face every morning. How're you feeling this morning?" Sean asked with anticipation as he reached for her hand to hold it between both of his.

Rachel could hear the excitement in Sean's voice and was especially pleased to give him her answer. Pulling his hand toward her, she then raised up to wrap her arms around him, the blanket falling to her waist, as she started to speak.

"I feel wonderful, darling."

Sean lowered himself to the edge of the bed, so she wouldn't have to stretch so far. Then, after a long, tight squeeze, he started kissing her neck. He worked his way to her sweet lips and made up for the last three days of being apart. Rachel finally pulled away and lay back on her pillow, gazing up into his eyes while holding his hands.

"I love you, Sean. Tonight we'll be man and wife, and you'll be here beside me."

"I love you too, Rachel. I'm so excited for the day to start and to hear you say, 'I do,' and to be honest, I can hardly wait… for tonight."

Rachel pulled him down to her and spent her kisses on his lips, revealing to him how excited she was also. After several moments of tender kisses, Sean stood to his feet to leave, but before Rachel let go of his hand, she slid out from under the covers, rising to her feet. Looking at her as she stood there, Sean realized he was holding his breath, taking in her beauty, as she again allowed him to see her in her nightie.

"Rachel, I can hardly put into words what I feel as I look at you knowing that you love me so much. I almost can't catch my breath, because of the way you excite me. I love you so much."

Rachel stepped up to him and put her arms around his neck as tears started to roll down her cheeks. Sean held her tightly, and when he heard her sniffling and felt her wet tears soaking through his shirt, he pulled back from her to look her in the eyes. When he saw the tears, he reached up and gently wiped them away.

"Why the tears, honey?"

"Because you make me so happy. I've never known a man's love before, and it's more than I ever dreamed. Kiss me again."

When Rachel was finally satisfied with his kisses, she turned, walked into the bathroom, and closed the door. Sean walked downstairs and ran into Mike coming from the kitchen.

"Hey, your mom is in the kitchen starting breakfast. You give the you know what to Rachel yet?"

"No, I just went upstairs and woke her up, got my fill of kisses, and now she's going to shower."

"Now would be the perfect time to lay the dress on the bed, and when she comes out of the bathroom, it'll be the first thing she sees."

"That sounds good, Mike. That's just what I'll do. When will you leave to pick up Hailee?"

"Now I wish I had told her earlier. I could have had her here for breakfast."

"Call her right now then. She might be an early riser and might be ready to go as soon as you can get there."

"That's a good idea."

As Mike was calling Hailee, Sean walked over to the hall closet and took the wedding dress from inside. After he carried it into the kitchen to show his mom, he was getting excited.

"Sean! How in the world did you get that? That's beautiful. Rachel is going to be so happy. You haven't told her yet?"

"No, not yet. She's taking a shower, and I think I'll go lay it out on the bed for her to see when she walks into the bedroom."

"That's perfect, Sean. You better hurry before you lose your opportunity. Oh, Sean, I wanted to give you this. It was your grandmother's wedding ring, and she wanted you to have it if you needed it for your future wife. I don't know if it will fit, but it should. I can barely get it on, but Rachel has longer, thinner fingers than I do."

"That's great, Mom. I didn't know what I was going to do. I couldn't find any jewelry stores open at all."

Mike walked in all excited. "She's already up and will be ready to go as soon as I get there."

"Great. The keys are on the counter, and we'll save you some breakfast."

Sean walked back up to his room, as Mike was heading for the door. Opening the door slowly, he peeked in to make sure Rachel was still in the bathroom. He couldn't hear the water running, so he knew he needed to hurry. Taking the clear plastic cover off the dress, he carried it over to lay it on the bed facing the bathroom door. After removing the hanger and smoothing it out, he stepped back to look at it. The sun was now up, and there was plenty of light to see the dress in all its shimmering beauty.

He heard Rachel moving around in the bathroom and was trying to decide whether to leave or wait for her to come out so he could see her face when she saw it. It would be a precious moment to treasure in his heart.

Before he actually made up his mind, the bathroom door started to open. He quickly stepped back against the wall and held his breath. All of a sudden, he realized that Rachel might walk out without any clothes on, not expecting anyone to be in the room, but it was too late to move. At that moment, he felt like an intruder rather than the loving groom. He didn't know what to do.

Rachel walked out into his view, and then froze, with her eyes on the dress. She was holding a towel around her, her damp hair hanging down across her bare shoulders. She squealed with delight as she moved forward to take up the dress, exclaiming, "Oh, Sean, you darling!"

As she reached for the dress with both hands, she let go of the towel, and it fell to the floor. Sean couldn't take his eyes from her beautiful form. He couldn't say a word. He was embarrassed for her and himself, for intruding on her privacy. However, try as he might, he couldn't look away or close his eyes.

Rachel picked up the dress to hold it aloft and to look at its beauty, but all Sean could see was the beauty of Rachel's naked profile. She spun around to carry it into the bathroom to look at it in the mirror, and as she turned, her eyes found Sean leaning against the wall.

"Rachel, I'm sorry. I…"

Rachel looked at Sean, realizing his embarrassment and loving him more because of it. It only took a second to decide what she wanted to do, needed to do, to ease Sean's embarrassment. She turned, lowered the dress to lay it carefully upon the bed, and then turned back to look again at Sean with nothing between them. Standing there watching Sean look at her from head to toe, she felt the heat of desire rising in her body once again. With love in her eyes and in her heart, she stepped up to him to put her arms around him to hug him tightly. As she felt his arms envelop her bare skin, she turned her lips up to his and kissed him over and over.

"I love you so much, Sean. Don't worry about this, in just a few hours you were going to see me like this anyway. I'm alright with it, sweetheart."

Their lips met again, softly and gently. Rachel leaned back to look into Sean's eyes, conscious of his eyes on her body, feeling an excitement she had never known. "Sean, you had me before the dress, and with everything you do, I love you more and more. I'm never gonna let you go. You are so dear to me."

She slowly stepped back, turned and picked up the dress, and walked into the bathroom to close the door behind her.

Sean took a deep breath, and then another, and yet another to calm his racing heart. He had faced death many times in battle, and none of them compared to the way he had just felt in Rachel's presence. What a woman! He was the luckiest man on the planet to find someone like her that loved him as much as she did. He walked back down to the kitchen to find everyone standing around visiting, glad that everyone was okay after the ten-day ordeal.

Turning to Joanna, he said, "Joanna, you need to go up to Rachel's room and see if she might need your help trying on her wedding dress."

"Sean! You found one?"

"I sure did, and it's beautiful. Mike just went into town to pick up the woman who sold it to me. She's bringing her sewing machine with her in case she needs to make some minor alterations."

"That's wonderful, Sean. You're such a darling!" Joanna hugged Sean tightly and then hurried up to Rachel's room.

Looking at his mom, Sean could see a question coming and answered it first.

"Mom, it was the sweetest thing I've ever seen, the way she grabbed it up and held it, and the look on her face is something I'll never forget." Among other things, he thought.

Beth wrapped her arms around her son to hold him tightly. "I'm so proud of you Sean. The way you've treated that dear girl makes me so happy. I love you."

"I love you too, Mom."

"Sean, when is the pastor coming out?" asked Mitch.

"Right after lunch. He has the directions, but I'll call him right after breakfast to make sure."

Mike arrived at Hailee's without incident before seven. There were still a few people driving around through town, but the traffic was probably down to less than five percent of normal. There were no schools operating anymore, and ninety-five percent of the workforce was no longer working. There were no office complexes open, nor insurance centers, no factories or manufacturing of products, no clothing stores, shops, or boutiques, nor restaurants or cafes… they were all closed. There weren't any stores open, except those selling groceries and only a few gas stations.

Most of the traffic on the roads now were people going to see their family or friends, looking to buy more food, or people leaving the city to escape the virus. The only other traffic was law enforcement, military, or government workers that still had important enough duties that they continued to work.

The whole of society had come to a halt as if all of humanity was standing still, with bated breath, waiting to see if the world would stand or fall, hoping that a news bulletin would come across the airways pronouncing a cure for the virus and that the world could return to normal. But they all knew that this was their new reality, fearful of their death, but more fearful of their survival. There were no answers, and although many were praying, everything continued to get worse. The weak were crying; the strong were taking stock; and the ones in between were frozen with indecision. Anyone who would step forth with a plan would draw many followers; they all were looking for someone who seemed to know what to do. For either the good or the bad, there would be followers willing to join themselves to any plan for survival. The world's new society was about to embark on an unprecedented journey into anarchy that would put history to shame.

Mike's thoughts about the future weren't rosy, but he could face the reality with confidence and hope because of his best friend that he had learned to trust and depend on for leadership. He knew the odds of surviving were slim, but with Sean and Mitch thinking and leading the effort, he was as confident as anyone could be about the future. And now that he had met Hailee, he was actually excited for what the future would hold. With a woman to fight for and to hold, a strong man was made stronger and would rise to the occasion to protect what was his. With Sean at his side, he was confident that they would succeed.

Walking into the apartment building, Mike was glad that he was able to take Hailee out of the city. There would be too much danger in the midst of so many desperate people, and he felt that things were about to explode as food supplies continued to dwindle. Knocking on her door, he was wondering how many people were living in the building and how they would survive the coming collapse. The door opened, and Hailee stood there, dressed in jeans and a white blouse, looking prettier every time Mike laid eyes on her. Her long, dark, wavy, hair made her look as beautiful as Rachel, only in a different way.

"Good morning, Hailee. Feeling good?" Mike asked. The question was becoming one of the most asked among his group, as everyone needed to assess their health all the time.

"Good morning to you too, Mike, and I'm feeling wonderful actually—physically as well as mentally. After you guys invited me out, I feel like a weight has been lifted off my shoulders. I hadn't realized how worried I've been until you guys released me from it, and now I actually have some hope to carry me forward."

"Hailee, about yesterday, you don't have to pay me that kiss. I was only kidding and trying to be humorous, and I'm sorry about that. You're still invited, of course. I'm not taking that back. Sean and I both like you a lot, and so we wanted to help you."

"Mike, does that mean you don't want to kiss me?" asked Hailee with an inflection of tone that indicated that she was hurt.

"No. No, that's not it at all. Actually, it was excitement and anticipation of kissing you that kept me awake last night and woke me up this morning. But I don't want our first kiss to be under false pretenses, but rather I want you to kiss me because you like me."

"If that's all the problem is, I can solve that right now." Stepping quickly up to Mike, she wrapped her arms around his neck and pulled him down to meet her sweet lips in their first kiss— a prolonged dreamy kiss with a promise of a future filled with more.

"Maybe I should have taken it as payment of a fee, because then I could just increase the fee or add surcharges…"

Hailee stopped his ramblings with more kisses, realizing herself that she was enjoying the closeness with Mike way more than she had been anticipating.

"Would you rather think of reasons to charge for kisses, or would you like free ones anytime you want them?"

"Well, now that you word it that way. Anytime?" Mike grinned at her.

"Right now?" he asked. She kissed him. "Right now?" She kissed him. "Right now?" She kissed him again, but longer that time.

"Alright," interjected Hailee. "Let me reword that, because I can now see that you're going to abuse the privilege. Let's make it anytime I want."

"That won't be fair. What if I need kisses more often than you? Where does that leave me?"

"What would be an acceptable compromise?" Hailee asked with a mock concerned look on her face.

"Anytime we see each other, anytime I come home, anytime we part, anytime we…"

"Alright. I see I'm the one that's going to have to make decisions in this relationship because you'll always be muddleheaded around me."

"We're in a relationship? That's so sweet. I guess I'll have to let all of the other girls know that they'll have to look elsewhere." Bending down to her, he kissed her long and lingering one last time.

"Can you guys take that outside? It's sweet and all, but really…?" Hailee's roommate spoke from the kitchen.

Pulling apart, Hailee introduced her roommate, Julie.

"Are you sure you'll be okay with me leaving?" asked Hailee.

"Sure, Hailee. John and Lee are coming over this afternoon to help me load my things and take me to their place. They're a little disappointed that you aren't coming too."

"That's alright. I just don't feel right around them."

"Are you sure you're making the right decision now? You've only known these guys for what, three days?" asked Julie, a little hurt at the slight against her friends.

"Yeah, I'm sure. I really like the two of them, and I think they'll be able to take care of me, if anyone can."

"Alright, Hailee. If you need anything, call me."

CHAPTER THIRTY

Sean and Mike were standing next to the minister in the front yard, decked out in their full military dress blues, with their medals and ribbons, white cover, and black shoes. They were two handsome and very striking young men, who would catch the eye of any young lady who happened by. The sun was still high in the sky, but it was well on its way in its descent to the horizon as the wedding was about to start. A slight breeze would lift every few minutes to stir the aspen leaves and the branches of the fir trees around the house.

There were eight chairs lined up for the six people that would be sitting, and the minister's wife was standing on the porch with a CD player to play the wedding song, as Rachel walked out to meet Sean.

Beth walked down with Mitch to take their seats, as it was ready to begin. Hailee came out of the house after her last second check on Rachel's gown, walking up to Mike to let him know he needed to go into the house to begin his walk with Leah, who was the bridesmaid. She then took a spot beside Beth and Mitch. Sean removed his cover and handed it to Mike to set in the house during the ceremony. Everything was ready to start. Mitch and Beth stood by their chairs, and Joanna and Steve stood across from them in front of their own. Steve had a camera in his hand and would be taking pictures of the wedding.

The music started, and the front door opened. As Mike and Leah stepped out, she took Mike's arm with her hand and they descended the stairs. Sean was looking for Rachel to see how beautiful she looked in her dress, waiting anxiously for her to step out.

As Mike and Leah separated to step to each side, the music changed to the wedding march, and then the doorway was filled with Kevin stepping out, followed by Rachel in her beautiful gown. Sean was beaming as he looked for her, but as his eyes took in her beauty in the wedding gown, he caught his breath. His eyes started to water, and his heart rate increased noticeably. Catching her eye as she stepped out on the porch to take her father's arm, Rachel also became teary eyed as she watched Sean reaching up to wipe away his tears. Descending the steps and then walking to the front, the minister asked his question.

"Who gives this woman away to be wed?"

"Her Mother and I," Kevin answered. Kissing Rachel on the cheek, he turned to Sean as he stepped close, and placing Rachel's hand into Sean's, he placed his own hands on the shoulders of both of them and pulled them together as he hugged them, then stepped over to Joanna and took her hand.

Rachel, being moved by Sean's show of emotion, wrapped her arms around him in a tight embrace, whispering to him that she loved him so much, and then turned to face the minister as he began.

"We are gathered here today to witness the joining of these two lives and hearts in holy matrimony. Marriage is a time-honored and holy pact between a man and a woman—a union of two hearts to share a life together through good times and bad. It's a promise to always be there for one another, to encourage and to build up, to watch over and to protect, to love one another, and to lift each other higher. Do you have vows for one another?"

"Yes."

"Go ahead and exchange your vows."

"Rachel, you are my one true love, the woman that I've always dreamed about to be my wife, my friend, my lover. I will respect you, support you, and encourage you as we go through life together. In hard times and good, I will hold you, protect you, and care for you, I will watch over you, provide for you, and serve you. I will love you for as long as I live."

"Sean, you are the man I love, the man that has shown me what true love is, and you will be my friend, my lover, my husband. I look forward to spending the rest of my life with you, loving you through the good times and bad, holding you, encouraging you, supporting you, and loving you for as long as I live."

"Do you have the ring?"

"Yes."

"Take the ring and place it on the third finger of Rachel's left hand."

"Sean, do you promise to love, honor, and cherish Rachel, to watch over her, encourage her, and protect her, to provide for her and to lay down your life for her, and to love her for the rest of your life?"

Looking Rachel in the eyes, Sean replied, "I do."

"Rachel, do you promise to love, honor, and cherish Sean, to watch over him, encourage him, and take care of him, to cleave unto him, support him, and to love him for the rest of your life?"

Looking Sean in the eyes, Rachel replied, "I do."

"Then by the power vested in me, I now pronounce you husband and wife. You may now kiss your bride."

Wrapping their arms around each other, Sean bent his head down to meet Rachel's warm, sweet lips in a long, tender kiss. Everyone stood to their feet and applauded the couple—most of them teary eyed.

"I love you, Rachel."

"I love you, too."

"Sir, I have that hand-delivered communication from the United States."

"Let's have a look at it."

Opening the satchel, they removed a folder and a DVD. Reading through the papers, the President turned to his aid and told him to call a meeting of his leaders right away.

Within the hour, everyone was gathered, and the President of Russia began the DVD so that they all could watch the message for themselves.

"Mr. President, I and my leaders have seen that China has been moving its forces in preparation of an attack and also the movement of your own defenses in preparation of that happening. I want to lay this out in as simple of terms as I can. At the current rate of growth of the spread of the virus in my country, we can see that our nation will, in the next four weeks, cease to be a nation with almost our entire population dying from the disease. We also realize that your nation and China may, in fact, escape the brunt of the effects of the virus. If that does happen, we also foresee that the U.S. will be open for invasion and acquisition of one or the other of the two of you.

For those Americans who are able to escape the virus, who will also have no defense against a future invasion, rather than letting them face that and be subjected to rape, torture, and murder, we are appealing to you and your basic human decency to give your word and promise to assimilate our remaining population into your own in a humane manner, in the hope that humanity will be rebuilt without the hatred and distrust that has originally caused this current crisis throughout the world. We have decided that if we had a choice in the matter, we would rather see your country and your people move into our country, rather than China's armies. In this hope and with your promise, we would agree to help you militarily if China launches an attack against you. Even now, half of our nuclear submarine fleet is waiting off the coast of China with three more positioned in the Mediterranean. With your word and your promise, we will be your ally and help defend you, but also join you in an attack against China. I did not trust our usual communications with this, due to all of China's hacking of our systems, and I would suggest that you should also be wary of their capabilities. We, and our nation, anxiously await your reply."

The video ended, and the silence continued, as they were all thinking of the seriousness implied in the message from the American President. They knew that conditions in the U.S. were worse than in their own nation, but to hear from the U.S. President the news that they would not survive as a nation was mind boggling and surprising. The U.S. had always been able to overcome all obstacles because of the greatness of her people, and to now see their total failure in the face of the advancing virus was heartrending and moving.

It was at that moment that all of them began to see the enormity and full scope of the danger from the virus, but also they realized that the survival of the human race was at stake and their nation could play a big part in the survival and rebuilding of humanity.

It wasn't long before all of them were in unanimous agreement with the plan the U.S. offered them. Arranging a reply in a like manner, the President of Russia soon had a message to return to the United States.

The mayors of Eugene and Springfield called a meeting with their county sheriff and city police chiefs and their associates. Attending the meeting were also their county's public health officials, who had been keeping track of the spread of the virus within their county, but more specifically within their two cities.

"Gentlemen, we're estimating that, within our county, we may have as many as eighty thousand people infected with the virus now. We have approximately twelve thousand cases with symptoms that are infectious, and we've lost about a thousand to the stage two of the virus with as many as four hundred turning to stage two today. That is, four hundred or more violent, contagious individuals that will be turned loose on the public today that will infect almost everyone they touch. And then, tomorrow, there will be as many again turning to stage two, and five thousand or more will also be initially infected the same day. Each day that goes by from now on, we will see a rising number of initial infections, stage one symptoms, and also stage two conversions.

"We're currently euthanizing all of those in the hospitals that turn to stage two, but the majority of cases are no longer coming into the hospitals. What this means is that our law enforcement people are going to see a huge increase in the number of stage two individuals that they will have to take down as soon as they can.

"Portland and Salem are in worse shape than we're in and have called out the National Guard to help control the crazy ones and the turmoil that they're causing. We have requested that the National Guard sends us some troops to help out in our county. Every city and every town in our state have reported cases, but none of them are as advanced as our three largest metro areas. The National Guard is immediately sending more ammo and M4s for our law enforcement personnel. Are there any questions?"

"How will we dispose of that many bodies from the public areas?" asked the mayor of Eugene. "We're already maxing out on our personnel."

"We'll have to take some of our other government workers that are now doing nothing, give them some hands-on training with our professionals, and put them to work. With protective gear and minimal training, almost anyone can do it. One thing is for sure: We can't neglect the body removal and disposal. Otherwise, we may be fighting other diseases as well. That's the best we can do."

"Are we going to be able to continue bringing in food for the people?" asked the mayor of Springfield. "Everyone's food supply that they stocked up at the initial bulletin is about to run out. When the people start looking for more food, there's going to be a spike in the crime rate, ranging from breaking and entering, theft, assault, and maybe even murder for the most desperate people. Since they still have power, the storage of food isn't a problem, but finding it is."

"We've been looking into that also, and we're trying to make sure all of the food processing plants up and down the Willamette Valley will continue to operate until they themselves run out of raw product. There is still a lot of grain to harvest to process into flour, and as the growing seasons continue to arise, we're making sure farmers have the fuel to continue doing what they do for harvesting as well as planting new crops. When it comes to the imports of any raw foods or processed foods from other areas, that's a different story. There will be many things that we have no control over."

"Have you considered that the two main staples, such as meat and bread, may be supplied in continuing survival quantities?" asked the mayor.

"Yes, we're working with the local cattle industry, butcher shops, local bakeries, and the flour processors to keep running as long as possible. The problem is getting it to the people who need it. With delivery to the stores, the ones who get there first, buy it all up to hoard it, and then the latecomers or the ones who won't leave their homes are starving. We're looking at opening distribution centers so that the existing food can be doled out more fairly."

"Then we'll have to have law enforcement personnel on site for that also. We're running short on manpower for all the things that we're called to do," complained the police chief.

"We'll just have to cope with it. Tough times call for tough decisions and for stepping up to the plate when it's your turn."

"Alright. Let us know when you have something a little more concrete for us to work toward, like schedules for the food distribution when you get it running and numbers to call for the body removal."

CHAPTER THIRTY-ONE

Sean and Mike were called back into work the day after the wedding, hearing that there were several hundred a day of the stage two conversions expected. It wasn't something that they were looking forward to and decided not to mention the details to the family, except for Mitch and Kevin. No use causing any unnecessary worry; it was worrisome enough as it was. Arriving at work, they were briefed with what was revealed at the meeting with the mayors and the public health officials. Both of them were issued their own Colt AR15 M4 fully automatic carbine topped with a 4x32 ACOG scope—a weapon that both of them were very familiar with. Along with the weapon, they were given ten full mags each and a thousand round carton of shells for the car.

Before they were even in the car and patrolling, there were calls coming in of encounters with the infected. It was to set the tone for the entire day, with another stage two taken out every couple of minutes. Sean didn't envy the body disposal crew who had now reverted to a flatbed trailer being pulled around by a parks and recreation pick-up truck. They were actually using three different crews to keep up with the numbers of those killed by the police forces, although occasionally one was put down by a civilian who was about to be attacked. By that time, most civilians, who were braving the open public, were carrying weapons for their self-protection.

Sean and Mike were both assigned patrols around the edge of town because of their experience and marksmanship abilities, being put to use more frequently than the farther out patrols around the county. It was mainly the city police department that handled most of the in town infected rather than the county sheriff, but they were still used around the edges as the city police had plenty to do. There were a couple of times they were called back to a previous kill site because the body disposal crew were being held up by another stage two trying to attack them. It was unreal how many stage two were roaming the public streets.

Everyone was realizing how much easier it would be to put down the stage one infected before they turned. However, the majority of them weren't in the hospitals, and so no one would know how to locate any of them. Unbeknownst to them, both China and North Korea had been putting to death even the stage one infected to better control the spread of the disease, which had definitely worked, but still that step was one that Americans were loath to take.

There was one incident early in the day that was more heart rending than any other, when Sean and his partner noticed a child moving down the street in an erratic manner. Getting closer, they could tell that it was a girl of about eight years old, and as they drove past, she attacked the car. Driving beyond her by a hundred yards, Sean exited the car quickly as the girl had chased them part of the way down the street.

Leaning against the solidity of the fender, Sean took aim with his scope on the girl's face, looking one last time at her countenance to make sure that he had to pull the trigger. There was a glazed look in her eyes, and her face was grimacing in pain and agony. With the red dot on the child's forehead, Sean squeezed the trigger and watched her go down. Hearing the deputy exclaim loudly that another one was coming up behind them, Sean turned and lined up the dot and squeezed the trigger again. Calling them in, they continued to patrol and listen to the other calls.

Among the other deputies, talk about Sean and Mike was starting to be passed around. They were unerring in their marksmanship, and no matter how hard the situation, neither of them shirked their duties. It didn't take long before almost all of the deputies wanted to be put on the roster with either one of them, and of course, because of that, the inevitable jealousy and hatred began to fester among two of the deputies toward them.

Many of their comments reached Sean's ears, and he knew that eventually there would be trouble between them. One of them was the deputy that had earlier taken joy in shooting the infected woman, as if it was a competitive shooting match. Hopefully, it would remain at the talking stage only; they could ill afford the loss of two more of their deputies.

Later that evening, Rachel noticed that Sean wasn't quite as attentive as he usually was, and when a chance arose to speak to Mike, she asked him about it.

"Sean seems to be a little quiet tonight. Mike, did something unusual happen today?"

"Well… Um, Rachel, this is some serious stuff. If I tell you, it's going to hurt, and you have to harden your heart to some degree to even hear it or it'll tear you up inside."

"Is it that bad?"

"Yes. Sean wouldn't even want me telling you, but I've already noticed how much it's affecting him. In warfare, there isn't anyone like you, Rachel, to talk someone down from something like this, but as much as you and Sean love each other, I think you can help him."

"Tell me, Mike."

"Today, just here around the Eugene-Springfield area, we had to put down almost three hundred people."

"My God! It's really that bad?"

"Yes, and it's only going to get worse. But that's not what got to Sean. Today Sean and his partner came up on an eight-year-old girl wandering in the street. She attacked the car as they drove by. Driving down the street a ways, Sean got out to take the shot. She was definitely stage two infected—glazed eyes, excessive drooling, aggressive behavior. There wasn't anything else Sean could do. She was heading for him as he took the shot."

"Oh, Sean. How that must have hurt!"

"Rachel, Sean and I have seen things in war, but that today affected him a lot. Later in the afternoon, another officer was faced with another child, about six years old. He couldn't do it, so Sean was called over. Six-year-old boy. If you could get him to your room and talk to him, love on him, let him know that there are things still worth saving and living for… anything to ease the pain…"

"Alright, Mike, I'll do that."

Rachel went up to her and Sean's room at bedtime and changed into her nightie. When she had to wait a while for Sean to come in, she realized just how bad that day's incident had affected him, especially as much as Sean had enjoyed himself the night before and again that morning. She was almost ready to go back downstairs to get him, when the door finally opened and Sean walked in. Instead of coming straight to her and giving her kisses and hugs, now he acted with indifference to her—almost like he had been hoping that she would have already fallen asleep. She was hurting so much for him that she was aching. Moving to the edge of the bed, she took his hand as he came out of the bathroom and pulled him down beside her.

"Sean, I love you."

"I love you too, Rachel."

"Then tell me what's wrong. You're not acting like yourself tonight. Didn't our lovemaking last night and this morning make you feel good? I was hoping for and expecting more of the same tonight, but the way you've been acting makes my heart ache. You're sure you still love me?" Rachel was using an approach she was hoping would stir Sean into talking about what had happened that day.

"Oh, Rachel, darling, I'm sorry. I've just got my mind on something else tonight. That's all. I love you more than anything."

Sean put his arms around her in a long, tight embrace, trying to take away her worry, but also trying to dispel what he had been thinking about.

"What happened today, Sean, that has made you act like this?" Rachel asked with tender emotion. "I know something hurt you today, and I also know that as many horrible things you and Mike have seen in war, things can still happen to you that can cause pain. I love you, darling, so much, and I want to help you, so please tell me what happened today."

"Rachel, this is too much for you to bear, nor can I burden you with this thing. I love you too much to hurt you."

"Sean, I'm stronger than you think, and my love for you will see us both through this. Don't you see that not sharing your troubles with me will hurt me more, because then I have to watch you suffer alone through your pain? I spoke my wedding vows to you yesterday, and now you won't let me hold you, encourage you, or support you. Let me support you, sweetheart."

"Are you sure, Rachel? This isn't pretty, and there's no way to sugarcoat it."

"Sean, just tell me what happened, and we'll figure it out."

"Today there was a lot of stage two on the streets. They were showing up every couple of minutes all across the county. If it wasn't happening to us personally, we were still hearing everything over the radio. And then I saw a girl walking down the street, not like someone going somewhere, but rather wandering in an erratic fashion. She looked about eight years old, and as we came abreast of her in the car, she attacked us. We drove down the street a ways, and I got out with my rifle. She was hurrying toward us, and as I raised my rifle with the scope on her face, I had to make sure she was stage two. Her eyes, the pain and agony on her face, the drool on her chin… I knew she was infected and what I had to do, but I had to make sure before I squeezed the trigger. I took her out. Then a while later, another officer was faced with the same thing, only that time it was a six-year-old boy. He couldn't pull the trigger. I was requested to go over and take care of it, because I'm the hard ass that could shoot my own mother if I had to. Rachel, I can detach myself somewhat when I need to, harden my heart for the task at hand, and then when it's done, I can look at it objectively and be about my business. That's the way I handled it today. But that's not actually what's bothering me…" Sean paused for a moment to order his thoughts before he continued.

Rachel, following his recital of what happened was also reading between the lines, and as Sean spoke his last words, she understood with a lover's insight, what he was about to tell her.

"Rachel, I'm worried over, uh… having children in the midst of this mess. After that happened today, all I could think about was you, and us, having unprotected sex. If you got pregnant, and our baby caught this, I don't know if we could go through that. From now on, there won't be any abortions if you get pregnant. So, I think we need to wait, but if I keep kissing you all the time, I can't wait; I won't be able to wait. So, I have to draw back from you so we won't. Rachel, I can't go through that." Sean's eyes started to water, and a single tear rolled down one cheek.

Rachel hugged him tightly, and her own tears started to fall. Holding him for a long moment, she felt his tears through her nightie, and pulling away from him, she reached up and wiped his tears away, holding his face in her hands as she looked him in the eyes.

"Sean, I won't get pregnant. There's nothing to worry about. I've been taking birth control pills, so everything will be alright."

"That package that your mom had me pick up… Was that the birth control pills?"

"Yes."

"But that was only five days ago. You could still get pregnant, because we didn't wait long enough for them to take effect. You might be pregnant already."

"No, Sean. When Mom could see how much I loved you, adored you, and that same love was returned, she took me down to the health clinic to get me started on birth control right away. She thought that since I had never known true love before and since you were a grown man with experience and needs… well, she was afraid that eventually I might succumb to your charm and my own growing desire. I've been on the pill for ten days, not four. The package you picked up was a larger supply that she called a friend of hers in the clinic to get in case I couldn't get anymore because of the virus."

Sean lowered his lips to hers in a gentle sweet kiss.

"Now that's the Sean I know."

Immediately, she felt his caressing hands and was overjoyed with the results of her efforts.

"I'll show you a part of Sean you don't know yet. Are you ready for this?"

She smiled. "Oh, yes, darling… I'm ready."

CHAPTER THIRTY-TWO

The next day was pretty much the same for the police force, but a little more in numbers for the stage two. There also seemed to be more children in the mix. Earlier in the spread of the virus, most parents had been taking their infected children to the hospital, but as more of them had realized that they were only going to be put to death, more and more parents were opting to keep their sick kids home, hoping that somehow or some way their children would eventually get better. Also in the mix was the simple fact that one or both of the parents had been taken to the hospital, leaving infected children home alone to fend for themselves and, eventually, turning to stage two all alone and somehow escaping the house into public.

The police force itself was still losing personnel that would end up with the symptoms—most of them from someone in their own family infecting them. Many kids that had been attending school, right up until the Presidential bulletin on day twenty-two, had come down with the symptoms on day thirty-one, and because of the family not taking precautionary measures, they also were infected. With up to five thousand people starting symptoms on day thirty-two and another seven thousand on day thirty-three, the virus was showing no signs of slowing. Eventually, the numbers would start to be skewed because of the fewer people left to infect were becoming more isolated and careful.

The military casualties accredited to the disease were climbing into the forty-five-percent range, and most police forces across the nation were about the same. Healthcare workers that had succumbed to the virus were approaching the fifty-percent mark. The larger cities that had been initially targeted by the terrorists were being overrun by the stage two infected. Even the military was having trouble putting them all down. Riots had begun in most of those cities, because the lack of food was resulting in the first hunger pangs of starvation. Most of the apartment house tenants had no extra food storage, other than what could fit in their small overhead freezer in their refrigerator. Once their meat, bread, and junk food were gone, all they had left was canned goods and noodles of some sort. As they began scavenging for extra food in the apartments that were left empty because the tenants had succumbed to the disease, fights were breaking out, and people were getting beat down if not actually killed.

As more and more people were leaving their apartments and houses looking for food, they were getting attacked by the stage two infected, and with so many people without weapons, new people were becoming infected to the tune of thousands per day. The starving people could not outwait the virus and had to eventually brave their fears in search of sustenance. People were breaking into restaurants and cafes, fast food joints, grocery stores, and other people's houses looking for food. Some of thc fast food places had simply closed because of the advancing disease, and yet their freezers were still full of meat and other frozen goods. As more people left the overcrowded cities for rural areas and then eventually the countryside, they were unwittingly spreading the virus to the least affected areas.

But on the other hand, the people living in the country always had more food stored at any given time, because most of them either raised their own beef or hogs and had a separate stand-up freezer for the storage of the meat that they raised or they had bought a side of beef from someone else. Along with the fact that many country folks had their own vegetable gardens, they also did a lot of their own canning of fruits and vegetables. For these reasons, many country folk could outlast city dwellers without having to resupply their food closets, but eventually they too would have to go out in search of food. With most of them owning firearms, they were better able to hunt or to procure meat from the cattle herd of the local rancher, which in turn may or may not turn into a gun battle. Confrontations would depend on the generosity or mercy of the owner of the cattle, or a lack thereof.

As society would continue to spiral out of control, it was going to boil down to the temperament of the one who had much, and if he was willing to share or not. Up to a certain point, there could be cooperation among the dwindling population, but as that same cooperation began to endanger a certain group or family, things could turn into a bloodbath in a hurry.

Both Sean and Mike had some conversations with Mitch and Kevin about the decline of society and the need to continually have a lookout on the farm. Through that discussion, it was decided that Steve, Mitch, or Kevin was to be on lookout every day, all day long, taking turns as was needed. As long as Sean and Mike were committed to helping the Sheriff's Office with the patrols, the three remaining men would have to provide the protection for the farm. Occasionally, even Rachel and Leah would sit at the upstairs window keeping watch, waiting patiently, for what exactly…? They weren't really sure.

"Mr. President, we've received communication back from Russia, and we're ready for you in the conference room."

"Okay, Bob, I'll be right there."

President Nathan Roberts was more than anxious to see the reply from the Russian President. His reply could mean life or death to the remainder of the American people, and he was hoping that he and his family would be included in those survivors. Without an agreement, there would be no hope of saving the last of his people from the horrors of being the spoils of conquest. Hurriedly, he made his way to the conference room to hear their reply.

As he entered the room, there were several others just arriving, and after taking his seat, a few more straggled in. As soon as all the seats were full, with several people standing also, a video from Russia's President started to play on several monitors around the room. All the people present could both watch and hear the message they were putting their hope in.

"Mr. President, I am Sergei Andropov, the new President of Russia. The virus has taken its toll in both of our countries, and because of that, we have been made aware of how important it is to survive so that mankind will not be wiped out. I and all of my cabinet members listened to your message with heavy hearts, and as you explained the condition of your country, my heart went out to you and your people. And because of your honesty to share with us the full scope of your situation and the gravity of your outcome and that of the human race, we are in unanimous agreement with your plan. If we are the ones to survive this catastrophic epidemic and the possible war with China, we will welcome your people into ours with open arms, even as you have embraced our own people throughout history.

"In the recent past, we have been allies with China to a certain degree with both of us profiting from our interaction. Now, as we've watched China's defensive maneuvers against us, we don't understand the aggression that has started, but we will defend against it. In all the years that we have faced each other down, we never truly had the worry that you would actually launch a nuclear attack against us without it being in retaliation for our own launch. However, it is not so with China. We know her better than you, and we know she will want to take your country for her own people. We also know that she will stop at nothing to get it. I believe that we now stand in her way. We will protect ourselves in the best way that we can.

"Our country was not infected to the degree that your nation was, but we still do not have the epidemic under control. We have realized that as soon as symptoms are started, we have to put the infected down immediately to slow the advance of the virus. Our people have been made aware of the seriousness of survival for our nation, and as hard as it is to do so, our people are cooperating with our decision. With that in mind, we would share with you our gratitude in what your offer has meant to us, not only the help militarily, but in your thoughts for us to become one people in the future. We have moved all of our uninfected that we have secured, through the program that you shared with us previously, into our nuclear resistant bunkers. They will be able to survive the attack for up to one year. If this turns into a nuclear war and we lose most of our population, we need you, if you are able, to retrieve our people from their bunkers and move them to the U.S. to become your people. In the documents with this communication, you will find the coordinates for all of those bunkers that you may rescue them as soon as you're able.

"This communication is all that you will receive from us until we are attacked or until we are sure that China will not do so. If they attack, we assume that you will know immediately and will know what to do in the ensuing exchange. If that happens, our own people will be in need of your assistance in the future, rather than the other way around. If my council and I deem it necessary to launch a first strike, we will send you a time at which we will launch one hour ahead so that you may prepare. Sincerely, all of my people thank you for your offer of friendship. Until we meet again, my friend."

For the last view of the DVD, the camera panned around their conference room, revealing all of Russia's leaders that would stand beside them in the future, and as each one came into view, his right hand raised to cover his heart in a solemn pledge.

Nathan looked around his own conference room at all the faces that were teary-eyed, if not downright crying, and he began to shed his own tears of relief and gratitude.

As soon as he had his emotions under control, he turned to his aid to get his attention. "Make a copy of this DVD and also a copy of the DVD we sent to Russia, and I will also make another DVD recording with a message to the Prime Minister of the UK. I want all three of them in a package delivered to England as soon as possible in the same manner as Russia. I want them completely aware of what's going on and that we are in a pact with Russia to help them against the Chinese and that they could join us in that effort."

"Yes, sir, I'll get on it right away."

Turning to the Secretary of Defense, he said, "I don't know how you need to work it out, but if China launches on Russia, we need to launch a counterattack as soon as possible. Figure out how we need to accomplish that, including contacting our submarine captains and putting them on high alert. We need to get all our missiles locked in for targets. Get your people working on it right away and let me know when it's all set."

The next day, Sean received a call from his dad, explaining that they had to put down two different stage two people who had wandered onto the property. He told him that he would have the county send out a crew and not to get near them. Things were beginning to get hairy, although there weren't as many stage two within the city limits that day so far. Each day's fluctuation in numbers could go up or down, but typically they were always on the increase. Things seemed to be going along okay, until the sheriff called in and said that he was infected. His son had been sneaking out of the house and had been infected by one of his friends. Not knowing that he had been infected, when he became symptomatic, the sheriff and his wife were also infected. That's when things really started to go bad. The undersheriff could handle running things, but the sheriff himself wasn't ready to relinquish control. Some of the deputies were thinking it was no longer any use to keep coming in when they had their own families to take care of, for every day away from them was leaving them in danger.

The lead health official for the county stopped by to fill them in on what the current numbers were and what they figured was coming. In an afternoon briefing at the change of shifts, he gave them the news.

"Worldwide, there will be five hundred thousand infected turning to stage two today. As many as two hundred million people will be infected today, which brings the total up to one billion so far. Fifteen million will begin showing symptoms today and will start infecting others. Here in Lane County, our numbers are considerably lower, but the percentages are still close. We may have up to thirty thousand infected today, five thousand starting symptoms, and several hundred turning to stage two. But a word of warning, there are only two more days of low numbers of stage two. The third day from now will be the beginning of tier three infected turning to stage two, which we estimate might be as high as two to four thousand in one day."

"Two to four thousand? How are we supposed to be able to handle that?" one of the deputies asked.

"We've barely survived the days we had four hundred, and now we have fewer men to help. Even the city police have lost twenty-five percent of their force. Without any military aid, we're doomed."

"There won't be any military help coming our way. The day we have two to four thousand stage two infected, the Portland area will have almost twenty thousand turning, so they'll have to keep the military up there and at Salem. On one other point, the mayors of both Eugene and Springfield are now infected with most of their staff and office personnel."

"Then who's going to keep leading us and making the decisions?"

"As far as keeping some food supplies being delivered, I'm in charge. As far as your duties, you can still take orders from your sheriff; he isn't even symptomatic yet. It's just that he won't want to come in and be around you guys to infect you, although he won't be contagious for another eight days."

"If we've lost forty percent of our local patrol force, how will we take care of that many?" The deputy that asked the question still needed a viable answer, rather than just rhetoric from another uninformed political ass.

Sean decided to add his thoughts. "How many deputies are still stationed at the county jail and the courthouse?"

"I'm not sure of the exact number, but at least ten or so. I can find out," answered Lonnie, the undersheriff.

"Find out and then reassign all of them to patrol. We won't need them at the courthouse anymore and maybe just leave a skeleton crew at the jail, because you won't be moving prisoners anymore. Bolster the jailer numbers with some reserve deputies that aren't trained or experienced with patrol duties and get the more experienced deputies back out in the field. Would that work?"

"It would certainly help. I'll make some calls right away and see what we can get arranged."

"Also see if we can get more ammo down here too for the M4s. With that many stage two just around the corner, we don't want to run out of ammo."

"You're right. I'll see what I can do."

CHAPTER THIRTY-THREE

One of the two that was jealous of Sean in the department suggested that they start patrolling with one deputy per vehicle to increase their patrol capabilities. Sean nixed the idea, because any time a deputy stepped out of thc car, he needed someone to watch his back. The two deputies and one of their close buddies decided to go it alone anyway, and the undersheriff, because he wasn't actually ready for leadership, let them do it.

Around mid-morning, the single deputy that followed the lead of the other two that hated Sean called in to say there were two stage two infected and gave his location. As he took out the two, another one came running up behind him and before he could fire, he was taken down and bit several times before he could free himself. Eventually taking out the one that attacked him, he called it in to let everyone know what had happened. Everyone listening could tell that he was crying as he talked.

When he finished, he threw some serious expletives at Ed, the deputy that talked him into going it alone. Ranting about a comparison between Sean and him, he called Ed a wanna-be leader that wasn't really worth a damn. He also said that he hoped Ed got his in the end.

Unfortunately, at the end of the shift, the bitten deputy waited for Ed to drive up, and as he got out of the car, he shot him four times in the chest and once in the head as he lay on the pavement. Looking him over, he spit on him. As other deputies came running up, he put his pistol barrel against his head, just above his ear, and pulled the trigger.

Then they were short two more deputies. From that moment on, all of the deputies asked Sean for advice on how to handle certain situations and showed him a lot of respect. There was still one more deputy that didn't like Sean, Jack, the one that Sean had reprimanded for not showing respect for the ones he was killing. The attention that Sean was receiving began to eat away at Jack like a festering sore, but he knew that there was nothing he could do about it. He would bide his time, and in the future, if an opportunity presented itself, he would take Sean out.

Mitch had been out back checking the fences to make sure none of his cows could get out. When he walked back into the house, Beth let him know that he needed to return a phone call. He didn't recognize the number, but the name wrote down was Joe. He immediately called him back.

"Hey, Mitch, this is Joe."

"Yeah, Joe. You been getting along alright? Anyone sick?"

"We're getting by, Mitch, but just barely. Everyone is still healthy, but people are dying all around us. We haven't been outside in over a week, and I've been too nervous to go to the store."

"You've got a son don't you?"

"Yes. He's almost eighteen, and also a daughter that's sixteen. I'm lucky I haven't lost anyone, because they've both been calling friends for the last ten days, and now over half of them are gone and some that are left are infected."

"Joe, I'm assuming that you want to get out of the city?"

"Yeah, Mitch. We just can't take this anymore. I've seen at least ten people killed by the police on our street. Some of them were our neighbors."

"Alright, Joe, my offer still stands. How many days have you been holed up?"

"Since two days after you guys came in and bought all that ammo. I sold all my guns and ammo and almost all of my camping and survival gear. There wasn't any more reason to stay at the store, so I've been at home ever since. Why?"

"If you've been in the house, and that includes all of you, for at least ten days, and no one has come down with any symptoms, then you should be in the clear. You sure neither one of the kids snuck out in those ten days?"

"Yeah, I'm pretty sure. I can check to make sure." Mitch could hear Joe asking questions and someone answering. "No one's been out of the house except to step out in the yard and look down the street."

"Sean told me that one of the sheriff's kids snuck out and got infected and now his whole family has got it. We've got to be careful. None of us here has it, and we're getting along alright, but we have to be careful about letting anyone else in or it could kill all of us."

"I understand, Mitch. We're good. So… can you take us in?"

"Yeah, Joe. How much stuff will you need to bring over? Do you have a camp trailer?"

"Yes, I've got one. It's a fifth wheel, thirty-six foot. You want me to bring that?"

"That would be great, just in case the sleeping arrangements are getting tight. Is it at your house or a storage yard?"

"It's here, behind the fence. This is pretty new to me, Mitch, so what all should I bring?"

"Most of your clothes and boots, but not anything the family's not gonna wear. You'll be limited on space. No furniture, of course, except maybe camp chairs, guns and ammo, any food you have left, keepsakes that you don't want to lose, stand-up freezer if you have it, bedding and any personal stuff you need. Don't forget any medicines you have. You may never get any more of those. I'll give Sean and Mike a call and have them stop by after work and give you a hand. Start loading everything you want to take in the trailer, and if you load anything in the car or truck, be sure to carry your gun and never go outside alone. I'll give Sean your number, and he'll call you for your address and line it up. Sound good?"

"Yeah, Mitch, that sounds real good… and thanks. This means so much to me."

"Don't mention it, Joe. You'll be helping us too. The more people and guns we have the better we'll be able to survive. I'll see you tonight, and if you got any more questions, just give me a call."

Just before dark, Joe and the boys rolled in with Joe's wife driving her own car. Mitch and Kevin had moved his trailer out beside the barn to make room for Joe's trailer next to the RV septic dump that Mitch had installed for his own trailer. If they wanted to stay in the fifth wheel, it would be all set up for them. Sean's truck was loaded down with all the big stuff that wouldn't fit in the trailer, and he backed up to the barn to unload.

After Mitch had guided Joe into place and he climbed out of his truck, the two gripped hands tightly in an understanding of mutual agreement and appreciation. As Joe looked around the group that had come out to welcome his arrival, he noticed that everyone had either a pistol on their belt or a weapon in their hand, women included.

"Joe, this is my wife, Beth. Sean's wife is Rachel, and Rachel's family is her brother, Steve; her sister, Leah; her mom, Joanna; and her dad, Kevin. And this dark-haired beauty is Hailee, Mike's girlfriend."

"Hello, everyone. I wish this could have been under more pleasant circumstances. This is my wife Abigail or 'Abbey' for short, and this is my son, Ryan, and my daughter, Riley. Just let us know what you want us to do, and we'll be more than happy to help."

"Joe, the most important thing is to always carry a weapon with you. We've killed two of the stage two here, and there's likely to be more as the numbers climb. Sean was told that the day after tomorrow, as the tier three infected turn to stage two, there could be as many as four thousand in Lane County. Up 'til now, the most they've had is four hundred or so in one day. It could start getting a little more exciting around here shortly. Sean and Mike have been bringing in extra food supplies daily as they're already in town. Other than that, we keep watch and try to amuse ourselves with games or reading," explained Mitch.

"I can tell you right now, things are going to be better than we had it at home. We want to thank you for letting us come out. We really appreciate this."

"Have you had dinner yet? We've got enough to feed you if you're hungry."

"That sounds wonderful, Mitch. We haven't had a good meal in a couple of days."

"Come on in then. We can help you unpack after you eat."

Sean was finding it extremely difficult to leave Rachel in the mornings, as he was increasingly worried about her and the family as each day went by. One more day of several hundred to take out and then the first big day tomorrow. He was going to need to check on the ammo delivery to make sure that they got it in, or they would be in trouble tomorrow when the big wave started.

Thinking about the numbers, the police force and deputies would be putting down about twenty people per hour on the current day for twenty-four hours straight, and then it would all start again the next day, but it would increase to about two hundred per hour, depending on how many were in the hospital and would be euthanized. If they didn't get more ammo, they would be overrun with infected, and there would be no way to stop all of them. With that many roaming the street, no one would be safe in town. As more people were out scavenging for food, things could get ugly in a hurry.

Thinking about the best and safest way to take out so many, Sean was thinking about an elevated position that would be mobile, easy and quick to fire off of, without the possibility of an infected coming up on their blind side. With so many to take out, it would be dangerous every time they got out of the car to take the shot. The top of a one or two ton panel truck would be ideal. If they could either weld or bolt down a chair and shooting platform, and maybe a safety rail and with a harness they could take out a lot of infected quickly and in a safe manner.

As soon as he entered the office, he shared the idea with Lonnie, the undersheriff, to see what he thought about it. By the end of the day, they had two panel trucks set up and radio sets for the shooter to communicate with the driver. All of the body disposal crews had been armed once they had their first altercation, but it was still necessary to have a shooter with them because of the inherent danger with so many infected.

The following day, Sean was chosen to ride one of the panel trucks and the other was the designated sniper for the department. They worked so well that Lonnie had two more fixed up that day for the city police to use the following day. The body disposal crews started using sixteen-foot dump-bed trailers to decrease time at the pit and to get back to work faster. They had already replaced four people on the disposal crews because of the virus, so there was a continually decreasing pool of workers for them to choose from. Along with four more deputies starting to show symptoms and several staff members in the office, their numbers continued to be depleted.

By the end of the day, another deputy was showing symptoms, and the city police departments weren't faring any better, so much so, that if they lost ten more they would be in danger of everyone quitting and fending for themselves. Without any military to help, they were going to lose all of their men, and the city would be overrun. At that point, anyone venturing outside would be attacked and infected.

At the end of their shift, Sean let the undersheriff know that Mike would drive the panel truck home that night and back in thc morning, and the two of them would take out as many as they could in both directions. Sean had his M4 and a sniper rifle with a 6x24x44 powered scope on it, and before they left the department, they loaded up several cartons of the 5.56 shells and more mags for the M4s.

On the way home that night, they stopped by the store, but there wasn't any food left to buy. They would try again in the morning, and instead of taking the direct route home, they made one more pass through the city's edge that was their patrol and took out another thirty-two infected before leaving town.

Sean climbed in front as soon as they were past the edge of town and called Mitch to let him know what was going on so they wouldn't get nervous when they drove up.

Arriving home, Sean pulled the men aside to let them know how things were going in town.

"We've lost seven deputies to the virus and over half of the office staff. Two deputies called in and said they were finished and that it was useless. The city police departments are also similarly affected. The body removal crews are being depleted, and tomorrow they said there might be four thousand stage two starting. That means, every hour, there might be about two hundred infected to put down around the clock. That also means that by the time we get to the office in the morning, we'll be taking out all the ones that might have turned over night. We might have five hundred to kill on the way to work."

"Would you like Joe and me to drive in and help knock down a few?" asked Mitch.

"No. Mike and I don't want you guys leaving the farm. There might be some of them showing up around here tomorrow with that many turning. If anyone here gets infected by one stray, it'll ruin everything we have here. It's bad enough that Mike and I are going out, but we're always protected, and we know what we're doing. If we lose any more men, we'll have to consider quitting. We're also at that point that all the people that aren't infected, and who have been holed up, will start going out to collect food. If anyone shows up here, you'll have to be ready for that."

"And what should we do if that happens?"

"You'll have to use your own judgment, Dad. If you feel all scratchy inside when you're talking to them, like it just doesn't feel good to you, send them on their way. If it's a stray kid or female, you'll have to find out their situation: Are they sick? Is anyone in their family sick? Why are they alone? Where are they from, and how long it's been since they were around anyone that was sick? If you feel good about taking someone in then we'll have to do the shop quarantine plan that we discussed earlier. If you have any questions about it, you can call me."

"Alright, Son. That's pretty plain and simple. Let's go in and eat dinner; it's all ready."

CHAPTER THIRTY-FOUR

The Russian President called a meeting of his Cabinet and military leaders to discuss new intel on China's maneuverings and what their response should be.

"Andrei, if we launch a first strikc, what's going to be the best way to avoid their missile defense systems?"

"The best way would be to infiltrate across their border at all of their missile defense locations and then by either lasing the target and sending in small missiles to take them out or we blow them up with shoulder launched rockets. We could also send in our jets, under the radar, to the farther away sites and take them out. Either way, we might lose a lot of men; but if they were successful, it would make our first strike more effective."

"And if we just launch without that preparation?"

"I think that at least fifty percent of our cruise missiles will still make it past their defenses, maybe more. Missile defense is still like hitting a bullet with a bullet, and at the speeds that cruise missiles travel, there will be a lot of misses."

"How long will it take to set up and implement the plan for our men to slip in and take out some of their defenses?"

"At this point, not too long. Our men are already in place along the border with the necessary weapons. It's only a matter of getting them set up on a time schedule and with everyone's particular target. It will have to be orchestrated on a timetable so that it happens at the same time, causing our launch to take place within minutes of our attack."

"Are we all in agreement that China is planning an attack against us and that a first strike on our part would be our best course of action?" asked the President.

"China was the first to make a move without any provocation at all. That's enough to tell me they are at least thinking of a strike. If we wait for them to make the first strike, then we're finished."

"I agree."

"I also agree."

It was a unanimous decision among all his leaders.

"Work up a plan and let's get it going. If we can take out at least some of their defenses, and then beat them to the punch, we might survive. Let me know as soon as it's ready to go."

"Right away, sir."

Because of the workload they were expecting, Sean and Mike left earlier than normal the next morning. Sean rode in the cab until they reached the outskirts, only stopping twice to take out an infected wandering in a field. Once he was on top, dressed in several layers to stay warm, they immediately started a stop and go pattern of movement as there were quite a few stage two already out and about. By the time they reached the department headquarters, they had already taken out over a hundred infected.

"Sir, it's pretty crazy out there this morning. We hit the edge of town at 6:30 and from there to here, we took down over a hundred infected. Has everyone else shown up?" Sean asked.

"No, we had three more call in already with symptoms, and two others said it's just too dangerous to leave their families anymore. Lisa, in the dispatch, came in, and there were only three deputies besides you two. Two of them went out on patrol in the other panel truck. I could go out with the other deputy, but that would leave Lisa here all alone, and I don't think that would be a good idea."

"That's not looking too good. What do you think we should do? Will there be anyone here tomorrow?" asked Mike.

"The way we've been losing guys… you two might be the only ones that show up tomorrow," began Lonnie. "With several thousand stage two every day now, we'll be overrun. The county is too large for what few men we have left. The city police departments are still hanging in there, but they have more officers than we do. If you guys are going to keep making sweeps and keep coming into town every day, you should load up half of the ammunition we have left so you won't have to come back here to the office. There's no paperwork or reports to fill out anymore, so you might as well stay out in the field and take out as many as you can."

"What about you? Are you going to call it quits?" asked Sean.

"No. I'll keep coming in. If I have an officer to team up with I'll start going on patrol. I'm torn on whether to have Lisa stay or go. It's not safe to leave her alone, but I also feel like we need a dispatcher. It's not safe to even have her walk to the door from her car when no one else is here."

"What good is a dispatcher if there's no one to dispatch?" Mike asked. "Might be best to have her stay home from now on."

"I'll see what she has to say about that. She might feel safer here than where she lives. You guys load up that ammo and take a couple more M4s with you too. You never know if you'll need 'em and as long as there aren't any deputies here, no one else needs them. I'll call the military and see about getting another shipment of ammo before it's too late. If this thing blows completely up, the extra guns and ammo might save you guys in the future. If, by chance, we get more deputies coming back, you can bring the extra guns back if I need them. Okay?"

"Sounds good. Are we going to worry about body disposal anymore or are the crews still gonna show up?"

"I think they're still going to work, but when I find out for sure, I'll give you a call on the radio."

"Alright. You'll need to unlock the armory, and then we'll be on our way. Call us if you need anything."

Sean and Mike ended up taking fifteen thousand rounds of the 5.56mm, five hundred rounds for the .308 sniper rifle, about two thousand rounds of 9mm, a thousand rounds of .45 caliber, and decided to take four M4s with them. By the look of things, all the other deputies must have kept their M4s, and they were leaving four for anyone else that might show up. Mike also took a sniper rifle for himself, and as they were carrying the last load out, the undersheriff gave them a key to the front door and told them where they could find a key to the armory if they needed more ammo. Shaking hands with Lonnie, they loaded up the last of their things in the panel truck. Sean climbed up top and they took off.

Only going one block, Mike braked to a stop, and Sean took out three more before moving on. At almost every intersection he was able to take out one to three people in short order. He could see it was going to be a long day and knew he would have to trade off with Mike a couple of times throughout the day.

His dad called to let him know they took out a couple of stage two, and Sean reminded him to wear protective gear whenever they had to deal with a body. The best way to deal with it would be to tie a rope around the feet and drag it away with the four-wheeler.

Before they knew it, the day was gone, and they were headed for home. Keeping a rough tally, they let Lonnie know that they had taken out almost eleven hundred infected. Having kept in touch with the other crew of deputies, they had been able to correlate their patrol paths to be the most effective, and they also found out that another seven hundred infected had been taken out. The city police forces had taken out another two thousand or so, with Springfield still having about eleven officers and Eugene having seventeen. The forces were dwindling fast, and without military support, they would eventually disappear from the public scene. When that happened, it would be up to surviving individuals to take out the increasing numbers of infected. Sean realized that there wouldn't be nearly enough ammo to accomplish what needed to be done, unless they received another shipment from the military.

Jack Leland, the sheriff's deputy that was initially paired up with Sean when the first stage two infected began walking the streets, had stopped showing up for work. He had even kept his M4 and had kept two thousand rounds of ammo for it. He just didn't think they were doing that much good anymore, and he couldn't stand being around Sean and Mike for one more day—Sean especially. What a jerk. Everyone was thinking so much of him, but he knew better. He just liked being in the limelight. One of these days, he might get a chance to take him out. If he was to drive by on the top of that panel truck, he would be a sitting duck, and from his second-story apartment window, it would be so easy. And then if Mike were to stop, he would take him out too, as soon as he got out of the truck. He would show them.

His girlfriend had come down with the virus, so he couldn't swing by her house anymore. He was lucky she started showing symptoms during the couple of days that he hadn't been around. Otherwise, he might have become one of those stage two, and Sean would be putting him down. Getting bored living by himself, he started thinking about the lack of law enforcement and what that would mean. He could sure use some female company, and he knew where a good-looking sexy woman lived just down the street. She lived alone, and if he went to visit her and talked his way into the house, he could do whatever he wanted, because there wouldn't be any police to come investigating. He could do whatever he wanted and wouldn't get in trouble for it. He grabbed up his pistol belt and rifle and headed for the door.

"Mr. President, we've just received a message from the Russian President. It only said, 'In one hour.' Does it mean they're launching in one hour?"

"I would assume so. Get everyone in here right away."

"Yes, sir."

Ten minutes later, the Cabinet and Joint Chiefs were gathered in the room, and they were made aware of the message.

"Any comments? If this means they're launching a first strike, we need to launch with them," the President explained.

"Are we absolutely sure that's what it means? We don't want to launch a premature attack."

"We have to assume that's what it means. They can't come right out and say they're launching in case China is able to intercept it. They said we wouldn't hear from them until an attack started. I think we need to do whatever it takes to be able to launch with them."

"I think if we do that, then we need to wait for confirmation from our satellites to push the final button. As soon as we detect a launch, then we launch our arsenal. We would only be two or three minutes behind. That way, we won't be the first to launch."

"Let's bring up any satellite feeds that we have in the area and see what's going on. And then get things rolling so that we can launch our missiles as soon as we detect their launch. Are there any doubts about what we're going to do?" asked the President.

"If Russia has decided to strike first, then they must believe that they're in imminent danger of a first strike from China. They've decided to beat them to the punch in hopes of knocking out some of their retaliatory abilities," decided the Secretary of Defense.

"There's always doubt when you're about to embark on something that is ultimately going to cost several hundred million lives. The question is, are we ready to back up our promise to Russia. Regardless of the consequences. I think we should."

The President looked around the room at all of the expectant faces. "Are we all in agreement to launch with Russia? With a three minute delay to be on the safe side?"

All hands were eventually raised in the air. None of them really wanted to, but as they had reached an agreement with Russia already, they were ready to stand by it. Come what may.

"Alright, gentlemen, make it happen. Send a coded message to London to let them know what we're doing. As soon as we see a launch, we will launch ourselves."

For the next forty-five minutes, they were patiently waiting for the satellites to reveal a massive launch of nuclear missiles. Instead, many smaller explosions, non-nuclear, all along the Chinese border with Russia arrested their attention. All on the Chinese side. Zooming in, they could see that the Russians had tried to disable as many of the Chinese missile defense emplacements as possible. Within thirty seconds of those explosions, Russia launched two medium range rockets over China, which then detonated two large nuclear explosions, which emitted an Electromagnetic Pulse that knocked out most of the remaining missile defense of the nation, as well as most of the nation's electrical grid. Within minutes of that explosion, the rest of their massive arsenal of ICBMs from their ground-based silos was launched, while many of their submarines launched missiles from off the coast. There was also a launch of their bomber fleet out of their eastern bases, flying directly south.

"Launch our first wave of missiles."

"Yes, sir."

The order was given to NORAD, and within two minutes, another wave of missiles were erupting from the cold waters of the Pacific off the coast of China. Soon after, there was another wave of missiles, presumably from the English. In the next minute, there was a massive eruption of ICBM launches from all over China. Immediately upon their launch, there were numerous launches of Russia's missile defense network to intercept China's ICBMs and also their shorter range missiles. Within fifteen minutes of taking off, the Russian bombers released their low-flying, short and medium range missiles that didn't have to fly into space to reach their target.

All of the Americans were glued to the scene unfolding on the monitors, with so many missiles crisscrossing paths with one another. Soon there were explosions of light all over China's nation, and a few minutes later, explosions started taking place all over Russia. The Russian missile defense was only about fifty percent successful in knocking out China's missiles, and the rest were hitting all of Russia's largest cities, with three explosions in Moscow alone.

The Chinese had ten times the number of nuclear warheads that Russia or the U.S. thought they had, and if it wasn't for Russia's missile defense system, Russia would have almost been wiped off the map.

China, on the other hand, had approximately three thousand nuclear warheads explode around its nation, effectively removing it from future existence. Whoever didn't die in the actual explosions, would die a painful death of radiation burns, poisoning, or lack of medical care for their injuries. There would be no one coming to their rescue after the bombing—no military personnel, no doctors, no other nation's relief teams… absolutely no one. They were on their own. Even the ones that survived the horrendous bombing would eventually die because of the continued drifting radiation, the lack of food and healthy water, and the lack of electricity for the approaching winter. Even the theory of nuclear winter may have its effect, not just on China, but the whole world. It had been up to that time a theory only, and now it would be revealed as true or become another debunked theory of the thinking elite.

One aspect of collateral damage would be how much radiation would drift east on the prevailing winds and affect Taiwan, Japan, and eventually the West Coast of the U.S. With the virus already taking a heavy toll on Taiwan and Japan, with no end in sight, the radiation issue might not even come into play. One possibility of help would be the seasonal rain showers that were due. If they came quickly and were heavy and prolonged, they could effectively wash away a lot of the radiation as well as knock it out of the sky to prevent its spreading across the ocean.

All across the world, news stations were carrying videos of some of the nuclear blasts that were broadcast before they were knocked off the airwaves by the EMP shockwave. Taiwan was still broadcasting video that they had taken, and any other news organization that were close enough to the borders of either country were still broadcasting the images of the mushroom cloud pillars. Planes were being launched to fly closer to the devastated areas to film some of the destruction up close. Drones launched by the U.S. military were already airborne and closing in on the Capitals of China and Russia to see what was left of them. The President had his men trying to contact the Russian government to find out if the Russian President and his staff survived the bombing, but they weren't receiving any answers.

"How soon can we send in men to locate some of the bunker locations to check for survivors?" asked the President.

"It would be best to wait a few days at least to let the radiation dissipate somewhat. Even if we found them, it might not be feasible to remove them. With the virus still spreading, they might just as easily be infected with that and die. Our goal is their survival. If the bunkers were built to resist a nuclear attack, then they should be alright for quite some time. If the virus will virtually be played out in four weeks, then we could send in teams for their rescue, and by then the radiation will have depleted enough not to cause too many issues as long as our people stay protected. That is, if we still have the people and the means to perform the operation."

"At least make a record of what needs to be done so that if we ourselves don't survive this, those that succeed us will know what needs to be done. We will do everything in our power to honor our agreement with Russia."

"Yes, sir."

CHAPTER THIRTY-FIVE

Leaving two of the M4s with Mitch and some of the ammo, Sean and Mike drove the panel truck into town and started taking down the infected. They eventually worked their way around to the cardlock gas pumps that the county used to gas up their vehicles and filled up their tank. Sean stayed up top keeping a lookout, while Mike did the pumping. Leaving the area, they were taking out infected almost every couple of hundred feet. As they entered a residential area, with large leafy trees lining the streets, green lawns with shrubs, fences surrounding some of the yards, they knocked down several infected along one street as far out as two hundred yards. As the last one went down, a man came running from a house to get their attention. Sean swung his rifle and lined up the scope. Seeing the man's face, he barely kept from pulling the trigger.

"What are you doing? I almost blew your head off!" Sean yelled down at him.

"We need help! We're out of food, and my family is starving! Please! Please help us!" Something about the man tugged at Sean's heart. His pleas were almost too much for Sean; he was practically crying.

"How many of you are there?"

"Four. My wife and my two boys. They're only four and five years old."

"Do you have a car or a truck?" asked Sean.

"We've got a car."

"Why didn't you leave town before now. It's too dangerous here."

"I didn't know where to go, and the news bulletins said to stay in the house."

"How long since you had anything to eat?"

"Two days. We cooked the last of our noodles and rice and gave it to the boys."

"Is there anyone else alive on this street?"

"We haven't seen anyone. We called some of them that we had numbers for, but we didn't get any answers. We jumped the fence and broke into the house on each side of us to find some food, but it was all gone. They must have packed up and left town."

"Do you have any weapons at all?"

"No. We don't believe in guns."

"Sean, one coming up on our six," Mike spoke into his radio.

Sean turned, lifted his rifle and squeezed off a single round and watched a woman fall. Turning to look at the man again, he asked, "How about now? Do you still hold onto that hogwash?"

"No. I wish I had one right now."

"How many days you guys been holed up without any contact with others?"

"Thirteen days, maybe twelve. Why?"

"Are any of you sick? Got a cold, fever, cough, the chills…?"

"No, we're just starving. Why all the questions?"

"Because we're healthy, and we want to keep it that way. Being careful is the only way to make that happen." Speaking softly into his radio, Sean said, "Mike, I'll stay up top, and you can go inside and check it out. Make sure no one is sick and take our lunch with you. Wear your mask for now."

Looking back down at the man, he asked, "Have you packed up anything to go anywhere?"

"No. We started to, but then changed our minds."

"Go inside and start packing. I'd suggest all the clothes you like to wear, nothing that you won't be wearing, and extra shoes or boots, if you have them. You may be out of food, but if you have any cooking oil, salt, sugar, flour… I'd suggest you load that too. And, please hurry it up; we're sitting ducks out here…"

A few minutes later, Mike walked out, and looking up at Sean, he grinned.

"You should have seen how fast they wolfed down those sandwiches. They were as hungry as anyone I've ever seen. They're also packing as fast as I've ever seen anyone do. They don't want to be left behind."

"I don't blame them. No food, no weapons, no one to call for help, and two young boys to worry about... What do you think we should do with them?"

The breeze picked up for a minute, ruffling the leaves on all the trees along the street—a relaxing sound and out of place with all of the killing that they had been doing.

"Right now, or tonight when we go home?" asked Mike.

"For now we could take them to the department and then out to the house later. There might still be a few things in the vending machines for them to eat."

"I hope so. I could really use a candy bar myself right now. I was just about to eat my sandwich before I traded spots with you," explained Mike.

"I know, but just think how good it made you feel watching those kids eat your sandwich." Out of the corner of his eye, Sean saw another infected coming. "Got another down the street," he noted, as he raised up from the crouch he was in, raised his rifle, sighted it, and squeezed the trigger.

Turning back to Mike, he said, "You want to go check on them? We need to get going."

"Sure thing."

A couple of minutes later, the garage door opened and a fully loaded car started backing out. Mike walked out, jumped in the cab, and they all started down the street.

"I told them we would take them to the station for now and that we'd be stopping frequently to take out the infected. I also told them we'd have something figured out by the end of the day. They were okay with that."

"Good."

Arriving at the station a half-hour later, Sean took down another four infected before anyone could get out of the car to go into the building. The sun was past its Zenith, and the shadows were starting to lengthen. Leaves were blowing along the empty street as the wind would rise in a small gust, and many were piling up against the curb. All of the well-manicured lawn areas between the street curb and the buildings were becoming shabby looking for lack of care. The grass was tall and overgrowing the sidewalks, and with all of the falling leaves scattered everywhere, it was noticeable that no one was working anymore. Unlocking the front door, they all walked through, to see the undersheriff walking toward them, coming from a hallway to the back of the building.

"Glad to see you boys are still at it. What you got going here?"

"These folks got our attention as we were working our way through a residential area east of here. They're starving—completely out of food. We were going to leave them here for now and figure out what we want to do with them sometime this afternoon. Got any ideas?"

"Not me. I've got eight people at my house now, and our food supply won't last too much longer. Lisa moved in last night. She's single and really shouldn't be staying alone anyhow. We might have to start pillaging for food ourselves any day. What's the chances that any houses have any food in them now?"

"Slim to none. Most people stopped buying food six to eight days ago, and they've eaten it up before they got sick and turned, or took it with them when they left to get out of the city. You might get lucky, though, and find a house where someone left for vacation and never made it back home after the first bulletin. Did we get another shipment of ammo?"

"No, but they said if I wanted to come and get it, they would load me up, so I went first thing this morning. Filled the bed of the pick-up with ammo, mostly the 5.56 and 9mm. Mixed in some .45 and the .308. I asked about the mags for the M4s, and they said to take as many as I need, so I grabbed several crates of those, too. I parked the truck in receiving and locked the gates. You guys want to load up some more, you're welcome to it. Only one other crew showed up today, and they've been on the panel truck all morning. That sure has turned out to be good idea, Sean. Safe, quick, and easy."

"Yeah, Lonnie, I certainly like it. Like you said, it's safe and quick. Don't have to worry about your backside while you're taking down everyone out front. We better get back at it. Can you open the vending machines or do you not have a key?" Sean asked. "These folks are still hungry, and Mike and I gave them our lunch so we could use a snack, too."

"I don't have a key but I opened them anyway. Figured it wasn't going to matter anymore, and I was hungry too. Go ahead and help yourselves."

"If you want to unlock that front gate, we'll load up some of that ammo before we leave."

"Sure thing."

Sean called his dad that afternoon to give him a heads up on the family he was bringing out and wanted to get any feedback on it.

"Whatever you think, Son. They don't have any food to bring?"

"No, just some salt, pepper, sugar, some flour, and some other spices that Mike had them throw in. They were pretty hungry when we found 'em."

"I think we should be alright. We do need to butcher a steer pretty soon, though. Our meat supply is running low, and our frozen breads and rolls are too. We've got plenty of wheat in storage, though, that we can start grinding into flour to make our own bread, so we'll be doing our own baking in a few days. If the family wants to stay together, we can put them in one of the trailers. We'll figure something out, Sean, so bring them with you tonight."

"Okay, Dad, thanks. We'll see you tonight." Sean's heart felt lighter as he hung up the phone; he knew that they were making the right decision.

"Hey, Mike, looks like it's a go. I just talked to Dad about it."

"Yeah, I heard over the radio. How many more people do you think we can take in?"

"I don't have an answer for that, Mike. When we come across people in dire need, and especially now that there are so few people that are going to make it through this thing, we need to save as many as possible to repopulate the area. If we can figure out a way to keep them fed with current supplies, and by killing a steer every now and then, we should last until we can start growing as much food as we can next season. It might be a long winter. Our bigger worry may be too many people for the septic system and overloading it. That could make for a nasty scenario."

"If it comes to that, we could just go pick up a tank wherever they sell them, along with the drainpipe, and borrow a backhoe that no one is going to use anymore. You and I could figure out how to put in another complete septic system."

"You're right. That shouldn't be too hard to do. We can get any supplies we need now, at no charge… as long as we can still get fuel."

"You got any idea where to find the fuel delivery truck that comes out to your house to fill your dad's tanks?" asked Mike.

"I can give Dad a call and get an address. Maybe we can work our way over there and take a look."

"Sounds good. While we're at it, look up the address for any local bakeries, and maybe we could find the one that health guy was talking about working with. Maybe we could round up a bunch of bread."

"Alright, I'll call right now and find out."

An hour later, Sean and Mike were sitting in front of the William's Bakery building. They had already cleared out several infected on the street, and as they walked up to the door, they could hear some noise coming from the inside. The door was locked, and no one came out to the front at their knocking. They walked around to the back entrance, just as a man had walked out the back door. His arms were full of loaves of bread, and he was hurrying to his car that was parked only a few feet away. Sean and Mike ran up to him before he was able to unload and climb in. They were still in uniform, so the man wasn't too frightened, other than the fact of being surprised.

"Hey, you guys almost scared the crap outta me. What do you guys want?"

"Well, we see you just loaded up some bread, and we sure could use some. Do you have any more inside?" Sean asked.

"Yeah, I've got plenty. We stopped production for a few days, and then we got word that we needed to keep baking bread and that some government guy was going to come by and pick it up for a distribution center. He had a delivery truck bring us a lot of flour, sugar, and salt, and quite a few eggs so we could keep baking. He stopped by for two days to pick up bread for delivery, but then he missed the last two days. I don't know what happened."

"Tell you what, we could call the city police and see if they could use some of the bread. They might have some ideas on how to get it to some of the starving people around the city. The hard part right now is finding people that aren't infected. Let's get back inside where it's safe, and I'll use your phone to call and find out."

Calling the city police department, he let them know about the bread and where to get it and if they could maybe run a bulletin on the radio or TV to let people know about it and that they could pick up bread at the police station or leave their address for a possible delivery. The main thing was that people needed food, and if bread was available, they needed to be able to get it. Once Sean was done with the call, he was ready to load up some bread himself.

"By the way, this is Mike Taylor, and I'm Sean Dixon."

"I'm Bob Wilson. Glad to meet you."

"We've got fourteen people out on our farm, and we're just about out of bread. We just picked up a young family of four this morning that we're taking with us out to the farm tonight, and they were completely out of food. They hadn't eaten for two days. That'll make it eighteen to feed from now on. We've got four freezers to store it for a couple of weeks, so whatever you can spare would be great."

"Like I said, I've been baking, and that guy missed yesterday and today. There's more than enough for you guys and the whole police force. Do you want me to bake more tomorrow?"

"I don't see why not. Call the police department again tomorrow morning to remind them and see where they're at on their end. There's a lot of hungry people in town, and the police need to find a way to distribute it."

"I've got some cardboard boxes we could fill up with loaves. How much room you got for the bread?"

"We've got lots of room. We'll be stopping by the department headquarters, and our boss was just telling us he's got eight people at his house and their food supply was running short. We could take some for him too."

"Alright, we'll load it up and get you guys on your way. You're parked out front I'm assuming?"

"Yes. You got a weapon for protection?"

"No."

"Do you know how to fire a pistol?"

"Of course… I just don't own one," answered Bob.

"Here, take this one. 9mm with an extra mag. We'll meet you back here tomorrow, and I'll bring you a different one with some more ammo. Deal?"

"Deal… and thanks."

Sean quickly coached him on how to use it to make sure he would be there the next day, and then they were on their way. Sean took a few pieces of bread up to the top with him to satisfy his hunger. There was nothing like freshly baked bread.

"Hey, Mike, we'll work our way back across town to the office, give some of this bread to Lonnie, pick up our people, and then work our way past the petroleum supplier and see where we're at on that."

"Got it."

Pulling up behind the house, Sean jumped out to meet his dad and Rachel, excited about the bread and what it would mean.

"Guess what we picked up today? Come and see." He hurried to the back of the truck and pulled the doors open for all of them to see the several boxes of bread. "Freshly baked bread from the Williams Bakery. Mike and I already ate a whole loaf since we picked it up."

"You little piggies!" exclaimed Rachel.

Sean was pretty quick with a reply. "This little piggy went to market…"

"…and went wee, wee, wee all the way home," finished Mike.

"You two are incorrigible. What will we ever do with you?" asked Rachel with a smile.

Sean winked at her as he replied quietly, "I can think of a few things."

"Hey, Dad… I want you to meet our new friends: David, his wife, Lily, and his two boys, Dylan and Lucas. They've been holed up in their home for twelve days or so."

After introductions were over, Mitch asked them if they wanted a camp trailer to sleep in or if they would rather take a room in the house. They chose the camp trailer for the time being. After helping them to move their things into Mitch's trailer, he took them into the house for dinner and showed them where the bathroom was located. Sean and Mike with Rachel's help put away most of the bread into the freezers and then took three fresh loaves into the house for dinner. Sean and Mike would later move some of the ammo and mags for the M4s down to the bunker for storage, but first they had to get their fill of Beth's cooking.

CHAPTER THIRTY-SIX

That evening on the news, the devastation of China and Russia was shown. Sean and his group could hardly believe it; even with all of the devastation from the virus, two countries were still vying for world control. Now it wouldn't matter, because both of them were effectively wiped out.

The news anchor came back on the screen to speak on the attacks: "Apparently, the Chinese were the first to move more troops and missile defenses to their northern border. Russia, seeing the build-up, began preparing for an attack. That was actually several days ago. Then, yesterday, Russia launched a massive first strike to cause the first damage in hopes of stopping the retaliation of China's forces. There may be as many as one billion people killed in the nuclear engagement, with millions more dying from the aftereffects. With the devastation of the virus already wiping out the ability of the rest of the world to mobilize relief teams, there won't be any rescue crews able to help either country. If there are any survivors, they will be on their own. Our hearts go out to them.

"In other news, we ourselves here at WNN are operating with a skeleton crew. Most of our reporters are gone with the virus as well as most of our management. The few of us that remain have decided to keep gathering as much information as we can from other networks and reporters, to pass it on to our viewers. We're out of food, as are many of you, and if we leave here to try finding food to keep from starving to death, we may never return.

"We will now return you to your regularly scheduled programming. Good luck out there."

"It's not looking good out there, Dad. The world is really falling apart from all of the hatred and mistrust."

"I know, Son. Different people have different types of characters, and depending on who's doing the leading, we never know what might happen. There are so many different opinions that no one can agree as to what should really be done to keep the world moving forward and then when you get some real fanatics in charge, everything goes haywire."

"I don't know if there's going to be any coming back from this. If there's going to be any society, the remaining people will have to start cooperating with everyone else to be able to survive. If we can't get that to happen, we'll finish off the rest of us."

"It won't be that bad, Son. As people are coming to their senses because of all this death and destruction, everyone will start cooperating so that we can recover from this epidemic."

"I hope you're right, Dad, because I don't want to have to start killing people that aren't infected. Live and let live is what I want. But in the future, if we can make a nice go of it, and others see what we're accomplishing, they'll want one of two things: to either join us in our endeavors and have a better life for themselves, or they'll be envious of everything that we've made better for ourselves and want to take it all away. That's what I'm afraid of."

"Then we'll have to make sure that they don't. Son, you and I know how we feel, and we know the mindset of all those that are now with us. We're of the same mind and desire: to make our lives better and help others to do the same. If others come and want to help with that, we'll welcome them, just as we've been doing already. If they want to take it away, we'll kill every last one of them. And I'm counting on you and Mike to teach us how to keep us safe from those kind of people."

"Okay, Dad… first of all, now that we have enough people, we need to have lookouts in both directions from the house at all times. You can make up a schedule for the lookouts to trade off throughout the day, and everyone needs to help out to some degree, whether it is cooking, cleaning, fixing things, digging more spuds, or with the guard duty. Anything you can think of as the days go by, everyone has to pitch in and help, just so they stay busy. Of course, there will be down time, and it needs to be used for fun and games of some sort so that we can continue to live with one another. Otherwise, tempers will get short. But as time goes on, we'll figure out how to handle things better."

Rachel was sitting next to Sean, listening to the conversation, holding onto his hand, glad that she was able to find a man who was so strong and always seemed to have an answer for everything. It helped to dispel the fear that always wanted to creep in—that was always hanging in the air, waiting for an opening. Whenever she was with Sean, she felt that things would be just fine and that somehow they would make it.

Hailee was also present, sitting with Mike, listening to the conversation. Rachel and Hailee had hit it off right away and became good friends, and Rachel was so happy for Mike that he had been able to find a nice, down-to-earth, intelligent woman to stand by his side, especially after he had lost the rest of his family.

"At night, we need to make sure all doors are locked, and with the motion sensor lights, we'll be able to know if anyone comes up in the dark. We need to stash a couple of mags for the Colt AR15s in several locations around the place in case we get in a firefight and run out of shells—some in the barn, the shop, just inside the front and back doors, and maybe some out by the pig pen. Everyone needs to carry a weapon outside and to always try to have a partner when you're out of the house. It's harder to sneak up on someone if there's two people, four ears that hear, both having senses and reflexes to help from being grabbed. We can't foresee every contingency that'll come up, but we'll try to cover most of them."

"How much longer do you think you and Mike will be patrolling? You two might be the last ones to keep showing up."

"It might only be for a couple more days. The city police still had about twenty men on patrol today, but they're losing men almost every day just like us. We can only play it by ear. If the stage two ever stop increasing, we could have a turnaround; but in six or seven more days, there might be over ten thousand stage two in one day. Every day after that it could be increasing until it hits thirty thousand. What then? At that point, it might be best just to stay home and let them die out. But I haven't heard how long they'll last before the disease actually kills them. If we could butcher a steer and stock up on our bread supply a couple of days before the big increase of stage two, we could all lay low here for a week or more and see how it goes?

"What bothers me the most about it, is that we have the food here to live through it, but as the stage two increase, all the uninfected people living in the town will be starving to death because they won't be able to leave their house to look for more food. I don't know what I can do about it."

"Tomorrow, try and contact all the local radio stations that are still broadcasting and have them run a bulletin to tell anyone still in town who are uninfected to call the Sheriff's Office and give their address. If we can't bring them here, maybe you can take them enough bread to survive until the worst of it is over."

"That might work, Dad. I told that same thing to the city police today. I'll find out tomorrow if they were able to do it. Have you talked to any of your close neighbors lately to see how they're all doing?"

"The O'Reillys and Fergusons are still good, but I haven't gotten through to anyone else. Here's an idea: The Ross's had a milk cow; I've milked her a few times for them when they were gone. If they're not home anymore, for whatever reason, we could bring that milk cow over here for our own use."

"Sounds great. A cold glass of milk with some cookies is beginning to sound delicious. We haven't had any milk in two weeks. Keep trying to get a hold of anyone else close by. We should try to stay up to date on everyone we can that are out this way," added Sean.

"Hey, you know what?" exclaimed Rachel. "We still have our steer back at the house. If we could run by there tomorrow and he's still there, we could butcher him."

"That would work out real well, Rachel. That way we could save all of our close ones for later in the winter," replied Mitch.

"That's a good idea. You and Kevin could butcher that steer out and have it loaded in a couple hours or less. You could take Rachel to watch your back, that would leave Joe, Steve, and David to guard the house while you three are gone. I think that would work beautifully."

"Alright, it's settled. Tomorrow, the three of us will go do that."

"Go ahead and let everyone know what the plan is for tomorrow, so they can prepare for it. Mike and I will be gone early in the morning, but you guys wouldn't have to leave too early. Once you get back from that, maybe send Kevin, Steve, and Rachel back over to their house with

Kevin's truck and bring back their couch and loveseat for our living room. As many people as we're getting, it would be nice to have more seating. Even the dining table and chairs might be a good idea."

"Okay, Son. We'll take care of it. In the morning, you could take a few packages of steak and burger with you and give it to the sheriff, if he shows up. You said they were almost out of food, and with some extra meat to go with that bread he got yesterday, they'll think they're eating a feast. I'll see you guys in the morning."

Early the next morning on the way to work, Sean noticed Mike looking him over. He thought Mike had a smirk on his face a couple of times.

"What? You got something to say?"

"Not much. Just noticing how tired you look. Are you getting enough sleep? You and Rachel have been going to bed earlier than everyone else, so I'm a little surprised to see you looking like this. With everything we've got on our plate, you need to be on the top of your game."

"I know, but Rachel's been keeping me up late every night, and then she wakes up in the morning at my first movement… and then sometimes she even wakes me up in the middle of the night. She's like a kid who's been wanting a certain toy that she's been watching all of her friends getting and yet has had to wait for hers. Now that she's finally got one and found out how fun the toy is, she never wants to stop playing with it. She's wearing me out."

"Aw… I feel so sorry for you, Sean. You want to lean over here and cry on my shoulder?"

"You're the one who asked. It's not my fault."

"You lucky son of a gun. That's all I got to say."

"Well, if you would romance that little gal of yours a little more, you might be able to talk her into marrying you. Then you'd be having the same problem as me. What do you think of that?"

"I think so much of her already. I'd marry her today, but it just seems so soon. At least you and Rachel had four weeks together before the world turned upside down."

"That's just it. With the world going to pot, it calls into play different rules to play by. It's in these kind of times that Hailee sees you for who you really are, and you see her for who she really is. There's no time to put on a façade to hide the real you. The both of you would get exactly what you're already seeing, and if that excites you, then maybe you should have a serious talk with her tonight when we get home. She might feel the same way about you, and if something were to happen to either of you before you can consummate your love for one another, that would be a real shame."

"You're right. It would be a shame to miss out on having her love on me the way Rachel is on you. I care about her right now more than I have any girl in my life, and if she feels the same way, maybe she would be agreeable to a short courting process."

"It's worth a shot, buddy. The worst that could happen is that she wants to wait a few more days, or weeks, or months… Just think, if she said yes to a wedding tomorrow, you'd be in seventh heaven, and I'd be asking you, 'How come you're so tired?'"

"Alright. I'll do it," Mike conceded

"Let's drive back by that fuel truck on the way in and check it out."

Ten minutes later, they were driving by the fuel delivery yard and were very careful taking out several infected before they stopped at the office. Going up to the door, they knocked several times, and after there were no answers, Sean knocked the glass out of one of the small squares of the door window, reached through, and unlocked the door.

Looking around the office, they found some keys with a tag on it for the tanker truck. Taking them outside to the truck, they tried them in the door and then the ignition. The truck started right up. Checking out all of the gauges that were on the truck, they could see that it had a full tank of gasoline. They must have filled it prior to the morning start, and then everything shut down before the next time they delivered.

"Well, there's five thousand gallons of gas for free. Got any qualms about taking it?" Mike asked.

"The way things are going I'm not bothered in the least. If we don't take it, someone else probably will, and I think if we're going to plant fields of crops to feed as many people as we can, we deserve to have it. Now that I've thought of it, I'll call Dad and find out where he buys his seeds for planting. We could stop by there and appropriate some seeds for crops. It's almost time to put seeds in the ground for winter wheat."

"Good idea, Sean. We need to be thinking of other things that we can be appropriating as well… if it's not stealing."

“I think, at this point in the game of survival, everything is free for the taking, so let’s not worry about it. Should we wait ‘til tonight or take it back now?”

“If we take the keys, it should still be here tonight. Let’s head into the office and see if Lonnie wants that meat we brought so that he can get it back into a fridge or something.”

CHAPTER THIRTY-SEVEN

Arriving at the office an hour later, slowed down by all of the infected, Sean and Mike found that the only ones that had come in were Lonnie and Lisa, and that they were the last line of defense for the areas that the sheriff's deputies were patrolling. There were still two or three over at Florence and a couple more in Cottage Grove, but those cities would need them for their own troubles.

"Lonnie, we brought you some goodies. Come out to the truck and get your presents."

Following the two outside, opening the back door of the panel truck, Lonnie looked in the cardboard box and froze.

"Are you guys sure you can afford to give up that much meat?" He looked at Sean and then Mike. His eyes started to tear up, and he turned away, reached up, and wiped away his tears before they could see them. Both Sean and Mike could feel a lump in their own throats at the show of emotion from Lonnie.

Reaching up a hand to place it on Lonnie's shoulder, Sean tried to ease his mind. "Don't worry about it, Lonnie. We've got enough to give you some. We'll probably be bringing more before long. My Dad and father-in-law are going to butcher a steer today, so we'll have plenty."

Turning back to the boys, he looked at both of them as he answered. "Sean, you and Mike have proven yourselves worthy of the job we gave you already, and now you've proven yourselves of way more than words can describe. Thank you so much for helping me and my family."

"Will you take back all those pretty words when we tell you that we broke into a fuel supply office this morning and are planning on stealing a full fuel truck?" Sean asked with a smile.

"Really? Breaking and entering? I like your style, and let's just say if you don't tell anyone, I won't either. A full fuel truck? You guys are thinking big. I like that. Got anything else you're thinking about confiscating? Because that's what we're gonna call it from now on. Got some more ideas rattling around in that head of yours?"

"Well, let's see. We were talking about ta— um, confiscating some seed from a ranch and farm store so we can plant winter wheat and more crops next spring. If this virus is about played out through the winter, we'll need crops to feed everyone. We don't know how many people we'll have gathered by next spring, but I think we need to be prepared for the worst. By the end of winter, we may have several hundred hanging around."

"I was right when I said you guys are thinking big. That's real big. I like that type of thinking. How many people do you have right now?"

"Eighteen for now, but we might find more though. We don't know what else to do. We were talking about maybe holing up for the next couple of weeks and just letting the stage two die out on their own, rather than shooting them all, but then we started thinking about all the people that are scattered throughout the city and starving to death. We don't like that idea at all. Mankind will need everybody that we can save to start over—especially if we have another nation move in and try to take over."

"You guys are getting bigger and bigger the longer you talk. You got a new government already planned out too?"

"No," Sean chuckled. "No, we haven't gotten that far yet. Mike might make a good President, though. For now, we just want to figure out how to save the ones we can and plan for winter survival. You got any ideas?"

"How many more people can you guys handle out at your place?"

"That's a good question. We have a four bedroom house, a shop, and a barn. We have three camp trailers now with people in two of them, only one connected to the septic tank. We've got room for several more trailers, and Mike mentioned that we could… confiscate a backhoe, septic tank, and drainpipe and put in another system to accommodate more trailers. Of course, more trailers entail more confiscating. If we don't get in trouble for all of the confiscating, we might be able to make a go of it."

"How many miles from town are you? If you're far enough, the stage two shouldn't be too big of a problem."

"We're about twelve miles from the outskirts of town. Dad's only taken out four so far, but as the numbers skyrocket in a few days with the third tier starting to turn, we might see more out that far."

You've got more room for trailers, and there's still lots of farmland too?"

"Lots of farmland. Dad's only been able to call two of the neighbors, so we would have to assume that the rest are gone. That makes even more farmland for us to take over if we need it. We could always confiscate a new tractor and other equipment, and since we have the fuel to gather as much stuff as we want, we should be able to survive. The biggest thing is that we have to be careful about taking in only healthy people. If we take in someone who may be infected but not symptomatic yet, we have to be able to quarantine him for ten days minimum to keep the rest of us safe. If our core group can adhere to the safety rules, then I think we can keep ourselves healthy."

"I've got eight people with me. Would it be asking too much to let us join you? I know technically that I'm your boss here, but I also recognize that you guys are the real leaders with what's going on, and I'm more than willing to settle for being a grunt in your outfit."

"Sure you can come out, Lonnie. I was already figuring on that. We'll have to confiscate another trailer or two though. The master bedroom is empty, and if Mike would get busy with his girlfriend and marry her, we'd have another room in the house available."

"Do you think I could, with that reason you just stated, convince her to marry me? Just so we can consolidate bed space?" Mike asked with some renewed hopefulness. "If I can keep piling on the reasons for us to marry, do you think she will?"

"Just stick with how much you love and adore her and that you can't bear to be away from her every night. That should convince her, but be sure to throw in some timely kisses throughout."

"Alright! When I get home tonight I'll take her out on the porch and have a heart to heart talk."

"Good. Now we need to make some plans. What kind of people you got at your place, Lonnie?"

"My wife and my two older kids that moved back in about two weeks ago because of all of the turmoil. My son is twenty-two, and my daughter is twenty-five. Then, there is our Lisa and an African American family that lived a few houses down from me. They have two kids around eight or nine."

"Do you guys have a camp trailer?"

"No. We'll have to confiscate one."

"Joe's got a fifth wheel hook-up on his truck. Maybe we can get him to meet us at an RV dealer this afternoon. Lonnie, do you think it's okay to do all of this confiscating? I'd hate for an alarm to go off and have a bunch of city cops come in with guns blazing, shooting to kill for looting."

"I could give them a call and tell them what we're gonna do so they won't respond to an alarm. They would probably agree with it. Would that work?" asked Lonnie.

"Sure. That sounds a lot safer. Mike and I will get going. We need to thin theses ranks out a little, and I promised the bread man I'd stop by again today. The city police were supposed to try to get a bulletin on the radio or TV and let people know about the bread so they could call in their address to get a delivery if possible. If you want to take Lisa and go home right now, you could start loading all of the things you want to take with you. Clothes, extra shoes or boots, personal items, important keepsakes you don't want to lose, any food, spices, cooking oil, sugar, salt, anything that is useful. Don't bring a lot of clothes that you'll never wear. The women especially need to know that."

Mike had been listening, and now he had some thoughts to add. "Let's get this straight. Today, we need to take that truck out there, with all of the remaining ammo and weapons, out to the house. If we're all together now, we don't want to lose any of that to anyone else. We need Joe and his truck. We need an extra driver to drive the fuel truck. We need to stop at the bread store and load up more for us and find out about anyone else that needs bread because they're starving. I'm not saying we'll be doing the delivering, but we need to find out what's going on. In between all of that, kill as many stage two as we can manage."

"Yep, that's it! Okay, let's start right now with that ammo truck." Sean began. "We need to move everything from the armory into the truck, and then Mike and I will drive it to the fuel truck, grab it, and take both out to the house. We'll ride back here with Joe, get the panel truck, go find a fifth wheel, send him on his way, and then hit the bread store. Lonnie, you go home, load everything, and then meet us back here. Wait for us, because right now it's hard to tell how fast we'll get our part done. Alright?"

"Got it. Let's get the rest of that ammo and weapons loaded, and I'll be on my way."

"Don't forget to call the city police and tell them about the RV dealer alarm."

Sean had called home to give Joe a heads up on the trailer confiscation plan so he was ready to go as soon as they arrived. Sean backed the ammo truck into the shop and set Steve and David to unloading half of the ammo up on the loft floor over the work room that was located in the back corner of the shop. Explaining to them to stack the ammo around the back edges against the outside wall where there would be more support. The other half they were to divide between the bunker, tack room, and the loft in the barn. Mike parked the fuel truck at the far end of the shop behind the wall. Calling Mitch, he explained what was going on and that he only had Steve, Ryan, and David to stand guard as he was taking Joe with them. Mitch let him know that they had taken two trucks and had loaded up the furniture first and then butchered the steer. They were just pulling out of the driveway and would arrive within twenty minutes or so.

Sean called the young guys together and explained they were on lookout until Mitch and Kevin returned in a few more minutes. Jumping into the truck with Joe, they made their way back to get the panel truck. They had already looked up the closest RV dealer and were ready to get there with the least amount of wasted time.

As soon as they drove up to the dealer yard, they backed the panel truck through the gate and then removed it after it was knocked down. Driving down the aisle of the fifth wheel trailers, they were looking for a large RV with three slide-outs. They didn't need the two hundred thousand dollar one with the mahogany cabinets and the gold plated faucets. They just wanted a nice one with the slide-outs and, of course, all of the amenities.

When they found what they were looking for, they made sure that Joe's truck would be able to pull it. Since he had a Chevy four-door one-ton with the Dura-Max Turbo Diesel, there wouldn't be any problem. Backing Joe's truck under the trailer, they tried to hook it up, but they needed the keys to access the controls. Driving back to the dealer office with the panel truck, they checked out the door, and then had to knock out some glass to open it. Only a few minutes later, they had the keys for the trailer, and within twenty minutes, they were driving out the gate. Leading Joe most of the way through the infested streets, taking out as many as they could without littering the streets with obstacles to run over, they left him with clear sailing the rest of the way.

Within the hour, they were driving up behind the bakery, and as they pulled around the corner, there were two police cars already parked next to the baker's car with two officers standing guard beside them. Stopping beside the door entrance, Sean climbed off the roof, wearing his mask whenever he was around a stranger, and struck up a conversation.

"You guys collecting bread for yourselves or for delivery?"

"Both. All of our officers are short on food, and this bread is really going to help them and their families. And then someone called in yesterday and requested us to get out a bulletin on the radio, and the next thing you know we've got a thousand people calling for the bread. Most of them can't come to the station because there's too many walkers, so we're starting a delivery service it looks like."

"That's just great. Don't feel too upset over it, because when you show up with some fresh loaves of bread and get to watch starving kids putting it away, you'll be crying like babies," Mike explained. "You got two more guys inside?"

"Yeah, they're inside with the baker guy. There's a lot of bread here, and I hope it lasts."

"Me too." Sean replied. "If we can get some coordination going to bring more flour, salt, yeast and whatever else he needs to keep baking, it might save the lives of everyone that's still alive. Mention that to whoever is still in charge and see what they can do for it."

"Are you two Sean Dixon and Mike Taylor?" Things were beginning to click.

"Yeah. Why?" Sean asked, wondering if they were caught on security camera breaking and entering.

“You guys are a legend. Just the two of you have been taking out almost as many as our whole force. The rest of the guys will never believe I got to talk with you. You guys thought up the panel truck idea, too. Are you the one that called the station yesterday to set this up?”

“Um, yeah. Didn’t take a Harvard graduate’s degree to see what needed to be done with all of this bread. We’re gonna go inside now to talk to the baker.”

Both the city officers stepped up to shake their hands, but they were interrupted when Mike said something about an infected on Sean’s six. He spun, raised the M4 to his shoulder, sighted for just a second, and squeezed the trigger once… twice. The officers spun their heads just in time to see two different infected falling to the ground—one at eighty yards and the other out at two hundred fifty yards. One of them whistled low and long.

“That’s nothing. Mike would have knocked down both of them with only one shot, but he doesn’t like to show off.”

Shaking their outstretched hands, the two of them walked into the bakery to see Bob.

When they walked up to the baker and the two other officers, Bob was glad to see that they had made it back.

“Any trouble outside?” asked one of the officers.

“No, just a couple of infected down the street. So, Bob, I see our plan worked. You’re getting rid of the bread, and starving people are going to live because of you.”

“Yes, for a change, I feel really good about baking bread. Even most of the officers that are still working are almost starving and their families also. This is really going to help.”

“Good. I talked to the officer outside and told him to talk to the commander and see if they could figure out how to keep you supplied with ingredients so that you can keep doing what you’re doing. You guys might also keep a guard on this guy so nothing happens to him. From now on, it might not just be the infected that show up. It’s possible some bad guys could come in, take all the bread, and shoot the place up. This is important enough to protect it.”

“Sure thing. I’ll call the captain and let him know about it. You guys are with the Sheriff’s Office?”

“Yeah, we’re out of the Springfield office,” Mike answered.

“Hey, are you guys Sean Dixon and Mike Taylor?”

Mike looked at Sean with a goofy look on his face. "Yeah. I'm Mike, and that's Sean."

"We're so glad to meet you guys!"

Reaching out their hands to shake, Mike and Sean were a little uncomfortable with the idol thing going on, but what the heck.

Turning to Bob, Sean asked if there was enough bread for them to take some, and he promptly started handing them two full cardboard boxes to take with them. Mike started out with his, but Sean pulled a pistol out of his holster, handed it to the Baker, and received his back. Pulling two extra mags from his utility belt and two boxes of fifty shells each from his back pockets, he handed them over, also.

"Thanks for this bread, and I hope we see each other again."

Picking up the other box of bread, Sean started walking to the door. He could hear one of the officers asking the baker if he knew who those two guys were. His reply was, "Yah, two really nice guys."

Jack, hanging around in his apartment, occasionally plinking at the stage two that were down on the street, was starting to get bored again. Earlier he had heard the bulletin about bread, so he had called the number to get a delivery. There was an apartment that he knew was empty on the first floor, so he gave them that address and called again a few minutes later and gave them his own address, hoping to get two different handouts. For his room, he told them to just ring the bell and leave it outside the door. He had immediately went to the room below, broke in through a window and then waited for the delivery. It was only an hour or so later, and he had several loaves of bread for each address. Working the system.

Pacing around the room, getting antsier with every minute, he began thinking about that woman that he had visited the other night. Something about exerting power over someone else, especially in the context that he had, was exhilarating. And to know that he would never be punished, that was the best part. He still had to be careful in case a friend had been called in or someone may have a gun, but for the most part, it was all for the taking. The worse things became, the better for him it might become, especially if he was able to stay healthy. Sooner or later the virus would play itself out, and the guy with the most smarts, if he played his cards right, could be the one in control once things settled down.

As soon as it started to get dark, he would make another trip over to that woman's house. The other night had been so exciting. He'd need to watch the house for a little bit and make sure no one else had been invited over, and then he would probably have to break in, because he had a strong suspicion that this time she wouldn't open the door to anyone. It was time for the strong to take what they wanted.

CHAPTER THIRTY-EIGHT

Later that evening, Mike led Hailee out onto the front porch and sat down with her on the same bench that Sean had proposed to Rachel on. With the frogs and crickets still chirping, the moonlight casting darker shadows under the old growth fir, and the light breeze rising and falling, Mike began to share his heart with Hailee. The leaves on the few aspens that were growing along the front yard fence were rustling gently as the breeze whispered through them, and they could still hear talk and laughter coming from within the house.

"Hailee, I wanted to talk to you about something important that's been weighing on my heart… about us."

Hailee leaned into Mike and kissed him long and tenderly. When she pulled away, she tried to look into his eyes with what little light there was coming from the living room windows. "Does that help?" she asked.

"Yes, but I need a little more help…"

They kissed again tenderly and searching, feeling a rising desire within them.

"Hailee, do you care about me?"

"Yes, Mike, I do very much. It would be fair to say that I've never cared for a man more than I do for you."

"That's good, Hailee. That makes me feel wonderful. I can say the same thing about you. I've known a lot of girls throughout my time in the military and a few when I was in high school, but none of them ever captured my heart the way that you've done these last few days. From the moment I saw you, I was stunned with your beauty, the way you carried yourself, and your sense of humor. I think I've come to know you more in the last eleven days than I would have normally in three or four months, and I hope you've come to know me in the same way. I've seen your romantic side from day one, even though I know our situation hasn't been very conducive for romantic feelings, but my feelings for you are growing faster and deeper than they have for any other woman I've ever known."

Hailee reached up, put her hands on each side of Mike's face, and pulled him to her where she could spend her sweet kisses on his lips. She knew where Mike was going with his talk and realized that she desperately desired to hear his words of love. Once she used the word "love" in her mind, she realized that she also had fallen in love with Mike.

"I know, Hailee, that this is moving fast, but because of our situations, we've come to know each other more quickly and deeper than we would have otherwise. I love you, Hailee."

"Oh, Mike, I…" Hailee pulled his head down to her lips and revealed to Mike her feelings with kisses. Pulling back to look at him, she continued, "Every time you leave in the morning, I feel like something is missing from my day, and I don't recover from that until you're back here with me—safe and sound. I've just been realizing lately… that I love you, too."

Mike leaned toward her, took her in his strong arms, and lifted her to his lap as he lavished on her all the kisses that his love desired, and he felt Hailee's rising passion meeting his own.

"Hailee, darling… will you marry me?"

She smiled. "Yes, I will."

Their lips met again and again as they sealed the pact between them.

Straightening up so that he could see her beautiful face looking back at him, Mike asked the second most important question: "Hailee, how soon will you marry me? The thought of something happening to either of us before we have a chance to share the love we have for each other tears me apart every time I have to leave you behind. I can hardly sleep for wanting you beside me, to hold you in the night, knowing that I've found my one, true love."

Hailee started to cry, and the tears slowly rolled down her cheeks. Mike wiped them away, and then he kissed them as they continued to flow. Tasting her tears as he kissed her lips, he held her tightly until he could feel her responding to his love.

"Do you think you could find that preacher again?" asked Hailee, with her face resting against his shoulder.

"I will certainly try. I could go in, get his number from Sean, and see if he'll answer right now. It's not too late yet."

"If you can reach him, see if he can come out tomorrow afternoon… late."

Mike pulled Hailee to him and held her tightly once again, declaring his undying love for her.

Hailee's mind began to race with everything that needed to be done. "I'll need someone to take me back to my shop in the morning to get the dress that I want. Can that be done?"

"Absolutely. Sean and I will go first, and you could ride with Mitch. We'll make sure it's safe, get you started back here, and then we could finish out our day. Would that work?"

"Yes, but if you want me tomorrow night, you'd better go make that call."

She gave him a sweet little smile, and he again covered her lips with his.

In a secured area, the President was again in a discussion with his leaders.

"We need to get more aircraft into the area looking for survivors. It's just not right to wait," complained the President.

"Sir, there's still too much radiation. There is a large storm front moving in from out of the north carrying a lot of moisture, and it's already starting to rain. The longer we wait, the more the radiation will be washed away and dissipated, making it safer for our men. Also the longer we wait, the less our men will be sidetracked, trying to help those that are unable to be helped. If we wait until those ones have died, we will be less hampered in our efforts to save those that can be saved," explained the new Secretary of Health, Lester Hayworth.

"Alright, I understand your reasoning, but it doesn't make it any easier. We still need to figure out the logistics to how we're going to move into the areas, find the survivors, and how to move them back to here," replied the President.

"Our people will figure that out. What we need to know is where do we bring them that is safe enough to set them up without them being infected by the virus. The majority of our people are already infected right now. Nine more days for the symptoms to start, nine more for the symptoms to transform to stage two, and then the final seven to ten days of stage two to eventually kill them. Thirty more days, and the virus will be dying out. Thirty days of being careful, and then we may be able to go back to normal. If we wait two weeks for rescue efforts to start, by the time we're bringing them back here, it should be fairly safe from the virus," replied Lester.

"That sounds so good to hear: 'safe from the virus'. Will it actually be possible?" asked the Secretary of Homeland Security, Carl Lanthrop.

"Of course. Eventually, with the population reduced to less than ten percent of pre-virus numbers, there will be so much less contact between the remainder of the population. With so many of them scattered across the more rural areas, the virus will die out with no more new hosts to infect."

"So, eventually, we won't even need to have a vaccine discovered? Will it be that safe?" asked the President.

"A vaccine wouldn't hurt, because the virus might creep around the edges, only infecting enough people to stay alive, waiting until it can all of a sudden be reintroduced into a thriving, interacting society. Then it would again have the potential to wipe out that particular group in society, of course, without the worldwide spread it's had now. A vaccine would put the whole thing to rest, once and for all."

"Then let's make sure that our guys continue to keep looking for a vaccine."

"Yes, sir."

"What's the latest on the numbers of infected?" asked the President.

"If the numbers hold true, we'll have as many as eleven and a half million with stage two by the end of the day, with two and a half million of that total new today, and as many as eight million or so already dead by euthanasia or police and military. Most cities still have a carry-over of stage two from the last two days. Police forces are so depleted by the virus that they are unable to keep up with the stage two turnings. Our hospitals in all of our larger cities are now closed, with a seventy-five percent infection rate among the healthcare workers and doctors. The worst part of the scenario is that we may have as much as forty percent of our population on the verge of starvation and no way to solve the problem," explained Carl Lanthrop.

"We'll have two to three million stage two turning each day for the next four days, and then we'll see the start of the fourth tier infected turning to stage two, which may be as many as ten or eleven million in one day. We can't clear the infected we have now, so there's no way we're gonna clear ten million or so per day from then on," argued Lester.

"We have to keep trying. It's the only hope the survivors will have. Do what you can to keep distributing ammo to our troops and the remaining police forces. It would be good to keep the ammo manufacturing running also. We'll be in a world of hurt if we run out of ammo."

"Yes, sir. I'll get right on it."

The morning dawned with overcast skies, but without a weatherman, it was anybody's guess if it would rain or not. Sean talked Lonnie into taking the sheriff's patrol truck back to the National Guard Armory to get another load of ammo before they couldn't get any more. Taking Steve with him to keep him company and to give him something to do, they would be gone for several hours. Hailee rode with Mitch in his truck as they followed Sean and Mike in the panel truck. As soon as they reached the edge of town, Sean climbed up to the top of the truck, and they commenced doing what they were so good at. They both thought it was a shame that Hailee would have to watch what they had to do, so they held off on some of them, and tried to take out just enough of the infected to let them traverse the streets that led to Hailee's shop.

Arriving there, they cleared the street before they allowed Mitch and Hailee to exit the truck. Once the door was unlocked, Mike went in first to sweep the building and make sure that it was empty. Sean remained on lookout while the other three were in the shop.

It didn't take long for Hailee to try on the dress she wanted to make sure it was going to fit, and grabbing a few odds and ends, they were on their way. As soon as they had Mitch and Hailee back to the edge of town, they waved them on and returned to their work of clearing out the stage two infected. There were so many bodies everywhere on the ground that it was beginning to stink. It might be a good idea to stay away from the area because of the possibility of disease starting to spread from the bodies. Sean would have to ask some questions about it to see if there would be any danger… if there was someone to ask.

They had a police radio in the truck so they were keeping up on what was going on around town and were listening to many stories of the bread deliveries. They asked about the bodies and found out that they didn't really pose much of a threat as far as disease went unless they were to contaminate a water supply or aquifer. Eventually it was going to rain, and it would wash a lot of the decomposition liquids into the local rivers, streams, and ponds, which in Sean's mind could be a problem. But there were only two of them, so they wouldn't worry about it and would keep creating more decomposing bodies.

As the two of them continued their patrolling, they kept their eyes open for a rental yard with backhoes and trailers. Finding one, they took down the gate in the same manner as the RV dealer, broke into the office, and found the keys for a backhoe. Going into the yard, they found the one for the key and started it right up. It was already sitting on a gooseneck trailer with a fifth wheel hitch, so they gave Mitch a call to see if Joe could bring his truck down and pick it up. There was also a truck with a thousand-gallon tank full of diesel that the yard used to fill their equipment, so they requested another driver to take that back to the farm too. Rounding up the key for the diesel truck, they started it also to make sure everything was ready when Joe arrived.

Leaving the yard, they took down more infected within a mile or so and then returned to help Joe get things hooked up. Before long, they would have everything they needed to do just about anything they wanted.

Switching off throughout the day, they were almost ready to call it quits, when Mike noticed a curtain moving in a window. Mentioning it to Sean as they were beginning to move, Sean braked to a stop and slipped from the truck with his M4 to check out the house. The lawn was dark and green, but it was about eight inches tall from not being mowed in the last two weeks or more and Sean could see automatic sprinklers at the edge of the sidewalk. Mike remained up top to keep a lookout for infected, but he also had his scope trained on the door as

Sean knocked on it to see if anyone would open it. There was no answer, and trying the doorknob, he found it was locked.

"There's someone in there, and most likely they're starving or they're infected. Keep your mask on and be careful," warned Mike.

Sean knocked on the door again and began to speak, "We won't hurt you. We're here to help. We have food and can help you."

Sean could hear the deadbolt turning, and he stepped back one step in case an infected person opened the door. As the door swung open, Sean saw instead of an adult, a boy of about seven years. His hair wasn't combed; he was barefoot; and his blue jeans and shirt were dirty from many days of wearing.

"You have food?"

"Yes, we have a little with us, and we can get more."

"We're hungry."

A four-year-old girl and a three-year-old boy peaked out around their older brother. They had large eyes, and there was a look of hope on their faces as Sean mentioned the food. As the immediate area looked clear, Mike climbed down from the truck, grabbed what was left of their lunch and carried it up to the door.

"Where is your mom and dad?" Sean asked. The oldest boy took the food from Mike and handed each of his siblings the largest share of it, keeping only a bite for himself.

"They're gone. My dad's been gone a long time; he's in the army. My mom is a nurse at the hospital, but she's been gone a long time." The boy started to cry, just a little. "She said she would come back, but it's been a long time. My sister left to find us some food, but she didn't come back either."

"How long has it been since your sister left?" asked Sean.

"A long time. We were hungry, and she went to find us something to eat. Have you seen her?"

"No, we haven't seen her. Are any of you sick or not feeling well?"

"We're just hungry."

"May I come in and look around? We're policemen, and we're going to help you."

The oldest boy stepped aside and pulled his siblings with him out of the way.

"Do you have any more food?" asked the girl, hoping for something more.

"No, not with us, but we have more where we live. We'll take you with us, and you can eat all you want," Mike explained.

Walking through the house, checking the bedrooms and bathrooms first, Sean could see that the house was a total mess. With three kids alone and no one cleaning up after them, it looked like a tornado had gone through the house. Checking bathroom cabinets, he could see they were out of toilet paper, and there weren't any paper towels or napkins in sight. Going through the kitchen cabinets, all the food was gone—not even any sugar. There was no telling exactly how long they had been alone, but it obviously had been quite a while. Walking back to the kids, he asked if they had any clean clothes.

"Tell you what, you three go jump in the shower, and you wash them real good. I'll collect your clothes, and then we'll go get some food. You guys can live with us. Okay?"

"What if my mom or sister comes home, and we're not here?"

"I'll leave a note for them with my address and telephone number, and they can call us when they come back."

"Alright."

Sean gave Mitch a call and explained the situation. It looked like they had been separated by themselves for at least ten days and would be virus free. There shouldn't be any problems.

Turning to Mike, he asked, "Should we take them straight home or go find a clothing store first and leave this mess behind?"

"The Super Wal-Mart is close by. We could take a swing through and see what we could find to confiscate. We might have to break in though."

"I'll see what I can scrounge up in here, and then we'll decide. You go on outside and keep a lookout."

Finding a clean set of clothes for all of them, simply because they hadn't actually been changing any clothes, Sean opened the bathroom door and set them on the cabinet. Gathering up all of the dirty ones, he threw them into the bedroom and then walked outside to Mike.

"I found one set of clean clothes for them, but I think we need to swing by the store and check it out."

"Alright by me. Maybe there'll be a little food of some kind in there for them to eat."

After getting the kids packed in the seat, they made their way down to the store. Sean tried not to shoot any infected out front, but tried to rather wait until they were passed to take them down. Taking a half-hour to go one mile because of the infected, they soon arrived at the store to see that the front doors were busted in. Someone had driven a car all the way through the front doors and left it parked inside the front aisle. Leaving the kids in the truck until they could check out the building, they did a quick search, just to make sure there weren't any infected wandering around. There could be regular people hiding from them but it should be safe. Gathering the kids they walked over to the grocery section first and walked aisle after aisle, but the only thing they found was a bag of cookies laying on its side on the top shelf that had been overlooked. It wasn't long before it was all gone.

Mike had an idea, and as they neared the back of the store, he pushed through the double doors into the receiving room and looked around. There were a lot of covered or wrapped crates of product that hadn't yet been set out on the shelves when they decided to close their doors. Cutting the plastic off the crates and pallets, they were seeing canned fruit and vegetables, cans of soup, a wide variety of bags of chips, cookies, juices, and an assortment of frozen foods that had already spoiled. Opening up some cans of fruit, they let the kids eat them with their fingers and then some chips and a few cookies.

Mike walked over to a roll up door, opened it, stepped out, looked around, and then pulled a garbage can over to set in front of the door. He stepped back in and pulled the door down, but didn't lock it. He was planning on driving around with the panel truck and loading some of the food in it as soon as they were done with collecting clothes. Within forty-five minutes, they had collected plenty of clothes for the kids and had loaded up all of the food that was available.

Just before pulling out, Mike ran back up to the jewelry cabinet, picked out the prettiest wedding ring they had and then broke the glass to grab all of them. Not knowing which one would fit on Hailee's finger, he decided to take all of them. Seeing as how Sean didn't have a ring either, he grabbed up all of the solid gold wedding bands for men too. On his way to the back door, he grabbed up a handful of new release movies also. Seeing a cart close by, he put the movies in it and then moving to the next aisle, seeing what he wanted, he broke the glass case, grabbed four PS4 systems, and loaded up all of the available controllers for them. Stepping back to the game case, he loaded up all of the games for the system.

Looking at the glass enclosed cabinet case with the Xbox games and consoles, he gave it a quick thought, and then broke that case too. Taking three consoles, extra controllers and all of the available games, he was ready to go. Except for all of the series sets of current dramas on TV of course. Looking at all of the seasons of the Walking Dead, he had to smile. Why not? Grabbing all of the seasons of Game of Thrones, NCIS, The Mentalist, that Castle guy, and several others, he was finally ready to go. The apocalypse had a few advantages, but not many. It occurred to him he needed to hurry, or he would be late for his own wedding.

With all of the people that they were gathering, and probably a lot more in the near future, and as long as the electricity continued to stay on, they were going to need plenty of entertainment for everyone. Mike couldn't wait to see the look on Sean's face as he walked up to the truck with his cart full of goodies.

CHAPTER THIRTY-NINE

The minister arrived early, and the groom arrived late. What more could a person expect with the way the world was going? After getting the kids unloaded and into the kitchen, Mike and Sean hurried through their showers and again donned their dress blues for the ceremony. They held the ceremony in the same place as Sean and Rachel's, but there were a lot more people attending the second wedding.

Rachel was the bridesmaid this time, and Sean the best man. Hailee had asked Mitch to walk her down the aisle, since her own father had gone AWOL when she was only four and her mom and stepdad had moved to Illinois two years previously. The last two weeks she hadn't been able to contact them and had no idea whether they were alive or dead. But Mitch was only too glad to walk her down the aisle as a loving father would.

Sean and Rachel walked down the aisle together and then separated to stand at their designated places. As the music switched to the wedding march, Mitch and Hailee walked down the stairs and out into the grass.

"Who gives this woman away to be wed?"

"Beth and I do." Mitch hugged her, kissed her on the cheek, and then placed her hand in Mike's outstretched one.

Mike pulled Hailee to him, hugged her tightly for a moment, and whispered something in her ear. They then turned to the minister to begin the ceremony. By the time it was over, most of the people attending were in tears, as they watched Mike kiss his new bride. Their wedding vows were so sweet and beautiful, and it was touching for the people to experience something so moving in the midst of the world's downfall. Cutting the cake and sharing a banquet feast afterwards brought the group closer together and made them all feel like a big family.

Sean and Rachel were the last to speak to the newlyweds, and Sean's last words were: "You need to be on the top of your game tomorrow, so don't stay up too late."

First thing the next morning, Mitch started his tractor and began discing his fields. He had plowed them under quite a few days back to let the stubble decay and the dirt to set. Sean and Mike were going to pick up enough seed to plant about fifty acres in winter wheat, and the following day, Mitch would put the seed in the ground.

The night before, Lisa had decided to use the master bedroom and have the two small children sleep in the bed with her. The older boy would sleep on a cot in the room until the children became used to their new home. Everyone had been heartbroken over the circumstances that the children had been found in, and they all desired to make their new life as happy as possible.

Sean and Mike continued to do what they did best, taking out hundreds of the infected. The city police had been able to round up more crews to take over the clean up behind Sean and Mike, and once they got connected on the street, it was work, work, work. They left so many bodies in their wake that the body disposal crews would just follow them around. It was all two trucks with trailers could do to keep up with them. When one truck had to head for the pit, the remaining trailer would be full by the time they returned.

Neither Sean or Mike liked the idol worship that had started, but there wasn't anything they could do to thwart it, because no matter what they did, it was better, faster, or with greater numbers than anyone else could do. Soon the removal crews were spreading the word of what Sean and Mike were accomplishing. Before the day was half over, they had a third crew come out and start helping. Sean would empty his thirty round mag from one spot, and there would be thirty bodies to pick up. Mike was reloading mags every chance he had, and Sean would still use them up as fast as Mike could load them. The stage two were so thick that they were taking out thirty or so every two or three blocks of travel.

A couple of times, all three trailers were away, going to or coming from the pit. During those times, Sean or Mike would knock on doors if they were in a residential area to see if they could find more survivors just to kill time, waiting for one of the crews to come back. By the end of the day, they had traded off about eight times and had taken out more than three thousand infected. Once that news was passed around, Sean and Mike were going to be even higher on a pedestal.

By the end of the day, they were worn out mentally and emotionally with taking so many lives. Everyone that they took down, they made a conscious determination with their eyes and the actions of the infected, that they were stage two before squeezing the trigger. The last thing they wanted was to shoot someone who was only staggering from hunger rather than the virus.

When everyone was ready to head for home, Mike suggested they take a drive back to the bakery to see how everything was coming along with the food delivery. There were only a few stage two on the way, since the city patrols had been taking them down all day also. The baker was still on site with a deputy on guard and as they knocked on the door, the deputy opened up right away.

"How are things looking out there?"

"It was real busy for seven hours, but they finally started to taper off. The drive over to here wasn't bad at all. You shouldn't have any trouble heading home now." They had been walking into the building as they conversed, and as they approached the baker, Sean asked, "How's things shaping up?"

"Great. The police have lined up some people for making deliveries, and the bread has been going out all day. We're feeding a lot of people. Also, I've been getting deliveries of the ingredients, so I should have enough to bake another twenty thousand loaves. I've baked about three thousand loaves today, and that's up from a thousand the last two days. There's been a lot of people calling in for bread, and it might be the only thing they've got to eat to sustain them. I remember that one government guy was talking about butchering cattle and distributing meat, but we haven't heard back from him in four days now."

“I’ll give the police another call and see if they can round up a qualified butcher and maybe they can get something going. Meat and bread for every meal wouldn’t be bad if you’re starving otherwise.”

“That would be a good meal in these days. If everyone that we have left would now be extremely careful and not get infected, we might be able to make it,” replied Bob.

“I think most of the ones we’ll still be losing are already infected and don’t even know it yet. Only time will tell,” Mike added.

“Do you have some bread we could have? We’ve now got thirty people at our place, and the bread disappears fast. Last night, we found three kids alone in a house and took them home with us—a seven and three year-old boy and a four year-old girl. Both parents are gone, and an older sister went looking for food over a week ago and never came back. Breaks your heart to think of how many more like that might still be out there. Without going door to door, there’s no way to find out.”

“That’s terrible. It would be pretty dangerous right now going door to door, I suppose, with all the infected on the street. You might also open a door on an infected person, too, who has been trapped inside a house or apartment, and that could be extremely dangerous. I’m just a baker and am glad we’ve got guys like you to do those things.”

“I’m glad that we’ve got a baker like you, who’ll step up and do his part. What you’re doing is saving as many people as we’ve been saving,” Sean was quick to reply.

“Thank you, Sean. That means a lot to me. Go ahead and take those three boxes of bread, and when you need more, feel free to stop by.”

“Alright and thanks for your help. By the way, here’s my number and our house phone. Even if the electric goes out, the house phone will probably still work. Give me a call if you need anything.”

Mike reminded Sean that they still needed to swing by the farm store before they could head for home, and he was getting hungry.

“Got to keep your energy up, so you can stay awake? Is that it?” Sean asked with a smirk on his face.

“I don’t want to disappoint, now that I’ve talked her into it. I’m finding out what you were talking about… although you’ll never hear me complain about it. I’ve never enjoyed it as much as I have with Hailee. For some reason, it just feels right.”

"That's because you're doing it with someone you really love. Now you can actually call it making love for once in your life. It's been the same way for me, and it's so special every time we do it. I've never been happier. It's just too bad that it couldn't have happened under happier circumstances."

"That does explain why it's so satisfying. Thanks for the insight."

"You're welcome, buddy."

"Was there only one kind of seed that Mitch wanted?"

"For now. He's going to do some research to find out what else might be good to plant this time of year— Is that girl infected?!" Looking ahead and to the left, a young-looking woman was staggering along, holding a torn shirt across her naked body.

"An infected person wouldn't be trying to hold her clothes on, but she might still have the virus. We need to be careful."

"Okay…"

Pulling over and jumping out of the truck, making sure their masks were on, they intercepted the crying, frightened girl, who looked to be about seventeen. Mike put a hand on her shoulder to steady her, but they didn't want to get any closer because of the possibility of the virus. She had a bloody nose; blood was trickling from her swollen lips; and her left eye was puffy and turning a purple color. There were red finger marks on both of her bare arms, and she had a couple of bruises showing on her bare skin that wasn't covered with the tattered shirt.

"Are you sick?" Sean asked

"No. No, I'm not sick."

"Have you been bit? Were you attacked by one of the stage two infected?"

"No, I wasn't bitten. They were men, and they found me and my mom in our apartment. Two of them were raping my mom, and one of them pulled my clothes off. He hit me… and just kept hitting me…" She paused to wipe her tears, shaking with her recital of what happened. "And when he pulled his pants down, I jumped up, kicked him, grabbed my shirt, and took off running. I can still hear my mom's screams as they were…"

"Can you take us back to your apartment? How far is it from here?" asked Mike.

She pointed back the way she had come. "About five blocks I think. We need to hurry."

"Let's get in the truck and get over there."

Leading her back to the truck, Sean grabbed his coat and held it for her to put it on. As she put an arm through the sleeve, she dropped her torn and tattered shirt, exposing her young body, and Sean tried to look away as it fell, feeling so ashamed of the way some men could be. The coat was barely long enough to cover her bare bottom, but it was the best they could do. Getting in the truck, Mike draped his coat over her bare legs as she guided them to her apartment house. When they arrived, she told them the apartment number as they were getting out. Locking the doors, they told her to lay down and stay out of sight in case the guy was still looking for her and that they would be back in a few minutes.

Entering the building and working their way to the stairway, they moved upstairs, working the area as they were trained to do. Moving down the hallway, they could soon hear intermittent screams and painful moaning. Working their way up to a closed door with the correct number on it and moans and men's hoarse laughter coming from inside, Mike tried the doorknob to see if it was locked. He shook his head to Sean, raised his hand in a one, two, three count, and then turned the doorknob softly.

Sean whispered, "Now!"

Mike pushed the door open with a quick push, and Sean moved quickly into the room with his rifle up and searching. No one right or left. Mike followed right behind him, watching his back, as they moved forward toward the hallway and heard men's voices and a woman's moans.

"What happened to that girl we left you with?" one husky voice asked.

"She kicked me in the nuts when I pulled my pants down and took off running outside," Said a second voice. "I chased her as soon as I could, but I couldn't find her. She didn't have any clothes on, so when we're done here, we can go look for her. Is it my turn next?"

"Hold her still. I can't do this if she keeps moving," chimed in a third voice.

Mike signaled that there were three men in the room. Sean glanced at Mike, nodded his head, and then stepped quickly past the door with his rifle pointing inside to the right, covering two men. Mike instantly stepped up to the door, covering to left inside the room. Two of the three men had their pants off, and the woman was naked and bleeding.

All three were concentrating on the woman, holding her hands and feet. Three handguns were sitting on the dresser, and a rifle was leaning in the corner.

"Which one you want to shoot first?" asked Sean.

All three men froze. Two looked toward Sean, and the one in the act realized how vulnerable he was. The one closest to the guns, which were to the right, jumped and reached for a pistol. Sean shot him through the chest, knocking him down. The other two stood still. Mike stepped up and clobbered the guy doing the deed with a butt stroke to the side of the head, knocking him away from the woman.

"Now wait a minute…" started the third guy, raising his hands from the woman's body. "You can have her yourself. Keep the guns, and just let me go."

"Did you already have your turn?" Mike asked. The woman started to curl up on the bed into the fetal position to cover herself.

"Did you?"

They could both see that he had because of the blood that he still had on him. He started to whimper and cry, begging and looking for the same mercy that they had refused the woman and her daughter.

Mike lowered the point of his rifle and squeezed the trigger. He knew where it was going to hit. The man's private parts erupted into a gusher of red blood, and grabbing himself to stop the bleeding as much as to feel what was left of his manhood, he started to wail.

"Don't worry about what you just lost. You aren't going to live long enough to ever use it again anyway."

Mike squeezed the trigger again and shot the man's hand as it was holding the wounded spot. He cried out again and fell to his knees, begging Mike not to kill him. Mike squeezed the trigger a third time, putting a bullet through the man's heart. The one on the floor started to rise, trying for a grab at a gun, and Sean shot him through the ass. Twice. Going down to the floor, he started whimpering too. Mike stepped into the room and kicked him over onto his back so he could see his judgment.

"You guys are enough to make me puke. Picking on defenseless women. Beating them into submission." Mike had his gloves on, and he bent down and punched him in the face five or six times, and then he straightened up and kicked him in the ass another three times with his boot. "How does that feel? I can give you some more if you want…"

"Just shoot him, and let's get her out of here," Sean interrupted.

Mike squeezed the trigger twice, putting both rounds through his heart.

"Mike, get rid of those gloves and wash your hands… just in case."

Sean then stepped into the next bedroom, pulled the bedspread off the bed, and returned to wrap it around the woman. Speaking words of comfort and safety, he put one arm around her and the other he slipped under her legs. Lifting her off the bed, he carried her to the bathroom, and before he set her down, he explained, "Your daughter is outside in the truck, and she's alright. She was hit a couple of times, but that's all. If you want to take a shower, get their stink off you, you'll feel better. I'll go get your daughter, and you two can get some things together, and then Mike and I will take you to our home. We have thirty people with us. Our women will help you, and we have plenty of food. Okay? Do you understand?"

She nodded her head several times and wrapped her arms tightly around Sean's neck, not wanting to let go. She began to sob uncontrollably. Her whole body was shaking, wracked with her sobs, as she held tightly to Sean's neck.

"Mike, run down and get her daughter as quick as you can."

Sean stood there with the woman in his arms, holding her, comforting her with gentle words. Only two minutes went by before Sean could hear the sound of bare feet running through the living room.

"Mom! Mom!" Coming to the bathroom door, she stopped and looked at her mom in Sean's arms. "Mom? Mom, it's going to be okay."

The mother finally lifted her head from Sean's shoulder, looked at her daughter, and she began to cry again. Sean set her on her feet, waited for the daughter to hold her before he let go, and turned to the shower to start the water.

Once it was hot, he turned to the girl and said, "Get in the shower with her and help her wash. Scrub away everything. It'll make both of you feel better, and I'll look for some clothes for you. Take as much time as you need." Sean turned and left the room, closing the door behind him.

He looked at Mike and shook his head in sadness.

"Go in there, look through the dresser, and find something for them to wear. Pants for the girl; maybe a dress for the woman. I don't know. Do you think she can wear pants right away or would a dress be better?"

"Let's find both and let her choose."

"Okay, that's good."

Gathering the guns and putting them in a pillowcase, Mike looked down at the first one to die. Raising his foot, he stomped him twice and then kicked him away from the dresser. Mike started looking through the drawers for some clothes. It was the daughter's dresser, and he felt a little uncomfortable rifling through her stuff. Sean was in the other bedroom doing the same.

After they collected the clothes, Sean knocked softly on the bathroom door and opened it just enough to slip the clothes in and set them on the floor. The water was still running. They had no idea how long it was going to take, so Sean gave Mitch a call to let him know that they were going to be late. Finishing his call, Sean turned to Mike.

"We both knew it would come to this; it always does. But are you ready for it?" Sean asked.

"No, I'm not. You can never be ready for this. I was just thinking, what if it had been Hailee in her apartment that they had found? Or Rachel's family in her house? This pisses me off more than any other scenario."

"I could tell. Are you okay with the way it went down?"

"I'm alright. I'll get over it. What will haunt me is the way they were holding her down and the way she curled up in a fetal position after we stopped it. The way she clung to you after you picked her up and wouldn't let you go… that broke my heart."

"Mine too." Sean paused, thinking of that moment. "How much of the details should we tell anybody back at the farm?"

"Keep it simple. No need to scare them too much nor make them scared of us. What we did was harsh, but I wouldn't change any of it, unless it was to let them live a little longer to give them more time to think about dying. The first one got off way too easy."

"I agree. Let's go through the kitchen and see if there's anything worth salvaging."

The bathroom door opened, and the daughter was the first to walk out, holding her mother's hand. Gently coaxing her out of the bathroom, she led her into the living room, trying to decide what to do next. She had placed Sean's coat on her mother to keep her warm, thinking that her continued shivering was because she was cold.

"Do you have any aspirin, Tylenol, or ibuprofen that your mom could take?"

"Yes, it's in the bathroom. I'll get it."

"Bring all the medicine you have, and we'll take it with us. Medicine might be what we're short on," Mike explained.

Sean grabbed a glass in the kitchen, filled it up with cold water, and brought it back to the mother. When the daughter came back out with the aspirin, he handed it to her.

"Is there anything important in your room that you have to take?"

"I need my clothes."

"You can't go in there. There's three men in there, and they aren't alive anymore. I can get something out of there if you want, but we're going to stop at Wal-Mart on the way home. You and your mom can shop to your heart's desire. You can buy all you want for free—a whole new wardrobe for both of you, new shoes included, as many as you want. So with that said, is there anything here you want to take with you, like a picture album, personal papers, anything at all?" Sean asked.

"Yes, there's a couple of things." She started gathering some albums and other keepsakes and then walked down to her mother's room and started rummaging around. When she was done, they gathered everything and walked out. The mother was in pain walking, and she might even have gotten a concussion from the beating. Sean slung his gun across his back, picked her up, and carried her out to the truck, with Mike leading the way. Sean was thinking that maybe they could find one of those handicap scooters that he had seen before in the store; that would make things a lot easier.

"Later, if there's something you remember that you want from your apartment, we can come back and get it, although it might stink a little," explained Mike.

"Alright. Let's go shopping."

CHAPTER FORTY

The next day was more of the same, and Sean and Mike were getting sick of it. Sometime around mid-day, they had worked their way close to one of the remaining operating radio stations, which they had looked up the address for that morning, and took the time to go inside and talk to the deejay. Being in their uniforms the female deejay had no problem letting them in to talk. Talking with anyone was a good thing after being practically alone for two weeks.

"I'm Donna. How's it going out there?"

"About the same, we're putting down several hundred stage two every day, and we're getting tired of it," answered Mike.

"We'd like to give an announcement to the public if we may," stated Sean.

"Uh, sure. What's it about?"

Sean looked at Mike. "It's… a public service announcement…?" Sean started, with a question in the statement as he looked at Mike.

"Yeah, it's a public service announcement about protecting yourself, but also how we will protect and serve the public." Looking back at Sean, Mike gave a little shrug of his shoulders.

"Alright, that sounds good. You know what you want to say? Do you need to write it down first?" she asked.

"No, we're good."

"Okay, right this way." She led them down the hall and into her sound booth, where they could hear a song playing. She took the microphone and connected it to a mic stand for them to talk, and then she asked, "Are you ready?" Sean gave a head nod, and as soon as the song was over, she began to speak.

"This is Donna, and I've got here with me two gentlemen from the Sheriff's Office who have a public announcement to make." Stepping back, she hand gestured for one of them to step forward to start.

"I'm Sean, and my partner here with me is Mike. I want you to listen up to what I have to say. It might save your life. Yesterday, we came across a young woman, a child really, running down the street almost naked and frightened almost to death. She had been beaten and stripped by a man who was going to rape her."

Donna started to step forward, and Mike gently grabbed her arm and held her back, whispering in her ear to listen.

Sean continued, "She had kicked the guy and escaped from her apartment, leaving her mother behind, who was in the other room being raped by two other men. She led us back to the apartment, and as she remained in the truck, we entered the building and found her apartment. Walking in on the three men in the very act of rape, the woman was bleeding and almost unconscious, we killed all three men. They did not die easily. Actually, they were crying and begging for mercy, before we were finished. This public announcement is a warning. There are no jails to lock you up. There are no juries or judges to convict you and sentence you. We have no time to deal with you in the normal fashion. If we find you hurting women in this way, we will be your judge, jury, and executioner. There will be a speedy trial, and you will be found guilty and executed on the spot. Again, we will find you, and we will kill you. If you want to save your own life, then think of this warning before you do anything that you will regret. Thank you for your time."

Turning to Donna, Sean nodded his head and started to walk away. She grabbed his arm, hugged him, and whispered, "Thank you." She kissed him on the cheek and then quickly turned to take up the microphone.

As Sean and Mike were walking away, they heard her say, "All of you listeners, if you liked Sean's message, call the station and let us know. If you didn't like it, don't bother calling. Our number is…" Sean and Mike were out the door.

The nine men that were on their body disposal crew, three for each truck, as soon as Sean and Mike had walked out of the station's door, began to clap their hands and cheer. They had been listening to the radio as Sean gave his message, and they signaled for Sean and Mike to come over to the trucks. Sean could hear the radio Deejay talking as they still had the radio turned on.

"Hello, caller," they could hear Donna say. "So, did you like what the sheriff's deputy had to say?"

"Yes, I loved it. If that could have been the way that they took care of those things before this apocalypse, we would have a lot fewer people in prison, draining our tax dollars by taking care of them. Plus once the message got out that the sentence is harsh, it would deter others from ever doing it, which would further decrease our prison population. Thank you, Sean and Mike."

The next call, and the next, and the next… all went something like this:

"Hello, what do you have to say about the deputies."

A woman's voice: "I want their phone numbers and address so I can thank them personally."

"Hello, what do you think of the deputies?"

"Hello. I loved it. Those bastards got just what they deserved. Good for them. We need more cops just like them."

"Hello, what did you think about the deputies?"

"Hello. If they are the judge and jury, what if they're wrong, and they shoot an innocent man. Who's going to judge them?"

"Weren't you even listening to what he had to say. They were caught in the very act, dumb shit. Hello, what did you think of our two Deputies?"

"I think they're heroes, and we need to structure our future police force along those lines. If someone is caught in the act of a heinous crime like that, they should be killed on the spot and save the tax dollars. Thanks, Sean and Mike."

"Well, there you have it—a good sampling of how our county residents feel about serious crime in these trying days."

Sean walked away; he had heard enough. He should have had her record his message so she could replay it again and again, like a real public service announcement. Oh, well… that would have to be good enough for now.

"Nice speech for off the cuff."

"Thanks. Did I leave anything out?"

"The part where I shot off his balls? That might have had some impact on the listeners."

"Most likely. Want to go back in…?"

"Nah, I'm good. I think you got the message across."

"Good. Let's try to knock off a little earlier tonight and go get those seeds that we didn't get yesterday. Maybe we could go see the baker today and see what he thinks about fifty acres of wheat. He may have some recommendations."

"Sounds like a good idea to me."

As soon as they arrived at the William's Bakery, they noticed two police cars, and there were two deputies standing guard. As soon as the two of them walked up, the officers wanted to shake their hands again.

"We heard what you guys did, and thanks."

They walked into the bakery, and the other two deputies were carrying out more bread to load in the car. Stepping up to the baker, they shook hands.

"I've got a question for you. We're on a small farm, and Dad is wanting to plant some winter wheat. We were wondering if you have any ideas on what kind or how many acres."

"Are you talking just for personal use or to bring here for baking?"

"Some of both. Dad made a machine to grind the grain into flour, but I don't know how fine it would turn out to be. He's already got some spring wheat in storage that he just harvested six or seven weeks ago, but now he's wanting to plant fifty acres in wheat that most of it could be used for the bakery."

"Well, as an example, one acre of wheat would produce enough flour to feed a family of four for ten years. Fifty acres would supply my bakery for the rest of the year maybe. With one acre, I could bake forty-five hundred loaves of bread. Let's see… forty-five hundred times fifty… two hundred twenty-five thousand loaves of bread. What could we do with that many loaves? So, the best wheat for bread would be the hard red winter wheat. Tastes the best. I don't know how much more flour we might get delivered from the supplier, but it would be nice to know we had another supply when we need it."

"That's great. I'll let him know. He'll be excited to know that his fifty acres will feed so many."

"I'm glad I've had the opportunity to meet you guys. Your dad sounds like someone I'd like to meet someday; there's not too many right now looking to the future, trying to figure out how to save more people."

"If we all try to do our part, we might be able to make it."

"You guys want to take some more bread? There's plenty."

"Not yet. We've still got plenty, although it disappears fast when you have to feed thirty-two people," Sean commented.

"Thirty-two now? You guys have more people every time we talk."

"When we're patrolling, we seem to come across people who need help. What else can we do?" explained Sean. "With so many desperate people out there, we're going to miss a lot of them, and they might sit in their house and starve to death before we can help them. That's the real shame."

"How about scanning the radio? Find all the stations that are still operating and have them all put out a bulletin about the bread and to call in to get some. That way you're reaching more people, and we're able to save more. If some are in worse shape than others, those ones you could take out to the farm or find someone to take care of them, and we might be able to save a lot more that way. Use the Internet and TV also, and we might be able to reach everyone somehow."

"Sounds good. I'll talk to the police captain as soon as I can and see what they can do."

They were walking toward the door as they were talking, and as they stepped outside, a loud cheer erupted, with clapping and whistles. Looking around, they could see fifteen police cars parked around the lot, and twenty or so officers stood there cheering. Looking at Mike, Sean was wondering what was going on, and as soon as it quieted, the police chief stepped forward to shake their hands.

"We all heard your public announcement on the radio earlier, and when one of our guys told us you were here, we decided to come down and meet you guys."

"Well, we don't know what to say, but thank you."

"Thank you. You've put more fear into the criminals than they've had in years, and it might save some innocent lives. You've shown us all what we can do to help our remaining people. Thanks for the inspiration."

“Wait a minute… I don’t want all of you to leave here half-cocked and start killing anyone that might be a bad guy. What we encountered was a naked victim, leading us to the scene of the crime, and her mother, also naked, was in the very act of being raped by three guys. Two of the three men were naked from the waist down, and the woman was being held down on the bed while one guy was raping her. There was no question as to whether those guys were guilty, and they deserved to die, in a harsh manner no less. They beat those two women. If you come across a similar situation, by all means kill the perps, slowly if possible, but you have to be absolutely sure of their guilt. We don’t want our police force to get a bad rep for jumping the gun on certain situations. Then again, like I said on the radio, there is no functioning court of law anymore. Just be sure of your judgment.”

The police chief turned and looked at all of his officers. “What Sean has said is good advice. We don’t want to get carried away and start killing anyone we think might be guilty; we have to be sure. If we do catch anyone doing what they found, take care of them.”

Turning back to Sean and Mike, he again thanked them, and then all of the officers stepped forward to shake hands and to express their appreciation. As soon as he could, Sean shared the baker’s idea with widening the bulletins reach with all of the media outlets that were still operating to make sure they were reaching everyone that needed help.

“Wow! Did you expect anything like that to happen?” Sean asked as they were driving away.

“Nope. Never occurred to me in the slightest. Looks like we might’ve started something, though.”

“Let’s just hope it doesn’t backfire on us. Let’s stop by the card-lock, get fueled up, and then swing by that store and get that seed. We might want to look for some septic system supplies too, before long. We don’t want that system to fail before we get another in the ground. When we get to that farm supply store, we can look up a place that carries the tanks and piping.”

As Mike rolled to a stop by the barn with the panel truck, everyone could see a brand new, dark gray Chevy four-door pick-up truck coming up the driveway pulling a flatbed trailer with a septic tank strapped down on it, with a stack of sewer pipe lying alongside. Pulling around back, Sean backed the trailer out past the barn and parked it. Mitch came walking up to see what Sean had brought in. He was like a kid finding new toys or something every day, always thinking of something that needed doing.

"Hey, Dad. Was just thinking we might want to put in another septic system to handle all these people we're getting."

"Good thinking, Son! You're probably right. Our system is only rated for four bedrooms and maybe eight people at the most full-time. Even subtracting ten people for the bunker, we've still got over twenty people full time on the system. The only thing we need now to complete the job is a couple of dump truck loads of gravel for the drain-field."

"I've been thinking about that too. The county has a couple of trucks. We could confiscate one of them and take it down to the Springfield Sand and Gravel yard, find the keys to a loader, and fill up the truck. We could even bring some larger rock, with some smaller stuff to top it off to make a larger trailer yard, almost like a trailer park. Set up the septic to handle a lot of risers for the trailer park, and I think we'll be set. Maybe put in twice the usual length for the drain-field, and I think it'll last a while."

"Sounds good, Son. If you and Mike could get us the rock out here, Kevin and I could put in the system. I can run a backhoe, and not to mention, I put in the system for the bunker myself."

"Alright, we'll get started on the rock as soon as possible. In the meantime, we need to get your seed unloaded from the panel truck. Is dinner about ready? We're a little late, and we're starving."

"Rachel and Hailee are inside warming up your dinner right now. You two go ahead and eat, and then get cleaned up. I'll round up some help to unload that seed."

"How are Lucy and Emily doing today?" Sean asked.

"Your mom has been spending a lot of time with them. She said their bruises are really showing up today. Lucy is feeling better, but she still seems to be affected emotionally. Lucy actually asked to see you and Mike, so maybe you better check with your mom as soon as you can."

"Alright, I will."

Walking into the house, they could smell dinner and were anxious to dig in. Giving the girls hugs and kisses, they sat down to eat. Beth had come in, and before she was able to say anything, Rachel made a comment.

"Sean, it sounds like you and Mike are local heroes."

"Really?" Sean looked her in the eye and never batted an eyelash. "Why so? What did we do this time?"

"What you two did to save Lucy and Emily."

"Oh, you mean local like here in our local group. That's likely to happen since we're always bringing food home."

Rachel and Hailee could see that Sean was playing word games and steering the conversation away from the subject. Rachel would have to take the head-on approach.

"We heard you on the radio today, Sean. Everything you said, and we heard what all the people had to say who called in after your public announcement." Rachel watched as Sean slowed his chewing for one heartbeat, and then continued like there wasn't anything amiss. "Why didn't you tell us the whole story?"

"Rachel, what Mike and I did to those men was harsh punishment. We didn't burst into the room and shoot all three as they turned their weapons on us. Their weapons were on the dresser as two of them were half-naked and the third was asking for his turn. One of them was in the very act. I'm not going to tell you what we did… other than that the first one to die was the one that stripped and beat Emily, who was helping to hold Lucy, waiting for his turn, who reached for the guns on the dresser. He died too quickly to suit Mike and me. I should have shot him in the leg so that he could have suffered at least a little like the other two. Mike and I saw Emily, that darling, pretty, young girl running naked down the street, trying to hold a torn shirt over her body. We're the ones that heard what those three men were talking about as they were raping Lucy."

Rachel, looking in Sean's eyes as he spoke, could see his eyes starting to water, and her heart started to ache for him. Her reason for asking him about it hadn't been to condemn him, but rather to express her desire for him not to hold anything back from her. She wanted to know all the things that he didn't want her to know. She reached out and took his hand to hold it tightly.

Sean continued, "They were going to look for Emily as soon as they were done having their way with Lucy. If Emily had not escaped, they would have stayed in their apartment for several days taking turns raping both of them repeatedly. We couldn't stand the thought of those kind of men ever capturing you or Hailee, or any of the other women or girls that are here, that are now part of our family, and we both decided we would never have to worry about those three ever again.

"We didn't want to tell you all of the sordid details of what we did; we love you too much to burden you with all of that ugly stuff. That public announcement was an attempt to warn off other would-be rapists. If it will save just one girl from a rapist, then I'm glad I spoke from my heart for the whole county to hear. Mike and I are more than ready to back up our words with actions. That's all I have to say on it."

"That's good, Son, because we're all ready to back you up on whatever you did to those three." Mitch and Kevin had walked in just in time to hear most of what Sean had to say about the ordeal. Several other members of the group were right behind him, and most of the rest of the group had come in to listen from the living room. "Besides, it looks like most of the men in the county feel the same way as you and Mike. The only ones who disagreed were the panty-waist types who wouldn't lift a finger to keep their own sister from being raped."

Rachel wrapped her arms around Sean and whispered words of love into his ear.

"I'm proud of you, Sean, for what you and Mike have been doing, and I didn't question you on it because I disagreed, but that I want you to be totally honest with us on what you're having to face out there."

Sean pulled away enough to look at Rachel's face, wondering if he should tell her what was really happening out there. "Rachel, honey, Mike and I, yesterday, had to personally kill over three thousand people, one by one, lining up our scope on them and making a decision every time we squeezed the trigger. That was only one day for us. That's hard enough on us as it is and then we run into the likes of those three men. What we do every day is something we don't want to affect our loved ones back here. What we hold back from you is to keep you from looking at us like we're monsters or that we don't have feelings."

Sean had to keep pressing the point, because it was so important for them to see the reasons for their actions, to understand how they could keep doing what needed to be done. As he continued to watch Rachel, seeing her own eyes fill with tears, he couldn't keep from becoming emotional himself, and tears began to build at the corners of his own eyes. As he continued, the tears started to roll, "I love all of you people here, and Mike and I have promised ourselves to protect you from all of the bad stuff that's out there, and what's still coming. We just don't want you to stop loving us because we have to do these things."

By the time he was finished, everyone in the room was crying, seeing the tears on the faces of the two strongest among them. Day in and day out, they continued to do the hard job without a moment of complaint, and yet, continually, they were thinking of how to better the lives of all those around them—their immediate group as well as all those that were still living in the two cities. The two of them poured themselves out daily, and as their loved ones began to realize just how much they were dealing with, and suffering in their own way, they gathered around and held them, expressing their love and appreciation.

"Son, if you and Mike weren't who you are, two thirds of the people that are now here and safe wouldn't be here and nor would they be safe. You may not know it, but the baker guy called the radio station to tell what you and Mike have done to help everyone in the area, so when Rachel said that you two were heroes, she was basing it on what everyone already knows. We love the both of you guys, and we'll never feel otherwise, no matter what you have to do to protect us."

As Mitch wrapped his arms around his son, the tears continued to flow, and Beth stepped up to them and wrapped her arms around them both.

Rachel turned Sean's face toward her and said through her tears, "You and Mike are my heroes too."

CHAPTER FORTY-ONE

The first thing Sean and Mike wanted to do the next morning was drive straight to the bakery to talk to the baker. They had a plan to share with him. By the time they were able to make their way through the early morning wave of stage two, the baker was on the job, and two police cars were present. Entering the building, they could smell the delicious aroma of fresh bread, making them aware of their hunger. Walking into the baking room, they watched the baker operating his equipment, looking at all of the freshly baked loaves. As soon as he had time, Sean caught his attention.

"We've been thinking about the next wave of stage two infected. In two more days, there's going to be over ten thousand coming out across the county. These are people who were originally infected sixteen days ago, on about the twenty-ninth day of the attack. At that time, it had only been four days after the first presidential bulletin, and people still weren't protecting themselves from the virus. In two more days, there will be twice as many as we've had to deal with so far, and every day after that there will be even more. We won't be able to kill all of them. We were thinking, if you bake as much bread as you can for the next two days and have the police deliver twenty loaves to every location that they've already been delivering to, with a command to stay indoors for twelve days, the majority of the stage two will die off naturally. After that time, we start our patrols again, and delivering bread. Whoever is still alive, at that point, will most likely survive. Two more weeks after that, the virus will basically be played out, and we can start concentrating on rebuilding."

"That sounds like a good plan, Sean. Have you talked to the police captain and explained it to him?"

"Not yet. We were far too busy this morning just getting here. I'll call him right now and see what he thinks about it." Sean turned to go use the phone in the office and noticed Mike taking a huge chunk out of a freshly baked loaf. Seeing Sean looking him over, he held out the loaf for Sean to tear off his own piece. It smelled wonderful. Eating some bread on the way to the phone, Sean called the police department to talk to the captain. Explaining his plan to deliver extra food and holing up for ten or twelve days, Sean also wanted to know if they had been able to get a butcher started on some cattle.

"Yes, we've got packaged meat to start sending out with the bread. The butcher is cutting them up as fast as he can in all of the different cuts and a lot of burger. He's got a helper, and they've already butchered five steers."

"Have him butcher several cows, keep out the back-strap and tenderloin, and burger the rest of it. That will be very fast, and they'll be able to package three times as many animals. We have today and tomorrow to get that food delivered, and then we're going to be overrun with stage two. For at least a week, there will be huge numbers of infected every day. Maybe some of them will kill each other, but the rest will die normally on their own within six or seven days of turning. Six or seven days of turnings, and then another seven days after the last big day, and they'll mostly be all dead. If we can keep the healthy people locked away for twelve days or so with enough food to last, I think we'll be, for the most part, in the clear. So the more they can package for delivery right away, the more people we'll save. If you could locate where someone is storing the most recent harvest of potatoes, we could pass some of those around too."

"I'll get someone working on it right away. The spuds is a good idea and would really stretch out the food supply."

"Also arrange more bulletins with all of the available media explaining the plan so everyone knows what to expect and what to plan for," added Sean.

Jack had called again for food giving the two different addresses with separate calls and waited downstairs for the delivery. With the new delivery there were potatoes and several pounds of meat to go with the bread. He decided to use the freezer in the lower room to store some of the meat and had to lock the front door when he left to keep scavengers out of his stash. It seemed to Jack that apartment houses may have been the hardest hit with the virus, because of the closer association that the tenants had with one another. Many units had no people in them because they had been hit with the virus early enough in the outbreak to have been checked into the hospital, leaving their rooms empty.

Moving around from his unit to the one downstairs had drawn some attention from some of his neighbors, and starting up some conversations, he had started some seeds of thinking in their minds about his plans for survival. Some of the guys he talked to were a little on the rough side and seemed like they might fit right in with the types of things that he was wanting to do. He had to start somewhere, and as the virus would start to die out, he needed to have some things already in place. Somehow, he needed to start lining up followers that would embrace his philosophy of survival, no matter how ugly or controlling it may seem. He knew there would be a lot of men that would follow his ideals of using women as sex slaves; the trouble was how to find them.

Once the idea started to take root, he began knocking on all the doors in the apartment house to see who was still alive and to judge each one's character and whether they would fit within his criteria for followers. He also found out which units had any single women in them. As he continued his planning, he spread his recruitment to other apartment complexes that were close by his own. Keeping a notebook, he kept meticulous notes on who he thought would follow, who wouldn't, and what apartments had single women or only women living in them. He was always on the lookout for a woman who he could again visit in the night, like the ones that did not have any close neighbors that would come to her rescue if she were able to scream for help. Once he had built up a network of followers that agreed with his philosophy, everything else would be easy. It was only a matter of time.

That evening, Sean and Mike drove two dump trucks into the back area and dumped their loads in a pile close to where Mitch had dug the ditches for the drain-field. Lonnie and Steve followed with the panel truck and parked it in front of the house. As soon as they had eaten their dinner, the four of them left in the dump trucks to go get more rock for the trailer yard they had decided to make. They wanted to get all the rock down before the weather changed and rained on the ground, softening it up before they were ready. They left instructions to get two rolls of a membrane material out of the panel truck and spread it across the ground where they were going to lay the rock for the trailer yard. Mitch had already laid the pipe with the riser connections to receive the pipe from the trailers and had buried the line, so it was ready to lay the rock down. The membrane would keep the rock from disappearing into the soil as it softened through the winter. They were hoping to get all the rock that evening and then they could set the trailers up in a row like an RV park.

Steve was armed with both a handgun and rifle and was ecstatic about being invited along with the men on more important work outside the farm. It was only twenty minutes to the sand and gravel yard, and since they now had the keys for the loader, it wouldn't take long to load the trucks. A front-end loader with a six-yard bucket only took two scoops to fill a dump truck, so they were only at the yard for twenty minutes.

Mitch was already on the backhoe dumping gravel in the ditches as the boys were driving back in with a load of larger rock. Dumping both loads on the membrane, they took the time to watch Mitch spread it out to see if it was enough. It would take two more loads it looked like, and they were off to the yard again. Coming back with another load, they dumped it and immediately took off for a load of smaller stuff that could be walked across more safely.

By the time they returned, Mitch had the rock all spread out, and they were able to back the dump trucks onto the rock bed to start dumping their load at the back edge and slowly driving forward. They were, in effect, doing their own spreading.

It was almost dark, and they needed another load of rock. They would have Lonnie and Kevin get it in the morning, while Mitch was finishing up the drain-field.

It had been a long day for the men, and they were all ready for the evening to end. Finding Rachel, Sean led her up to the room and commenced to talk her into taking a shower to help wash his back. They used up a lot of hot water before they were done, and Rachel made sure that Sean realized how important he was to her. Loving on each other was their way of reconnecting with what was important in their lives and laying aside all of the fear and junk that was always encroaching on their minds. The future would be as bright as they could make it as each of them continued to work toward a common goal, waiting for the day that it was safe to start their own family.

The following morning, Sean and Mike headed into work; Lonnie and Kevin went after rock; and Mitch and the younger men worked on finishing the drain-field and laying the pipe and the membrane to keep the soil from filling in around the drain rock. By noon, Mitch had the entire septic system ready to use, and they commenced moving the trailers into position, by backing them in at an angle at each one of the risers for the waste pipe. All in all, the set-up looked extremely professional, and they were all proud of the accomplishment. All they needed was several more nice trailers set up for any future people that could show up at any time. Joe and Lonnie made several trips back to the RV dealer and had three more trailers set up by the time Sean and Mike returned.

After a quick dinner and shower, Sean and Mike decided to take their girls into town for a shopping spree at Kohl's. They had passed the store earlier that day and noticed that someone had already broken into the store, so there wasn't any fear about taking the girls and possibly getting shot at by the police. Steve and Emily had hit it off with each other and had asked if they could ride along. Seeing how well Emily had been improving after her ordeal, they welcomed them on the trip. Rachel's sister, Leah, couldn't be left behind either, and since she hadn't been away from the farm for so long, Sean couldn't deny her. Driving Sean's new four-door Chevy, there was room for everyone, and they were on their way. Taking weapons and facemasks, they were ready for a little fun on the town, even if it was only a trip to Kohl's for an hour or so. It had been quite a while since anyone but the men had been away from the farm.

Sean was hoping that they wouldn't run into too many infected while the girls were with them. It would probably scare them or repel them to see them have to kill someone. Arriving at Kohl's without seeing any infected up close; they were keeping a low profile to keep things as normal as they could. All four of the women carried handguns on their belts, and the guys had both those and their M4s.

"You four ladies can stay in the truck, while us guys take a quick sweep through the building to make sure it's safe," Sean instructed.

When they had gone, Emily was the first to speak. "You two are so lucky to have Sean and Mike. I think I fell in love with both of them when… they saved me. They never stared at my nakedness or made me feel ashamed of what my mother and I went through. They cared for us, covered us, and treated us with care and tenderness. They make all of us feel so secure, and even though they can be tough, there is also a softness and gentleness to them that comes out when you need it. I'll never forget them as long as I live."

"I know how lucky I am," replied Rachel. "I've seen his gentleness and his caring, tender side, and I'm glad I haven't had to see his hard side. But I also know the hard side is what's keeping us all alive. I've never loved anyone so much in my life."

"I feel the same way," added Hailee. "From the moment I met the two of them, I knew they were special. When Mike spoke his first words to me, my heart leaped. Of course, it might have been the uniforms."

The four girls all started giggling.

"Emily, what do you think of Steve?" asked Rachel.

"He's very sweet, kind, gentle, a lot like Sean I think, but not as confident. I think the more he hangs out with Sean and Mike, the more he'll gain in confidence. If some of their other traits rub off on him as he's learning, he'll be a lot like them as he matures."

"I think so too," replied Hailee. "He adores both of them and is becoming very proud of the fact that they've asked him to help out with things. Steve's asked me about you, what I think about you, and he really seems genuinely concerned about you. I think he really likes you."

"I hope he doesn't think less of me because… you know. That man touched me and saw me."

"No, Emily. He doesn't feel that way at all. He thinks you're pretty special to be able to keep your wits and to escape and to save your mom. I think he's taken a real liking to you," explained Rachel, as she took Emily's hand to hold it tightly.

"Here they come." Hailee had been watching for their return.

"All clear." Sean took Rachel's hand to help her out of the truck and Mike and Steve did the same for their girls.

As they started for the entrance, a man came around the corner of the building. He was walking slow, dragging one foot, and one arm dangled at his side. He was moaning and grunting as he moved toward them.

Sean and Mike looked at him and watched how he was moving and the noises he was making.

"What does that remind you of?" Sean asked.

"The same thing it reminds you of. If it talks like one, looks like one, and walks like one…"

"But still, those aren't real. This is. Go ahead and take the girls inside, and I'll take care of this."

"Why is he walking like that?" asked Emily.

"In the last stage of the virus, it starts to cause paralysis, and usually it starts with the feet. That one is one that we failed to get and has been stage two for several days. We'll put him out of his misery.

Mike led the girls through the door, and Steve hung back with Sean.

"Do you think I can take care of this one? I need to learn some time."

"Taking a life isn't something to look forward to, even if they're sick. But it can still affect you if you're not ready for it. You have to harden yourself to the act and realize it's for the greater good. They are still people, but they don't seem to realize even who they are. They're practically mindless, but they're in great physical pain and agony, because the virus is causing inflammation of the brain. Putting them down not only protects us, but also puts them out of their misery. If you're serious about wanting to do this, then at this distance I like to aim for the head to put them out immediately. Less pain for them. You sure you're ready?"

"Yes, this is as good a time as any."

"Kneel down, take the safety off, line up the red dot on the forehead, take a breath, and let it out, keeping the red dot on target. When the breath is gone, steady on the target, and squeeze the trigger."

Three seconds, four, five… Boom! The infected fell backward to the ground and laid still. Steve continued to look through the scope at the unmoving target.

"Is he dead?"

"Yes. A good clean shot. Well done, Steve."

"Thanks, but… I don't feel like giving thanks."

"That's good, because there's nothing good about having to kill someone. You just do what needs to be done and move on. You alright?"

Steve finally stood to his feet. "Yeah. It didn't feel like I thought it would. It makes me feel sad, sort of."

"I know what you mean. The whole thing is sad. They did nothing to deserve it, or to suffer because of it, and in the end, they lose their life for no good reason. Let's head inside and think about how the girls are enjoying looking at new clothes."

"Alright."

The lights were still on in the building, making it seem like just a normal day of shopping, minus the crowds and the chatter. Whoever broke in, must have found the switches and had turned them all on. The girls seemed to be excited with the looking and choosing. Not being worried about having the money to pay for what they wanted, they weren't limited to what they could afford. Before long, they had all made several trips to the dressing rooms to make sure their choices fit and looked good on them. Of course the guys didn't mind seeing the joy on their faces as they came out of the dressing room to model the clothes for the one who cared so much about them.

Sean, for one, couldn't keep from making remarks about Rachel that would cause her to blush. In turn, her blushing made him want to put his arms around her and whisper things in her ear that would make her blush all the more, which he did several times. The last time he did it, she whispered back that if he weren't careful, she would take him to a back room and make him live up to what he was promising.

All in all, it was a pretty nice evening for all of them—just to be carefree and laughing, not thinking about anything but each other and having a good time. For Sean and Mike, it was like balm to their souls to see four wonderful girls enjoying themselves so much, not having to worry what tomorrow would bring, but just totally immersing themselves in one of their favorite pastimes.

At one point, Sean walked toward the front of the store to look around to make sure all was good, and seeing a jewelry case, he walked over to see what was in it. Someone had broken the glass case and took the most expensive rings, but Sean was looking at the necklaces and seeing a thin gold chain with an 'R' attached to it and another one with an 'S', he took both of them, removed the letters and placed both of them on a larger gold chain. Steve came over to see what he was doing, and he picked through the jewelry to find something for Emily. Satisfied, they returned to the girls with a couple of carts, as they were finishing with their shopping.

None of the girls were going to return to the farm with the same clothes that they had on when they left, and they were all aglow from the excitement of trying on so many clothes and getting to take home everything they liked. None of them had ever been able to do that.

"Don't forget to pick out some coats for winter; it's just around the corner. Emily, you could pick out a coat for your mom too. As soon as you're done with that, Mom wanted us to pick up some bedding and pillows for several trailers and some cooking utensils, dishes, and silverware also. If there's anything else you can think of as we're shopping, feel free to throw it in." Soon after, the guys had to grab some more carts to hold all the things they were wanting. When the guys stopped at the men's section, the girls were quick to help them pick out a leather jacket and a warm winter coat, which only added more to their growing piles on the carts—plus, thick flannel shirts for the colder weather, new jeans to replace their old worn ones, new tennis shoes, and under clothes. It was nice having a wife to worry about how they were dressed, and it made Sean and Mike feel wonderful to have such a caring woman in their life.

By the time they made their way back to the truck, they had eight full carts of goodies. Sean had to go back in to get the rest of the carts, while Mike kept a lookout with the girls. They had a truck full of things and had to place the heavy boxes of silverware and dishes on the piles of clothes to keep them from blowing out on the way home. There was a lot of excited talk and laughter on the way home, and Sean was wishing that they had brought two truckloads of people to let them all experience the fun of shopping. It wasn't quite dark, and the store wasn't going to close, so he asked Mike and the girls what they thought of returning with some of the others to let them enjoy themselves before they shut themselves in for twelve days. The second trip wouldn't take as long because all of the trailer things were out of the way, and it would just be to pick out some clothes for several people. They were agreeable, so Sean called Mitch to line up some people that wanted to go, so they could head back into town as quickly as they could.

CHAPTER FORTY-TWO

With nothing to draw them away from the farm the next day, Sean had to stay up late to make good his promises to Rachel that he made back at the store. Then in the morning, after they slept in just a little, he again had to fulfill his boastful remarks to satisfy her desires. By the time they had showered, most of the breakfast was gone, and they were fortunate that Beth had set enough aside for the two of them.

"Thank you, Sean, for taking all those people to the store last night. This morning I noticed quite a change among the younger people—a lot more smiles and laughter during breakfast. They actually looked happy. Not to mention Rachel and Hailee are fairly glowing this morning," Beth commented.

"Mom, that was the funnest thing Mike and I have been able to do in three weeks. We really enjoyed it, and I just wish we had thought of it sooner. Then we could have done it more than once." Looking at Rachel, he added, "And the benefits for me were tremendous." He gave her a big grin that wasn't entirely lost on Beth. She was so happy to see that her son had finally found someone special to love that returned that love in the same manner.

"Your father and I were going to start setting up those new trailers with all the things you brought in last night. Do you and Rachel want to help?"

"No, Mom, I think I'd rather just lay low with Rachel and enjoy the peace and quiet. Maybe take Mike and Hailee around to some of the close farms and check on all of our neighbors, see who's still around and who's not."

"That would be a good idea, Sean. It would be nice to know who made it."

"After this plague runs its course and we draw a lot of people out here, it might be a good thing to have them move into all of the close farmhouses to keep us consolidated, so we can still work together for our survival. Just outlasting the virus doesn't mean things are going to go back to normal. There won't be any jobs at the banks, insurance companies, clothing stores, or malls and shops. There won't be any of that any time soon. We'll have to farm all of our produce, our wheat for our baking needs, raise all of our own cattle for butchering, and be pretty much self-sufficient. We'll probably go back to a bartering system of trading what we have for things that we don't have. Although with all of the surplus in the towns, and if we do a lot of collecting right away, it'll be awhile before we actually need anything from anyone."

"How many people do you think we'll have out here depending on us?" Beth asked with curiosity.

"It's hard to tell, Mom. By spring, we could have several hundred. It all depends on how many actually survive the virus. We won't know that answer for about three more weeks, and even then, without any government agency to go around looking people up and counting them, it'll be hard for us to count them with any accuracy. We're set up pretty good right here, even without the bunker. We can take care of all of our needs, except for medical, and none of the people that survive who live in city limits will have any way to raise the food they need to survive. All of the survivors will have to move into the more open spaces to raise their own food, to round up some cattle without an owner, and to raise their own beef. So eventually, almost everyone will have to become a farmer/rancher to survive. With most of them knowing nothing about doing that, we could end up with a lot of dependents quickly."

"When that happens, will there still be trouble for us?"

"Mom, I don't want to worry you too much, but yes there will be trouble. Whenever a society is trying to assert itself and to figure out how to operate, to sustain itself, who the leaders are going to be, and how it's all going to work, there are always going to be those who want to control everything and everyone. With a lack of law and law enforcement, we'll effectively be living back in the old west, with a lot of amenities, of course. It might come down to who has the most guns and ammo and the best leader. We'll have to wait and see how it all plays out. I'll guarantee you this, Mike and I will do our best to protect us, our followers, and then all of the new society that grows up. If we run into people that want to control everything, and make everyone a slave to them, Mike and I will treat them the same way we treated those three rapists—fast and no mercy. That's the only way to save society until a new government can be formed to start over."

"Even if that sounds a little harsh, I trust your judgment to do what's right. Don't ever lose sight of what's right."

"I won't, Mom. You and Dad and Rachel will keep me on the straight and narrow. I'll go round up Mike and see if he wants to go for a ride."

Leaving Rachel to talk with Beth, Sean headed into the living room to grab a hat off the rack, and Lucy was just coming out of her bedroom.

"Good morning, Lucy. Are you feeling better today?" Sean asked.

Beth and Rachel heard Sean's greeting and began to listen to their exchange.

"Yes. I'm better. I… I wanted to thank you for saving… us, and bringing us to your home. Emily has really taken a liking to it and has made some new friends. We've been eating better than we have in over a week, and Emily told me about the trip to town yesterday. It made her feel really good."

"I'm glad, Lucy. If there's anything you need, be sure to let me know, or Mom."

"Everyone has been so good to me, but I… I still feel, so dirty… and unworthy… to be here." Lucy started weeping, and Sean took her hands in his.

"It's alright, Lucy. None of what happened was your fault, and no one thinks less of you because that happened. Just keep your head up and keep moving forward. Every day that goes by, that other day gets farther and farther away. Someday soon, you won't even be thinking about it."

"But still, what man is going to want me now that I've been… been… used?" cried Lucy.

"Any man that's worth winning your heart won't even give it a second thought. He'll see your beauty and your inner strength, and he'll love you for who you are, not for what you've been through. Lucy, don't ever think those thoughts again. You're a fine, beautiful woman, and I'm sure any man will see that once he gets to know you. Things will be fine, I promise you."

Lucy was still crying, and Sean moved closer to wrap his arms around her and just hold her with the comfort that two strong arms can provide, whispering words of comfort. Beth and Rachel had been listening and had peeked around the corner to see Lucy wrapped up in Sean's arms, still crying. Rachel put her own arms around Beth as she also began to weep, feeling Lucy's sadness, but also the tender heart behind Sean's gracious words to build up and encourage the distraught woman. To see the woman's emotional pain and mental distress, and Sean's reaction to it, she could now better understand Sean and Mike's actions against the three rapists.

After a few moments, Sean led Lucy by the hand into the kitchen to hand her off to his mom, noticing that her own eyes were watery and her nose was red. He took Rachel by the hand, and his parting words to Lucy were to keep her head up, that things were going to get better. Walking out the back door with Rachel holding his arm, he looked over the new RV parking and admired it.

"I love you, Sean." Rachel reached her hand up to Sean's cheek and looked him in the eye. Giving him a quick kiss, they continued out to the trailers, looking for Mike.

"Hey, Dad, is Mike out here with you?"

"No. I think he took Hailee on a walk down by the river… to the north."

"Thanks, Dad. You need my help for anything?"

"No, Son, you go ahead and take it easy and spend some time with Rachel. You deserve it."

Walking over to the panel truck, he retrieved his M4 and continued walking up the river looking for Mike and Hailee.

"Maybe we should let them alone for a while—same thing Dad told me."

"Okay. What would you like to do?"

"I've already done all of those things." He smiled at her, pulled her to him, and gave her a tender kiss. Every time he would say something like that and show her that pearly white smile, her heart would melt like hot wax, and she would become putty in his loving hands. She adored him as much as anyone ever could.

"We could get a blanket and go lay in the pasture by the river and watch the clouds go by."

"If we lay down anywhere on a blanket, watching the clouds go by will be the last thing you'll be doing. You'll have to think of something else."

"Is there something wrong with wanting to love on my beautiful wife all the time?"

"No, but there's a time for that, and there's a time for other things. Right now it's time for other things," explained Rachel.

"Okay, let's take a walk over to the neighbor's house and see if anyone's home. We've got our weapons, so we should be safe."

"Let's go."

Walking down the driveway to the bridge, they stopped, and Sean threw a few stones into the water, watching some small fish scatter at the disturbance of their home. The sun wasn't very high in the sky yet, and their shadows were out in front of them as they strolled along. The blue sky was littered with scattered white clouds, non-threatening, and the two of them continued out to the road. There were pole fences lining the driveway to keep the cows in the pastures, and as they reached the pavement, they turned right toward Sweet Home and walked on to the next driveway taking off to the left.

Holding onto Rachel's hand while they strolled along, talking about the future, was peaceful for Sean, compared to the last couple of weeks. He would never tire of being in Rachel's sweet presence, and as he walked along, he inhaled her fragrance from the shower that morning. Just as they were about to turn into the driveway, Rachel pointed at something shiny across the river, inside the edge of the trees.

Sean, shading his eyes from the eastern sun, looked for about five seconds. "It couldn't be." He raised his rifle, looked through the scope for three seconds and then lowered it, then turned and started walking up the driveway.

"Could you tell what it was. It looked like it was moving." Sean turned his face to look at her, and with a smile, he explained.

"It's a good thing we didn't go looking for Mike and Hailee."

"Why's that?"

"Because we would have all been embarrassed. That was the two of them across the river that you saw. Didn't look like they had any clothes on."

"Sean, are you sure? I never would have thought Hailee would have done that out in the open."

"Doing it like that out in the country has its merits. Someday, I'll have to show you."

"No, you won't. I won't let you."

"Do you really think you could deny me anything if I turned on the charm and snuggled up to you?" He gave her that little smile.

"No… not really. But if we ever got caught I would scream and never let you do it again."

Sean stopped and pulled her to him, and with his arms around her, he said, "I would never put you in a position to get caught. I'd be more careful than that."

"Don't you think that's what Mike told Hailee before she got talked into it?"

"Probably. We'd just have to be more careful. That's all."

Approaching the house, a three-foot white fence extended all around the yard, encircling the house, to keep the animals out. Several old and tall poplar trees were standing on the south and west side of the house to provide shade during the summer months. There were a few chickens feeding in the yard and some outside the fence. The chicken coop was off to the south side of the house, and Sean could see several broods of baby chicks following the mother hen around, pecking at bugs and seeds on the ground. Sean called out a couple of times the name of the owner, and then walked up on the porch to knock on the door. Wrapping loudly on the glass at first, following it up with banging on the wood part of the door, Sean waited a whole minute and then tried the door. It was locked.

Walking around the house, he tried the back door, but it was also locked. Finding a bedroom window that wasn't locked, he removed the screen and slid it open. The blind was raised, and he spent a moment listening to the quiet inside the house. Pulling his mask from his pocket, he put it on, and handing his rifle to Rachel, he crawled through the window. He could smell the decomposing flesh as soon as he opened the window, but didn't want to mention it to Rachel. Taking his rifle as Rachel extended the barrel through the window, he told her to wait by the front door.

Walking slowly through the house, room by room, he found old Mr. Barrows. His wife was tied to the bed frame. He blew his brains out after he shot his wife of fifty years, with an old twenty-two long rifle pistol. Just enough power to enter the brain cavity, but not enough to exit and would expend all of its energy ricocheting around inside the skull until it came to rest, turning the brain to mush. Walking to the front door, he unlocked it and walked out.

"Old Mr. Barrows took care of his sick wife until she turned, and then shot her in the head. Before he turned, he shot himself. None of us deserved this crap. I'm glad we nuked those guys so that they wouldn't live to see what they caused."

Rachel hugged Sean tightly for a moment, feeling his tension release, and then she kissed him.

Walking over to the chicken coop, they checked out how many chickens were feeding around or inside the coop. Sean decided they needed to send someone over to catch them all and take them to the farm. They needed more layers, and they could use the young ones as fryers as soon as they had grown enough in size. With more people, they needed to continue increasing all of their animals to help supply the growing need for food. With a continuing supply of eggs, they could do both. Heading back to the farm, Sean noticed that Mike and Hailee were no longer in sight.

Getting back to the farm, Sean informed his dad about Mr. Barrows, also about all of the chickens and baby chicks running around, and the several steers, calves, and cows in the pasture. Mitch would find time later to take a cage in the truck with some of the youngsters to catch all of them and bring them over.

"Have you ever ridden a horse, Rachel?" Mitch asked.

"A couple of times, when I was quite a bit younger. Why?"

"Sean, why don't you saddle up three of the horses, and you could take Rachel and Hailee over there and chase all those cows over here to our property. Have Mike stay on foot and run the gates. Shouldn't take too long and would be fun for the girls."

"Okay, sounds like fun."

Forty-five minutes later, Sean had three horses saddled and was ready to go. All of the young kids were hanging around, excited by the horses. Sean took turns riding each horse around the barn to make sure they weren't over ambitious about dumping the rider and then started putting different kids in the saddle and leading them around. Mike and Rachel helped, loving the looks of excitement on the faces of the children as they rode a horse for the first time. When they were done, they let the teenagers take a turn riding around the barn by themselves. Everyone was enjoying themselves and laughing and joking with one another.

When it was the girl's turn to mount, the guys were more than helpful as they placed their hands on their wives to help them up into the saddles. At first, the guys led them around to let them get used to the feel of the saddle and the stirrups. Then, increasing their speed to a fast jog, they led them around the barn to get themselves settled into the saddle. Handing them the reins, explaining the ways of a rider with his horse, Sean jumped up into the saddle to give them some quick training.

"Mike, jump in the truck and park it out on the road, on the left side of our driveway, and then you can run up and open the gate for us. It's back up the road to the right about fifty yards. Keep your rifle handy."

Mike went first, and then Sean followed with the girls. Sean dismounted to open their gate into the pasture before they reached the bridge, and he then continued to lead the girls across the bridge and into the pasture on the other side of the road. Kicking up his horse into a gallop, he yelled back to the girls to hold on with feet, legs, and hands as their own horses sped up to match the gait of Sean's horse. Circling around behind the animals, as they were already starting to bunch up with the abnormal activity going on, Sean started to push them back toward the gate. The girls got their horses off to the side, out of the way. As the cattle trotted past them, their horses took after them of their own accord.

"Pull back on the reins a little. We don't want to crowd them and cause them to panic."

Mike was standing to the left of the gate, so if the animals made it that far, they would turn back down the road toward the other driveway. Sean had to do a some quick riding to keep the cows from turning away from the gate, but as they figured out they weren't going back out into the pasture, they went on through and then down toward the truck. Mitch and Joe had walked out to the road to help block their way, forcing them down the driveway. The cattle balked at the bridge some, and as Sean pushed them, they headed down the path into the water. Chasing them up the other side, they again started up the driveway, and when they saw Lonnie, David, and Kevin standing in the road, they turned through the gate into their new home. Following them a little ways to push them closer to their own cows, Sean returned to the gate and the girls.

They walked the horses back up to the barn, where the kids were waiting for another turn to ride. Each of them took the youngest child and held them in front of them as they rode the horses around the barn a couple of times and then dismounted to let the older kids try it by themselves. All of the adults stood around watching the kids having fun, and Beth and Lucy started bringing out glasses of iced tea for everyone. There were a few lawn chairs around, and Sean and Mike walked to the shop to round up a few more. Everything seemed so normal for a while, with everyone forgetting about their troubles and just enjoying the moment, the sunny weather, and watching the kids having fun on the horses.

CHAPTER FORTY-THREE

Late in the afternoon, Sean and Mike wanted to take a swing through town, at least the edge of it, to see how bad it was going to be with all of the infected. Lonnie wanted to ride along to check it out also, so they invited him into the truck. Driving the panel truck into town, they reduced speed once they crossed the McKenzie River, because they could see a lot of movement. Taking out his binoculars, Sean looked everything over that he could see. There were a lot of infected, with a lot of them fighting with one another, going to the ground, biting, and hitting—no wrestling moves, boxing, or jujitsu, just animal like fighting. Handing the binoculars to Mike, he let him take a long look at what was going on. There was no way they would have killed that many, and there were going to be added even more than that throughout the night and the next day, and then more and more for several days.

"I see a police uniform in the crowd. That's not good." Mike handed the binoculars to Lonnie for a look-see. They backed off and drove around by another road to take a look a little farther on, and it was the same. It was discouraging to see so many infected roaming the streets. They had killed so many already, and to see that many at one time made them realize just how bad it actually was.

Lonnie picked up the mic for the police radio and started talking, trying to raise anyone, but with no replies. Sean pulled out his cellphone and called the baker.

After a few rings, he answered, "Hello, Sean, is that you?"

“Yes. Mike and I are sitting at the edge of town looking things over. Doesn’t look good here over on the northeast side of Springfield. Where are you located?”

“I’m on the southside of Eugene. I hate to even look out the window; it’s so bad. Most of them are fighting with one another, but I haven’t noticed if they’re killing each other or not.”

“You got plenty of food to last?”

“Yes, we’ve got bread, meat, and potatoes… thanks to you and Mike.”

“That’s great, Bob. Have you heard anything from anyone else, the police, friends, relatives, even from out of town?”

“A couple of friends are doing okay, and I talked to the police chief just a little while ago. He said that five more officers called in with the symptoms. It’s not looking good really, other than a lot of people have enough food to hold them for the next twelve days.”

“Bob, if you run into any trouble, feel free to call me. Mike and I will come over and pull you out. How many are with you?”

“My brother and his family, his wife, and two kids”

“Alright, be sure to call if anything comes up”

“Okay, and thanks, Sean.”

The call ended, and Sean turned back to Mike.

“That’s all I need to see, Mike. Let’s head back home.”

Arriving back at the farm, Sean explained to the adults what the town looked like and that it wouldn’t be safe walking around after dark anymore. Once everyone separated to their sleeping areas, they were to remain indoors until first light, and even then, they needed to be careful walking into the open, lest there were any wandering infected drifting in overnight. He reminded them again to keep a weapon with them at all times. After dinner, he didn’t want any of the kids, and that included teenagers, walking around outside without an adult with a weapon, just in case. Every door needed to be locked every night so that everyone would be kept safe while they slept. They would keep a continuous guard of three people throughout the day. With the motion sensor lights, they would be aware if anyone showed up during the dark hours and would then be able to take care of the intruders. It was just getting too dangerous to take any unnecessary chances.

"Mr. President, we've just got word that twenty-five people in the compound have come down with symptoms. They're in the process of moving them out right now. They'll have to find them someplace outside to stay, until…"

"With the outside being overrun with stage two, how will they find a safe place for them? And what about food and care for them?"

"There are plenty of empty houses and apartments or motels that they can use, and they'll have to give them some of our food to live through the first of it. After that, they won't need any."

"It seems so cold to be talking about our associates and fellow workers that way," complained the President

"There's nothing else we can do, and there's no way to sugarcoat it. As bad as it is, we can no longer get accurate numbers on the infected. With so many roaming the streets, none of the government workers are going to work; hospitals are all closing; and there's no one left to report the numbers. We are assuming that the number of infected in the U.S. may be up to ninety-five percent or more, and almost all of them are now in stage one symptoms. If anyone is lucky enough not to have symptoms today, and continue to stay isolated, they have a good chance of surviving."

"My God. We may be reduced to less than five percent of our population? That's unbelievable. Do you think the rest of the world is the same way?"

"The three countries that had a good chance of fighting it off have all been nuked out of existence. I would imagine that the remaining countries are as bad off as we are or worse. There's just no way of telling."

"How is it coming with the rescue efforts in Russia?"

"Our reconnaissance planes, drones, and satellites are all sending back photos. There are a few airstrips that they can land on and then unload vehicles to drive further in to find the bunkers. They are lining things up to start even as we speak."

"If we're successful in recovering survivors, where are we going to put them? Has anyone been doing any research into that?" inquired the President.

"There may be several locations, but most of the far south locations have been eliminated because of the extreme heat conditions and most Russians may not acclimate to it very well. Too far north and the agricultural advantages are eliminated, and it needs to be a location with plenty of surface water in case the electric grid eventually fails. Some of the best locations that they've come up with include the Willamette Valley in Oregon—close to the coast, has good access to the Port of Portland, plenty of flowing water, mild winter conditions, plenty of cultivated ground for survival, and plenty of food processing plants and electrical power generating dams in the area. It actually has everything needed to sustain a society except for oil reserves and other natural resources. With help for that coming from California, I think it would be very doable. After researching it, I wouldn't mind living there myself."

"Do we have any data on how hard it's been hit with the virus?"

"It wasn't originally targeted, but once the virus got a foothold, it's been hit as hard as anywhere else. There'll be plenty of empty homes for the survivors if that's what we choose. I believe it would be ideal for reestablishing a thriving community."

"Keep researching it and make me up a list of what you find. We don't necessarily need to place all the survivors in one area. There may be key areas in the nation that will need a new labor force to keep the wheels of the new economy rolling, so keep that in mind."

"Yes, sir."

"How are our own survivor groups doing?" asked the President.

"Good. Once we got past the initial purging and set up the groups in their new locations, we haven't lost any of them yet."

"Do we still have military personnel surrounding them with protection?"

"We've lost some of the military with several groups, but they were able to purge out the infected without complete loss. With other groups, we haven't had any infection."

"That sounds good. I'm glad we've had some success with something."

Sean and Mike continued to take Steve with them, but also added Joe's son, Ryan, to the group. If anything happened to the two of them, they needed others to take their place that knew what to do and could handle themselves in adversity. Continuing to investigate the surrounding farms, they were keeping track of the empty ones and the ones that were still occupied. Finding a few people on a handful of farms, they began to share some of their food with the most desperate ones to help them get by until more supplies were procured.

Mitch and Kevin butchered another steer and a hog, and having his own meat grinder, he was able to make his own burger and sausage. Mitch had brushed up on his skills to cure, flavor, and smoke his own bacon and hams, which helped with meal variety. Mitch also started grinding some wheat so Beth could see how the bread baking would turn out with fresh flour. The bread tasted wonderful. Processed flour lost a lot of the things that made the flour tasty and more wholesome.

The following day, Bob called and asked if there was any way that Sean could come by and pick up his family. Having so many infected right outside their windows was making them all extremely nervous, and no one was getting any sleep. The only weapon they had was the pistol that Sean had given him, and not being proficient with it, they were afraid to try to come all the way across town by themselves.

"Let's take the panel truck, Lonnie driving, and at the edge of town, we can both hop on top. We won't be going fast through town, and there's a handrail, so we can take an extra chair in case we need it. We can strap it down for safety. With both of us shooting, we can make our way through town faster. We'll take a box full of loaded mags and reload some if we need to once we're at his house."

"Sounds good. Let's go."

Giving the girls a hug, a kiss, and a word of encouragement, they set out. Having Bob's address on his phone, they used MapQuest to lead them there. From the time they crossed the Willamette River, they were stopping every two hundred yards or so to knock down the infected. Trying to take the shot just as they walked to the edge of the road so they wouldn't be creating a roadblock, Sean and Mike were going through mag after mag of ammo.

Arriving at Bob's house, they knocked down at least twelve infected, only two of them close. Lonnie backed into the driveway, right up to the garage door so they could load some stuff into the back of the panel truck.

Climbing down to the driveway, Mike stepped out to the street to keep an eye on it, while Sean opened the back doors of the truck. Lonnie stepped out next to Mike to watch his back, while Sean went to the front door. Bob opened it with a big smile and a hearty handshake.

"Thank you so much, Sean. This means so much to me and my family."

"Don't mention it, Bob. Is everyone healthy?" Sean asked the number one question.

"Yes, of course. If they weren't, we would have all stayed here and died. I know how important it is to stay isolated from everyone else."

"Okay, do you have anything loaded yet?"

"Yeah, the cars in the garage are full, but we didn't have room for everything."

"The door on the truck is open, you can load some things in there if you want."

"Alright, I'll tell Clint to open the garage door."

Bob turned back into the house, and a minute later, the garage door was rising. As they were loading things, Sean stepped out to talk to Mike and Lonnie.

"Hard to believe that this virus is killing so many people. Makes you wonder where it's going to end."

"What I worry about is once we're in the clear in several months, is there a possibility of it sprouting up again?" asked Lonnie. "How long will we have to be careful?"

Mike, looking down the street, answered his question. "We'll always have to be careful, anytime someone new shows up that you can't guarantee is clean. Limited contact until we're sure of it."

"I'm gonna climb back up top and start reloading those empty mags. Be best to have them all full when we start back."

By the time they were ready to leave, Sean had finished reloading the mags and was ready to move. Lonnie climbed in and Bob and his brother drove the two cars. Using the door opener to close the garage door as they were pulling away, Bob and Clint followed close to the truck, not wanting to get separated. Driving back through town, they couldn't tell that there was any difference in the numbers on the same streets that they were on only two hours before. They could see a swath of bodies on the ground, but that was the only difference. After an hour of slow traveling, with having to run over some bodies because there were so many, and with the live ones still walking around, it was too dangerous to get out and clear the streets.

Eventually, they were able to reach the outskirts of town and were able to speed up with less infected in the way. Once they crossed the

McKenzie River, Lonnie pulled over for Sean and Mike to climb up front.

Arriving home, Sean could tell that Rachel was relieved. She was already aware of how many infected were out there, so she worried every time they went out. Giving Sean a long hug first, she was introduced to Bob "the baker" Wilson and his family. Clint and Gina were his brother and sister-in-law, and their two kids were girls Angie, age ten, and Tina, eight years old. Mitch had the family of four move into one of the new trailers, and Bob was placed in the next trailer. They were going to run out of trailer space again, and if Mike thought it was okay, they would try to get a couple of more the following day. One thing that Sean took note of was that when Bob was introduced to Lucy and Emily, He perked right up with excitement. Sean didn't know if Bob knew that Lucy was the one that was attacked, but he suspected that he knew.

Once everyone was settled, Mitch showed all of them around the house and what they had going on. Explaining the rules of protection, about the guns, and not being outside after dark, Mitch gave a pistol and holster to Clint and told him never to go anywhere without it. After giving both him and his wife a quick lesson on how to handle it safely, the dinner call came, and everyone went inside.

Meals were getting to be more of a buffet style set-up, with everyone walking along the table and picking what they wanted. With so many people to cook for, it was getting more difficult figuring out how much to cook. Hopefully, they would have enough for the new people. There were three loaves of Beth's freshly baked bread with the newly ground flour, and the baker absolutely loved it. Getting her recipe, he wanted to compare it to his own baking ingredients to see if the flavor difference was entirely the unprocessed flour. He could hardly wait to bake some of his own bread with Mitch's flour.

Ex-deputy Jack Leland had found several men that would follow his lead, and in so doing, the first thing they had done while the city was shut down, was to attack several of the women in their own apartment house, killing seven different men that had tried to butt in. He found it odd that there were so many people who had no weapons other than their kitchen knives. He knew that the area was made up of many highly liberal democrats and figured that was why. With their stand on gun control and their belief that they weren't needed in a civilized society, he was assuming that was the reason why. What most of them didn't understand was that the gun enthusiasts wanted the right to own and bear arms for just such an emergency that they now had, among other reasons. Now, the liberals stand on gun ownership was going to come back and bite them in the ass, very hard.

Jack found it very amusing pondering the whys and wherefores of people's actions, because now, all the rules that they lived by were null and void, and he and his followers were going to take full advantage of the situation. As more and more of the stage two were appearing, Jack and his followers would bide their time with their new women until the infected started to die out. He had no idea how many people would be left in the end, but he wanted to be the one in control of all those who were left. It would be his own personal kingdom, and he would have the most beautiful harem of girls.

"Lonnie, is there any way to get more ammo and weapons from the armory?" Sean asked.

"I've got a number to call. Let me try it and see."

Lonnie made the call with his cellphone, and after a couple of minutes, he turned back to Sean. There's no answer. I'll keep trying and let you know if I get through."

"If we lose almost all of our military and police force and some unsavory groups rise up," Sean explained, "and they have weapons and ammo, it could be a lot of trouble for us. In situations like these in third world countries, a strong leader gathers around himself a small militia and begins to ride roughshod over all of the individuals that don't have anyone to protect them. They create their own little fiefdom to rule and pretty much do anything they want, which usually includes taking everything of value—everything that takes their fancy. The biggest and worst thing they'll do is take the prettiest and youngest women and turn them into sex slaves. Raping, torture, and murder all go hand in hand with those types of people. I'm sure that we'll see our share of that happening here."

"What can we do to stop it?" asked Lonnie, surprised and almost unbelieving.

Mike had come over and was listening to the conversation. "We kill them all."

"Eventually," Sean added. "If we want a society to grow up, be strong, and cooperate with all, we can't let those kinds of people live. The sooner we can put them down, the better off everyone will be."

"How do we find them before they start trouble?"

"I'm thinking on that. I don't know how yet, until they make themselves known. In a city this size, it'll be hard to track them down. It's not like we have satellite surveillance, helicopters, and a network of informants. I'm just telling you now so you know what we're in for. And it may not be just one group. There may be several that pop up in different locations, like a lot of inner city gangs. Some groups may not even be bad, like ours for instance, but they're just looking for the best way to survive. Those groups we can work with. But if a group gets a vile, evil person at the head of it, many of the members will become just like him, and if a group like that gains too much power and influence, it'll be hard to dislodge them."

Sean paused for a moment, and then he continued, "But even then, my hands aren't tied by the government bureaucrats. I will assassinate from ambush if I have to, once they go public. I'm hoping they won't get that far. That's why we took all the weapons and ammo from the jail and why I want to empty out the armory. I don't want a group like that getting more weapons and firepower."

"If it's that important, why don't we make a trip down there first thing in the morning? It'll only take twenty minutes or so to get there."

"Keep trying to get a hold of them, and first thing in the morning, we'll give it a shot. Might not hurt to get a hold of the police chief and explain the situation to him and make sure all of his weapons and ammo are safe. Wouldn't hurt to find out from him how many officers that he can still count on."

"Alright," agreed Lonnie. "I think Bob may have his personal number. I'll check." Finding Bob walking with Lucy, coming up from the bridge was a surprise. Lucy had seemed to be a little withdrawn since Lonnie had met her, but she didn't seem to be that way at all with Bob. He felt bad about interrupting them to get the police chief's number, but after listening to everything Sean had to say about it, Lonnie was becoming a believer and needed to make that call.

CHAPTER FORTY-FOUR

The following morning, Sean was having a conversation with Rachel explaining the situation.

"Sweetheart, everything will be okay. There are a lot of infected, but we can take care of ourselves. We won't be doing anything stupid, we're always careful. We're just driving to the armory, loading some ammo, and coming straight back. Simple mission."

"This has to be done? Are you sure?" asked Rachel.

"Honey, you said that you didn't want me to hold anything back. I believe this needs to be done before someone else raids the armory. If we can empty it, it'll keep any potential bad guys from getting enough weapons to take over the town."

"Alright. But be careful. Now that I've found you, I don't know how I would live without you. I love you."

Sean drew her up tightly, kissed her on the lips, and then looked her in the eye. "I love you too, baby. We'll be back in no time."

Meeting Mike and Lonnie out at the panel truck, they were ready to go. The first thing Lonnie had to say was to ask Sean if he had noticed a connection between Bob and Lucy. He had, and he hoped it would keep on growing.

Thirteen minutes to the McKenzie River crossing, and then Sean climbed up top to start taking out the infected. One hour of stop-and-go driving, and they were approaching the building. Lonnie stopped at the keypad for the locked gate and punched in the code. The gate slid back, and they drove through. Lonnie backed up to the loading dock, where he had loaded up before. The automatic gate closed behind them, and they all breathed a little easier getting out of the truck. As they walked up to the main door, it opened, and a sergeant walked out and greeted them. He was African American, six foot one, athletic, and clean-shaven. He looked to be about thirty-two and capable.

"How was the trip in?"

"Not too bad. We only took down just over a hundred. It's hard to tell if the numbers are slowing or not. We actually crossed town yesterday to pull out five people, and there seemed to be more then, but it might just depend on the area you're in. We could have taken down five times that number this morning, but we were only concentrating on clearing a path to get here," explained Sean. "Are you healthy? Feeling good?"

"Yeah, I feel fine. I haven't had any contact with anyone, 'cept for Lonnie, when he stopped by last. I've seen a lot of infected outside the fence though, and I've been wondering if I should be shooting them. But if I did that, there would be no way to move them, and they would start rotting and stinking."

"Good thinking," replied Sean, holding out his hand. "I'm Sean Dixon, and this is my buddy, Mike Taylor. It's good to meet you."

"Same here. Len Harding," he replied, as he shook Sean's hand and Mike's too.

"Have you heard back from your commander?" Lonnie wanted to make things clear before they proceeded.

"No. I got a hold of a couple of corporals and a private, but it looks like the military is out of it. With that last big turn, most of the military came down with symptoms, at least the ones that weren't AWOL. With the ones that remained, they tried to continue taking down the infected, but they just lacked the manpower. They had been trying to keep up with the body disposal too, and it was just too much."

"Who do you answer to now?"

"That's a good question. Most of the soldiers in the Portland and Salem area are just trying to survive now. When the large number of soldiers became symptomatic, a lot of the rest were exposed before they knew it. So now there won't be but a handful left that aren't infected."

"If that's the case, you want to throw in with us? It's not like you'd be AWOL if someone starts looking for you. With a loss of all of your men, you'll be joining forces with the Sheriff's Office, protecting the weapons and ammo from falling into enemy hands. That should keep you out of trouble if anything comes up."

"Explain to me again your reasoning behind this?"

Lonnie spoke up: "Sean, you go ahead and explain it to him the way you did to me last night."

"Okay, Mike and I were in the marines for four years and just got out at the end of July. Being stationed overseas, we've seen a lot of things, and what we feel this is going to come down to is…" Sean continued his explanations and thoughts on the situation they were now in. When he had finished, the sergeant was convinced of the need to take care of the weapons.

Lonnie took over, "If you want to join us, you will come out to the farm and live. We'll take all of the guns and ammo with us. We're expecting to draw a lot of followers through the winter, because we have the food to survive. Sean and Mike here are the team leaders. I'm the acting sheriff since we lost Sheriff Briles to the virus, but what we're facing now is a little out of my league. After watching these guys in action and listening to their ideas and plans, I've gladly submitted myself to their leadership. I take my orders from them, and even though they ask for my input, they are the bosses and will be your bosses. After hanging around them for a few days, you'll see why. I'm trusting them with my life and also with the lives of my family."

"Don't get the wrong idea," began Sean. "I never declared Mike and I the bosses. My dad is the one with the farm and also had most of the ideas on how to survive. Mike and I are more of the muscle part of the set-up. We do have some of our own ideas on how to achieve the ideals that my dad has started for the survival of as many people that we can save, and because of our experience with bad people, we know how to deal with that kind of element under the circumstances. One thing you do need to know is that this'll be no picnic, and there are no longer any rules for dealing with the criminal element. This is what we were faced with last week…" Sean filled him in on every detail of the rape of Lucy, leaving nothing out, no matter how small, including everything that he and Mike did to the rapists.

"For at least a while, we will be judge, jury, and executioner for that type of behavior. If you're agreeable to that, then join us in saving as many people as we can," Sean finished.

The sergeant held out his hand to Sean who took it in a firm grip, signifying a partnership between men of action.

"I'm with you. If we get to save people from that kind of stuff, I'm with you all the way." Shaking hands with Mike and Lonnie, they walked into the building to watch the sergeant open up a secure room with the weapons and ammo. They looked at all of the weapons and ammo that was stored, and it was a lot—not to mention all of the MREs.

"If there's anything that we don't take, how safe is it to leave here? Can this place be broken into if no one is here?" asked Sean.

"If someone wants in, they'll get in, so I would say that nothing would be safe to leave behind. We've got an M35 cargo truck here that we could load up along with yours. Might take two trips to take it all, but that's okay."

"Alright, let's start loading."

Opening the roll-up door, he jumped down, walked over to the truck, started it up, and backed it up to the loading dock beside the panel truck. Climbing back up on the dock, he grabbed a pallet jack and pulled it into the storage room. There were over a hundred M4s, a crate full of 9mm Berettas, several sniper rifles with scopes, and over three tons of ammo. In crates, there were three hundred thirty-round magazines for the M4s and another crate with extra magazines for the Berettas. It was a good thing they were taking all of it with them. If that much firepower fell into the wrong hands, it would be lights out for whoever tried to stop them. Using the pallet jack to move the crates, it didn't take long to get it all loaded. The M35 was a two-and-a-half ton truck, so they could realistically carry over three tons with no problem, and the panel truck was a one-and-a-half ton truck. But, even so, since they couldn't actually pick up the crates to stack them, the load was almost all one layer.

Only taking an hour to load it all, the sergeant went to his room to retrieve all of his personal gear. Once that was done, Sean pulled out the lunch that Beth had packed for them, including one for the sergeant, and they sat down on the loading dock to enjoy it. The sergeant had been reduced to eating the MREs, since the rest of his food was long gone, so he was delighted with the lunch.

"How do you have all of this food?" asked the sergeant.

"My dad has a farm with cattle and hogs, with an orchard and garden, and he raised a crop of wheat that he still has stored on the place. He was close to having it sold when this plague broke out. He made a small grinder for the wheat to make fresh flour for bread baking, which is what your sandwich was made with, and since he was a pretty serious doomsday prepper, he had a lot of stuff stored away for something like this. He had about fifteen rifles, three or four pistols, and maybe ten thousand rounds of ammo with a reloading kit for all of the rifle calibers. Like I said, he was serious about it. Two days ago, I checked on our neighbor and found out him and his wife had died of the virus, or rather two bullets to the head because of the virus, so we rounded up his fifteen head of cattle and pushed them over onto our place. We'll run short on some things before they can be replenished, but we'll have bread, beef, and some pork for quite some time. After this plague dies out, we'll round up more cattle, plant more wheat, look for more hogs to confiscate… and we'll be looking pretty good to start growing a society by next year. If we're lucky enough to get some specialists that could help in manufacturing items or food processing, most of our troubles will be over."

"That sounds real good to me, Sean… starting over. Hopefully, there won't be a bunch of countries wanting to move in and take us over. With Russia, China, and North Korea gone, that only leaves the Arabs maybe that would hate us. Maybe with a fresh start and more help for other countries, we can make the world a better place," replied Len.

"That's what we're hoping, but there's still going to be the criminal element that will want to control things. If we can be successful in eradicating those ones, I'll be happy. Let's head for home."

Sean rode up top again, and Mike climbed in with Len. He was going to get his first experience with the stage two infected and was quite impressed with the set-up on the panel truck. Watching Sean knock down one infected after the other in a quick fashion, with what looked like all head shots, he was impressed with his marksmanship. And Sean wasn't even shooting the close ones to the side, but was sticking to clearing a path for the trucks out front.

Arriving home, they had to figure out what to do with all of the weapons and ammo. If someone were to case the place and see an army truck, they might assume that there would be weapons and ammo and might attack them to get it. They might be able to back it into the shop, if it would fit, and throw a tarp over it or maybe out behind the shop.

They could set a few rifles in every closet in the house, bunker, and trailers, with some extra mags and ammo for each. Just in case. But that would be good for only about fifty of them. Maybe a few in the workshop, some up on the loft floor, but then still they had all that ammo to take care of. Sean would have to talk it over with Mitch and Kevin to see what they could come up with. They still had a lot of ammo from the first trip, and the sheriff's truck was still loaded with it. They were up to their ears in ammo.

As they were crossing the bridge, Sean could see four saddled horses with riders out in the field riding around, and he couldn't help but smile. Joe's son, Ryan, and Rachel's sister, Leah, were laughing and having fun with one another, riding around one another. Her blond hair was flowing in the wind.

Seeing Rachel come hurrying from the house as they drove up, Sean jumped out and gave her a big hug and a kiss before introducing Len to the family. Everyone was quite impressed with the load of stuff they brought back, but Len was even more impressed with the variety of people that they had accumulated, the RV parking with full hook-ups, and all of the new trailers. He had also caught a glimpse of the five thousand gallon fuel truck and the smaller one too. He had seen all of the cattle in the fields with the horses, the orchard, and the garden. It was all just like Sean had told him it was—not to mention the beautiful setting with all of the old-growth firs, the green fields, the river, and the picturesque setting of it all. He was beginning to realize that Sean and Lonnie had meant every word that they had said; they were thinking big and he liked it. He was finding himself very glad he had made the decision to throw in with them and become a part of rebuilding the area. It made him feel really good inside.

"Hey, Dad," started Sean, "we passed a propane dealer, and I saw a delivery truck sitting there. I think it might be worthwhile to go get it. We could use it to refill all the tanks on the trailers. With winter coming on, they'll be going through a lot more propane with the furnaces running."

"Sounds like a good idea, Son. When do you want to get it?"

"The sooner the better, I think. You never know when someone else might get the same idea. As soon as we get Len settled and figure out what to do with all of the weapons and ammo. Besides, your trailer and Kevin's might be close to empty already."

"Having a tanker truck here through the winter would certainly help out. When you get there, find out if they have any twenty-five gallon tanks and what it would take for hoses and connections to use those for the trailers. Be less time re-filling if we could do something like that."

"Alright. I'll take Lonnie and Len with us and start breaking them in on the confiscation process. Maybe Lonnie's son, Dwayne, and Steve too. Ryan looks like he's having too much fun with Leah on the horses, so we don't want to interrupt that. We'll take the panel truck and the Chevy with the flat-bed trailer in case we find some of the twenty-five gallon tanks to bring back."

Inside the secure bunker, close to the Pentagon, the Secretary of Defense sat down with the President in his makeshift office.

"Alright, sir, we've got two C130 cargo planes on the ground close to Moscow. They've unloaded the trucks and personnel to start their search."

"How's the radiation levels?"

"It's been almost two weeks, and it's been mostly raining for one week. Some of it was heavy downpours, so the radiation levels are at a minimum. They're still wearing protective gear, but there shouldn't be any problems. We should know more by tomorrow at the latest. The worst thing will be, if they find a bunker entrance buried with debris. They'll have to bring in some machinery that could push it out of the way. We've also flown in some C130s from our base in Alaska, landing outside Vladivostok. There may be more Russian people to transplant to U.S. soil than at first anticipated. There is a lot of area in eastern Russia that wasn't targeted by China, but there is still the virus to worry about. It looks like Vladivostock was also targeted by one of the original terrorists but later than the initial targets. With the more information that the CIA has gathered, it looks like the terrorist group sent out a second wave of terrorists with the virus, who targeted less densely populated areas in hopes of covering even more geographic areas."

"How soon could they begin transportation of the people to U.S. soil?"

"If they bring anyone, it would be people that aren't in bunkers, and it may be too dangerous to just start loading people if they don't know who is or isn't infected, pre-symptomatic. It boils down to the same problem we faced with finding healthy people for our 'Survival of

Mankind' project. On top of that, we don't have the food to feed a lot of people for the time it would take to find the healthy ones."

"They'll have to figure out a way. It wouldn't do any good to transport one hundred seemingly healthy people, and then have all of them come down with the virus, infecting even our own people. And with our government, local or otherwise, can we contact anyone, anywhere for help in the redistribution of the Russian people?"

"Right now, we have less than a hundred contacts with local or state governments across the nation that are still answering communications. And out of those, the majority have no functioning ability to do anything. It looks like we may have to wait until the virus is actually played out before people start crawling out of the holes they've been hiding in and start to reassert themselves. Even then, without a viable local government or any law enforcement, our experts are predicting that most areas may spiral into anarchy—whether partial or complete is unknown. They would be just as apt to shoot the new people as to help them, or turn them into slaves, using the women and girls for, you know, using all of them to better their own odds of survival and control. It may be decades before there is any semblance to a nation again, if at all."

"That sounds pretty bleak. Our experts need to start figuring out ways to keep that from happening," stated the President. "Once things settle down after the virus, we'll have to take stock of what's left of our military, train up some new recruits, and then deploy them region to region to bring back some semblance of righteous order, killing off the bad guys if we have to. It might end up being like a lot of small civil wars all over the country. If some of the ruling bodies don't have everything they need to survive, like gasoline and oil products, we could dangle that in front of them to change their philosophy. Any way you look at it, life will be hard without it."

"If their philosophy is rape, murder, and complete ruthless control, I'd say just dispose of them and their main leaders that condone it, and then let the common people start ruling themselves, with our assistance, of course."

"Now our talk sounds like what our foreign policy has been around the world for the last fifty years. I don't want to be controlling, but rather setting things straight and what is right. Everyone deserves a chance at life without someone's foot on their throat. But naturally, the ones who want complete domination are against anyone who is a threat to their ideals, but the bottom line is that when their ideals are to crush all those that are less powerful, stooping to rape of the women, making slaves of the common people, to murder all those who oppose you, then that's when stepping in to stop the injustice is acceptable. That's what we're about. Hopefully, this time around, we do a better job of it. Keep me up to date on what's happening."

CHAPTER FORTY-FIVE

Mitch took some of the kids to the farm next door to catch the chickens to add to their own. Before they left, Lucy decided she wanted to do something different, so she hopped in the truck to help out. Steve went along also to carry a rifle, to watch over the group, just in case. Some of the chickens took some chasing, and while the younger crowd were involved with that, Lucy decided to check out the inside of the house. Smelling the decaying flesh as soon as she opened the door, she recalled something that was said about the neighbors and suicide. Finding the bodies, reading the story, she picked up the revolver and checked the loads. Nine shells, three fired, six still good. Placing the pistol back on the bed, she continued her investigation and reached the conclusion that it would be a good place to live. One or more of the families could move over to the farmhouse and relieve some of the overcrowding at the main farm. It seemed like a good idea.

As they were driving back to the farm, Sean and the boys were just returning from town with two propane trucks and a flatbed trailer with several two hundred fifty gallon tanks loaded. The rest of the evening the men were busy unloading the tanks with the tractor and a chain to lift them into place, and then hooking up the longer hoses to the trailers. By the time they were finished, all of the trailers were hooked up, and the tanks had been filled from the tanker truck—another nice idea and a good job performed on getting it finished.

After dinner, Sean pulled Mitch and Kevin aside for a private conversation. Not wanting Lucy or Emily to overhear what was being said, they walked outside by the barn to talk.

"I've been thinking about Lucy. She's an absolute dear, and I hate to say what I've been thinking about… but the day she was attacked was eight days ago. If any of those men were sick at the time, like had just become symptomatic but not long enough for the others to notice, there is still a possibility that Lucy will come down with it in the next day or so. Emily is a possibility also, but she only had contact with one guy, and it might not have been enough to infect her. I just don't know for sure, but for the good of everyone else, it might be best to isolate the two of them for the next two days."

"If that's the case, we need to keep them away from one another also, in case not both of them are infected. It would save at least one of them," Mitch concluded.

"I don't even know how to approach her with it. It breaks my heart to just think about it, after what she's already been through. If we do this, we don't have a place for both of them to stay separately. We're out of trailers, and it would be best to keep them out of the house until we're sure."

"What do you suggest we do to solve that problem?" asked Kevin.

"The only way is to run back to town right away and pick up another trailer. We get it set up and then move Bob or Len into Lucy's room, or even both of them can sleep on our cots for the next two nights. We would then put each one of the women in each trailer."

"That would work. Son, do you want me to talk to them while you go get the trailer?"

"No, Dad. I have to do it. I'll take Rachel with me. I already talked to Mike about it on the way into town, so I'll give him the go ahead to take Joe and maybe Ryan for back-up. I guess that's it. And thanks." The sadness in his voice was easy to pick up on, and Mitch realized that it was weighing heavily on his heart. He put his arms around his boy and gave him a hug before he let him go.

"Oh, Dad, you could explain it to Bob and Len. I know we just got Len settled, but this is important."

Walking into the house, Sean nodded at Mike to give him the go ahead, whispering to take Joe and Ryan. He then found Rachel, led her out onto the front porch, and sat down on the bench.

"I remember this bench. You proposed to me on it." She then started kissing him, trying to cheer him up; she had noticed the sadness that was riding him.

"Rachel, I've got something hard to do, and I want you with me while I do it."

"Sean, what is it? Is something wrong?"

"I don't know if something is wrong, but it's been eight days since Lucy's ordeal. Dad and I think we need to separate her and Emily for the next two days from the rest of us and each other. You know, just in case."

"I understand. This will break her heart to have to do this. I hope it's not the straw that breaks the camel's back."

"That straw will be if either one of them comes down sick. But right now, the thought of having to tell her is breaking my heart. Dad offered to do it, but I really feel I should be the one."

Rachel put her arms around Sean and held him tightly for a long moment. When she felt the wetness of his tears on her shoulder, she also began to weep for him. When she had herself under control, she pulled away, looked at him, and then raised her hand to his face.

Giving him a soft and gentle kiss, she asked, "Do you want to talk to her now?"

"Yes. I just sent Mike and Joe to go back into town to get another trailer. That way we could put both of them in two different trailers, and it only has to be for two nights. If everything turns out, both of them can move back into their room together."

"Alright, let's go talk to them."

Entering the house, he didn't see either of them in the living room, but walking into the kitchen, both of them were helping with the dishes. Seeing that they were close to done, he asked Lucy if he could have a few words with her… and Emily. Leading them into an empty living room, Sean had both of them sit down on the couch while he slid the coffee table out enough to sit on the edge of it.

Taking her hands in both of his, with Rachel taking a seat beside her, he began, "Lucy, all of us here have come to care a great deal about you. This is really hard for me to say, and I don't want you to feel that we don't care for you. You know I care deeply about you?"

Lucy had tightened up a little at the start of the conversation, because it started to sound ominous. But she also knew that Sean was telling the truth. She nodded her head quickly several times, not trusting her voice to speak. Her grip on Sean's hands had tightened noticeably.

"When you were attacked, did you notice if any of those men were sick? Did they have a fever or sweating profusely, coughing, anything that would make you think that they might've been infected?"

"No. Nothing. It happened so quick that there was only a couple of minutes before they grabbed us, and after it started, I wasn't paying attention." Her voice was wobbling a little. "Do you think we might be infected?"

"Lucy, I'm not thinking that you are, but we have to be careful. Even when we thought that one of us could still come down with the virus, four days before our wedding, every single one of us had to sleep in a different bed, even our moms and dads. We had to wear a mask all day and not have any physical contact with anyone else until the ten days was up from our last contact with outsiders. It was hard to do, but it was the only way to protect everyone else in the group if one of us were infected."

"What do you want us to do?" Immediately Lucy realized what it was about. Not about her, but about the virus. She understood, and after living with them for eight days and hearing what Sean and Mike were doing every time they went to town, she didn't blame them for this at all. But it did hurt to know that her ordeal wasn't completely over.

"Mike has gone to town to pick up another trailer. That way we can have you sleep in one and Emily in another. You can still come out, but you need to wear a mask for two days whenever you're outside and around anyone, and you have to wash your hands often."

"For how long exactly?"

"Tonight, and then two days, and the morning after if you feel good when you wake up, it's all over. Then you and Emily can both move back into the bedroom… or live in the trailer, if you prefer."

"Okay, Sean. I understand. I know you're just protecting everyone. That's what you do. I know, too, that you're protecting Emily from getting it from me, and I'm glad that you've thought of it." Lucy released Sean's hands to wipe away her tears, and Emily had her arms around her mother, comforting her. They both knew that if either one of them came down with the symptoms, it would most likely be Lucy and her alone. Rachel also had an arm around her and a hand holding on to her arm. After a moment, Lucy started to stand, and quickly Sean stood and took her arm to help her to her feet.

"Sean, could you… could you hold me?" Her small voice was breaking, and all of a sudden, the tears started to flow once again—not all were Lucy's. "The way you did before, when you saved me?"

Sean wrapped his arms around her, as his own tears started to fall, and after a brief moment, he bent down slightly, slid one arm under Lucy's legs, picked her up and held her tightly, fully in his protective arms. Lucy buried her face against Sean's neck and continued to weep, as Emily and Rachel wrapped their arms around them both. Beth and Mitch soon walked in from the kitchen, wrapped their arms around the close-knit group, and added their love and tears.

The following day, Bob went out of his way to spend time with Lucy, taking her out of the trailer, walking with her down to the river, sitting close to her at mealtimes, sitting in the shade on the porch, talking and laughing with her… Toward the close of the day, taking a walk through the pasture, Bob asked her if she was feeling good, and when she replied that she was feeling wonderful, he took her hand in his as they continued to walk.

"Bob, why are you spending so much time with me today? Surely you aren't that interested in me?"

"But I am. When I first found out that Sean had rescued you, I wanted to meet you and let you know that all men aren't like those guys. And when I met you three days ago, I realized that you were a special lady. I've seen how well you've raised Emily, and how hard that must've been, by yourself, and I've been wishing that I had met you earlier in my life. I know I'm not the man that Sean and Mike are, but I was hoping that you liked me."

"Oh, Bob, I do. But you shouldn't be thinking that way until we're sure that I… I'm okay."

"That may be true, but I wanted you to know that I'm very interested in you now, and when everything is okay, I hope that we can continue."

"Bob, that's the nicest thing anyone has said to me in a long time."

They had been heading back toward her trailer, as it was approaching dark, and when they stopped at her door, Bob asked, "Lucy, may I kiss you good night?"

"Bob, it wouldn't be safe for you."

"If you become sick, it won't be until tomorrow. Then I'll never get to kiss you. To kiss you once, to find out what that's like, I am willing to take that chance."

Lucy, with tears in her eyes once again, leaned toward Bob, raised her hands to his face and kissed him long and gently.

"Thank you, Bob." Looking into his eyes for several seconds with her hands still holding his face, she kissed him quickly before saying good night.

The next morning, with the sun barely up, Bob was at Lucy's door, waking her up. Opening the door in her fairly new Wal-Mart pajamas, she looked at Bob with a smile.

"I feel wonderful, Bob. Would you take another chance and kiss me again?"

Bob stepped up into the trailer, wrapped his arms around Lucy and held her tightly. Once he was satisfied, he kissed her long and tenderly. Lucy was the one that finally disengaged, feeling her passion rising. It had been a long time since she had feelings for a man, and now that she was once again feeling desire, and feeling the same thing from Bob, it scared her a little bit. She had thought that after being attacked the way she had, she might never find love and desire from or for another man. Now that she was finding it, she might lose it all by the following morning. Realizing that if it went on, it would be harder for her and Bob both if things turned out badly the next day, and she began to pull back.

"Bob, we can't keep this up. In a way, you've made me so happy, to know that a man can still find me desirable and attractive, has touched me deeply. But if I get sick tonight, it will be all the harder for you."

"It's too late to save me any pain, Lucy. I realized that yesterday, as I spent more and more time with you, that you're the perfect woman for me. If I lose you tonight, it's going to be the most painful thing I've ever faced. It'll be taking my future away."

Lucy wrapped her arms around Bob and began to cry. "First Sean, and now you. The two of you have saved me, and I'll never forget it. Now, you'd better go. If Sean catches us kissing, he'll want to quarantine you too."

"If that quarantine was with you, it wouldn't be so bad." Lucy pulled him into her arms one last time and spent her remaining passion upon his lips.

Before Sean had reached Lucy's trailer, he heard the door close, and Bob came walking around the front of it with a big smile on his face. As soon as he saw Sean, the smile mostly disappeared.

"Good morning, Bob. You almost look like the cat that swallowed the canary. How's Lucy this morning?"

"Wonderful. Just wonderful. She's feeling great by the way," was his cheerful reply.

"I'm glad, Bob, that you and Lucy are hitting it off, but you might want to slow down, at least until tomorrow morning."

"It's too late for that, Sean; I'm already smitten. She's excited me more than any other woman has in the past fifteen years."

"That's great to hear, Bob. Does she know that?"

"Yes, and she feels the same way I think."

"That's wonderful! I told her that she would find someone that would see her true beauty. It saddens me that it had to happen right now though."

"I'm looking at it like if she does have the virus, she won't have to go thinking that no one would want to love her. Because I think that I do. If she is well, then we've got a good start to a wonderful relationship."

"Okay, Bob, I completely understand. The love of a good woman has tremendous value. I'll poke my head in and say good morning."

Sean walked around to the door and knocked and hearing Lucy say to come in, he opened the door. Lucy was sitting on the couch wiping the tears from her eyes.

"Did you hear what we said?"

"Yes."

"Lucy, I'm so glad that you and Bob have met and that he has taken a real shine to you. I can't begin to express how much I want you to be well tomorrow so that you can find real love with Bob."

"I know you do, Sean. But, it is what it is. Like Bob said, I'm glad to know that someone could still love me that way, and I think it will be easier for me to face the end, if that happens, knowing that I found it."

"That's wonderful to hear, Lucy. Breakfast is almost ready. You can come over in your pajamas if you want and then take your shower later, or I could have Bob bring you over a plate."

"If Bob comes back over, he'll want to kiss me again, and I don't think that's a good idea. I feel wonderful right now, but if the virus is in me, it'll start showing up pretty soon. If you could bring me a plate, I would appreciate it. And if Bob wants to bring it over, let him know why not."

"I can do that. And Lucy, I want you to know that if everything is okay tomorrow morning, I want a big hug too."

Tears started again and with quivering lips Lucy said, "Okay, I'll reserve you one."

Sean left the trailer and knocked on Emily's door to see if she still felt okay, and when he was invited in, he found Steve already sitting on the couch with Emily in the chair. He could see that Emily had also been crying, and Sean realized that she must have heard everything that he and Bob had talked about.

"Good morning, Emily. Steve. You feel good this morning?"

"Yes… at least I did until I heard you and Bob talking. It made me happy and sad at the same time. To know that Mom hasn't found love in several years, and now that she has, she might lose it all tomorrow, is so heart wrenching."

"There's three scenarios that might happen. You could both be well. You could be well, but she could get sick. You could both be sick. Let's hope for the best one, and then we'll go from there. I would suggest, for now, if you're both feeling so wonderful, you might want to go over and give your mom a great big hug right now, just in case it's the last one. Steve and I will bring you both some breakfast. Oh, and also, I wouldn't recommend any more kissing until tomorrow."

Both Emily and Steve started blushing.

CHAPTER FORTY-SIX

Jack was beginning to get antsy. They had already taken over three apartment complexes; he now had fifteen guys following him, and they had twenty-five women and girls. The rest were killed or kicked out into the street where all of the walkers were. The young boys were a nuisance, because any time he or his men wanted to do anything to their mom or sister, they were continually in the way, so the boys were kicked out also. Jack didn't really care for anyone but himself, and once he had started down the road he was on, he became even colder and more hateful. Before long, his followers didn't even like him, but they did fear him—not to mention he had at least some plan to survive, and that was the one thing that all of them were lacking.

There was one thing that Jack was disappointed in, and that was the fact that in three entire apartment complexes, they had only found one rifle and three handguns with minimal ammo. The first chance he had, he wanted to stop by the Sheriff's Office and take any ammo and weapons that were still there. Once they had those, he would have to look into the chances of getting into the armory. Surely there would be some weapons and ammo there, but they would need to be better armed to do so. Once the infected thinned out to make it safe to walk around, he would organize his men into scavenging parties, checking every house for food and weapons. The more he thought about it, houses might turn up more weapons than people living in apartments might.

Looking around at his dirty apartment, he was realizing more and more that they needed to find a better looking, more comfortable residence, like a motel with a pool for instance, but that might not work either. Maybe a more upscale hotel or apartment house would be more appropriate. They would need more food storage capabilities, because if the bread and meat delivery thing started back up, they would try to get as much as they could and hoard it for the future. He was wishing he had found out where the bread was coming from. That might be a good thing to get control of. Then his people would have as much as they needed, keeping them satisfied, and he could hold it over others as leverage. He had to start somewhere and that seemed like a good way to begin taking control and exerting his influence over a larger portion of the surviving population.

If only those walking dead would hurry up and disappear, they were holding up all of his plans. He wouldn't mind speeding up the process, but he didn't want to use up any more of his ammo unnecessarily. If he couldn't find any more soon, he would be in trouble.

Walking through the building, room by room, checking on his men, he found one young girl, a teenager, who he'd like to spend the night with. Some of the women that they now had were content to be included in a survival group, not minding what they had to do. They thought that some of the men weren't so bad, but most of the rest of them were giving some fight every time. He might eventually have to get rid of those ones too, but they had some advantages to go along with their refusal to cooperate. He was willing to give them a few more days; it was hard to throw away a good-looking, sexy, young woman.

Throughout the day, Bob stayed by Lucy's side, following her, talking, sharing his past, learning about her, making Lucy's possible final healthy day as happy as he could. Steve was doing the same with Emily, but of course, they weren't really expecting bad news for her. Emily and Lucy would often come together to talk and laugh about silly things, talking about the past, reliving good moments between them. They were both frightened of the future, but were bravely putting their best faces on to make things better for the other. Eventually though, the day had to come to an end, and neither of them were able to hug one another goodnight or either their new boyfriends. It was a hard parting for all of them.

"Lucy, I'm sleeping on the porch, so I'll be up at first light, and I'll come and check on you first thing. Be ready for some serious kissing though. And, Lucy, I want you to know how much I enjoyed today, just taking it easy, getting to know you better, just being in your presence. I hope today was as good for you."

"It was as good as it could get, Bob. I really enjoyed hanging out with you too, and I'm really looking forward to that kissing in the morning. Goodnight, sweetheart."

After saying goodnight and stepping into the trailer, Lucy closed the door and removed her mask. She leaned against the closed door and began to weep. She had been feeling soreness in her throat and a slight fever for the last hour. She had been formulating a plan on what she should do and had located all of the motion sensor lights so that she would be able to avoid setting them off in the middle of the night. She had been able to get her hands on some writing materials the day before, as soon as she decided that she would sneak away if she became sick from the virus. Now that she was feeling the onset, she knew what she needed to do.

At one point during the day, when Bob was pulled away for a few minutes, she had grabbed a frozen loaf of bread from the freezer just inside the barn. She had been able to sneak a few small things out of the pantry, but she didn't want to push her luck too far or someone might realize what she was doing. She believed she had enough to sustain her until the sickness took her completely. Placing all of her food in a pillowcase, she took the bottle of cleanser and a rag and began wiping down everything in the trailer to get rid of any of her germs, so as not to infect the next person to stay in it. Taking a small bag and packing all of her clothes and personal items in it, she was ready to leave, but before she did, she sat down to compose three letters—one to Emily, to Sean, and to Bob. She needed to explain her reasoning for leaving, although she knew Sean and Bob would realize it as soon as they found out that she was gone.

To Emily she wrote, "My dearest Emily, I love you so much and have always been so proud of you, especially the fine, beautiful young woman that you've turned out to be. To see how happy you've been with Steve and how he treats you makes my heart ache to watch you grow in your future happiness. Honey, I'm so sorry that I have to leave like this, but if I stay, I might infect some of the people that I love most in the world and that thought tears me to pieces. If I go, none of you will have to watch my decline, and I can't put Sean, who saved me and gave me a reason to continue living, through the ordeal of having to take my life. I could never bear the pain of that, and I will never allow that to happen. I'm sorry, sweetheart, that I won't be here for you when you get married, but remember that my last thoughts will be about you and your happiness and how dearly I love you."

To Sean she wrote, "Dearest Sean, my savior, my comforter. You saved my life and that of my daughter. For this, I can never repay you or thank you enough. You helped make life bearable again, and I love you for that. Tell Rachel that I love her and your parents also. Your mom has been so good to me. Tell Mike I love him also, and that if I ever had sons, I would want them to grow up to be just like you and him. The two of you are the finest men I have ever met, and I will truly miss being around you. I now have a fever, so there is no reason to explain to you why I'm leaving, you already know. Please don't try to follow me. There is no reason to stop me or to bring me back. Let me go my own way, and if it gets to be too much, I will take my own life. I will try to go far enough away that you will never see me walking around. I love you, Sean, and thank you."

To Bob she wrote, "My dearest, sweetest Bob, I love you. I've only known you for five days, and I truly love you. These last nine days I've come to love so many people on the farm, for their kindness, generosity, and their care for me. But you, Bob, hold a special place in my heart, revealing to me that I could still love a man and that a man could still love me. I'm truly sorry that we couldn't continue this beautiful relationship that we've begun. But always know that I will treasure your kisses 'til the day I draw my last breath, dreaming of being in your arms once again. Thank you for what you've given back to me. I will always love you. Yours Forever, Lucy."

Leaving all three notes on the table, she gathered her things, including the pistol on her hip and a rolled blanket. She turned out the light and left the trailer as quietly as she could. Walking straight away from the trailer to avoid the motion sensor lights, she walked down the slope, slipped through the fence, and continued through the grass, until she was close to the river where she turned back to the driveway. Slipping back through the pole fence, she crossed the bridge, and when she reached the pavement, she turned right toward Sweet Home. She didn't actually relish the thought of heading toward Springfield, because of all the walkers from the city, but rather she was hoping to find an empty farmhouse several miles away where she could be protected from the night cold and have a comfortable place to die.

Walking for three or four miles, she stopped to rest and eat a snack. It was still dark, but she had only two hours or so left before daylight, and she was assuming that Bob would be at her door at the break of day in anticipation of all of the kisses he was going to receive. Finding her gone, he would probably come driving down the road looking for her. Resting for only a few minutes, she continued walking for another four miles, only resting when the road had a steeper incline up a hill. It was close to daylight when she ate another snack and drank some water, turning her gaze back down the road, looking for headlights. Pushing on for a couple of more miles, she began to get nervous about finding a farmhouse that was empty and also not getting caught out after daylight. She picked up her pace, and as the sun was coming up, she crossed a fence heading for a farmhouse that she could see nestled back against a cluster of trees about a third of a mile from the road.

Walking across the field, trying to keep a large tree between her and the house, she approached the fence line with a row of shrubs and bushes growing along it. Crawling up into the bushes, she wanted to watch the house for a little while to see if there was any evidence of occupation. She also wanted to stay under cover in case Bob came driving along the road looking for her.

Setting her pillowcase down, she pulled out the bread and ate a couple of slices. Laying her head on the bag of clothes, she pulled her blanket over her and promptly fell asleep. Not feeling well and being up and on the move all night, she slept soundly for several hours. When she awoke, she discovered that a squirrel had come up, chewed a hole in her sack of bread and eaten almost all of it. She began to cry. Must she starve as well as suffer the disease? Once she had pulled herself together, she started looking over the house in the full light of day and decided that no one was in it.

Crawling up the fence line and following it around to the back of the house, she continued to watch, finally deciding that it was safe to approach. Sneaking up to a back window, she looked inside, and seeing no movement, she continued around the house, looking into all of the windows. Nothing. Trying the back door first, she found it unlocked, pulled her gun, and disengaged the safety. Opening the door, she entered slowly and walked throughout the house, finding no one. Not turning on any lights, she began checking cupboards and shelves for food, but it looked like someone had already emptied everything. The water faucet still worked, and the hot water line was still hot. She could take a hot bath for as long as she wanted.

As she was thinking about the bath, a noise was starting to intrude on her thoughts, and she quickly realized someone was approaching the house in a car, coming up the driveway. Quickly moving to the front window to see whether she needed to run or hide, she could see Bob driving his car as it came to a stop. She wore no perfume so that wouldn't give her away, so she could hide in a closet, slip under a bed, or run out the back door and try to hide in the trees before she was seen. She was almost panicking in indecision. She couldn't let him find her, or he would wish to stay with her, and he himself would become infected.

Moving as fast as she could quietly, she grabbed up her stuff and was slipping out the back door, just as she heard the front doorknob turning. Running into the trees and brush, she quickly ducked down behind the thickest cover and laid flat on the ground.

She could hear him calling out her name, and her heart ached. She could hear the desperation in his voice. She heard the back door open, and after a long moment, the door closed. A minute later, she heard the car drive away. Listening to the departing rumble of the car traveling down the highway to the north, she finally stood up and walked back to the house. It was so quiet in the cool afternoon air that she could still hear the tire rumble on the pavement over a mile away. Carrying her things to the bathroom, setting them down, she walked to the front door and locked it, and then went to the back and locked that door. She started the bath water, ate a snack while she waited for it to fill, and then undressed and lowered herself into the steaming water.

The following morning, she decided to go further, in case in his desperation, Bob rechecked the house. She had been so hungry the night before that she now only had two pieces of bread left and a couple of small snacks. Not sure that she should walk on the road for fear of being seen, she started walking cross-country, paralleling the road, which made for harder walking. She stopped more often, and her hunger was greater with the exertion. Not finding a house, she raked together a pile of leaves, curled up under a tree with her blanket, and fell asleep; the virus was taking its toll on her strength.

The next morning, she finished the last of her food and went back to sleep. Awaking in the late afternoon, she was still fatigued and her fever had worsened. Drinking most of her water, she realized that she might be in trouble. She couldn't think straight, and she didn't know for sure which direction it was back to the house she had stayed in. Going back to sleep, she was awakened in the early morning hours by the footfalls of an animal moving around and smelling her.

Barely able to make out the moving shape of a dog, she began talking to it, and as it started to growl at her, she pulled out her pistol, lined up the sight on its center, she squeezed the trigger as Sean had showed her. The dog yelped and jumped away, and then all was silent. Exhausted, Lucy fell asleep.

Feeling the warm sun shining on her face, Lucy awoke, and looking around, she tried to remember where she was. After several moments of thinking, she remembered leaving the house with the bathtub and walking for most of the day. The pistol was still in her hand, and she recalled shooting at the dog in the moonlight.

Standing to her feet, looking around, she could see the dog laying only thirty feet away where it had died. It looked like someone's farm dog and hoped that the owners were already gone. Lifting her pillowcase, she found that it was empty. Her food was gone, and she was starving.

Looking at the dog, repulsed by the thought, she reached for the knife in her pocket that Mike had given her for her protection. Her thoughts being overridden by her hunger, she approached the dog and began to skin the back leg from the backbone down to the knee. Soon having a large piece of bloody meat in her hand, she realized she had no matches or lighter. She didn't know which way to go to find a house and she was starving. She began to cut the meat into smaller pieces and began to eat the bloody meat one little piece at a time. It was all she could do to eat it raw, but she needed strength to keep walking, and after she drank the last of her water, she skinned and cut the meat off of the other leg.

Gathering her things, she continued walking north, looking for another house to take refuge in.

By dark, she hadn't found a house, but she had crossed a small stream and refilled her water bottle. Slicing up some more of the dog meat, she ate as much as she could stand, drank more water, and then curled up to sleep.

In the morning, she again ate some of the meat, drank the rest of her water, refilled the bottle at the stream and then continued on her northward trek. Within an hour, Lucy came across another house, and after making sure it was deserted, she entered it and soon found some food to eat.

She turned on the stove, cooked up the remainder of the dog meat, and with some food that was in the cabinet, she ate her fill. Still cold, she started the water in the bathtub and was soon drifting off to sleep in the steaming water.

CHAPTER FORTY-SEVEN

It had been five days since Lucy had walked away, and Sean was still feeling the pain of letting her go. Lucy was right in what she had done, but Sean wasn't sure which hurt the most: having to put her down himself before she turned or sitting comfortably at home knowing that she was out there all alone suffering through the illness. He still wasn't sure that he should not go look for her, but now it would be harder to find her. If he did, and she was already gone, he would like to see that she had a proper burial.

It would be an almost impossible task to find her, for they didn't even know which way she went. Although one direction would be out, there was still a lot of area in three directions, and they didn't know if she would have stayed on the road or cut across the countryside. With all of the grass and leaves on the ground, there would be hardly any tracks to follow, and Sean would probably be limited to checking abandoned farmhouses, hoping she found one to hole up in.

He had been waking up every night, dreaming about Lucy wandering alone in the wilderness, being chased by bad people and by the infected. Rachel told him that he had even been crying in his sleep. Sean was being tormented by day and by night over Lucy's predicament.

While he had been absorbed in those things, Bob had talked Mitch into planting a hundred acres of wheat instead of fifty. They couldn't have too much wheat, and if there were more survivors than they anticipated, the wheat would disappear faster than they expected. Their survival may be linked to their wheat production and maybe to what they might be able to find still stored on some farms. Until they were able to start scavenging parties and send some out to farms to specifically look for wheat, they had to plan on surviving on what they alone could produce. With Mitch's current stored wheat and the flour that was already at the bakery, they could bake enough bread to last until the new crop was to come in.

Bob had spent three days driving around and checking all of the farmhouses within six or seven miles with not a sign of her. Bob had taken it hard, and Sean thought that maybe if he had helped Bob in his search, then he wouldn't now be facing all of the torment that he was. In searching for something to do to keep his mind off of Lucy, Sean had decided to clean out the farmhouse across the road in preparation to moving a family or two over there. Reducing the load on the septic systems, giving two families a feel of having their own place, and just taking possession before anyone else did all seemed like good reasons to get it done. Of course, all of the farmland around the house would come in handy also.

Getting antsy one day, Sean talked Mike, Lonnie, and Len into going into town for a look. Driving the panel truck and the Chevy to the McKenzie River, they parked the Chevy, and Sean and Mike climbed up top on the panel truck, while Lonnie drove and Len rode along. Knocking down a few infected without even stopping, they continued to get deeper and deeper into the city of Springfield, utilizing the whole road to miss as many bodies as they could. There were so many bodies, because the first five days of the large, fourth tier infected had already died. Newly turned stage two were well on the decline, and Sean felt like they had finally turned a corner with the numbers, although, at that moment there were more on the street than any day that Sean and Mike had been working. But, still, it made Sean glad that it was finally noticeable that they were actually on the downhill slope of the disease. Five or six more days, and they would be in the clear.

They made a loop around back toward Eugene to check out the region, and the walkers were still thick. Just before they decided to turn back south toward home, driving through a residential district, a young man came running out of a building trying to get their attention. Actually a teenager, maybe.

"He's not stage two," Mike commented quickly to make sure Sean didn't drop him. Sean told Lonnie over the radio to stop, and he and Mike commenced to drop all of the stage two in range so that the uninfected guy wouldn't get attacked. As soon as the man realized they weren't going to shoot him, he held still while they continued to shoot. When they were done and the echoes of their shots had died away, Sean signaled him to approach a little closer.

"What were you doing running out in the middle of all those infected? We could have killed you."

"I had to stop you." They could hear the waver in the man's voice and knew that he was highly agitated. "It's too late for me anyhow; I'm already infected. I was thrown out of my building in the middle of this mob, and there was nothing I could do but run. Eventually I was bitten, several times, before I could get away. That was seven days ago."

"Why were you thrown out, and who did the throwing?" asked Sean.

"A local guy picked up a few followers and started taking over several apartment complexes where I lived. They killed a few guys. Others joined them, and they were raping all of the women, even the teens. I tried to stop it, but I had no weapons. I was able to beat down one guy, but then four more helped him out. They thought it would be funny to throw me outside with all of these walkers. There was nothing I could do."

"How many guys are we talking about? And how many prisoners?" Mike asked.

"At least fifteen guys. Almost double that in women, I think. If you give me one of those rifles, I'll go back there myself and kill all of them."

"Do they have any weapons? How were they able to kill those men?"

"I only saw one rifle, and it looked a lot like one of those you're using. Several of them had handguns. That was about all I saw before they threw me out."

"Where at are those apartments? What's the address?"

He gave them general directions and then the exact address. "One more thing. After I was bit and escaped to another building, I was watching their building from an upstairs window, trying to think of what I could do, and I saw them throw seven boys out into the street, from twelve years old all the way down to four. All of them were attacked before I could get back down to them and most of them had then fled as best they could."

"You know it's too late for you?"

"Yes, I know."

"Have you had any food?"

"No. I haven't had anything for the last three days. Before that, I caught a dog. It was okay, but a little meat by itself isn't much of a meal."

Len grabbed their sack of snacks that they had thrown in, just in case they were out longer than they were expecting, and stepped out of the truck and tossed it over to the man.

"Thank you so much." Reaching into the sack, he started eating before they were completely done with the conversation. "My name's Jason."

Sean climbed down off the truck, his gloves on and slipping on his mask as he hit the ground, leaving Mike up top to cover. He opened the back door of the truck, grabbed a Beretta, two extra mags and a couple of boxes of shells. Closing the door, he stepped up to the open door and asked Lonnie to hand him a police radio. Turning it on to make sure the batteries were good, he walked over to the guy.

"Dammit, I'm sorry, real sorry. We can't take you with us since you're infected, but here's a police radio. We'll bring more food into town with us tomorrow, and we'll come back here to give it to you. We'll call you on the radio to locate you. Here's a Beretta 9MM, two mags, and two boxes of shells. It should be enough to protect yourself. Like I said, we'll bring you more food tomorrow so that you won't starve before you turn. Again, I'm so sorry."

"What will you do now?" he asked.

"We're going to those apartments right now, and when we find 'em, we're going to kill all of 'em." Mike from up top gave the answer.

"Can I go? I'd sure like to do some of the killing. I need some payback. I know the layout, and I could help."

"Do you know how to shoot a gun?" asked Sean.

"I know how to shoot it, but I've only used a revolver."

Giving him a quick lesson on cocking, safety, and changing out the mag, Sean watched him do it and then had him repeat it three more times in a row. He might be taking a chance, but he wouldn't be contagious for three more days.

"Looks good. If you run completely out of shells in the mags, here's how to load one." Removing several shells, then slipping them back in, Sean was satisfied. "Climb up top with me and hold on."

Fifteen minutes later, they were parking a couple of blocks from the first apartment. All five of them moved forward, little by little, with Sean and Mike leading the way, Lonnie covering behind, and Len watching the side streets as they crossed. The four of them, wearing their masks and gloves, just in case, were keeping cover to not stir up the infected. There seemed to be fewer in the area, and there were quite a few bodies already on the ground. Leaving the two at the door, Len followed to the hallway to watch their backs, as Sean and Mike cleared each room one by one.

Finished with the first floor, they moved to the second. Still no one. Returning to the other two, they needed some more information.

"Which building were you living in?"

"Third one from here."

"Is that the one that they had the women in?"

"That's the one that I saw it happening in, but they had previous women in the next apartment from here. Afterwards, as I watched, they moved other women and some of their stuff to the building I lived in. I don't know if they had decided to just keep moving as they advanced or what their thinking was. After that first day, I kept moving, looking for a gun everywhere I went, but without any luck. It's been almost six days since I was here."

"Alright, let's move to the next building. Once they've started moving and advancing, there's no telling how far they've gone."

Leading out, they advanced to the next building, finding seven male victims in a downstairs room, but no one living. Again to the third building, there were eight or so bodies stacked outside, around the corner from the entrance, which would indicate they stayed for a while and didn't want the building to stink. Once they started clearing the rooms, they found one woman upstairs, naked, beaten to death. She must have put up too much fight, so they got rid of her… but not before they used her up. Judging by the small stretch marks, not all that old, on her stomach and hips, she was probably a mother to one of the boys that they threw out to the walkers, and judging by her age, maybe the four-year-old. Sean and Mike both read the same details, but it was Mike who made the comment.

"She was a mother to one of those youngest boys they threw out. She fought to the very end."

"I don't think I've ever wanted to kill someone so bad in my life," Sean added.

"I'm with you, buddy."

"Let's move down the line, clear two more buildings, and see what we find."

Meeting up with the other two, they explained the situation.

Jason had been looking around, and then exclaimed, "My car's gone. And there's several others missing out of the parking lot. I distinctly remember a lot of cars in the lot."

"Alright. They're probably no longer in the area. If several cars are missing, they've probably run out of food, and they've moved the whole group to another location. More people to take over and more women to abuse. They've probably already hit the next two buildings, and there's no way to tell which direction they've gone. Let's go ahead and clear the next two complexes to make sure, and then we'll head back to the truck."

Once they had finished, finding several more bodies, they asked Jason what he wanted to do.

"I'll stay here in my apartment for tonight and try to find some keys to another car. If I can find some, I'll start driving around, looking for my car, movement of people, or dead walkers by bullet rather than natural causes. Maybe there's some kind of trail for me to follow."

"Alright, we'll head for home now. We'll bring you enough food tomorrow for at least a week. We'll contact you on the radio, and if you haven't found any keys, we'll round you up something to drive. Let's plan on meeting here tomorrow and discuss what else we can do."

"Alright, guys, and thanks for this and the food. I'm just glad that if I never find those guys before I'm toast, you guys will finish the job."

"Count on it. We'll see you tomorrow."

On the way home, they stopped at a car dealership and picked up the keys to a new Chevy Camaro. Starting up the car, listening to it run, Sean explained, "Jason lost his car, his life, his future, but in my book, he's quite a man. I think he deserves to have the last few days of his life driving around a nice car."

"Great idea. I'm really starting to like the way you guys think," replied Len.

"You don't have anything to drive either, Len. Do you see anything you'd like while we're here?" asked Sean.

"Anything? And can we get in trouble for this?"

"No. Ask Lonnie. This is official police business. We're confiscating everything we need to operate. What do you want?"

"I've always wanted one of those Chevy Colorados."

"What color?"

"Do they have black?"

"Let's see. Jump in, and we'll drive the lot and look."

Climbing in, Sean took off spinning the wheels, testing how much power was actually under the hood. Racing around the lot, almost out of control, they found the trucks they were looking for, and they did have a black one. Running inside the office, Sean found the key, handed it to Len, and told him to go try it.

Stopping at his own truck where they had parked it earlier at the McKenzie River crossing, Sean left the Camaro in its place, and had Mike drive his Chevy to the farm. They would pick up the Camaro in the morning on their way to Jason. Jumping into the Colorado with Len, he found out just how nice a vehicle it was.

Lucy woke up late, still had a fever, and walked out to the kitchen, opened up a can of soup and heated it up for her lunch. There wasn't a lot of variety, but she wouldn't starve. It was hard to tell if the owners skipped out to the mountains and took most of the food or just what happened. Maybe they ended up at the hospital after being infected early. After eating, Lucy took another long hot bath, glad that she at least had a comfortable place to stay during her last days. While in the bath, she dreamed of what life might have been like with Bob and continuing to watch Emily growing into a beautiful young woman. It would have been so nice.

Sean had thought very highly of Bob and had nothing but good things to say about him. She knew he was a good kisser, she had really enjoyed that part. When he had come looking for her, it broke her heart listening to him calling out her name. He really seemed like he actually loved her, and the thought of that made her feel so good.

Continuing to lay there, her mind was wandering, and she was trying to figure out how many days she had been gone. Was it four? No, it was at least five. She had killed the dog about the third day, fourth day? Ate the meat for two days, which was yesterday. And now the current day. She'd been away six days, she thought. How long would the sickness last before she turned? She was sure that she heard ten days, but she wasn't sure how bad off she would be by day nine. Should she end it all that night? The next night? What if she waited too long and then she turned? Would it hurt? Would she even know if it hurt? Or would she know anything? She was getting a little nervous just thinking about it. But right then she didn't feel bad enough that she needed to end it all, just a little fever, headache, and a little sore throat. She'll wait and see.

Another night and another morning. She didn't seem to be any worse. Another hot bath, more soup, more daydreams. As long as the symptoms didn't get any worse, it should be okay to keep on living. Besides, she wasn't sure if she'd be able to pull the trigger. Going back to sleep, she dreamed of Bob and marrying him, and Sean was the best man.

CHAPTER FORTY-EIGHT

Len was driving the Camaro, following the panel truck through town, trying to run over as few bodies as possible. The car could actually high center on one if he wasn't careful. They had over a week's worth of food in the car for Jason, some of the best stuff they had, to make his last days as good as they could make it. Sean and Mike had taken a liking to the young guy, and Len was the same way. He had been showing some real courage and backbone, and Len liked that too. Jason was at the same building, and Sean, wanting to get an early start, had used the radio to wake him up. The sun was barely up, and they were almost there. There wasn't a very good chance in finding those guys now that they had moved on over three days ago, but Len knew that it was important to at least try. They might even get lucky. It was worth a chance.

Only a few seconds after they drove up, Jason came running out of the door to check out the car. Yellow, just like the movie. How cool were these guys?

"Thanks, guys. This is great."

"I thought you deserved something nice," explained Sean. "All your food is in the back seat if you want some breakfast."

"You know what? I really wish I had known you guys earlier. I like the way you guys operate. And now, since my days are numbered…"

"We would've liked that too, Jason. I'm sorry that it can't be."

"You have any new ideas on finding these guys?"

"Yeah, I'm getting an idea on how to find them," began Sean, "but it might take a few more days. For now, we need to just drive around and look the area over. We'll continue to move west, like they have, and maybe we'll pick up on something. They're looking for food, weapons, and more women. Where will they find those?"

"Just like here, apartments will have the greatest concentration of people, but the food is anyone's guess. With four or five complexes searched and only a handful of guns, maybe individual homes will have more guns," guessed Jason.

"I'm thinking that the key to finding them will be food. There are people scattered all over, and weapons are intermittent and scattered, but what they need to live, first and foremost, is food. Where will there be any food in the city?" asked Sean.

"Most houses and apartments, with living occupants will be out of food. There would be scattered homes that occupants left early and never came back, like on vacation, early virus infection, or they bugged out. Any homes like that may have a cache of food, but even some of those have been found already, likely most of them. But with everyone locked down tight because of the stage two, maybe there are more left than we think. Your neighbors know when you're gone, and if they're starving, they'll break into the house they know is empty first, but the ones farther away may be left alone," Lonnie explained.

"Without any operational stores now, where is any food?" asked Len.

"There isn't any. Other than people who were real prepared, like Dad."

"Do you think they left the town for the country homes?" asked Mike.

"No," began Sean. "Not enough women out there, or shelter, and the prospect of finding enough food for a gang their size, would be marginal. They could, of course, butcher a cow and have plenty of meat, but they would be short of the other things. And moving that many people around might use up all of their fuel. I've been thinking about it since yesterday. If they were in these apartments, and they received bread from the police delivery, we would be able to find the names of all of the tenants. If we could identify all of the dead bodies, then we could narrow down the list of suspect names."

"But names won't do us any good if we don't have a clue as to where they went," concluded Lonnie.

"Just say if we had a complete tenant list, and we start up a new delivery of bread, radio bulletins and the works, ask for their names as they call in for a delivery, compare the new names with the old, we've got our culprits. Names and new delivery addresses. Then Mike, you and I go to work."

"Sounds like it might work," chimed in Lonnie. "We can go to the office, get the names of all of the tenants, call up the police chief, and see if they kept track of any names and addresses. Getting those, we do a cross reference, and we've got the most likely culprits. Jason, since he's already infected, could go through the pockets of all of the dead people in these three buildings trying to identify them for elimination from the list."

"Do we really have to wait for more bread for delivery before we start advertising it?" asked Len. "What if we run the bulletins as a ruse to start getting the requests, with names, and the addresses with the largest concentration of names on the list will be our target."

"That's exactly where I was heading, Len. You're reading my mind. I think that's our way to find them. We know they're heading west from here and will be looking for a good place that will house all of the gang and prisoners, which could be a nice motel or an upscale apartment house, but most likely won't be separate residential homes. That would divide his forces too much. Okay, Jason gets to work here; we go to the office and do what we can. We need to contact the police chief and run the plan by him and get any information on names and addresses. As soon as that's done, we can start bulletins on all of the media outlets, monitoring the names that come in. Once we have our target area, we can set up a surveillance crew, deliver some bread from our stockpile, and watch how it goes down. Then decide on our next move," explained Sean.

"Sounds good, let's get started."

"Jason, you got that radio, you can contact us directly, but when you have as many names as you can find, call the Sheriff's Office on the phone and save the radio batteries. Oh, and eat as much as you want because we can bring more if you need it."

"Alright, and thanks again."

"Sean, here's the names of everyone that lived in those three buildings. You're never gonna guess whose name is on it," exclaimed Lonnie.

"Someone we know?"

"Yes. Someone that has one of our guns."

"One of our deputies? And he's the ringleader?"

"You tell me, you rode with him for a few days: Jack Leland."

"That figures," soliloquized Sean. "He had a little bit of a dark side come out when we started killing the stage two. He was enjoying it way more than I thought would be good for him. I didn't realize it would turn into this."

"We never know, do we? Some people hide what they have inside because of civilization and the penalty for their bad side. But if there is no penalty, and he gives free rein to his bad side…?"

"Anything might happen, and the more he gets away with, the worse it gets. It grows like a cancer, consuming more and more, and he's gone off the deep end. His only cure will be what we can give him. The sooner we can implement this, the more people we'll be able to save. Give the police chief an update on what we've found and what our plans are. I'll get the number for that radio station I used and see if Donna is still around. If we're gonna start the bread announcements again, it might be good to start it for real. It's been twelve days since the last delivery."

"You're right. Everyone is probably out of food or close to it. Maybe you ought to give Bob a call, explain our plan, also that it's time to start baking again. Just a heads up for tomorrow."

"Okay, I'll do that as soon as I find out about Donna."

The phone rang, Lonnie answered, talked a minute, started writing names, and then hung up. "That was Jason with some names. He even found an ID for the naked woman. He must have gone through every apartment looking for purses, discarded wallets, and paper mail. Pretty thorough job. I find myself liking that young man more and more. Too bad we're gonna lose him."

"Exactly how I feel."

"Guess what name wasn't among the dead."

"Jack's."

"Correct. My guess would be, especially with one of them carrying an M4, that he's the leader and instigator."

"Alright, we have our first answer. Let's start working on the rest of it."

It was only a few minutes after noon by the time Police Chief Ray Latham had his office secretary in front of the computer looking up records for food delivery from before the lay-off. It wasn't long before she found Jack's name and address included on the list. Ray was able to contact a couple of radio stations and the local TV station, which had two people living on site. Before one o'clock, they had announcements starting to run on both radio and TV, and Mike had met Mitch and Bob at the McKenzie River to take Bob into the bakery and get started.

Sean had driven his own truck with Lonnie, which had been at the Sheriff's Office for over two weeks, over to the city police headquarters. Ray was trying to get a hold of any remaining officers and then the workers on the body disposal crews to line up people for food delivery as soon as they could.

Within the hour, there were hundreds of calls coming in for food delivery. One caller wanted to know where the bread was coming from, and the receptionist had been instructed not to give out the true answer but only that a private party was offering it. Within an hour and a half, they had five hundred names, and looking them over, Sean and Lonnie had already picked out twelve tenant names from Jason's apartment area. Although the call requests had come through at different times, every one of the twelve names had requested a food delivery to an upscale apartment house close to downtown Eugene. The room numbers were randomly selected on both stories of the building, trying to make it look like a realistic occurrence.

"It looks like we found them," Chief Latham exclaimed. "At least twelve of our names are on the delivery list, but checking how many times the building was given for a delivery order it adds up to seventy-five. There won't be that many men there; I think they're trying to hoard some of the food for their group. Of course they're hungry, just like everyone else, but if you cross reference any other apartment complex, you won't find that many requests. Most buildings would be a handful at best, and they have seventy-five. These guys are bad to the bone, not caring about anyone else. I vote we kill every last one of them. Surely there is a special law pertaining to what they're doing during a crisis."

"There is a law," Sean replied. "You commit rape and murder, and the penalty is instant death. That's my law. That's righteous law. When we move into that building, we are going to kill every man in there, unless he's tied up as a prisoner. The way society is, there may even be a few women in there that need to be put down. We'll do our best to find out."

Sean continued, "I want to get Mike back from the bakery and then do some surveillance for the rest of the day, probably throughout the night, so we can get a good count on the assailants through the windows—not to mention a count of the women and girls. See where everyone is located, what room Jack is using, and maybe how many weapons they may have. What we need are some special operations weapons and accessories."

"You mean silencers?"

"Yes, that's exactly what I mean. Do you know where we can get them?"

"Our SWAT team has some. I'll check into it right now."

After giving Mike a call, he showed up with the panel truck a few minutes later and had the foresight to load up about twenty loaves of fresh bread. Shortly after, Jason showed up in his bright yellow Camaro. Keeping Jason out by his car to reduce the risk of infection, Sean explained the scenario to his group. With high-powered binoculars and cameras to record video of the assailants, they were going to watch the place until the next morning and see what would be their best course of action. With a hostage situation and weapons involved, there was a strong possibility that innocent people were going to die before they had it resolved.

Moving into position in an adjoining building, Sean and Mike looked things over. With orders not to use any lights and open doors slowly to keep from drawing attention, they walked down the hallways of both floors checking the rooms. The gang had already been there and left their calling card with several bodies scattered throughout. Closing all the doors on the opposite side of the hallways to reduce the possibility of light interruption from the back windows, Sean left Lonnie and Jason with instructions to watch only, take notes, take video with the camera, and never move fast anywhere, to reduce the risk of catching their eye.

They were to crawl up to the windows and back out. The main thing was to be careful not to draw attention.

Sean and Mike took Len with them to the building on the opposite side of the target building. Clearing that building also, room by room, they found the same thing. Closing certain doors and leaving others open, the three of them spent the next hour watching and evaluating. They could see both men and women moving around with some of the women with their hands tied. Apparently, they were allowed some movement. Not expecting any help from the outside, and with the walkers moving around on the streets, the men weren't expecting the women to try to get away. There were men and women on both floors, scattered randomly throughout, and Sean recognized Jack on the upper floor. While he watched him, there were several men approaching him and leaving, as though reporting and taking orders.

Sean and the group all had headsets on for their own communication. It seemed like there were about fourteen men inside, but there might be over thirty women and girls, many of whom had bruises and black eyes. Sean and Mike were burning with anger. They had their silenced pistols and silenced sniper rifles, and they were ready to do whatever was necessary. Leaving Len upstairs in the second building, Sean and Mike walked back down to the entrance where they could keep an eye on the other building's entry door.

Ray had approached the area and stopped two blocks away. He was bringing two more officers with weapons and gear to see the layout. Before they left the vehicle, they became aware of an approaching vehicle from a side street heading for the apartment complex, with four men and two females in it.

"Sean, this is Ray. I've got two more with me. I'm two blocks away to the west. A car just drove by heading to you. Four males, maybe two females."

"Got it."

"Think we should shorten the odds?" Mike asked, looking at Sean.

"If it looks doable. I'd rather get it done now and keep those women from any more suffering, especially these two new ones. Here they come. Cover me and play it by ear. Keep it quiet."

Sean leaned his rifle in the corner, propped the door open with the doorstop, and walked out across the parking lot, heading for the other entry door as the car was approaching. Reaching the door, he took a quick look inside, and not seeing anyone, he opened it and walked in like he knew what he was doing. After the door was closed, he could barely hear the car pull to a stop and the opening of the car doors. They had parked about thirty feet away, only forty feet from the doorway where Mike was hiding. Not giving them time to even close the doors, Sean stepped back out, took a quick study of what was going on, and decided what he would do and also what Mike would do. All four men were out of the car, and two of them were reaching in and jerking two females from the seats. When the girls grabbed for something to stop their exit, their captors hit them, and then jerked them unceremoniously to the pavement.

"Hey, Jack said he wanted a look at those girls first thing."

"Who are you?"

"Sean, the new guy. Hey, tell that guy not to do that." Raising his left hand to point at the guy in the back, he reached with his right to pull his silenced handgun from behind his back. As all eyes turned to look, Mike shot one in the head and then another, both on his side of the car, while the girl was still on the ground. Sean lifted his gun, shot the one with his hand on the girl first, and then the closest one he shot in the face as he turned back to cry out. Just like that, four men were dead.

Looking at the girls, Sean put a finger to his lips.

"See that guy right there? Go to him, and he will hide you in a room while we take out the rest of these vermin." They nodded and immediately hurried to Mike. Sean checked the car, and the keys were still in it. He started it and pulled it out of sight of the building. Hurrying back, he dragged the four bodies up to the edge of the building, out of sight of anyone looking out the windows. Couldn't do anything about the blood though. Everyone on his crew had listened in on the incident.

"Lonnie, Jason, Len, Ray… Mike and I are going to clear the downstairs first, quiet and quick. The building that you're in, get downstairs and move with us, room by room. Watch through the window and cover us. Ray, drop one guy in the west building and have him meet with Len. One man per room and advance down the line, one man at a time. Ray, you and your other man come to the entrance, south end. You'll see me."

"Got it."

Sean could see Ray and his men come around the corner of the first building. Giving him a hand signal, he signaled one man to drop off, and Mike met him at the door and explained it to him more clearly. Mike came out and walked up to Sean behind Ray.

"Mike and I will lead. There's a stairway just inside the door. When we get just past it, one of you will turn and face the corner of the stairwell. Any male comes around that corner, you put two quick ones, dead center. When he goes down, pull him toward you so he won't be seen from upstairs. The other of you will kneel and face down the hallway. If anyone walks out while we're in a room, two quick ones, dead center. Clear?"

"Got it."

"Let's do it."

CHAPTER FORTY-NINE

In the secure bunker close to the Pentagon, Glen Williams, the Secretary of Defense was in a meeting with the President and his other top advisors.

"Mr. President, our men in eastern Russia have been successful in separating several plane loads of potential transplants from other possible infected. The clean ones are not totally guaranteed, but with interrogation and an interpreter, the ones they believe are safe haven't had any contact with any sick person in over ten days. Others have been honest about their association with sick people and are willing to wait a few more days to prove their health."

"How many then are ready for departure?" asked the President.

"Close to seven hundred at their present location. Three C130s could have them on our West Coast in about ten hours or so."

"Have we decided on the best place for relocation?"

"With the ones from eastern Russia, the best place would be the Willamette Valley in Western Oregon. There is a place in Northern California, north of Redding that also shows promise. Our satellite images of the Willamette Valley close to the Eugene-Springfield area, shows recent fieldwork, within the last several days. Over a hundred acres of cultivation. That suggests that someone is thinking of the future and is planning for long-term survival."

"That's the most encouraging news I've had in the past two months. I'd love to meet the men that are involved with that. Can you tell with any certainty how many people are living in the area of the cultivation?"

"Over thirty, but the only thing we know for certain is that there are both adults and children involved. Also, they are using vehicles to drive back and forth into town. Scavenging for supplies or looking for survivors? We don't know, but from older images, we can see that they keep increasing the number of camp trailers on their farm—apparently for the continuing increase of people that they have."

"This is sounding better and better. I'm assuming that they've figured out a way to tell if someone is healthy enough to take them in. Is there anything else you've been able to find out?"

Infrared pictures tell us that there's a lot of heat coming from a certain location. Having checked into it, it's a bakery. And we've seen the same vehicle parked at the bakery and at the farm. These people are really thinking and are planning their future survival."

"If they were only feeding their thirty people, couldn't they do that with the house oven? Baking several loaves a day? And if they're using a bakery, how much heat would it take to show up on your pictures?"

"You're asking all the right questions. The amount of heat we've seen from the bakery would suggest that they're baking thousands of loaves a day. They're feeding more people than what they have at the farm. These people would make good government leaders. They're out to save every survivor in the area and are using their heads on how best to achieve that. I almost wish I were right there with them, listening in on their conversations and plans. Besides, freshly baked bread daily? That alone is enough to make me wish I was in their group."

"Have you been able to pick up on any other activity in the area? Can you tell how much of a hit the community has taken, as far as the virus goes?" asked the President.

"I can tell you that we've seen a large pit filled with bodies, so I would have to say they were keeping up with body disposal for quite a while. Like everyone else, though, it all came to a stop when the fourth tier infected started to develop stage two. No matter where we look now, the streets are littered with bodies in every city. Most of our on ground military is no longer functional. Once things calm down and everyone comes out of their holes, we'll probably find quite a few military personnel. Rounding them all up to have a viable, on-the-ground military is another matter. Right now, there are still too many walkers to differentiate between the infected and healthy population. We have picked up radio and television bulletins advertising bread delivery."

"So they're baking thousands of loaves of bread, and then advertising delivery if you call in?"

"Yes. That's exactly what it sounds like. So they're saving the survivors, but they're also getting a good count on how many people are still alive and virus free. Going back in time on our satellite video, they were baking bread for about a week before the tier four conversion, a lot of bread, and then they shut it down for twelve days, starting again today. That suggests that someone was really thinking early and were baking bread before everyone starved or had to start scavenging for food, which would have pushed more healthy people outside with the stage two infected, resulting in more infected. The increase in baking just before the shutdown gave the survivors enough food to stay indoors and weather the tier four invasion. And now they think the worst of it is over and are starting back up. Like I said, these guys have earned my respect and admiration."

"Mine too. If we had people all over our nation with that kind of ingenuity, we could come out of this good enough to recover. Is there an airport large enough to land the C130s close to that location?"

"I believe so. The Eugene Municipal Airport is only seven miles from town. There are clear runways, and once they land, I would suggest attaining a car from the rental agency at the airport, driving straight to that farm and having a talk with the leadership. The best way to guarantee the survival of the Russians would be to develop a working relationship with the people on that farm."

"I agree. Find me a phone number for that farm, and we can find out where they stand in their survival plans and if they would be agreeable to helping to integrate the Russians. With the extra labor force supplied by the Russians, they could plant more crops and increase their own survivability. Not that I'm talking about slave labor, but rather more people working together for the good of all, which is what I'm picking up from what you've told me. I think when I explain to them what our plans are, they will be agreeable. I think the worst problem we'll have to face is the language barrier."

Taking the lead, Sean advanced to the first doorway on the right, which was open. Stepping into the doorway quickly with his pistol raised, he completed a quick scan of the room. With Mike behind him, Sean continued across the main room to the bathroom door and then the bedroom. Nothing. Returning to the hallway, they stepped across and entered the first room on the left side of the hallway. Nothing. Advancing to the next door, they could hear a girl's voice ask a question. Couldn't be much older than fifteen. Sean stepped in quickly, with his gun raised.

He found a man sitting in a chair with his hands on the girl. No one else. Sean clucked his tongue to get the girl's eyes on him as he squeezed the trigger. The man's head bounced away from Sean like he had been hit with a rock to the temple. Mike held up his finger to his lips so that the noise that escaped the girl was minimal.

Sean eased up to her, and whispered, "Is there another one in this room?"

She shook her head.

"There's two girls in the bedroom."

Sean picked up her shirt and handed it to her to cover her naked bosom. "Stay here."

Stepping to the bedroom door and opening it, there were two women lying on their stomach on the bed with their hands tied behind their backs. Sean whispered to the girls to wait for him to come back to get them as he was untying them.

"You're safe. We have men outside, and as soon as we're done, we'll take all of you where you'll be fed and taken care of."

"Okay."

Sending the single girl in with the others, they walked back out to the hallway and the next room. Nothing. In the next room, some small noises could be heard. A voice in his ear stated, "Two men and one girl in that next room. Girl in the bedroom alone, two men at the dining table."

Sean, replaying the previous room in his mind, stepped through the door facing the table, with Mike right behind him. Mike covered right just in case, and Sean took the head shot on the first one and two in the chest on the second man. Easing into the bedroom, they opened the door to see a young woman lying on the bed, crying.

"Can't you leave me alone? Pleeease…?" she begged.

Stepping closer, Sean whispered, "We're here to help you. Get dressed, and we'll be back to get you in a few minutes."

Stepping across the hall, there was nothing. Moving down the hallway, Sean heard Lonnie's voice, "One man on our side, laying on the bed."

Taking the left room first, they opened the door and stepped in. No one in the common room or the bathroom. Stepping up to the bedroom door, Sean reached for the doorknob, and Mike waited. The door opened, and Mike shot once, twice. Across the hall, the door was open. Footsteps could be heard at the end of the hallway. There was a man coming into the hallway from the stairwell, one step, two… two shots, dead center. The man fell, making a small noise, but a louder thunk when his head hit the wall. There were more footsteps as another man stepped into the hallway, looked at the body, then… two more shots as he started to call out, and he fell.

Releasing the mag, Sean slipped in another quickly, sliding the near empty one in his pocket. Turning right into the room, they cleared it, found two more women tied up on the bedroom floor, released them, and then moved down to the last two rooms. Both were empty of men, but there were two women in each bedroom. Getting them all to dress, he led them down the hallway to the next girls. Telling them to wait, the girls could see two police officers at the end of the hallway.

With Mike facing down the hallway in the other direction, Sean went into the bedroom to get the other girls. Bringing them out, they continued to the next girl, brought her out, and then to the last three. Sean led all of them to the last room and sent them all into the bedroom to wait.

"Everyone move to the top floor, same procedure. Six perps down, ten women safe. There may be as many as fourteen men upstairs…"

"Sean, there's another car coming up the street."

"Crap. Mike, we've got to step out as soon as they leave the car and knock them down. They'll see the bodies. It's got to be fast. I'll go first and take the left side. You two stay just like you are and cover, just like you've been doing."

"Got it."

They heard the car pull to a stop, and the doors started to open. Sean could hear a whisper in his ear, "They're stepping out, four men, shit, there's three more women… dragging them out… walking forward toward the entrance…"

Sean stepped out quickly, stepped immediately left, with Mike right on his heels stepping forward. Thirty feet away, the women were dragging back, digging in their heels, knowing they didn't want to go in the building. All eyes turn toward them, but it was too late. Muzzle flashes blinded them. The first two men fell with head shots, and the next two both got double tapped in the chest, falling away from the blast. All three women were frozen in fear, lying on the pavement from their backwards pull, all of a sudden having no resistance, as the men dragging them died. Sean raised his finger to his lips, and then pointed at the officer in the entrance door of the next building. The women nodded their heads and scrambled for safety.

Both Mike and Sean put in a new mag for the upstairs—full mags on their left side, empties on their right. Re-entering the building, Sean nodded his head at the two inside. Advancing slowly up the stairs, Sean peeked over the top. No one was in sight.

"First three rooms on the right, all have men and women," Len related his report.

"Same on the left," Lonnie said, seeing the same.

"Ray, keep your head low, but keep watch."

Ray gave a small nod.

Jack was in the middle room, on the right. Sean moved forward, eyes roaming, gun following. Listening at the open doorway, he held up two fingers to Mike. Stepping quickly in and to the left, Mike followed, aiming right. Two men at the table were playing cards, and music was playing from a CD. One shot to the head of the one closest. Two to the chest of the other one, just as he started to move.

Mike turned and softly closed the entry door. Checking the bathroom and then walking up to the bedroom door, they could hear a girl's whimper inside. Opening the door softly, they could see a man naked on top of a woman. Mike holstered his weapon, slipped up close, grabbed the man's long hair, and yanking it back, he wrapped his arm around the man's throat, dragging him from off the girl. Applying pressure for forty seconds, the man was long gone. Laying him on the floor, Mike took a pillow, put it over the man's head, and then shot him through the skull.

"Get dressed. We'll be back for you," Sean instructed.

Crossing the hallway, they entered the second room. There was one guy sleeping in a chair. Sean stepped closer, so a pass-through wouldn't go into the next room, and then he shot the man in the forehead. Opening the bedroom, they found four women, all tied up. Untying the ropes, Sean told them to find more clothes, and they would be back.

Slipping down to the next room on the left, they could hear voices talking.

"That little bitch scratched me good."

"What'd ya do to her?"

"I beat the hell out of her, and then did it to her while she was unconscious. Serves her right. They all need to know who rules the roost. When the other girls see what she got for scratching me, they'll think twice about it next time."

"She might not be any good for several days then."

"Who cares? There's plenty of them, and we get more every time we go out. You see that last one that Jack beat to death? What a waste of good flesh."

Sean poked his head past the door's edge quickly to get the lay of the room and the men's location. Looking at Mike, he whispered, "I'll take the one at the table, his back is to us. One just walked to the bathroom."

Moving into the room, Mike split off to cover the bathroom, as Sean came up behind the seated man. Moving quickly, he wrapped his arm around the man's throat, and with the other, he started putting pressure on the side of the head.

Whispering in his ear, he growled, "You're dying. You'll never hurt another one of these girls." A strong quick pressure, and the struggle stopped. Laying him down, he pulled his pistol to cover Mike, just as the other man came out of the bathroom.

"Hey."

The man turned to look, and Mike jabbed out a fist to his throat hard, crushing it and preventing the man from crying out. As the man gagged and raised his hands to his throat, Mike took him to the ground and pulled his knife. He showed the knife to him, and then he slipped it between two ribs, slowly, and then into his heart. "You don't rule the roost."

Pulling it out, Mike set the knife tip under his chin and pushed it up through his mouth, pinning his tongue and driving it up into his sinus cavity. Pulling out the knife when the struggling was done, he wiped it on the man's shirt and replaced it in the sheathe.

After standing to his feet and drawing his weapon, Mike and Sean advanced to the bedroom. Opening the door, they found another girl naked on the bed—no pulse and not breathing. She had been beaten to death. Pulling the cover over her body, they looked at each other. Walking back into the common room, they heard footsteps in the hallway. Edging up against the wall, Sean could see a man walk past their room, heading straight for Ray. They heard two muffled shots and the tumble of a body. Easing up to the door, Sean poked his head out quickly to see Ray dragging a body down over the stairs. Good man.

Crossing the hallway, they entered the opposite room. The shower was running, but no one was in the room. The bedroom door was open, and they eased up to it to see a man sleeping, bare chest, the rest of him under the covers. Mike aimed and squeezed off a round. The head jerked and a small explosion of blood and brain matter flew over the opposite side of the pillow. Opening the bathroom door, Sean stepped up to the curtain and pulled the edge to peek in and make sure it was a woman. It was.

Softly, he said, "Miss… Miss?"

"Can't you leave me alone long enough to take a shower? Please go away."

Sean pulled the curtain back a little so that she could see him holding his finger to his lips. He then opened his hand to flash his badge. "Take your time, and don't come out until we come to get you."

Her eyes started to redden, and her face scrunched up, as she started to cry at the realization of being saved. She nodded her head up and down several times in acknowledgement. Stepping back out in the hallway, they began to back away, toward Ray and the stairs.

Descending the steps down to the landing, Sean whispered, "We'll go down to the opposite end and start over, working our way to the middle. We'll save Jack's room for last. He may be the only one with a rifle."

"Okay."

Dragging the body to the bottom of the stairs and around the corner, they hurried to the other end of the hallway and up the stairs to begin again. Speaking to his crew, he let them know they were coming up the opposite end and then waiting in the stairwell for their "go ahead" reply.

"We're set."

"We're set too. First room on the west side has one male sitting in the chair, two girls sitting on the bed talking."

"Room on the east has two girls in the living room. I don't see any males. Might be in the bathroom."

"Let's go."

With full mags in, Sean and Mike started to advance to the first room with one male. Walking into the room, noting nothing to the kitchen side, Mike head shot the guy sitting in the chair just as he saw them. Walking to the bathroom, Sean made sure it was empty before opening the bedroom door for Mike to enter. Shushing the girls, Mike told them they would be back for them and to hold still. Exiting the room and entering the one opposite, there were the two women sitting on the couch. Holding his finger up to his lips, Sean eased up to them and asked if there were any men in the room. They answered no. Having them follow him to the hallway, he had them go across the hall to sit with the other two women.

"The next room on the west, women in the bedroom… I can't see any males in the room." Len's voice.

"On the east side, one man in the bedroom… he's talking to someone, but I can't see who." Lonnie's voice.

Easing up to the next room on the east, choosing to clear the one with the male subject first, they cleared the front room, kitchen, bathroom, and then stepped up to the bedroom door. Gently turning the doorknob, Sean looked at Mike and then pushed the door open. Mike stepped through with weapon raised. A man was sitting on the edge of the bed, with his pistol slightly behind him, and two girls kneeling on the floor in front of him. The girl who wasn't busy looked at Mike, but kept quiet, as she watched him extend his gun barrel to the man's temple. The man tensed up even more than he already was, and as soon as both girls scrambled away toward Sean, Mike squeezed the trigger. Sean told them to get dressed and to go in the bathroom and wait.

Stepping across the hall, they entered the room with only women. There was no one in the front room. As they were about to enter the bedroom, Lonnie stopped them.

"One male is heading toward the hallway."

Sean quickly spoke, "Ray, if he comes your way, let him get close. Otherwise, let him go."

"He's in the hallway, maybe going straight across. I lost him." Lonnie's voice.

Len's voice: "I got him, he's walking over to talk to Jack… He's walking back to the door. He's out, and the door's closed."

"I saw him. He turned north toward you guys. Lost him." Lonnie again.

Mike had stepped into the bathroom, while Sean slipped into the bedroom, startling the girls, but only slightly. Keeping them quiet, Sean stepped over to where the door would have to open all the way, before he could be seen. By then, it would be too late. He could hear footsteps approaching the door and then the rattling of the doorknob. Mike would have been more quiet. Muffled noises, and then a body falling to the floor.

"All clear, Sean," over the radio.

"Get all your clothes on. We've only got two more rooms to clear, and then we're leaving. As soon as you're dressed, come out to the living room."

As he was talking, he was untying two of the girls and then letting them untie the other three. "No talking, and be as quiet as you can. You might find more clothes in the closet if you need some."

Sean opened the door, walked out, and then closed it softly behind him. Mike had pulled the body out of the way.

"Five girls, all of them tied up."

"Which room next? Save Jack's for last?"

"The man you just took out was the only one that was in the last room you haven't cleared, except Jack's. There are some women in that room, though." Lonnie's voice.

"Jack is the only male left that I can see. He has at least three women—two in the bedroom and one on the couch with him." Len again.

"Alright. Len, you stay put and keep your eye on him. Everyone else come to the top of the stairs. I'm not sure how this is going to go, but we'll check that last room first to make sure we're clear, and then it's time for Jack. I hope I don't have to kill him too quickly."

When the girls came out of the bedroom, some of them wrapped in a sheet or blanket, Sean signaled them to stay quiet, and then led them into the hallway and pointed them in Ray's direction.

“Ray,” Sean whispered, “put them in the room to your left with those other girls.”

CHAPTER FIFTY

Moving softly to the hallway, Sean looked at Jack's door and could see that it was closed. Easing down to the last room across from his, with the door still open, Sean and Mike slipped inside. Moving to the bedroom after seeing the rest of the room was empty, they eased open the bedroom door. One woman was tied to the bed, naked. Four more were sitting on their knees on the floor with their hands tied behind their back, and their feet tied to their hands, with tape over their mouths. The last man didn't want to hear their words of reproach as he was abusing the one on the bed. Mike realized he had killed the man all too quickly. All of them had died too fast. Sean could see that all of the girls were at varying degrees of undress, and as they realized that Sean and Mike were there to save them, they all began to weep.

Pulling his knife out, Mike reached behind each one and sliced through the tape between their wrists first so that they could stand and remove the rest of the tape themselves. Sean quickly cut the girl on the bed free, while keeping half of his attention on the door. Mike then lifted her to her feet, handing her to Sean, while he pulled the bedspread off the bed, threw it to the floor, and then pulled the blanket free and wrapped it around her. Mike then pulled the sheets loose and gave them to the other girls to wrap up in. Leading them quietly to the hallway, he sent them all toward Ray.

"Ray, put them in the room with the other girls and then come up here."

When Ray had arrived, Sean could see Lonnie, Jason, and another officer at the top of the south stairwell. He signaled them to stay put.

"Len?" Sean whispered.

"Still on the couch, he's got a bottle of something that he's drinking. Alright, the girl is walking toward the bathroom. Go! Go now!"

They had already tested the doorknob, and it was unlocked. Mike pushed the door open, and Sean rushed in facing the couch. Mike followed, facing the opposite direction, and as Ray came in, Mike turned toward the couch, watching both the bathroom and bedroom doors. Jack was a little slow in his reaction, sitting in his boxers with a bottle of beer in his left hand. Reaching for his pistol on the arm of the couch to his left, by having to reach across his body to grasp it with his right hand, he wasn't fast at all. Sean squeezed the trigger once, shooting Jack's hand, turning it into a bloody mess, and the gun fell to the floor. His M4 was leaning against the chair five feet away. With Jack holding his bleeding hand, Mike opened the bedroom door to see two girls sitting on the bed with their hands taped to their ankles, knees to their chest, with no clothes on.

"So if it isn't the high and mighty Sean Dixon and his puppy dog tag along," sneered Jack.

Mike cut the girls loose and told them to get dressed. Closing the door, he stepped over to the couch, and looking down at Jack, he pulled out his gloves and slipped them on. Quickly, he struck down for Jack's face. Since Jack saw it coming, he had jerked aside, so that it wasn't as powerful a blow. Unsatisfied, Mike handed his gun to Sean, and then grabbed Jack by the throat with one hand and hit him several times in the face. By the time Mike was done, Jack's nose was broken and smashed, two of his front teeth were knocked out, and his lips were in ribbons.

"See, I didn't need Sean to give me an order to do that, nor did I have to obey an order to stop. That was all my idea. I'm just softening you up for the rest of what you got coming." Receiving back his gun from Sean, Mike stepped over to the bathroom door and knocked on it.

"I've got thirty men, and they'll never let you get away with this. You won't get out of the building alive." The noise coming out of Jack's broken mouth was hard to understand.

"Jack, you're the one who won't get out of the building alive. By the way, you only had twenty-six men and they're already dead. Ray, check every room upstairs and take all of the girls to the downstairs hallway quick as you can. Len, there are ten girls downstairs in the first room on the south end. Get them out into the hallway."

"Already on the way. Nice job, Sean. You too, Mike."

"Ray, have one of your guys go next door and get those five girls from the cars that we saved. We left our rifles just inside that entry. Grab those too, please."

Sean walked over to the table and picked up a half a roll of duct tape. The bathroom door opened an inch, and the last girl looked out to see what was happening. Walking back over, Sean handed his gun to Mike, grabbed Jack by the neck, and jerked him off the couch. As the girl watched, Sean placed his foot on Jack's back and held him to the floor. She opened the door wider to see everything that Sean was doing. He pulled Jack's hand up and wrapped his wrist with duct tape. Pulling the other hand over, he continued wrapping the roll around both wrists as tightly as he could. Pulling the tape out four feet, he twirled the roll until the tape was made into a rope and then wrapped that around until he reached the flat part of the tape, and then continued a few more wraps to keep it all in place. Starting over, he wrapped the wrists again and then made the rope once more and pulling Jack's feet up to his butt, tied it around the feet and then wrapped it all again. He opened the bedroom door, the girls inside were dressed and wondering what was happening.

"Ladies, don't worry. Everything is over. You're safe."

Sean then stepped over to the closet, opened it, and pulled all of the clothes off the closet pole. Grabbing the pole at one end, he jerked the plastic holder from the wall, and taking the six-foot pole, he cut a ring around the center with his knife. Leaning the pole against the wall at a forty-five degree angle, he stomped it in half. He now had two rods about three feet in length. They should work nicely.

The girls had stood and watched Sean's workings with perplexity, not understanding any of it. He took them by the hand and led them out into the living room. He handed each girl one of the rods and then jerked Jack up to his knees. Jack knelt there, not knowing that Sean had handed the girls anything. Mike pulled the two girls around in front of Jack so that he could see his victims.

"Are you going to punish me some more, Sean? I get it. I get to face my accusers." He started laughing.

"Girls, is there anything you'd like to say to your captor?"

One of the girls raised her stick and brought it down over the top of Jack's head, again and again. She stopped when she was breathless. The other one swung her stick across his face, repeatedly. When she stopped, Sean stepped up.

"Ladies, I need to take this guy downstairs where the rest of the women are waiting. I'm sure they might want to participate or at least watch." Turning to the girl standing in the bathroom, he asked, "Would you like a turn?"

She shook her head in the negative. "Mike, you want to pick up that pistol and grab his rifle? We'll take it all with us."

Grabbing Jack by the armpit, he dragged him out of the room and down the stairs, not caring if he dislocated his shoulder with the rough treatment. By the time they arrived at the bottom of the stairs and turned the corner, all the women were assembled in the seven-foot wide hallway. Propping him up on his knees, Sean took the two sticks and held them out.

"This man has been found guilty of assault, kidnapping, rape, torture, and murder. His sentence is unanimously agreed upon. Death. Do any of you ladies have any last thing you'd like to say before the sentence is carried out, or perhaps you'd like to take part in the sentence? Step forward if you want." Immediately, there was a surge forward by several of them. "Now, now, ladies, you'll have to take turns."

Handing the rods to two women, each one took a turn at striking Jack across the face. Two more. Two more. And then one of them bent down and ripped his boxers off. All of a sudden there was a knife being held out, razor sharp. When the woman saw it, she looked up at the face of the man offering it and saw a smile—Mike's face. Taking it, she knelt down, reached out to Jack with one hand, grabbed it, pulled, and then sliced. She then grabbed his sack, squeezed as hard as she could, and then sliced away the rest of his manhood. Jack was howling in pain and agony, crying out for mercy, tears streaming down his unrecognizable face, blood pooling underneath him.

Another woman stepped up, took one of the sticks, and was cursing him as she struck his face and jabbed his empty crotch over and over. Not every woman participated, but they all watched, some enjoying the agony that he was suffering. There was no telling how many of the women had been raped before, but it was safe to assume that probably thirty-five to forty percent had been either raped as an adult or molested as a child with most of them never seeing any judgment or penalty against the one who did it to them. But they were all finding justice this time. Jack had fallen over with weakness, blood loss, and pain.

"Jack? Jack? Can you hear me? I told you not to fall in love with the killing and now look where it got you. The pain you're suffering now still doesn't compensate for what you've done. Would you like to say you're sorry?"

He nodded his head but couldn't get any words out. Almost half the women were crying at the decrepit spectacle that Jack had become.

"Ray, could you take the women over to the next building. And then we need to decide what to do with them. We could sure use a bus right now. Watch out for walkers when you're outside."

As the last of the women walked out the door, Sean looked down at Jack. His breathing was quick and shallow, not able to get enough oxygen delivered to the different parts of the body. He was only moments, maybe seconds from cardiac arrest from the magnitude of his blood loss. There was now a six-foot pool of blood on the floor and still growing. Sean considered the humane thing might be to end it with a bullet through the brain, but then he pictured in his mind the four-year-old boy that had been sent out with the walkers, the older boys, the young mother that had fought back because of losing her son and getting beaten to death for it, after she had been repeatedly raped by no telling how many men. He needed to suffer as much pain as possible before he died. The door opened, and Jason walked back in. Coming up close, he watched Jack's final moments.

"We found the young mother that you beat to death, after kicking her young son out to the walkers. I hope you could at least feel sorry for that one." Jason was still plenty pissed off.

Nothing.

"I'm the guy that tried to stop you. Your men beat me and then kicked me outside with the walkers. Now I'm infected, and I owe my death to you. But for now I'm still alive, and I get to watch you die, less than a man."

Jason rolled him over onto his stomach, then placed a foot on his back between the shoulder blades, and applied enough weight to keep him from breathing. It was over in seconds. Jason just wanted him to feel the suffocating horror, for just a few seconds, which all those women felt whenever he or his men were on top of them. His own personal death sentence was secondary to what those women suffered.

Once it was all over, Mike turned to Sean. "What should we do?"

"I could call Dad, have him and Joe bring the two four-door Chevys down with plenty of food. I don't think it would do any good to take them to the farm. We can't house all of them. We could find a motel with kitchenettes maybe, set them up in it with the clean rooms and nice beds. Bring in some food, maybe have a couple of our women stay with them for a couple of days, so they don't feel alienated. We could stay a couple of days ourselves to make them feel safe and protected and then decide on their future after that. The walkers are on the decline now, so there shouldn't be much danger."

"Alright, that sounds good. I can't think of anything better. You make the call, and I'm gonna make another sweep through the building. I want to make sure we didn't miss a girl that crawled into a closet to hide or something, and then she'd be left all alone and afraid. I'm a little nervous about it. I'll pick up any guns I find also."

"Go ahead, that's a good idea. The thought of leaving one behind isn't very appealing."

Over the radio, Sean said, "Ray, I'm gonna go get the panel truck. Send one of your guys out, and I'll walk with him. Have a couple of guys start gathering pillows to throw in the panel truck to sit on for as many women as it will hold. We need a motel for all of these women for a few days until we figure out what to do with all of them."

"Got it."

Turning to Jason, Sean asked, "How you feeling, Jason? Any symptoms yet?"

"No, none. I think I'm still a day away from the usual time it shows up."

"What do you want to do now? You can't be around anyone after tonight."

"I'd like to say good-bye to the women. I… I knew two of them from my building."

"Alright, go on over. I've got a call to make."

"This whole thing went down a lot easier than I thought it would," commented Jason.

"I agree. But seeing the ones driving up at the start, realizing we could deplete their numbers right away, I made an instant decision to start. With the silencers, none of them realized they were under attack, and you have to remember that they weren't expecting anyone to be out and about, or anyone to even know about what they had been doing. They weren't expecting any kind of a rescue effort and didn't have any guards posted. That was their downfall: no planning. I'm just glad we were able to effect a rescue without losing any of the girls. If we had waited until morning, the way we'd been thinking earlier, more girls would have been raped and beaten."

"I'm just glad it turned out as well as it has," responded Jason. "Thanks, Sean, for letting me help with it."

Pulling out his cellphone, Sean called his dad. Explaining the situation first, he asked him if he knew of a suitable motel that would work out.

"There's several motels out in the Gateway area. They would be close enough to us for easy access, and there's a mall close by with a lot of clothing stores to take them to. You said most of them don't have anything but what they have on?"

"Yes. But some of them are even wrapped in sheets and blankets without anything else. They've been treated pretty ugly. If we could transport all of them there and get them fed and situated for the night, we could shuttle them over to the mall tomorrow, maybe a third at a time. They could get cleaned up tonight, get some good rest, and tomorrow they'll wake up with a brighter future."

"That's a good idea, Son. Should I have Mom cook things here or bring the fixings down there to the motel?"

"Throw in a variety of things, snacks, canned fruit, vegetables, and the fixings for a nice meal. I'd like a couple of women to come along to stay the night. When it's all done, you can take Mom back up to the farm."

"Okay, Son. We'll meet you there. Give me another call when you pick out a motel."

"Alright, I'll see you in a little while."

"Mike, how's it going?" asked Sean over the radio.

"Just about done. I'll be there in a couple of minutes. Go ahead and get the truck. You can start passing out some bread as soon as you get back. I imagine all of the women will be extremely hungry. I doubt that the bad guys would have been too generous with whatever food they've been able to find in the last week."

"Okay. I forgot you brought some bread. I'll hurry."

Once Sean had the panel truck in front of the building, he took several loaves of bread inside and passed them around. "Ladies, there is one question I need to ask of you. Did any of you notice any of the men showing any symptoms of the flu in the last couple of days? This is important. Think about it. Were any of them coughing, feverish, sniffling… anything that would resemble the flu?"

No one could recall any symptoms, which sounded good, but it still weighed on Sean's mind. It would be easier to quarantine them than to take the risk. He would talk it over with Mike and his dad.

"Jason, we'll need your help to get the women over to the motel, and after, you could stay for dinner. What do you say?" asked Sean.

"I'd love to, Sean. It's nice to have company for a day. All I've got to look forward to is solitude."

"I know, buddy. That's why I offered. But also because I like you."

"You do? That makes me glad. Whatever you need me to do, Sean."

Utilizing Jason's car, the two cars the bad guys had drove up in, Ray's car, and the panel truck, they were barely able to load everyone for the trip over to the Gateway area. There was a six-story motel on the north end, and it had a kitchen for the in-house restaurant. The clothing stores were all within eight blocks, which would make it easy to access. The motel had a pool and hot tub. Some of the rooms had hot tubs also, and with everything still working, Sean thought it was a perfect set-up. Giving his dad a quick call, he let him know their location.

Taking the women into the lobby, Sean and Mike needed to do a room sweep before they felt safe. Leaving Jason with the women, the rest of the men, starting with the ground floor, went from floor to floor, checking every room and closet, including the stairwells. There were a couple of bodies that they had to assume were dead infected. Noting their location, Sean would have Jason help with their removal later.

Finding the room keys, they assigned all the women rooms on the second floor to keep them close and easy to keep track of. Once they were sure it was safe, Sean sent Mike and Lonnie to pick up Bob and a lot of bread for the women and their crew.

"Ray, you want to take your guys and start some bread delivery? Were you able to line up more men for that?" Sean asked.

"Yeah, we were able to find several men that we were using on the body removal crews, still healthy. We could get started with that before dark, although we won't get a whole lot done before then. But the more people we can start helping, the sooner they'll start breathing easier. Some of them, I'm sure, are already out of food. It's hard to ration yourself when you're so hungry to start with. Sean... I ... I want you to know that we never could have pulled this off without you and Mike. We never would have realized it was even going on. If we hadn't stopped them, there's no telling how powerful they would have become or the havoc they could have caused. I've never seen two guys like you and Mike before or ever had the privilege of working with anyone like you. I'm proud of you guys and our military that could produce two guys such as you've proven to be. Thank you." Holding out his hand, Sean met it with a powerful grip and strong emotion.

"Thank you, Ray, but remember the whole thing was a team effort, starting with Jason. That young man has some balls and some smarts. And you and your men backed us up the whole way. From now on, that's what it's going to take to be successful in rebuilding our area. I just hope that the rest of the country has been as fortunate to have some people left over who have society's interests in mind rather than their own. So thanks for your help, Ray."

Mitch showed up about ten minutes after Ray and his men had left. Beth, of course, had come, and so had Rachel, Hailee, Riley, and Karen. The three orphaned children had also come with Karen, since the adults had been hoping that the presence of children who had lost their parents might spark some interest in the hearts of some of the mothers who had lost their own children. Immediately utilizing the kitchen and getting things underway, Beth then went with Sean and Karen with the kids up to the second floor. Rachel, Hailee, and Riley had stayed behind to continue the meal, allowing the older and motherly Beth and Karen to go and visit the younger women and girls to comfort them in ways that only a mother could. The women that survived the ordeal had paired up for the rooms, since many of them had already bonded during their captivity. There had been clean robes hanging in each unit for the occupants to use, and they had all taken a cleansing shower by the time that Beth and Karen started knocking on doors.

Room by room, the elder ladies with the children visited the hurting women, comforting them and letting them know that a nice dinner would be ready to eat in a half-hour. Sean, once he had his mom started, returned to the kitchen to be with Rachel, as she cooked the meal.

"Sean, right after I talked with you, I received a call from the federal government. Guess who?" Mitch asked excitedly before he made it to Rachel.

"No guessing, Dad. Was it important?"

"Yes, I think so. If the President of the United States is important. Apparently, they wanted to talk to the man who owned the farm that was planting crops and having all of the bread baked. They were trying to figure out where to transplant several hundred or up to several thousand Russians. Since they picked the Willamette Valley as one of their locations, they were looking it over with satellite and noticed the new cultivation. The more they watched the area, they could tell that the bakery was in operation. And also, they heard the bread delivery ads on the internet. They said they were very impressed with the way we're working for the future and wanted to talk to the leaders to discuss our future and how to integrate the Russians into our new society. What do you think of that?" asked Mitch.

"That sounds like good news, Dad, as long as they don't send us a bunch of outlaws and worthless people. If they're good people and want to work together for the good of mankind, I'll make it work somehow. When did they say to expect them?"

"Probably tomorrow. They're practically starving now, so we'll have to start feeding them right away," explained Mitch.

"I'll have to talk to Bob about it and see how much flour is still at the bakery. With that and what you have, we'll need to figure out how long that will last and for how many people. If Bob thinks we have enough until the new crop comes in, then I see no problem with it. Do you?"

"No. Like you said as long as they're good people and want to work, that's all that matters. First thing tomorrow, though, I need to start preparing a lot more ground for some more wheat. You can never have too much wheat."

"That sounds good enough for me. For now, we need to figure out how to take care of these young women and girls. They're at a crucial place right now, and they need some TLC just like Lucy needed."

"Alright, Son. I have a number for you to call. They were anxious to hear back from you, especially since the first load of people will be here tomorrow."

"Okay, let me have it. As soon as I talk to Rachel for a couple of minutes, I'll give them a call."

CHAPTER FIFTY-ONE

"Hello. This is Sean Dixon. From Springfield, Oregon. You wanted to talk to me?"

"Yes, I did. I'm Nathan Roberts, the President. Now Mitch is your dad, right?"

"Yes. That's who you talked to earlier."

"You're the one that just led a successful operation against a gang of murderers and rapists?"

"Yes, I guess you could call me the leader. My partner, Mike, I consider my equal, but he usually follows my lead. Plus I had the sheriff and the police chief for Eugene in the group along with an army sergeant, two other police officers, and a male victim of the gang, who we found and had turned us onto them. He was also helping throughout the entire operation."

"How many women did you save?"

"Thirty-seven. Some of them were as young as thirteen."

"How many men did you have to kill?"

"Mike and I killed twenty-five. Most of them with a pistol shot to the head. Others with various means. The police chief killed one, and the ringleader, who was a former deputy, I let the victims take care of."

"I see. How was that done?"

"I taped him up so he couldn't move, found some wooden rods and let the women take turns beating him. A knife came out and one woman cut off all of his manly parts. Between the beating, the bleeding to death, and the one male victim that was thrown to the walkers to get infected, he didn't survive."

"Sounds like a just punishment. Thank you for ridding us of such bad characters. Your dad told you of what we talked about?"

"Yes, he did. You plan on sending out seven hundred people tomorrow?" asked Sean.

"Yes. Maybe a little less than that. We're sending three C130s from Russia—men, women, children, of all ages. Should be free of the virus, but not absolutely guaranteed. The one big thing I need is as much bread as you can afford to send back to Russia."

"If they're not guaranteed, we'll have to keep them quarantined for ten days. After getting our group to survive, we can't take that chance of infecting everyone. If they're agreeable to the quarantine, and they will be fed, of course, everything will be fine. As for the bread going back, I know we can send some."

"Okay. I understand that. I don't see any problems with that. I want to tell you why we're doing this. Normally we would be concentrating on our own people, but we made a deal with Russia before the nuclear war between Russia and China." The President went on to explain about the original offer that was made to Russia and their acceptance and what Russia wanted in return if the nuclear war wiped them out. "That's why it's important to try and save as many Russians as we can, and we're running out of time. Even the bread going back on the return trip is going to keep alive more people until we can transport all of them. Will you be able to feed them until your dad has harvested another crop of wheat?"

"I won't know that for sure until I can talk to my baker. He should be here in less than twenty minutes. He has a certain amount of flour and other ingredients at the bakery, my dad has a certain amount of wheat to grind into flour, and we may be able to find flour supplies at a processing plant. Once the virus is done and all of the walkers are dead, we can start searching for more flour or wheat that is in storage. With the number of cattle around, we will have plenty of meat, but we won't have much in the way of fruits and vegetables. We'll have to get past another growing season to see what we can raise and harvest."

"With the extra man-power from the Russians, do you think you can make a go of it?" asked the President.

"That depends on if they're workers or not. If they're criminals, I don't have much use for them. I can say that I will make it plain that if any of them turn into the ones we just killed, we will kill them also. As long as they want to cooperate and work for good, I don't think we'll have any issues that we can't solve."

"Good, good. When the planes leave, they're going back to pick up more starving people. If you could spare some of your bread to send back with them, it would be appreciated."

"I think that we could do that. So, we need to round up some buses it looks like, take them to the airport, with enough bread to satisfy their immediate hunger, several truckloads of bread to load on the planes, arrange housing for seven hundred people, all by when? Tomorrow afternoon?"

"If they leave Russia at 7 P.M. their time, flying east towards the rising of the sun, crossing six time zones, they would arrive at your location at 11 A.M. your time, tomorrow morning."

"That's cutting it a little close. Not only do we have all of the preparation to do, but also there are stage two infected everywhere still. That complicates matters somewhat."

"Can you have the bread at the airport to tide them over until you have the buses rounded up and the other preparations done?" asked the President.

"I think that may be the only thing we'll have ready. If we pick out several motels for them to live in, under a ten-day quarantine, we still have to do a sweep of each building to make sure that there are no infected in any of the rooms. We only have so much manpower, and we still have to protect and feed our own. Even the airport needs to have a sweep done before they can enter it safely. You see what a large order you're giving me?"

"I realize it's a lot, but under the circumstances it's the best we've got. Those people are now starving; some haven't eaten in more than two weeks. Eastern Russia was never loaded with food to begin with and most of it is too cold to grow much. We can't leave them another day. The first planeloads will leave tonight. You'll just have to do your best, and that's all we can expect. Is that clear?"

"That's clear. What about an interpreter? They'll need to know how to understand what I'm telling them to do."

"There will be several people on each plane that know how to speak English. They are prepared to operate as interpreters. That's the best I can offer you."

"Alright. I'll see if I can make it work. Have you had any contact with other parts of the world? How is everyone else doing?"

"I'm not sure if anyone is doing as well as your group is right now. There may be others though, that are normally living off the land that are continuing to do so, but your group has an excellent start on rebuilding the future."

"If you can communicate with people across the nation, they might be able to find someone who knows how to run a bakery, and if they could do the same thing we've done, they might start saving lives immediately. Most bakeries would probably still have some supplies to start baking right away. The hardest part will be finding people to deliver food but also people that are still alive. Using the radio stations is almost the only way."

"Thanks for the counsel. I'll pass it on as soon as we're done. And, Sean…? Thank you. I mean that from the bottom of my heart. Give my thanks to your dad, your crew, and everyone that's a part of your organization. Your story has been very uplifting to all those that are here and to me also. I look forward to the day that we can meet and talk face to face."

"Thank you, Mr. President. It's been good talking with you."

Before the women and girls came down for dinner, Sean and Mike had the tables set with dishes and silverware, and three large pots of spaghetti with hamburger and sauce stirred in, plates of garlic bread, and bowls of green beans. There were glasses with ice and several pitchers of tea spread among the tables. It was probably going to be the best meal most of them had sat down to in quite some time. To see a meal like that prepared and set up made Sean and Mike feel good about themselves. Anything they could do to make the women and girls feel good and have a brighter outlook for their future was not too much for them to strive for. Having Jason stand by, watching the door and just keeping an eye on things as they helped the women with the preparations, was a great help. Sean noticed Riley looking Jason over several times, and when she wasn't looking, Jason was looking her over. It was sweet, but would only end in heartache.

As the women started showing up, Sean and his group heard exclamations of surprise and gratefulness coming from all of them. It had been a month since any of them had sat down to a home-cooked meal, and being half starved, even the smell of the food to them was delicious. Many of them were crying as they sat down at the table. To go from one extreme to another in a matter of two or three hours was very taxing on their emotions. They were involved in the very worst that mankind had to offer, and now they were being treated like they were royalty, within reason, of course. Nothing was expected of them, except to enjoy themselves and recover from the nightmares that they had been subjected to.

The five new girls hadn't been subjected to all that the other ones had, but had still watched some of their family members, boyfriends, or just good friends killed in front of them, trying to fight off the invaders. They had also experienced vile talk, beatings, groping hands, and the fear of what was to come. To be free and safe once again, touched them all to the core of their being, and all night, they were expressing their appreciation to Sean and Mike, for theirs were the two faces that all of them remembered as they were freed of their bonds and captors.

Rachel and Hailee lost count of how many times that their husbands were thanked with a long hug, by smiling women and crying women and the two of them could see a lot of hero worship beginning. Rachel and Hailee didn't hold anything against the women for showing their affections toward their husbands; they also knew that Sean and Mike were heroes. Besides, what woman in her right mind wouldn't love the two men? Everything they did stirred people to care about them, no matter their age or their sex. Women wanted to be with them, and men wanted to be them. All Rachel and Hailee could do was to glory in the fact that they were the ones who got to go home with them, and in the end, to go to bed with them. But still, to see so many women that their own husbands had saved from dire conditions made the two of them extremely proud of them.

Sean stood to his feet to address the women as the meal was at an end. "Ladies, I'm hoping that this meal is a revelation to you that things are going to be okay, and that from this day forward your lives will be improving. I am so sorry that this terrible tragedy had been perpetrated on all of you, and I hope that you will be able to look forward from now on and looking back to your past less and less as each new day arrives. I want you to know that my mom, Beth, and my dad, Mitch, along with my wife, Rachel, right here, and Mike's wife, Hailee, sitting right there, are here to help you move forward and receive new hope for your future. The man sitting over there is Bob Wilson, the man responsible for any bread that you've eaten in the past three weeks. I also want you to know that my friend, Jason, sitting right here, took a serious beating trying to save you at the beginning. He was then thrown into the street by your captors to be bitten and infected by the stage two walkers… and that was their undoing. For instead of giving up, Jason found us and made us aware of your predicament, showing us where it all happened. Beginning at that point, we were able to find your location. It is because of him that you are all saved today."

There were many thank you's spoken for Jason, and as he began to cry, many of the women also started shedding tears. Sean found it hard to continue talking because of the emotion that tried to overwhelm him.

"The virus that has killed so many is finally on its downhill journey, and we're hoping it will be completely over in another week. We still have to be careful, and it would be best for you to stay here for ten days to make sure all of you are okay. I also want you to know that I talked to the President of the United States only an hour ago, and he is aware of everything that you've been through and wishes all of you a better future.

"He also made me aware of the fact that they will be bringing several thousand Russian survivors into the area to replenish the population and to help rebuild our society… starting tomorrow. Mike and I have many responsibilities in making that work, so you may not see us very much in the next few days. I'll have to bring in a few more people to help take care of you and keep you safe. I hope that you will be okay with that.

"We wanted to take you down the street in the morning to the mall for you to pick out a new wardrobe for each of you, but now my time will be limited. There's still enough time to take some of you shopping tonight before dark. I know that some of you may want to go to your room and rest, since it's only been three hours since you were captive, but if any of you feel up to it, Mike and I would be willing to take you tonight.

"Tomorrow, the Russians are scheduled to arrive around eleven a.m. There will be many families. They should all be virus free, but to make sure, we have to quarantine them just like you, for ten days. But we have to find places for them to stay, and as large as this motel is, it would be ideal to house most of them. Once they are here, for quarantine to work, we need for all of you to stay as isolated as possible. That way if one person starts showing symptoms, not everyone will be infected. I'm saying all this because the next ten days will not be a walk in the park. You'll face a lot of boredom, and I hope you will bear through it and obtain a better future."

All of the women stood to their feet and expressed their appreciation for Sean. To hear a message of such hope and to see a member of the same sex that had abused them, show such care and respect for them, moved them deeply. For many of them, it renewed their faith in men, that there were some that could be trusted and loved, and who could actually love them back.

"I know all of you are in your robes, but any of you who don't feel up to shopping tonight, go back to your rooms when you're done and the rest of you we'll take to the mall right away."

There were only a few that walked away to their room, the ones that had been more severely beaten and raped only hours before. All of them made their way up to Sean, Mike, and Jason to hug them and speak of their thanks and appreciation for all that they had done for them.

Using the panel truck and the four door Chevy, they made two trips to ferry them all to the mall, and leaving Mitch, Beth, and Bob at the motel to watch over the rest, the three men were able to guide and protect them as they forgot their troubles while searching for a new wardrobe. All three of the men were happy to see the women totally engrossed in their "shopping," not worrying about price or even volume. If they liked the way something looked, they found their size and went to try it on. Many of them seemed to be pleased over the fact that in the last four weeks of forced starvation, they had shrunk several sizes and could now wear a lot of cute outfits that were too small for them earlier. Sean was amazed that they could still find joy, even in the little things, so soon after what they had all been through. They gave him hope that everything would be alright.

Before it became too late, Sean called his dad to see about lining up others to come down and watch over the women in the morning. As soon as they would show up, Mitch could go back to the farm and start cultivating more ground for a couple of hundred acres of wheat. Maybe even three hundred. Once they had the wheat production, they might need to start delivering bread to other counties. It would be best to be prepared.

Every large city had at least one bread bakery, and sometimes three or four. But not every county could grow their own wheat. Mitch also needed to have the people bring more beef for the freezer so they would have it for future meals. With all of the new people, they would need to butcher several steers right away. Mitch would mention it to Kevin. Sean needed to look into rounding up some more wrapping paper or getting a vacuum sealer with a lot of bags, or both.

Once he was done with his call, he turned his attention to Rachel.

"Rachel, darling?" asked Sean.

"Yes, sweetheart?"

"There's a pool at the motel. Do you want to pick up a bathing suit of some kind? We could go swimming tonight. I've had a really tough day, and I could use some TLC and some alone time with my beautiful wife."

"Will we be alone, or will a lot of the other ladies like to join you?" teased Rachel.

"I'll make sure we're alone. I can't do what I want to do with anyone else around."

"Ohhh… that kind of TLC."

"What other kind is there?" asked Sean, with a silly grin on his face.

"Alright, I'll oblige your fanciful whims. I'll go pick one out right now. I'll get you one too."

"But I figured that I wouldn't need one…?" he said with a straight face.

"You're not getting into the pool without one. Otherwise, I won't join you."

"Alright, fine… have it your way."

When Mike heard the word pool, he mentioned it to Hailee, and so she also picked out a bikini. She'd love to model one for Mike and have him help her pick one out, but then he would get sidetracked from his job of protecting everyone. Well, there were still Sean and Jason. She picked out a couple of cute ones and had Mike follow her to the men's dressing area for a little privacy, without telling him what she was going to do. She had a lot of fun, a lot of fun, modeling a bikini for Mike. So did he. More fun than she had anticipated. It was all Mike's fault, of course. He talked her into it. Hopefully no one else heard anything.

Sean watched Mike come walking back from another location with Hailee all smiles. When Mike noticed him looking, he gave Sean that "cat swallowed the canary" smile, and Sean knew what had happened. Maybe he should ask Rachel to model some bikinis for him, and he could have a smile like that. It was worth a shot. A little while later, Mike watched Sean and Rachel walking back from another section, and Sean gave him that same smile. Nothing wrong with a little healthy fun and games with your wife.

By the time everyone was ready to go, Jason also had a few clothes picked out. What the heck. He might as well go out in style. He already had the nice car, so why not the clothes to match. After they had put everyone to bed and got Jason set up with a rollaway bed in the lobby, Sean and Mike had their women in the pool for some fun—just some goofing around fun and relaxation. After a trying day with their emotions, some fun with their wives was just what they needed. Both couples were bonding more and more in a deeper relationship with one another.

CHAPTER FIFTY-TWO

Sean, Mike, and Bob were leaving before the sun was up. They had a lot on their plate with the Russians coming and the food distribution to continue. Jason also followed along in his car. Since he was still feeling good, he could help drive some buses over to the airport. Mitch was the only one left to hold down the fort, but with all of the exterior doors locked, there wouldn't be any trouble. Joe, his wife, Abby, and their son, Ryan, were on their way in to take Mitch and Beth's place, while their daughter was already at the motel. Lonnie was coming in also with Len, and he was dropping off his son, Dwayne, at the motel to help with the protection detail. Still at the farm were several men for protection, so everything was covered.

Dropping Bob at the bakery, expecting some of the officers to show up soon to start the food delivery, Sean and Mike continued to a school bus barn to see if they could confiscate a few of them to ferry the Russians to the motel areas. It didn't take long, and with Lonnie and Len catching up to them, they were able to have twelve buses at the airport, waiting on the tarmac, all by nine o'clock.

Returning to their vehicles, they swung by the bakery and loaded as many loaves as they could into the panel truck and into Len's new Colorado. They made four trips, using up almost all of Bob's bread to give to the Russians to send back on the planes. Bob had started using one of the officers to help him with the baking. Most of the process was automated, but there were still a few things that needed people to accomplish it, especially when they were baking thousands of loaves.

When they made their final trip to the airport, they would take even more. They were all so busy throughout the morning that the time just disappeared. Unbeknownst to them, their progress was being monitored by the President via satellite, and he was very pleased with what he was seeing.

Everywhere that they drove during the day, they were taking down a few infected, but it was beginning to taper off. A couple of more days and almost all of the walkers would be on the ground. After that, there would only be an occasional late bloomer to worry about. What was on Sean's mind throughout the day was how long to keep Jason around. He spoke about it with all of them, including Jason, and whenever they would be in any close proximity, masks and gloves had to be worn. Around 10:30 a.m., they checked out the closest motel to their own and cleared all of the rooms. It was only three blocks away, and it could hold two hundred forty people if they were in family units. They would fill that motel first and then put the rest in their own. Sean didn't want them to be too far away from one another.

Lucy woke up lonely and afraid. The sheets were damp from her fever, and she didn't want to sleep any more. She had a dream about turning to stage two and that Bob and Sean found her wandering and had to shoot her as she began attacking them. She still had her pistol, but she was afraid of the pain she might feel if she shot herself. What if she partially missed, and it didn't kill her, but only created a lot of pain before she turned. She kept thinking of a lot of reasons not to end it, but she knew that she had to do it.

Fixing herself some soup for breakfast, she found a magazine to read, and then spent a while again in the bathtub. She was still feeling a fever, and she had been taking Tylenol for her headache. The fever seemed like it just wouldn't go away. Several times throughout the day, she went walking outside to just cool down in the colder air. When the chills would start to come back, then she ended up back in the house covered with blankets.

Thinking about the days since she left the farm, she couldn't place them all, but counting from the start as far as she was sure of, she would count the days backward from the current one, and she kept coming up with the eighth day… maybe the ninth day? She just wasn't sure. Maybe she had one more good day, and then the following day she would turn, late in the day. She would wait one more day before killing herself. She could spend it remembering all of the things that her and Bob had talked about and the way he made her feel any time he looked at her. She would wait.

Sean's phone rang and it revealed a restricted number. Assuming he knew who it was, he answered. "Hello? This is Sean."

"Sean, this is Nathan Roberts. I see you've been busy this morning. You've got the buses lined up, and you've been to the bakery several times."

"Only trying to accomplish what you asked, sir."

"Thank you, Sean. I called to let you know the planes are only about fifteen minutes out. I've talked to the pilot and also the project leader. They know you'll be waiting for them and also about the return cargo that you have for them. Were you able to produce enough bread for our needs?"

"I believe so. Since I don't know how many more people you'll be delivering or how many you have waiting, I wasn't sure how many loaves you needed for the return trip. We've got two hundred loaves to pass out to the ones arriving, and we've got on site about thirty-five hundred loaves for the return trip to Russia. We also have the equivalent, in packaged meat, of about two steers. I'm assuming that the ones that will still be left behind can still cook meat? And also we've loaded up one more batch of bread for our last trip to the airport. We'll arrive there in about twenty minutes or so."

"Sounds good, Sean. I'll contact them and let them know. Have you found suitable housing for the Russians that will suffice for quarantine?"

"I believe so. The motel, where we have the thirty-seven women located, is six stories, with a kitchen. It will have plenty of room, and there is another motel only three blocks away that we've already cleared for occupancy. As long as the Russians know about the quarantine and what it means, I think we'll be alright. The hardest part for us right now is that we only have so many adults, and now we'll have two locations to have to watch over and prepare meals for. It's going to stretch us a little bit."

"With the virus and everything else that's happened, we're all being stretched. That brings up my next statement. The C130s will return to Russia, pick up more people and return. Probably in about thirty hours, you'll have another six hundred or so people to get settled and to take care of. I know it'll be hard to accomplish, but we don't have any viable alternatives. You and your group are the only ones that we know about that are rebuilding with any kind of plan or hope. Just to have a bakery and the ingredients to operate on a large scale as you've been doing moves you to the top of the list. It would be more accurate to say that there isn't any list, only your name. There is no one else. That is why we picked you."

"I understand."

Sean had walked to the end of the bakery building, thinking deeply about what the President was telling him. "This first load of people will be the ones most likely uninfected?"

"Yes. Our men interrogated them all extensively and made it abundantly clear about the importance of their honesty. Each succeeding group may be less positive about their health."

"Then maybe I can use some of the first group to start helping with the increased workload. We need more people cooking to feed all of the new people, and we need search parties to locate and procure more flour supplies and other ingredients for continuing the baking. The reason why we decided on bread is because it's the easiest to make in large quantities and is rich enough in nutrients to keep people alive. Once we know that we can produce enough for a growing population, we can then start concentrating on other aspects of rebuilding. Right now, there are so many bodies in the streets that it's hard to drive anywhere without running over some. Removing the bodies alone will be a huge undertaking in itself."

"With protective gear, you could put to work, right away, several hundred Russians doing just that. If you have the fuel for it," stated the President.

"As we move forward, that is going to be the biggest problem we'll be facing. Fuel for that as well as the farming we have to be engaged in, and all of the less minor things we'll be doing. We'll have to take a survey of all of the gas stations and see what we'll have available and how long it'll last. It'll be tough if we have to revert back to horsepower."

"I'll start working on my end and see what it'll take to get some more fuel rolling in your direction. Just keep setting goals and work toward them as you can. That's all we can ask. Thanks again for the good work, Sean."

"Thank you, Mr. President."

Just as Sean was putting his phone away, with his mind on the new aspects of what needed to be done, a man came around the corner of the building. Sean, raising his eyes to see who it was, realized too late that the man was a stage two infected. With the man jumping at him, Sean's reflex was to raise his arm to block him off, and he felt the man's teeth sink in. Pushing him away, drawing his weapon, Sean put two rounds into his chest.

Sean couldn't believe it. After everything they had done to be careful, every precaution, and now this. How would he ever tell Rachel? Her heart would break. Hurrying into the building, Sean asked Bob if there was a first aid kit, and finding it for him, asked what he needed it for.

"I got a scratch outside, and I want to make sure I get it clean. Where's the restroom?"

"Go down that hallway, and it's the second door on the right."

Cleaning out the bite as well as he could, even to the point of cutting it a little deeper to get the anti-bacterial soap in farther and to get the antibiotics in deeper into the flesh, Sean was heartbroken. Now he wished that he knew if that first guy that he saw get bit had survived. He had a little hope, but not much. He wasn't sure if he was even ready to tell Mike about it. He might suggest cutting the arm off but Sean couldn't face that. It was one thing to be in an army hospital with wounds and you wake up without a limb but to make a conscious decision to cut your own arm off when you're not even sure it needs to be done, was something else entirely. It might be fairer to Rachel to tell her about it and see what she would recommend, but he wasn't ready for that either. Why wasn't he more careful? Why didn't he have Mike with him to watch his back? Why didn't he go inside to talk? He kept asking himself the obvious questions, but no matter what answers he had, it was too late to go back and change it. He was the only one to blame for what had happened.

Calling the President, he now had one important question to ask.

"Mr. President, this is Sean again. I wanted to ask if there's been any success in finding a cure for the virus yet. It would sure ease up the strain if we knew that getting bit was no longer a death sentence."

"No, Sean. Our people haven't come up with anything yet. They haven't stopped trying though, so there might still be some hope. Have you had anyone bit lately that you're asking for?"

"There is one young man; he's nineteen. He tried to stop that gang in its early development and was beaten and then thrown out in the street where he was eventually bitten. He's still with us, but after tonight, he'll be contagious. I really hate to lose him. He was instrumental in putting that gang down and saving all of those women."

"I see. I'm afraid there isn't any good news for that. Our guys are still working hard at it, but no luck yet."

"Thank you. If something else comes up, I'll give you a call."

Mike walked up and noticed the look on Sean's face and the bandage on his arm. "What's up?"

"Just talking to the President about the Russians. They'll be landing in about ten minutes so we need to get a move on."

"What's with the bandage?"

"Scratched myself outside. It was bleeding a little, so I put some stuff on it and wrapped it."

"Let's go then. We're all loaded."

The first plane was on the ground before they arrived, and the second one was circling for approach. By the time the second plane was taxiing toward them, they could see the third approaching the airport. The army officer approached Sean to introduce himself.

"I'm Colonel John Stanton. You're Sean Dixon?"

"Yes, I am," answered Sean, extending his hand. "We have bread to hand out immediately. Would you like to offload your passengers first or give it to them on the plane?"

"Since the plane isn't equipped for handling this many passengers, I think it would be best to unload first."

"Alright. We'll bring the truck up with the bread, and you get them out here."

As the Russians were eating the bread, the second plane was disembarking, and the third plane was on the ground. Sean still had questions to ask.

“I’d like to address the people as soon as I can,” stated Sean. “I want to lay down some immediate ground rules and let them know how this is going to work.”

“Sounds good. I wouldn’t mind some of that bread myself.”

Sean walked up to the truck, grabbed a loaf, and handed it to the colonel.

“Take a few slices, and then take the loaf in to the pilots.”

“How fresh is this? It’s wonderful.”

“Just baked a couple of hours ago.”

Thirty minutes had gone by before everyone was unloaded and eating their fill of bread. The planes were all shut down with the crews standing by, eating the freshly baked bread.

Sean jumped up on the tailgate of the truck and with an interpreter standing close beside him, Sean was ready to begin his speech. Raising his hands to quiet the crowd, Sean noticed a pilot step up beside the truck.

“Sean, be sure to speak loud so all of them can hear you. Some of them actually understand English.”

“My name is Sean Dixon, and I’ve been asked to help in your relocation to fulfill the promise of my President made to your President before the nuclear war with China. First of all, I want to say welcome. Welcome to America. I want our relationship to be beneficial to all of us. We’ve survived the worst of the virus and are now starting to rebuild and to expand our survival capabilities. There are still infected out there, so you must be careful in everything you do. Now, we all work and do what we can to help the progress of all. There are many things that need doing, and since we already know what we’re facing here and have some of the answers to move forward, we'll look to you and your people to help us. I’m sure all of you can understand the concept of working to survive. In our new society, we aren’t better than you, nor are you better than us. Moving forward, we will be one people, helping all others to survive, and enjoying life together as best we may. I don’t know if your life here will be better than the one you had in Russia, but it’s the best you will have from now on.

“My first rule: Respect one another. My second rule: Honor all women as your mother and as your sister. My third rule: Work hard toward making our future as bright as it can be. That’s as simple as it gets. One warning: The last group of men that decided to take women for themselves, raped, and abused them, we killed every last one of them. The same goes for you men. If any woman is attacked and hurt in any way, whether it is an American woman or one of your own, I will kill you. Let me repeat that. I will kill you if you hurt any woman. Now let me say this: If one of your men meet one of our women and the two of you fall in love and want to get married, that is fine by me. That is a good thing. If one of your women meet one of our men and the two fall in love and want to marry, that is a good thing. Do not hurt any women, work hard, and we will all survive."

The whole crowd, when the interpreter had finished, erupted in a cheer and applause. They were more than agreeable to Sean's simple rules. Even the pilots and army personnel were clapping. Before he knew it, the Russians swarmed him, wanting to shake his hand and hug him in one of those Russian bear hugs. The women also took their turns at hugging and kissing him on the cheek. Soon after, the flight crews went looking for fuel trucks to refuel the planes for the return journey. The pilots helped to load all of the bread and meat into one of the planes, and Sean's men had immediately started loading people into the buses for transport. It would take at least two trips to get everyone over to the motel. Once Sean and his group were finally able to take a breather, he had the interpreter ask for any leaders of the Russians to meet with him and his guys to discuss what was needed and expected.

Using the conference room at the motel, he related to them the story of the women they rescued to reiterate the importance of honoring and respecting women. He also let them know where they stood on the flour and the bakery and what was needed to continue the work. Also, they discussed the need to start a more extensive body removal program and that also there would have to be men armed everywhere they went for protection from the stage two infected. Did they have anyone that knew anything about butchering cattle? Yes. They continued to work out details of everything that Sean could think of that needed handling. The Russians could make up teams to work together on every aspect of what Sean wanted, and with a helper from the Americans to guide them and also to carry a rifle for their protection, they would be ready to start right away.

Sean brought in Ray to help figure out logistics, vehicles, trailers, and American manpower for guiding and protecting. Handing out the Beretta handguns from the armory, Sean and Mike gave all of them lessons on their operation, and they were ready to start. Traveling with the Russians long enough to acquaint them with the basics of what they were to do with the body removal, Sean and Mike dropped out to pick up an extra truck. They took three other Russians with Dwayne also, outside of town, where some cattle were roaming, and they explained to them to butcher three steers and bring them back to the motel. Sean called Bob to find out where his flour normally came from and any of his other ingredients also. They were trying to make sure that the bread baking would continue to operate. Sean had Joe swing by the mall to pick up wrapping paper for the butchered steers and some knives suitable for cutting it up for packaging. He also lined up the women that hadn't shopped the night before to ride with Joe and Ryan to the mall so they could pick up their new wardrobe and personal items.

Soon, they had Russians working on everything that Sean and Mike could think of. They also separated a couple of Russian families that were farmers and moved them out to the abandoned farm across from Mitch's house to help Mitch with anything he needed. Sean was to find out that the Russians were hard workers and very industrious. They were all so appreciative of the chance that they had been given at a new life and were great visionaries of what the future held for them in this new land.

CHAPTER FIFTY-THREE

As busy as Sean kept himself, eventually he was going to have to face his dilemma. Jason had continued to work alongside everyone else, showing no signs of the virus. Sean was beginning to wonder if there was any chance that a bite might not be a sure infection. What a blessing that would be for him now, but even if Jason never came down with symptoms, there had been many on record of catching the infection through bites received from the stage two. So there would still be that chance for Sean, but he could never take that chance with Rachel. He could safely stick around for eight days, but after that, he would need to leave. He now understood Lucy's actions even more acutely than ever before.

By the end of the day, the Russians had impressed Sean and Mike with their work ethic, their dedication, and their resolve to make their new home everything that they could, and Sean and Mike let them know how they felt about it. Throughout dinnertime, which was at the larger motel, Sean and Mike were shaking hands and thanking all of the Russians that they could. Even walking outside for a moment, they could see armed Russians guarding the sidewalk between the two motels for all three blocks.

"You know, Mike, these Russians look like they're going to work out great. It's good to see all of the manpower that they're providing. This is going to make it a lot easier on us. These guys are taking the bull by the horns and handling it beautifully."

"I'm finally getting a comfortable feeling about our future. With all of the help, we'll be able to get so much done a lot sooner. Makes me feel real good."

"I hate to be a spoiler, Mike, but I have some bad news." Turning to look straight at Mike, he tried to stay strong. "It's as bad as it can get. I haven't told anyone yet, and I don't know how I'm going to tell Rachel."

"The scratch on your arm wasn't a scratch."

"No. I was on the phone with the President. I wasn't paying attention to what was going on around me, thinking about all of the things he was dumping on me. I should have gone inside or had you with me, but I didn't. When I got off the phone, a walker came around the corner, surprising me out of my thoughts. I threw up my arm to block his reach, and he bit me. I killed him, but it was too late for me. I cleaned it, cut it open, and cleaned it deeper, but I don't know if it did any good. I have to believe that I'm infected so that I don't infect any of you guys. How will I ever tell Rachel? Or my folks?"

"The same way you just told me." Mike wrapped his arms around Sean and held him while both of them shed their tears in silence. "I'm so sorry, buddy." Pulling back, Mike tried to laugh through the tears, "You weren't kidding when you said you had bad news."

"I'll only be good for another eight days, and I'll have to leave like Lucy did."

"Are you sure that's what you want to do?" Mike asked with deep concern.

"Yes. Although we talked about it earlier, I would never want you to have to go through that with me, to remember that you had to shoot your best friend. I'd much rather suffer the sickness and everything it has than make you do that."

"Alright. I know what you're saying. But still we could figure out something that would ease your suffering."

"I'll have to give it some thought. Right now, I need to go see Rachel. Oh, what do you think we should do with Jason? If he's going to get symptoms, it'll be tonight or in the morning. Should we send him away or tuck him away safe and wait to see what happens?"

"If we send him away, he might shoot himself because he would think it's over. If we keep him here, he won't end it too soon. There's always a chance that he might not turn."

"Have a talk with him for me and make sure he stays here. Tell him if he wakes up ill, to wear a mask and stay away from everyone, and then you and him can arrange something in the morning. You know what has to be done with everything else. Since we got a good start on it today, tomorrow should be easier. With more Russians coming in maybe tomorrow night, you can take some of the Russians with you and scope out another motel down the street, maybe two of them. I want to keep the new batch separate from this first one. And it might be best to actually quarantine the second batch. I think I'll take Rachel out to the farm and tell all of them tonight."

"Alright, buddy. Maybe I'll see you tomorrow night."

Taking Rachel up to their room, Sean let her know that they were going out to the farm for the night, maybe even two nights. Collecting their things, they were soon in his truck and heading down the street. An idea had hit Sean earlier, so he had prepared a plate of leftovers from the kitchen and a loaf of bread, and had them set aside to grab on his way out. Rachel wasn't sure of what to make of the food or Sean's actions. He seemed to be preoccupied, like he was that one day when the thought of having children was bothering him. The thought of that reminded her that she had forgotten to bring her pills from the farm. Not only that, but she had forgotten to take one the day before.

It wasn't long before she realized that Sean missed his turn for going back to the farm.

"Sean, is something wrong? You missed the turn back there."

"I was thinking that maybe we would swing by another motel for tonight. There's a Best Western just up the road. It has a pool, and we could be all alone for a whole night. No one else around to worry about hearing us or interrupting us. I know it won't be a honeymoon, and there won't be any room service, but I just thought it would be nice for one night."

"Okay, honey. That sounds wonderful."

From that moment on, Sean was having a hard time driving, because Rachel was getting excited and wouldn't keep her hands to herself. Fortunately, there weren't any cops out and the motel wasn't far. The front door to the lobby wasn't locked and the light was on, but Sean hadn't seen any other lights on in the rooms as he drove up. Carrying their things into the motel, Sean locked the front door and then walked behind the front desk to find a room key for one of the rooms with a hot tub. Taking two keys for the room, they walked down the hall just past the door to the pool, and opened the door into their room. The bed had been made and the room cleaned before everything went haywire.

Sean kissed his woman, told her he needed to look around before they could do anything else, and then left the room. Checking out the poolroom first, he walked over to the windows and pulled the blinds down for more privacy. Feeling the water it felt a little cool, and it smelled salty—a new style of pool water that lasted longer and took less maintenance. Turning on the hot tub to check it, he then went to the front desk to find the key for the pool maintenance room. Turning up the heat for the pool as high as it would go, knowing it would take overnight to get anywhere, he then turned up the heat a couple of degrees on the hot tub. Checking the water with a strip, he added some chemicals to the hot tub. Continuing his walk through the motel, both floors, he found all of the room doors were locked, no noises and no lights on except the hallways, poolroom, and lobby. Placing a chair with its legs through the bars of the front lobby doors, Sean felt as safe as he could possibly make it. Walking back to the room, opening the door, Rachel was undressed, lying on the bed.

"Rachel. I'm always breathless every time I see you like that. I… I checked out the motel, blocked the front door, pulled the blinds in the poolroom. How would you like to go for a swim? Without your bikini?" Sean was practically holding his breath waiting for her reply. He was so excited about it that he could hardly think straight.

"I'd love to. You're sure it's safe?"

"As safe as I know how to make it."

He walked over, sat down on the bed and kissed her, caressing her lovingly. Quickly, he stood, picked her up, snagged a robe off the hook, and carried her to the poolroom. She didn't do any arguing, just kept her arms around his neck and her face snuggled up against him.

Setting her down next to the hot tub, he turned and put a chair up against the doorknob so that it wouldn't open inwardly. Turning back to Rachel to see her already in the hot tub, he slowly undressed while she watched him. Watching her in return, he stepped over to the control and turned on the jet streams and the bubbles before joining her. Sean wanted the night to be the best night that they had so far, because it might not ever be the same after he told her what happened.

A long while later, after a couple of swims in the cooler pool water to cool down from the hot tub, Sean was holding Rachel between his legs, when she realized he had some tape on his arm. Earlier, he had a long sleeve shirt on during dinner, and had taken it off just before getting in the tub. She had been too excited to notice it at the time, but now that they were a little calmer, she looked at it and asked him about it. He was quiet for a long moment, and she thought he wasn't listening.

"Sean, what happened to your arm? The tape is all red from the water. Are you bleeding?"

Immediately, Sean stood her up and started out of the tub.

"Let's go back to the room. I forgot about the bandage, and that it would get wet."

Handing her the robe, he picked up his clothes and his gun and stepped over to the chair. She took his clothes from his hands so that he had better control of his weapon. As he moved the chair and then walked through the doorway holding his gun out in the ready position, she started laughing.

"Do you know how funny you look walking with both your weapons drawn?"

She laughed some more and when he looked down at himself, he realized how funny the situation was. He started laughing with her.

"It's all your fault. If you weren't so pretty and sexy I could keep it under control." He pulled her up tightly and kissed her passionately.

Once they were in their room, they stepped into the shower to remove the tub chemicals and while they were there, Rachel pulled back the tape and then the bandage.

"Sean! Why didn't you tell me about this? I could have put something on it. We'll have to go see if we can find some antibacterial ointment in a first-aid kit. That looks terrible. Did you cut it?"

"Uh… yes, I did. Hurt like blazes too."

"I should say so." When they had dried off, Rachel took his arm and looked at it closer in the light. Holding it up and turning it, she all of a sudden froze.

"Sean, what is this? How did this happen?"

She started crying.

"Sean, is this a bite? Tell me the truth."

She looked up at him with tears streaming down her cheeks. At his silence, she knew the answer. As tears started to fall from his eyes also, her knees almost buckled.

Sean pulled her up tightly in a warm secure embrace and held her as they both cried.

"I'm sorry, honey. It was my fault. I wasn't paying attention, and a walker came around the corner of the building. I raised my arm to fend him off instead of jumping back. My mind was on all of the things that the President wanted me to do, and I just wasn't thinking straight. I'm so sorry."

Carrying her to the bed, Sean laid her down and then joined her, wrapping his arms around her.

After several minutes of weeping, Rachel finally asked, "What are we going to do? Is there anything? Does this mean for sure that you're infected?"

"I'm not sure, honey. I don't have a definite answer for any of your questions. First, I cut the bite deeper to clean it better and rubbed a lot of antibacterial ointment into the wound. If it helps or not, I don't know. I called the President to ask about a cure, if his guys at the CDC have had any luck yet, but they haven't. Our only hope is that Jason, who is nine days infected with several bites, doesn't come down with symptoms tomorrow. If he doesn't, there may be some hope, but if he does, then there isn't much hope at all."

Rachel started to weep again, and Sean could feel her tears pooling against his skin.

"Sean, make love to me again. Take away this pain and make me feel better."

Sean tried his hardest to make up for his mistake in the only way left to him. It was the most tender lovemaking he had ever been involved with.

In spite of the late night, Sean was up early and gave his dad a call to tell him he was coming out to the farm and wanted to talk with him. He then called Mike to let him know what he had done in case he had found out that he hadn't made it to the farm the previous evening. When he bent down to wake Rachel, she pulled him back into bed, and they again made love. Afterwards, sharing breakfast and taking a shower, Sean noticed that she hadn't taken her pill.

"Don't forget your pill, honey."

"Sean, I forgot to take one two days ago and then left the farm without them. I'm sorry. I… now I don't think I'll start back up."

"Rachel, sweetheart, you can't stop. What will you do if you get pregnant, and I'm… and I'm not here? Is that what you want?"

"Sean, if I can't have you, I'd love to have your baby to raise. That would help take away my pain."

"What if you finally meet another man and you fall in love? Do you want a child to be in the way of that?"

"Honey, do you honestly think I could ever fall in love with someone else after loving you and being loved by you? You are the man of my dreams, before I married you. Now after, I found out you're much more than I ever dreamed of. You're my knight in shining armor and no one will ever replace you or be able to fill your shoes. To raise your child is my only hope of happiness if you're taken from me."

Sean's eyes started to water again as he heard Rachel express what he meant to her. Rachel placed her hands on Sean's face and kissed him tenderly.

"Maybe we should take another swim before we leave? There's still time."

"No, Sean. We need to go talk to your mom and dad right away. Maybe tomorrow night we could come back, with more food and do everything again."

"Everything?"

"Uh-huh, everything."

Finding a key for the front door, Sean locked it on their way out to keep it safe for their next visit.

Sean spent the entire day on the farm, hanging out with his parents and Rachel. Telling them about his injury had been hard, but not quite as emotional as with Rachel. Although, when his mom broke down, Sean lost it, then Rachel, and finally Mitch also. The hardest part was realizing that they had survived the worst of it; Sean had saved hundreds if not thousands of lives through his untiring effort; and continuing to do so, he got bit when least expecting it. But since life goes on, they continued to function and worked around the farm. Mitch was in the fields across the road, and Sean was making the rounds with those still on the farm to make sure everything was going well.

As the day went by, Sean could see that Steve and Emily's relationship was growing, although Emily carried with her a sadness that Sean was all too familiar with. Her mom would be turning to stage two today, if she was still alive, and Sean was sure that Emily had been keeping track of the days. Leah was definitely moping around. She had been spending a lot of time with Ryan, and now he was in town with his dad, helping with things. Leah was only two years younger than Rachel was, so Sean could imagine that she was more than capable of developing a strong love for a man and that she was missing the one she had set her eyes on.

Sean answered his phone, seeing that Mike was calling. "Hello?"

"Sean, how's it going, buddy?"

"As well as could be expected, I guess. Rachel took it extremely hard—harder than I did. It was hard on Mom and Dad too. Everything has been going so well, so it was a complete shock to all of them. I just feel so bad about it, but there's no going back to change it now. How is it on your end?"

"The other motels are ready. The Russians are working their tails off. Bread is being delivered like crazy, and we found a supply of flour at a plant that was ready to ship. We're sending out bulletins on the radio and TV requesting anyone that knows how to work at the plant to call in so we can keep processing the wheat that's in storage. Every time we find something that needs a specialized worker, we advertise it, and then we get a call—most of the time only one, but sometimes more."

"That's great, Mike. That's some good thinking. If we have enough trained workers step out and take over the parts we need doing, things will run a lot smoother. How's Jason doing?"

"Good. No symptoms, and he's up and running. He's really been a help. It was his idea to start the radio bulletins for the workers that we need. If he comes down with symptoms tomorrow, I'm gonna be real sad."

"You won't be the only one. There'll be a lot of crying if he comes down with the virus. You need to be sure to make him wear a mask at all times. Symptoms could start at any time, and we don't want anyone else to get infected. Are we getting any better count on how many survivors we have?"

"Yeah, as a matter of fact we are. Our bulletins are asking everyone to call in if they're able to so that we know how many are left and through that we've found out that in the Eugene-Springfield and surrounding area there may be as many as four thousand people. Some of the calls are coming from farther away even. We're telling people that if there's nothing keeping them where they're at, to drive into the Gateway Mall, and we'll get them a place to live close so that they can have access to our food. Then we will put to work those who can."

"That's another good idea. Consolidate everyone for now, and as things get better, people can then go back to where they came from. The disturbing part is that Lane County had a population two months ago of almost four hundred thousand. Now we're down to less than ten thousand, if there's more survivors farther out that is. There may still be a lot along the coast and in all of the small isolated areas. Do you need me for anything today?"

"No. No, you stay with your family today, buddy. Maybe even tomorrow. If something comes up we can't handle or I need some ideas, I'll call you. Just take it easy."

CHAPTER FIFTY-FOUR

Mitch and Beth had decided to move back into their bedroom in the house, since the bunker wasn't really necessary anymore, and in just a few more days, everyone could be moving back to their homes with the disappearing stage two. Everyone would still need to carry a firearm, even then, because all it would take is one walker to infect someone. What happened to Sean proved that out. It might be best to give it a full two weeks before people could really start to feel safe.

Sean was sitting down with the family for lunch when his phone rang. Looking at the caller ID, it was restricted. "It's the President," he announced to his family. He switched it to speaker-phone as he answered it, "Hello?"

"Sean, good afternoon. How's it going with the new citizens?"

"Wonderful. Those guys are as busy as bees. Whatever we show them to do, they jump right on it and then take over. If we're not careful, this will be the new Russia."

They could all hear the President chuckle.

"That's good to hear. I also heard that your welcome speech was very well received, and you were almost trampled by the Russians trying to thank you. It was a very nice speech by the way—very moving actually. No wonder the Russians took such a liking to you. Did you write that by yourself or did you have help?"

"You heard it?"

"Yes."

"Well, no, I didn't write anything. When they were all gathered, I just wanted to explain to them the situation, what I expected from them, and what they could expect from me. It was all off the cuff actually. Didn't even put that much thought into it beforehand. It just came out. How did you hear it?"

"One of my men recorded it and played it for me to hear. I told him not to lose it, that I wanted it, so I can put it in the national archives or the historical database. I want that speech recorded for all to hear some day. I believe, Sean, that you made history yesterday with that speech. The pilot rigged up a PA system in Russia this morning, or last night, whatever, and played it for all of the Russians that they have gathered. They cheered for five minutes. You're their new hero and are all looking forward to working for you and America. I've even had the crew send it to all the other crews to play, as they've found more Russians in bunkers across Russia. Your family should be very proud of you, Sean."

"We are, Mr. President," Mitch spoke up loudly to make sure the speaker-phone picked him up. "We're all very proud of our son."

"Mr. President, I've got one bad report. I was careless yesterday when I was on the phone with you, walking outside around the bakery, and a walker bit me right after talking with you. That was one of the reasons I called you back to ask about a cure."

"So you think you're infected now?"

"I believe so. The bite was deep and broke the skin."

"And you gave your speech even after you were bit?"

"Yes, of course… I take my responsibilities very seriously," explained Sean.

"I see. This news really ruins my day, unless I look at it like I'll keep my job a while longer. Once everyone finds out what you've done, you could be the next President of the United States. I'll need to fly out there and meet you in person in the next several days then. I don't want to miss out on meeting you and your family face to face. I'll give the CDC another call and see if they've made any progress at all yet."

"Mr. President, write this number down. My buddy, Mike, who's been with us through all of it, making decisions with me, is stepping up and taking my place for a couple of days. If you want to talk to him directly, you can call his cellphone." Sean gave him the number.

"Okay, Sean, that's good. If it's at all possible, the Russians that are arriving tomorrow morning… they're really expecting to see you there. Could you be there?"

"Yes, I think I can handle that. What time will that be?"

"I'll have to check into that and get back to you. Thanks again, Sean, and also your family. Spend some time with one another, and I'll light a hotter fire under those boys at the CDC. Good-bye."

Sean wanted to run back into town to get more wheat seed for planting, and Rachel refused to stay behind. If her days with her beloved were numbered, she was going to be with him every hour of the day. Leah was missing Ryan, and so she invited herself on the trip. Swinging by the motel to drop off Leah to hang out with Ryan, if she could find him, Sean and Rachel continued to the farm supply store. Sean rounded up what they needed and then some, and then stopped back by the motel to have a look around and see how all of the girls were doing. All of them were still so thankful for Sean's work in setting them free, and they weren't shy in letting him know about it, even with Rachel standing there.

As they were driving to the bakery, Rachel looked at Sean with a smile.

"No matter how thankful they are, they'll never be as thankful as me. Look what I get every night… and in the morning."

"And if you keep talking like that, you'll also be able to say in the afternoon. Talking like that is almost like teasing."

"Who said anything about teasing? I'm dead serious. Do we have time to stop by the motel room?" Rachel asked with one of those smiles that Sean couldn't refuse.

"Well, I guess we can spare a little time. Only on one condition though…"

"What's that?"

"You have to promise to quit when I say it's time to go."

"When you say it's time to go, I'll see if you really mean it. Is that good enough?"

"That's good enough for me. I can be there in two minutes."

By the time they arrived, Sean had three near accidents and hit the curb twice. Rachel really wasn't teasing.

Arriving at the bakery, the two of them greeted the Russian that was standing guard, and almost didn't get away. Walking in and finding Bob, Sean was to find out that Mike had told him what happened the day before.

"Sean, I'm so sorry about what happened. Rachel, I don't know what to say."

He hugged both of them unabashedly, expressing his deep affection for them both.

"So, I see you have some new help," Sean began.

"Yes, the Russians want to help with everything. They're so thankful for being saved, and they don't want to be a burden on us, so they want to work hard to do their part."

"That's good to hear. With so many things to do, I know it really lightens the load on Mike and me. We can concentrate on other things that take more than just labor. They've been a real blessing to all of us."

"I agree, Sean. With their help here, it frees up more people who know the area to deliver more bread."

"Have you been receiving any of the new ingredients yet?"

"Yes, they started arriving just before lunch. They were even able to get more bags for the bread from where I previously had them made. Except for two people in my life, everything is looking up."

"I know Bob. It still hurts me too. I also know it hurts more to see a woman walk out alone than it does a man, but in a few days, I'll have to do the same thing. After all my talk about having Mike put me down if I became infected, I finally realize how hard that would be, and I would never want to saddle anyone with that memory for the rest of their life. I care too much for all of you to do that."

Rachel couldn't hold back the tears, and Bob's started once he saw hers. They hugged one another, as Sean stood there watching. Getting their emotions under control, Bob turned to Sean with a question.

"Did you stop by for something in particular? Do you need anything?"

"No, Bob, I just wanted to see you and talk. That's all. You've become one of my good friends since this thing started, and I've grown to care about you."

"Thanks, Sean. I care a lot about you too. I need to get back to work. I'll see you tonight at the farm?"

"Sure, we'll be there."

Driving back to the motel to pick up Leah, Rachel was thinking about Bob. "Bob is such a sweet man. He isn't quite like you, but he is very nice and has a lot of good qualities."

"I know. It just broke my heart to see how hard he had fallen for Lucy. I think they would have been so good together. It's still hard to believe that Lucy's gone."

"I'm glad that Steve has taken such a liking to Emily. That has really helped her to move forward after the loss of her mom."

"Me too," replied Sean.

After stopping at the motel, they decided to let Leah stay the night, because she hadn't been able to see Ryan yet. Almost all of the guys were out working on things, so Sean and Rachel headed back to the farm with the wheat seed for Mitch.

The following morning, Sean and Rachel were both at the airport to watch the landing of the planes from Russia. Sean was asked to speak, and taking the stage again on a tailgate, he was applauded by the Russians for several minutes before he could even give his speech. He was able to remember most of it, and he had to add that he was so happy with the work and effort of their comrades that he could hardly wait for them to join in on the work, after they had to be separated for nine more days to make sure they weren't infected.

After all the cheering and thanking had finally quieted, the planes were loaded with food for the return trip, but the pilots and army personnel wanted to sleep for a few hours in a real bed. The Russians had even more buses and drivers this time, so the whole group was shuttled over to the new motels in one trip, and Sean and Mike were able to ferry the pilots and their men to the large hotel for lunch and some relaxing sleep.

After some visitation with the men during lunch, Sean and Rachel were able to talk with Mike for a while before he had to head out.

"I didn't see Jason anywhere. Is he okay?"

"He's feeling wonderful still. So, he's out doing something—helping the Russian crews with this or that."

"That's such good news. What day is this for him?"

"It's at least his tenth day, but he thinks it's day eleven. He was bit three times, Sean. Isn't that good news?"

"It's wonderful news. If he survives three bites, and I only had one… that's the best news I've had since Rachel said she'd marry me."

"So if he doesn't get sick, you might be okay? Is that what it means?" asked Rachel, with hope in her voice.

"Rachel, hold on. It means that there's a slim chance that I'm not infected—a very slim chance. And it might mean that something in Jason is fighting the virus that other people don't have. We don't know for sure. Mike, have you gotten any leads on any doctors? Are there any left?"

"You know, I don't recall that anyone has asked. This afternoon I'll get that out on the bulletins right away. If Jason does have something special, maybe a doctor might be able to find out what it is with a blood test. The sooner they can start testing, maybe they can figure something out in time for you."

"That would be great. Do what you can, and when you see Jason, find out how he's feeling and let me know. Right now, the most important thing would be for him to narrow down for sure how long ago he was bitten. If he's actually past the tenth day, then we know something is up with him."

"I'll get right on it, Sean."

Sean was awakened early the next morning at the Best Western with Mike on the phone.

"Hey, Sean, Jason just called me. He's got a fever, a little nausea, and a headache. We moved him over to an empty house a block away and got him set up with food and whatever else he wanted. He was talking about ending it all, so I told him that you had been bitten. Of course, he wouldn't believe me, because, you know, you're the indestructible, larger than life Sean. You're invincible. He thought I was just trying to make him feel better, so I had to explain the whole thing to him before he believed me. I told him that your only hope was that he would survive. If he kills himself, he'll be taking away the only hope that you and Rachel are holding onto. That really got to him. That's right, isn't it?"

"Yes. I told that very thing to Rachel the other night. It'll destroy her if I tell her he has symptoms. Maybe I'll wait a while to tell her."

"Jason checked with the two women at the motel yesterday, that had been living in his apartment building when Jack moved in, and they both agreed on the date it all happened. Jason didn't start showing symptoms until today, which would technically be twelve and a half days since he was bitten. There might still be something there that will help us. A doctor called in yesterday, and he was trying to round up a couple of others that would know how to isolate the virus and try to figure out if there is something different in Jason's blood that would explain why it took so long for Jason to become symptomatic. So don't give up hope yet."

"Thanks, Mike, for the call. Keep me posted."

"I will, buddy."

Talking Rachel into taking another dip in the pool and some time in the hot tub, an hour or so later, they were ready to leave. Just before they left, Sean cleaned out the hot tub as best he could and added the chemicals it needed to function properly. There was no telling when they would be back.

Arriving at the farm, Sean talked to his mom and dad about what Mike had told him. Everyone was grasping at straws of hope for beating the virus, but underneath they were all filled with fear and were trying not to show it. Hanging around the farm for the day, Rachel was doing things with some of the kids, helping them to enjoy the life they now had. Sean drove over to the farmhouse next door to check on the Russians, to see how they were doing and what they were working on. He was immediately the center of attention. One of the men could speak some English, and he was continually letting Sean know how grateful they were for being allowed to live there and to work with Sean's dad. They had been working hard to clean up the farm and make everything beautiful. Sean let them know what had happened to the previous owner and his wife, without going into the actual details, when asked how such a nice place for farming was empty. Barely escaping the attentions of the Russians with an excuse that he had many things to do, Sean made his way back to the farm.

By midafternoon, Sean was getting antsy and was thinking about heading back to town. Rachel was out beside the barn playing with a couple of the girls when one of the boys came running up from the hog pen yelling that there was a walker down at the edge of the field.

"Sean! Sean! There's a walker down at the edge of the field. Johnny said it just came out of the trees. Bring your rifle."

Sean ran over to the barn, took Johnny by the hand, and asked him to show him where it was. Hurrying out to the back of the hog pen, Johnny pointed down the hill. Sean could see someone stumbling along, actually falling down and getting back up.

"Johnny go back over to Rachel." Sean raised his rifle, wanting to knock down the infected before he got too close. Actually, it looked like a female. Putting the scope on the woman, judging the distance, ready to squeeze the trigger, he noticed the shape first and then the face. Getting closer with every stumbling step, Sean noticed that she was avoiding crossing into the freshly worked field. When she raised her head, Sean took a long look, and not absolutely sure, he took off running to close the distance. Rachel watched as he ran farther out wondering what he was doing. As Rachel continued watching the scene, Sean came to a stop, raised his rifle again, and Rachel prepared herself to hear the boom of the rifle. Sean lowered his weapon and turned back toward Rachel.

CHAPTER FIFTY FIVE

The American rescue teams around Moscow had brought in the equipment needed to clear the thousands of tons of debris from the entrances to two bunkers and then had moved it on to two other bunkers a few miles further out as teams began working to transport those that were inside the first two. One of the bunkers had the Russian President and his parliament inside. They were all healthy and were surprised that the Americans had moved in to find them as quickly as they had. The President was all smiles, as he realized that the American President had kept his word.

Walking outside, into the bright sunlight under a blue sky, seeing the mountain of debris that had to be removed to get them out, he realized the magnitude of what the Americans had accomplished. They had to truck all of the survivors many miles to an intact airport that was sufficient to land the C130s. All the way across, he was looking for all of the familiar buildings that he had just seen a month before, but he couldn't find any of them. His beloved city and country were totally destroyed.

Once his tears and those of his compatriots started to fall at the sight of their city, they continued to weep all the way to the airport. Once at the airport, the Russian President was finally able to talk to the American President, full of gratitude and thankfulness.

President Nathan Roberts shared the news of transporting thirteen hundred survivors from eastern Russia so far and that they were daily in the process of delivering more. Nathan shared with him about Sean Dixon and what he had accomplished on his own in the region to which they had delivered his people and all of the food that they had sent back to Russia to keep his people alive until they could be transported to the U.S. He then played the recorded speech by Sean to his people right after they had arrived on American soil. All the Russian President could do was shed tears as he listened to the way his people had been received.

"Since you and your fellow survivors are closer to our side of the country, you'll be transported closer to us. I believe it would be best to spread your survivors out across our country that our two peoples will intermingle and in the future inter-marry, to make one people out of two. Hopefully, all of your people will feel the same way."

"Eventually, we will call ourselves Americans. Russian Americans and I hope that our two peoples do become one. I gave you my word, and you have given me yours. You have kept your word, and I will keep mine. I am glad to call you my friend."

"We have found people to start up bakeries in our own area, and as more and more survivors come out of their hiding places, we are beginning to recover the same way that Sean's group has done on the West Coast. The bad news is that in Sean's area, the original population was around four hundred thousand, and now that might total around ten thousand. They still don't have an exact number of survivors, but it doesn't look good. If the rest of our country holds to the same ratio, which it probably won't because Sean's early intervention saved many more of the local people than otherwise would have survived, our entire population might end up around six to eight million people. We have no estimates yet on how many of yours have survived. This is going to be a long process of finding them and then transporting them to the U.S. I have to warn you that we may also find opposition in many areas from gangs that have banded together for survival. Not all of them will be made up of good people. Sean and his friends actually killed off a gang that was starting before it got out of control."

"That is to be expected in these types of situations. I hope that you will be able to protect us or arm us so that we may rid ourselves of those kind of people."

"I will do what I can. Our military was hit extremely hard also, and as more of them start coming back together, I'm hoping to restore order.

Sean himself and his number one man are ex marines, and I had been planning on sending them into tough regions with some other military personnel and restoring order. However, Sean was infected five days ago, and we still have no cure. In time, we will figure out what to do."

Sean raised his hand to the side of his mouth to carry his voice farther as he yelled out, "Rachel! Go get Emily, quick."

Rachel watched as Sean ran down to the infected person, which was starting to resemble a woman, grabbed the woman to keep her from stumbling, and then lifted her in his arms, hugging her and lavishing kisses on her. All of a sudden, it hit Rachel what was going on. She took off running for the house to find Emily, yelling out her name the whole way. Everyone came running, pouring out of the house to see what all of the yelling was about, and Rachel, seeing Emily, grabbed her by the arm and began to pull her toward where Sean was.

"Sean wanted you Emily. He... he... you have to come and see! Hurry!"

Rachel continued to pull her in Sean's direction. At Rachel's excitement and urgency, Emily started to run with Rachel still holding onto her. As they cleared the back of the barn, both of them could see Sean hurrying toward them carrying a woman in his arms. When Emily saw the hair coloring and the profile of the face snuggled up to Sean's neck, she froze.

"Mom? Mom! MOM!" Emily screamed the last word and took off running as fast as she could make her legs move, closing the remaining distance in five seconds. Grabbing her mom's face, kissing her and caressing her, Emily had tears streaming down her face.

"She's a little dehydrated. Let's get her into the house, and then we'll talk," explained Sean.

Carrying her into the house, there were many hands that had reached out to touch Lucy, and there were many encouraging words. Setting her on the couch, someone brought a glass of water, and Sean helped her to drink it.

"Mom, I thought you were gone. How? Why aren't you sick?" asked Emily, kneeling in front of her mother with her hands on her legs.

"I don't know, honey. I was sick. I had all of the symptoms for days, but I couldn't bring myself to end it. I kept waiting and waiting. I lost whole days, but I kept writing down when I thought a day went by.

There were cans of food in the house I found, and that kept me alive. The tenth day came, I woke up and was still here. I hadn't turned. I thought that maybe I had the days wrong. I was still a little sick, but then another night… and then I woke up yesterday feeling fine. I'm just very weak and tired. By the end of the day, I decided that I was going to be alright. My food was about gone, so when I woke up this morning I decided to come back here. I was lost, and it took a long time to get here. I ran out of water and food… and then Sean found me, again."

Lucy turned her face to look again at Sean with eyes of adoration.

"Where's Bob. I was hoping to see him right away."

There was a look of disappointment on her face as she spoke.

"He's at the bakery, Lucy. After not being able to find you, he's kept himself busy baking bread for everyone. We've gotten a bunch of Russians relocated here to live, and so we've needed a lot of bread to feed all of them. We started bread delivery again, and we even sent several thousand loaves back to Russia to keep them from starving to death. The President wanted to stop by in a few days to meet all of us." Sean explained.

"If you want, Lucy, you can take a shower, get cleaned up, and Sean and I can take you into town to see Bob," suggested Rachel.

"That's sounds good."

Lucy reached forward, placed her hands on Emily's face and bent forward to kiss her, looked at her face, and then wrapped her arms around her. "I love you, Emily."

"I love you too, Mom."

While Lucy was in the shower, Rachel suggested to Emily to pack some clothes for her to stay the night at the motel with Bob. That way they could have some privacy for themselves. And if Emily wanted to go also, she should take some clothes for the next day. Sean let Beth know that he didn't want anyone else to know that Lucy was back, that he wanted to surprise Bob with it. Hopefully, he wouldn't have a heart attack.

Sean and Rachel packed some food and leftovers from dinner the night before, loaded them in the Chevy, and when Lucy was ready to go, they drove into town, stopping at the closest clothing store on the way to the Best Western Motel.

Lucy filled in more of the details of her survival as Sean asked her questions, and then he explained to her his plan for her reunion with

Bob to see if she was agreeable. She loved it, so at the clothing store, she and Emily picked up a swimsuit for the pool and one for Bob to wear. At the motel, Sean unlocked the front door and picked out a room key for a hot tub room on the bottom floor. Leading the girls to it, he checked it out and then went back to bring their things in. Giving another card key to Emily for another room, he explained to her that Lucy and Bob might want to be by themselves. He also explained that he and Rachel would be in a room also to make sure everything was safe and that they had stayed there the night before. Leaving Rachel with Lucy and Emily, who had two guns between them, Sean locked the door and drove to the bakery.

It was almost time for Bob to wrap it up, and Sean gave Mike a call to tell him about Lucy and what they were planning for the reunion. Mike thought it was a great idea.

"If Lucy had it and survived, she might also be a key to a cure. Tomorrow we need to take her to the doctors I've got lined up and see if they can figure it out. Jason was a start, but Lucy is an even better key to the mystery. If they can figure out what saved her, you could be next."

"I've been thinking the same thing. Maybe I should call the President and let him know about the both of them and he could pass it on to the guys at the CDC. They might find it very interesting and might want to fly them there for some specific tests."

"Give him a call then and see what he says," agreed Mike.

"If I have Bob ride with me, I'll bring him back to the bakery in the morning. How's everything going on your end?" asked Sean.

"Great. It's hard to estimate how many bodies we've removed, but I'd say over ten thousand. We have enough cattle butchered that the walk-in freezer at the motel is full. I've sent a bunch out to the farm; we've located a warehouse full of spuds; and a processing plant we checked out had a lot of packaged frozen vegetables in storage that were ready for shipping. That's huge. They kept processing, even after deliveries had stopped so their storage freezers were packed. And they're not just veggies, but flavored ones too, like teriyaki stir-fry. I can hardly wait to dig into those ones."

"That sounds so good, Mike. I'm glad that you've been able to find so much. Are you about done?"

"Yeah. There'll be some Russians continuing to work; they hardly know when to stop. They're all so happy to be here. Why?"

"If you could stop by somewhere and get some kind of stove, hot plates or something to cook some things on, microwavable bowls and plates, along with Hailee, change of clothes, swimwear, some of those veggies, and some steaks, enough to feed seven or eight of us for the evening… we'll have a little feast at the Best Western to welcome Lucy home. Sound good?"

"Absolutely wonderful! I'll call Hailee and have her gather up what we need from the motel and then grab her on my way to the store. I'll get there as soon as I can."

Sean walked into the bakery to find Bob almost ready to shut down. The aroma in the bakery was mouthwatering.

"Hey, Sean, good to see you. I was talking to my Russian helpers today, and apparently, they all know about your condition. They cried when we talked about it. They told me that all of them are very saddened by the fact that we're going to lose you. They barely know you and are crying over it. You should feel proud, Sean, that you've affected so many people so deeply. I don't even know where all of us would be today if it hadn't been for you and Mike doing the things you've done. I'm proud to have you as my friend."

Sean hugged him for a moment, touched by the words and saddened that he would no longer be able to continue in life with all of the friends that he had newly acquired.

"Bob, I was thinking you could ride with me tonight on the way home. I'll bring you back to the bakery tomorrow morning. I wanted to spend a special evening with some of my friends tonight, a special dinner… you know?"

"I know. I'll be ready to go in just a bit."

"I'd like to take several loaves of fresh bread with us too."

While waiting for Bob, Sean walked out to his truck and slipped inside to give the President a call. Shouldn't be too late on the East Coast, but one never knew.

"Hello?"

"Mr. President, I've got some news for you. It may be as good for you as it was for me. That friend of mine that was bitten three times, pertaining to that gang, he didn't come down with symptoms for twelve and a half days, and even now, it doesn't seem to be very serious. We have no reason or answer why it has happened."

"That's very interesting, Sean. The guys at the CDC have heard about a couple of cases like that, but they couldn't track down who it was to be able to run tests. If you know the guy, maybe we can get him over here, and our guys can start trying to figure out why that's happened."

"I've got one more bit of news. We lost a woman a while back. She was healthy, but had been raped by two men, so we quarantined her for the last two days of the ten days to guarantee that she was virus free."

"What happened to the two men? Need I ask?"

"The same. Mike and I killed all three of the men involved. Only two had actually raped her. Anyway, the night of the tenth day, she was looking good, but right at bedtime she came down with a fever. She snuck away around midnight, taking a few provisions, thinking that would bc best. She was armed and had planned to commit suicide once she decided for sure that she had it. Her boyfriend looked for her but with no luck. As the days went by, she kept track, and so did we. She was sick for ten days, and then she came back today and is no longer ill."

"What!? She had it, and now she doesn't?" asked the President with excitement.

"Correct. She had been gone for twelve days. Sick for ten, but now healthy for two full days and counting... We've got a couple of doctors lined up to look at both of them tomorrow, but I don't know how far out of their field this is. If you want to call your men, explain what has happened to see what they've got to say, and then call me back. I think this could be important."

"I'll call them right away. I'm sure this might be what they're looking for. Two survivors and the answer should be in their blood. If nothing else, they may have developed antibodies for the virus that can be transplanted… to you first and then others, and then a vaccine might be acquired. I'll get back to you right away. And thanks, Sean, I hope this works… even if you might take my job away."

Sean smiled. "No worry about that, Mr. President. I'll talk to you later."

When Sean arrived at the motel, Mike's truck was already there and also another vehicle from the farm. It looked like Kevin's truck. A new barbecue was set up outside the lobby, and steaks were already cooking. Sean had just called Rachel to let her know they were almost there and to keep out of sight. They had planned to bring Lucy in after Bob was in the room.

"Thanks, Bob, for coming out. This means so much to me."

Sean was telling the exact truth. He was so excited on the inside to see Bob and Lucy's reunion.

"Don't mention it, Sean. I'm happy that you consider me such a friend. You know I'd do anything for you. You saved my life and those of my family, and now I consider you my best friend in the world."

Leading Bob into the lobby, Rachel met them, and after she hugged Bob, she continued to lead them into the poolroom where Mike and Hailee had a table set up with hot plates, a microwave, and a small refrigerator. The smell of the hot tub chemicals and the pool water itself, with the heaviness of the humidity, was so different from the feel of the outside air. There was also the smell of cooking vegetables that was very tantalizing; Sean and Bob were starving. Everyone gathered around, including Rachel's brother, Steve, whom Rachel had invited, and Bob felt like all of them were watching him.

"Bob," Sean began, "we had a surprise today, and we wanted to share it with you."

Rachel was standing at the door, and when Sean gave her a signal, Bob turned to look as Rachel opened the door. Emily walked in, with a beautiful, happy smile on her face, and Bob was trying to guess what was happening. A few seconds passed, and then Bob saw more movement as someone else started to come in the door. All of a sudden, Lucy was standing there, fresh, clean, and healthy. Her hair was pulled back in a ponytail, and she had on a pretty, little, blue colored sundress that reached down to her knees, and little white shoes on her feet. She was beaming with a beautiful smile for the man she loved.

Bob stood there, unable to believe his eyes. As tears began to fall, he started walking toward Lucy. As he held out his hands, Lucy rushed into his arms, and the two of them held each other tightly as they sobbed in each other's embrace.

Rachel hurried to Sean, crying uncontrollably, while Emily joined Steve, and Hailee was wrapped up with Mike. There was not a dry eye in the room, and Bob seemed to be past the danger point of having a heart attack.

Mike quickly left the room to check on the steaks, wiping his eyes as he walked across to the door. The rest of them held back, giving Lucy and Bob all the time they needed. Before much time had passed, Lucy was receiving all of those kisses that Bob had promised her. Before anyone could say anything, Lucy turned and led Bob from the room, with Bob flashing Sean a grateful smile through his tears as he was going out the door. The rest of them looked at each other, smiling through their tears, and then got down to the business at hand of getting a meal ready.

Thirty minutes later, the lovebirds hadn't made it back yet, so they started the meal without them. Barbecued steaks, cooked vegetables, baked potatoes, and freshly baked bread. With much laughter and talking, sharing their happiness over Lucy's safe return, they were almost finished by the time Bob and Lucy joined them. Lucy's hair was no longer in a ponytail, and she had whisker burns on her cheeks and neck. But even her red skin couldn't deter the beauty of her beaming face as she looked at all of them in appreciation of what they had made possible for her.

The rest of the evening was spent frolicking and playing in the pool, sitting in and around the hot tub, telling stories, reminiscing about their experiences, and eating cold leftovers. All of them had grown close, and every new thing that they experienced drew them closer, caring more deeply for one another.

CHAPTER FIFTY-SIX

Another day, and more Russians had been delivered, with the airplanes again carrying food on their return trip. They were assuming that there would be possibly four or five more trips; every day the Americans were finding more and more survivors. The doctors were starting the tests on both Lucy and Jason, wearing protective gear, since Jason was still symptomatic. By the end of the day, they hadn't found out anything other than both of them had antibodies to the virus in their blood. Why or how and what they could do with the information was beyond their skill. They sent all of their findings to the CDC, but what needed to be done was that the two needed to go to Atlanta for further testing. Advertising on their radio bulletins for a pilot that would be capable of flying to Atlanta was begun. By Sean's sixth day of infection, they still had no way to get the two to Atlanta. Jason's symptoms had disappeared overnight, and Sean was starting to get worried about what he should do.

Clean up of the streets, the baking of bread, and food delivery continued to take place. More and more of the Americans started coming out of their homes and began helping in whatever way that they could. More specialists started popping up as they realized that the virus had finally run its race and was at an end. Processing plants and butcher shops began to operate. Workers that could repair electrical lines went back to work. People who worked at the hydroelectric dams started working at the dams again, doing maintenance work and checking water flows and whatever else had to be done to keep the dams operating properly. There was no cash and no payments other than the food they received to survive. People were cooperating to the fullest to make everything work once again, but with so few numbers that one man had to do the work of five. People started to be trained in areas that they knew nothing about because that's just the way it had to be.

The President never showed up because he had no pilot to fly anywhere. All available pilots were working on transporting Russia's people to the U.S. By Sean's eighth day, one of the C130 pilots who could fly a Learjet was ordered to find one, fuel it up, and fly Lucy and Jason to Atlanta.

Bob had another baker show up that knew how to operate all of the equipment, so Bob was going with Lucy to Atlanta, not wanting to be away from her ever again. Before they left, they shared one last meal with Sean and the original group.

All of his closest friends had stayed at the farm the night before he was leaving to seclude himself from infecting any of them. Beth and the women cooked up a feast for his departure, and after the meal, Sean felt inclined to say something to all of those that he loved.

"Two months ago, the only ones of you that I knew, were my family and Rachel's family… and, of course, my best friend Mike. I've come to know you in the time since this thing began, and I've come to love you all and to care deeply for you. I've looked after you and tried to make the life you now have worth living. I hope that I succeeded. But I also want you to know that I couldn't have done it without your help and support. It's taken a team effort to get us this far, and I wish the best for all of you as you move forward in this new life."

Sean looked at all of them and spoke their names. "Jason… Len… Bob… Lucy…," longer pause, "Emily… Lonnie… Joe… Ryan… Steve… Leah… Kevin… Joanna… Hailee, thank you for meeting with me so that I could buy Rachel's beautiful dress. You'll never know what that dress did for me. Maybe someday Rachel will tell you. Mike, your unwavering trust in me gave me the confidence I needed to continue making decisions for everything we did, and you were always there, backing me up. My Darling Rachel, you are the light of my life, and I hope that we won't be apart for long."

Sean was finding it difficult to talk. As he looked at each person and spoke his or her name, the person started to weep. "None of us know whether I will return or not. If a cure is found in time, through Lucy and Jason and their tests, I might make it. I didn't want this meal to be too melodramatic, but if I never see any of you again, I wanted each of you to know how special you are to me, and I couldn't have asked for better people to have gone through this with. I love you guys."

Everyone was crying, unabashedly for their savior, friend, brother… not knowing where they would now be if he hadn't come into their lives. Everyone stood and gave Sean their hugs, love, and kisses. Lucy was crying the most, and as she hugged Sean, she whispered something in his ear. He immediately bent down to slip an arm under her legs, lifted her, and held her in his arms. Everyone understood what it signified, and they cried even more, especially Rachel. She knew that Lucy was in love with Sean, and it didn't bother her in the least. Sean was Lucy's hero and always would be.

Long after everyone else had turned in and Jason, Lucy, and Bob had left to catch their flight, Sean spent some quiet moments with his parents, Rachel, Mike, and Hailee. They all understood that the odds were against them, but they were still hoping.

The following morning, Sean was going to load some food in his truck and go live in a house by himself somewhere. He would let them know where he would be once he found a spot to stay. He spent his last night with Rachel, but kept his distance, sort of. He didn't want to take the chance of delivering the virus to her during their lovemaking. Neither one of them slept the whole night, holding each other and talking about the what-ifs. They talked about baby names just in case Rachel was pregnant and Sean wasn't able to come back. Rachel decided that if she had to raise the baby alone, she would name the baby Sean if it were a boy. If it was a girl, she decided on Lucy. Sean was agreeable with both names, but they would discuss the boy's name more later, if possible.

The next morning, after loading his truck, everyone gathered around to see him off. When it came time to get in the truck, Rachel wouldn't let go of him. She clung to him and just kept crying. Kevin and Joanna pulled her from Sean's arms and held her as he drove away.

Mike and Hailee went back to the motel so that Mike would be closer to the Russians and keep things moving forward. He was glad that he had plenty to keep himself busy, but even then, he found himself wondering what life was going to be like without Sean. He and Sean had been part of each other's lives for over four years, doing everything together, whether it was work or play. Life would take a lot of getting used to without him.

Sean spent half the day looking for a house to spend his final days in. He was driving around in an area where houses had a pool in the backyard, large expensive homes. He hadn't seen a walker in a couple of days, which was a good thing. When he finally found a house, the front door was open but not broken, which would indicate that the occupants had probably turned into walkers and then disappeared down the street. The house was intact. Everything seemed to work, and it had a pool and a hot tub. He checked the house through every room and closet, not wanting any surprises, including the poolroom out back and even the tool shed. Sean was thorough with everything.

That night, he lay awake thinking about Rachel and how her heart was breaking. He was haunted continuously about the day he was bitten, thinking about why he reacted the way he did. If only he could relive that day, the lives of so many would now be different.

As he lay there, a dog started howling outside—probably missing his master, but maybe he was trapped in a backyard and was starving to death. Sean decided to check on it first thing in the morning. He hated to see an animal suffer unnecessarily, nor did he want to listen to a dog howling all night.

Through the night, he had nightmares about starving to death, even as Lucy had for a time and also Jason, not able to find any food, starving until Sean and Mike had found him. Sean's dreams were wild and remorseless, mixing things up and also showing Rachel running through the streets looking for him until Jack found her, took her to his room, and just as Jack was about to… Sean woke up, sweating..., from the dream, not from the virus.

Thinking of how crazy his dreams were, Sean's mind drifted to Lucy and Jason. What could they possibly have had in common to have escaped the clutches of the virus? No one else ever had. If simply being immune was a possibility, then out of so many billions of people, there should have been more. However, no one had heard of anyone else being immune.

If immunity wasn't the case, then something else must have triggered their recovery. Something that both of them had gone through… an experience that the two of them shared. What did they both have in common? The puzzle pieces of his mind swirled. Then, all of a sudden… everything clicked into place! Sean thought that he had the answer. He immediately arose in the pre-dawn morning; he was going to put it to the test.

That day, putting his theory to the test wasn't very pleasant, but it had to be done if there was any hope for his recovery. Lucy had gone through the whole ten days of symptoms, but she already had the symptoms when she had left the farm. Jason on the other hand, only suffered two days of symptoms, but he had no symptoms when he did the same thing that Lucy had done. If that was the reason for the way things turned out, then according to Sean's reasoning, he would have to go through at least half of the symptoms. He could handle that; it wouldn't be much worse than the duration of a bad flu. He found a calendar and marked down the day and time of when he started and also the day he was bitten. Now he had some hope for his future if his reasoning had any merit.

Sean called Mike first to see how things were going and to let him know where he was staying. No one else could know, or Rachel might find out and come looking for him. As soon as Mike had heard anything else from the CDC or Jason, Bob, or Lucy in regard to the testing that they had started, he would immediately give Sean a call.

Sean found himself praying quite often for his recovery and also for all of his loved ones in case he didn't recover. Sean didn't really think it would do any good, because he figured that at least three or four billion people had been praying for two months and apparently almost all of those prayers were unanswered. If there was a God, then surely, He would have seen fit to save a lot of innocent women and children, but they all died a terrible death. Most likely, if the evolutionary thought was true, then what had happened to the whole world was just the outcome of stupid and uncaring people and may have happened at any time, regardless—just like with North Korea and their EMP bomb and a satellite. If they would have had a little more time before the virus hit, they would have used that on the United States. If there is no divine hand in the works, then any bad thing might happen. For this thing to have happened, it would point to the probability of there not being any

God. Regardless of his musings, it did happen, and he was infected and had a good chance of dying.

He called Rachel to get his mind on something else, but listening to her cry didn't help much either. He let her know that he would probably be sick by the next day when he called her so not to worry. Lucy had survived ten days of symptoms, and Jason also had survived three bites with only two days of symptoms. There was still time. Rachel wouldn't let him hang up until his phone had died. Even then, she was crying as the phone shut off. It broke his heart to hear her crying. Digging out his phone charger, he plugged in his phone and then turned it back on. He still had the house phone, but he didn't want to take a chance with the caller ID.

Looking the house over, he realized how nice of a place it was. It had a home theatre room as well as the pool and hot tub, and a Jacuzzi in the master bath. It also had a tile walk-in shower, granite countertops, some hardwood floors, and a tile floor in the kitchen and dining room. It had to be over a million-dollar home, and now it had no owner. The virus killed rich people and poor people alike, showing no favoritism. No matter how much money someone had, eventually the virus would have worked its way into their home through kids, hired help, or friends. Since the rich were always out in the crowds, whether actors, singers, athletes, oil moguls, or any shakers or movers, they were always involved with many people, and in so doing, most of them had caught the virus and were now dead. All the wealth in the world couldn't buy them health with the virus on the rampage.

Sean realized that in the new society, all of the world's wealth would be shuffled among the survivors, but much of it, especially real estate, was practically worthless. The real value would be in the answer to the question, "Can you do something that will help your fellow man to survive?" If the answer was yes, then that person would have societal value. Even if a wealthy person still lived, his money was on paper, with little or no value.

Who would want worthless cash, when anything they wanted they could find among the abandoned homes and stores? A new society might be better set up by everyone being able to receive food, medical care, and basic clothing. Once the existing supplies of clothes ran out, then basic clothing would be on the list of provided essentials. Also, food would be basic to survival, and there would be no way to go out and buy a meal at a restaurant if you wouldn't work and help to better society. But when it came to fuel, the one commodity needed to go anywhere, or to do the fun things in life, it could be regulated according to a person's involvement in society and the work that they accomplished. Everyone who could and would work, would get credits for fuel and or even for air travel and other fun things. The basics for survival would be handouts, but everything else would have to be earned.

The biggest problem would be someone taking over an abandoned house and someone else wanting it. There could be fights and squabbles over such things, but why not just go down the street and find another house? Or car, or boat, or truck, or trailer…? The list was endless—from large items to small items, from houses to shoes, from trucks to jewelry. With so few people, everyone could get what they wanted by scavenging. But the key would be, what good is a boat if you don't have the fuel to use it? Same with a car or truck. Fuel could be the commodity of value.

Sean soon fell asleep with his thoughts scrambled, and he dreamed about Rachel and their first time on the McKenzie River.

Two days later, the scientists had isolated the antibody that caused Jason and Lucy to survive, but they still hadn't figured out what triggered it in the first place. There was a chance that they could separate the white blood cells, and with just the plasma, they could inject it into an infected person. However, they would only have enough for a couple of people. Still they wouldn't have a vaccine or a cure. The answer still eluded them. Finding an infected person in the area, they sedated them and set them up with an IV with the plasma. Running their tests might take longer than Sean could spare. It would take at least several days for the antibodies to work, since Lucy had the symptoms for ten days. Even with that, they still wouldn't know if it would reverse the stage two infection. Stage two might be too far along and wouldn't give the antibodies enough time to grow and increase to a viable, healthy conclusion.

Jason and Lucy continued to remind them of the urgency for Sean. Even the President had told them to use all haste to find a cure that would be able to save Sean. Bob and Jason were in daily contact with Mike, letting him know about their progress, or the lack thereof. If they took too long to find out if the plasma was going to work, it might still be too late for Sean. Going over Jason and Lucy's testimony repeatedly, they were finally able to recognize a possibility that may have triggered their survival. Following that, they began looking for information on what they thought was the cause… and also, they needed a dog.

Sean was in his third day of symptoms. He spent a lot of time laying down, thinking about his life with Rachel, how beautiful it had been, and also what the future could hold if he were to recover. He had talked with Rachel several times a day and had told her not to call him. If he were asleep or not feeling well, she would fret even more for his lack of answering the phone. He had finished his special meals, taking three days, hoping that it would be enough to do for him what it had done for Jason and Lucy.

Mike had called him every day to give him updates on Jason and Lucy and also his own progress with the town and its recovery. Mike let him know that Rachel had called him several times, digging for information on anything that Sean had told him but not her or anything that he may have been holding back. Sean wanted to share with Mike what he had done, and his reasoning for it, but he didn't want to get his hopes up in case it didn't work out. That would hurt too much.

On Sean's fourth day of symptoms, Mike called to tell him that the scientists had a lead, but weren't yet able to test it fully, but the cure might have something to do with a dog.

"Didn't Jason say something about finding a dog and eating it for food? And then he had been without anything for three days?" Mike asked excitedly.

"Yes, Jason ate a dog."

"What about Lucy? Did she ever say anything about that? But how would she have eaten a dog? If she didn't eat one, then they're theory is useless," Mike concluded.

"Mike, I'm going to tell you this, but don't tell anyone else. I don't want you to get your hopes up too high, but... Lucy also killed and ate a dog. It woke her up growling, and she shot it. Later, she decided to eat the meat because she had been out of food for two days. She was still outside and had no matches or a lighter, and so she ate small pieces of the meat raw. For most of two days."

“Then that’s it! You need to eat a dog. I’ll see if I can find one. I’ll pass the word around, and I’m sure we could find several with everyone looking.”

Mike was finally excited for once in the past ten days. With the news that Sean had given him, he was ready to do whatever it would take. But that’s what Sean didn’t want.

“Hold on, Mike. That’s why I didn’t tell you. I already ate a dog. For three days. The first two days raw, like Lucy did. It wasn’t real good. The third day I cooked it. The first two days, I ate nothing but the dog to be as much like Lucy as I could be. I won’t know if it will do any good until another two days. Lucy was four days with symptoms before she killed the dog and started eating it. She was well seven days later. Jason was two days infected, eight before symptoms, when he started eating the dog he caught. It took longer for him to get symptoms and then only lasted two days. It’s almost like the earlier start he had, it gave his body more time to develop what he needed to fight the infection. More so than Lucy’s did. If the ratio of recovery holds true, I might start recovering tomorrow. Only time will tell. Say nothing about this to Rachel. She would get her hopes up, and if I don’t recover, she would be even more devastated.”

“Alright, buddy. I’ll call you first thing tomorrow morning. If the symptoms are gone, how long should you wait before going home?”

“If I feel good tomorrow, I would want to wait at least one more day to make sure I’m not contagious. I think by tomorrow night, we should have our answer.”

“Alright, first thing in the morning.”

CHAPTER FIFTY-SEVEN

Two days later, early in the morning, it was bright out, with a few gray clouds scuttling across the sky and very cool. The date was November 6th. Sean spent some time in the hot tub, relaxing and thinking of how he wanted his reunion with the light of his life. He could call Mike and have him arrange to bring himself, Hailee, and some food for dinner. He would have Mike stop by to pick up Rachel, telling her that Sean requested to see her again before any more time went by. That sounded honest enough. When they came to the door, Sean would open it, and Rachel would see him healthy and well. He would also have Mike call him to let him know when they were leaving the farm. Immediately after, he would call his dad and tell him he was going to be fine, that he wanted to make sure before he had told anyone and that he wanted to surprise Rachel. He would come down the following day and see everyone. Sounded like a good plan, except that he hoped Rachel had a strong heart. She was young and should be able to handle it.

Calling Mike, he found out that the President had called and said that by the next day, he would be bringing a cure for the disease. The guys at the CDC had finally come through and were in the final stages of developing the solution that could be injected in two shots in two days. Apparently, the cure was a particular enzyme, or was it a protein, that dogs had in their blood that is normally not found in humans. It actually made dogs immune to the virus. Although dogs are very susceptible to rabies, when the terrorists had altered it, it created a virus that only humans could get. The enzyme, when ingested by people, would help jumpstart the immunity building process.

Mike had felt inclined to tell the President that it was all well and good, but Sean wouldn't need any. He could bring some in case they needed it for someone else, but Sean had already figured it out and had eaten a dog himself. He told the President that no one knew yet, so don't give it away.

Sean decided to forego his plan and just drive down to the farm. Afterwards, the four of them could come back to his hideaway for dinner and to stay the night. He explained to Mike the set up that he had—that there was a pool and hot tub, a theatre room if they wanted to bring a good movie to watch, probably something for the women of course. There was a built-in barbecue on the patio for the steaks, a small selection of wine for the women, and beer in the fridge for the men. Everything was perfect. All Sean needed was his wife and his two best friends for it to be complete.

Mike was going to have the entire group back at the farm by 5:00 p.m. Sean could drive up any time after that. Mike told Sean he might have to forego their dinner plans because everyone would want dinner at the farm, and it just wouldn't seem right to take off too soon. He could bring some beer though, if he had enough to spare.

No one knew that Sean was coming to the farm, but all were thinking they had been gathered to hear the news about the cure for the virus. Beth and Rachel had made dinner, and as everyone was gathered around the table to begin the meal, Mike stood to his feet and began talking.

"The President called to say he'll be here tomorrow about five o'clock with a cure for the virus. He's bringing Bob, Lucy, and Jason with him. He also will have the Russian President with him, and so he will want all of the Russians gathered for a speech. Both of them wanted to meet Sean and all of us too. He said he had something for Sean besides the cure and wanted to give it to him personally. So, tomorrow, we all need to be at the airport at five o'clock."

As he finished, they could hear a truck coming up the driveway and then stopping out front. Mike was looking at Rachel at the time, and when she registered the noise of the truck, she quickly looked up at him. Mike began to grin. He couldn't help himself. He winked at her and nodded his head toward the front of the house. That was all it took for Rachel to take off running for the front door.

Jerking the door open, she could see Sean coming around the back of the truck carrying, of all things, two twelve packs of beer. He gave off the look of just coming home from work with some beer, but Rachel could tell it was for show. She gave out a cry of delight, as she started towards him. Sean quickly set the beer down, and Rachel flew into his arms, crying. With tears running down her cheeks, she kissed his face all over. With her legs wrapped around Sean's waist, he stumbled around in the grass, still a little weak and wobbly. Gently going to the ground before he fell, Sean ended flat on his back with Rachel on top of him, still lavishing him with kisses.

Everyone else poured out into the yard and shed tears of joy at Rachel's happiness to be reunited with the love of her life.

Two hours later, Sean decided it was time to go. The beer was gone, and he knew where there was more.

"Sean, you can't drive anywhere. You're half drunk," Mitch let him know.

"I'm not drunk. I only had six… I think."

"But you haven't had any in so long, you're no longer used to it," explained Rachel.

"Mike can drive. He's okay."

"He's just as bad off as you. We can't go anywhere."

"You can drive. You haven't had any. I'll tell you where to go. I put the address on my phone. I've got big plans for you tonight, so we need to go."

"Alright, Sean, then let's get you in the truck, and we'll go."

"Mike and Hailee are going too. There's a pool, and you'll need some clothes, I think… or not."

"Alright, honey, I'll get my things, and then we'll go."

"Dad, we'll be back tomorrow, and we can all go into town."

"Okay, son. We'll be waiting. You go and have some fun, and we'll see you tomorrow."

Sean hugged both of his parents goodbye.

"What are you guys cryin' for? I'll be back."

"We're just so happy to have you back, sweetheart," Beth explained. "That's all. We love you so much."

"I love you too, Mom."

Rachel came back down the stairs carrying her overnight bag, while Mitch took Sean by the arm to make sure he didn't fall down the porch steps, and Hailee and Joe helped Mike out to the truck. Once the guys were in, Mike said to not forget his things in his truck. Joe grabbed everything he could see and put them in the back.

All of them could hear Sean say something about more beer.

"Once we get there, you can't have any more beer. I've got plans for you mister, and if you drink any more, you'll be useless to me."

Rachel's words carried to them all just before she closed the door. With all of them laughing or crying, they watched the two couples drive away, and their hearts were filled with joy.

The following day, there were almost ten thousand people gathered at the airport, almost half of them were Russians gathered to see their own President. Someone had found an elevated flatbed trailer and had pulled it in to use as a stage. The sky was blue, a few clouds were drifting slowly across the expanse, and the sun was well down in the afternoon sky. The temperature was still a comfortable sixty-four degrees, and everyone was excited to see the proceedings. As soon as the plane landed and had come to a stop a short distance away, a former airport worker moved a ramp into position for the occupants to disembark.

Bob, Lucy, and Jason were the first ones out the door, and they made a beeline for Sean as soon as they were on the ground. As the hugs began, the cheers erupted. The two Presidents emerged from the plane to a belated applause; because they were so new in their respective offices, no one actually recognized them. They hugged Sean and Mike and shook hands, and the Russian President kissed both of Sean's cheeks. The applause erupted anew and lasted for several minutes. Once they were on the stage, with a makeshift PA system in place, everyone moved up to hear what was to be said.

"Ladies and gentlemen, I am so happy to be here today, to meet the men that have saved most of you. This is a special day, because we also have a cure for the virus. We've sent the information to everyone we could locate around the world so that they can start their own production of it and start saving their own people. We owe all of this, including the cure for the virus, to these young men and their small group of people.

Without their bravery, foresight, ingenuity, and thoughtfulness for others, we might all be dead, or at least facing a more bleak future than we are now."

Looking at Sean and Mike and beckoning them to come up on the stage, the President turned, received a small box from an assistant, and opened it.

"Sean and Mike, for your bravery and leadership, I want to present you with the Congressional Medal of Honor. As marines, as officers of the law, you deserve the highest honor for everything that you've done, for not just your people, but for all who have come to you for help."

Placing the medal over Sean's head, he then shook his hand and hugged him tightly, as a father would his own son. The President whispered in his ear, "I'm so glad you're healed, Sean. I'd like to discuss a few things that we need done elsewhere that you and Mike could set right."

The crowd erupted in applause, cheering, whistles, and shouts.

"Thank you, Mr. President."

Turning to Mike and placing the medal over his head, the President then shook his hand and gave him the same embrace that he had given Sean. The crowd once again erupted in applause and cheering.

"Thank you, Mike, for standing with Sean, your friend and your brother, for helping to make the decisions and for being willing to go the distance, no matter how hard."

The Russian President stepped forward and took the microphone.

"Sean, Mike… I also want to present to you the highest Russian honor: The Hero of the Russian Federation. For welcoming my people with open arms, for feeding them, accepting them, and giving them a new life, thank you."

Reaching forward, he pinned the medal on Sean's shirt, shook his hand, and then hugged him. Everyone could see the emotion of the Russian President and the tears that were on his face as he hugged Sean. The crowd again cheered loudly, with the Russians making themselves heard.

Turning to Mike, he also placed the medal on his shirt, shook his hand, and embraced him. The whole gathering erupted in cheers and wept for the heroes.

Sean and Mike were soon hugging their wives and looking out over the crowd… thankful to be alive.

ABOUT THE AUTHOR

Jim Norman lives in Oregon with his wife and their four adult children who live close by. He is fifty-eight years old, has been involved in construction work for forty years, and is an avid outdoorsman, who enjoys fishing, hunting, and hiking.

While playing the video games *The Last of Us* and *Call of Duty: Black Ops*, killing zombies, he often wondered what kind of real virus might produce a zombie-like creature and how it might come about. Following that up with imagining the world events that might surround such an event that would spiral into chaos, this story was born.

Made in the USA
Monee, IL
05 March 2020

22641800R00273